THE
TRAIL TO
BUDDHA'S
MIRROR

Also by Don Winslow

A Cool Breeze on the Underground

THE
TRAIL TO
BUDDHA'S
MIRROR

Don Winslow

ST. MARTIN'S PRESS   NEW YORK

Design by Judy Dannecker

Library of Congress Cataloging-in-Publication Data

Winslow, Don.
    The trail to Buddha's mirror / Don Winslow.
       p.   cm.
    "A Thomas Dunne book."
    ISBN 0-312-07099-3
    I. Title.
    PS3573.I5326T7   1992
    813'.54—dc20   91-40334
                                                       CIP

First Edition: March 1992

10 9 8 7 6 5 4 3 2 1

To Mark and Marcella

A NOTE ON PROPER NAMES: We have used the Chinese *pinyin* system of Romanization except in cases in which the older forms are more familiar to Westerners, such as Chiang Kai-shek, Kuomintang, etc.

Formerly I constructed a thatched hut in the mountains, and passed several summers and winters there, subduing my passions and destroying desire.
—Sheng Ch'in, *A Guidebook to Mount Emei*

PROLOGUE
Dad's Knock

He never should have opened the door.

Neal Carey knew better, too—when you open a door, you're never really sure what you're letting in.

But he had been expecting Hardin, the old shepherd who came every day at teatime to sip whiskey with him. It was raining—*had* been raining for five solid days—and by all rights Hardin should have arrived for "a bit of wet to take the chill off."

Neal pulled his wool cardigan tighter around his neck, edged his chair a little closer to the fire, and hunched down lower over the table to read. The fire was waging a brave but losing battle against the cold and damp, which was miserable even for March in the Yorkshire moors. He took another hit of coffee and tried to settle back into Tobias Smollett's *Ferdinand Count Fathom,* but his mind just wasn't on it. He'd been at it all day, and now he was ready for a little conversation and a spot of whiskey. Where the hell was Hardin?

He looked out the small window of the stone cottage and couldn't see a thing through the mist and driving rain, not even the dirt road that climbed up from the village below. His was the only cottage on this part of the moor, and on this afternoon he felt more isolated than ever. He usually liked that—he only hiked down to the village every three or four days to pick up supplies—but today he wanted some company. The cottage usually felt snug, but today it was suffocating. The one electric lamp didn't do much to brighten the general gloom. Maybe he just had cabin fever; he had been up there for seven months, alone save for Hardin's visits, with only his books for company.

So he didn't stop to think when he heard the knock. He didn't look out the window, or ease the door open, or even ask who was there. He just got up and opened the door to let Hardin in.

Except it wasn't Hardin.

"Son!"

"Hello, Dad," Neal said.

That's when Neal Carey made his second mistake. He just stood there. He should have slammed the door shut, braced his chair against it, jumped out a back window, and never looked back.

If he had done those things, he never would have ended up in China, and the Li woman would still be alive.

PART ONE
The China Doll

1

Graham looked miserable and ridiculous standing there. Rain sluiced off the hood of his raincoat and down onto his mud-caked shoes. He set his small suitcase down in a puddle, used his artificial right hand to wipe some water off his nose, and still managed to give Neal that grin, that Joe Graham grin, an equal measure of malevolence and glee.

"Aren't you glad to see me?" he asked.

"Thrilled."

Neal hadn't seen him since August at Boston's Logan Airport, where Graham had given him a one-way ticket, a draft for ten thousand pounds sterling, and instructions to get lost, because there were a lot of people in the States who were real angry at him. Neal had given half the money back, flown to London, put the rest of the money in the bank, and eventually disappeared into his cottage on the moor.

"What's the matter?" Graham asked. "You got a babe in there, you don't want me to come in?"

"Come in."

Graham eased past Neal into the cottage. Joe Graham, five feet four inches of dripping nastiness and guile, had raised Neal Carey from a pup. Taking off his raincoat, he shook it out on the floor. Then he found the makeshift closet, pushed Neal's clothes aside, and hung up the coat, under which he wore an electric blue suit with a burnt orange shirt and a burgundy tie. He took a handkerchief from his jacket pocket, wiped the seat of Neal's chair, and sat down.

"Thanks for all the cards and letters," he said.

"You told me to get lost."

"Figure of speech."

"You knew where I was."

"Son, we *always* know where you are."

The grin again.

He hasn't changed much in seven months, Neal thought. His blue eyes were still beady, and his sandy hair was maybe a touch thinner. His leprechaun face still looked like it was peeking out from under a toadstool. He could still point you to the pot of shit at the end of the rainbow.

"To what do I owe the pleasure, Graham?" Neal asked.

"I don't know, Neal. Your right hand?"

He made the appropriately obscene gesture with his heavy rubber hand, which was permanently cast in a half-closed position. He could do almost everything with it, except Neal did remember the time Graham had broken his left hand in a fight. "It's when you have to piss," Graham had said, "that you learn who your friends are." Neal had been one of those friends.

Graham made an exaggerated pantomime of looking around the room, although Neal knew that he had absorbed every detail in the few seconds it had taken to hang up his coat.

"Nice place," Graham said sarcastically.

"It suits me."

"This is true."

"Coffee?"

"You got a clean cup?"

Neal stepped into the small kitchen and came back with a cup, which he tossed into Graham's lap. Graham examined it carefully.

"Maybe we can go out," he said.

"Maybe we can cut the dance short and you can tell me what you're doing here."

"It's time for you to get back to work."

Neal gestured to the books stacked on the floor around the fireplace.

"I *am* at work."

4

"I mean *work* work."

Neal listened to the rain dripping off the thatched roof. It was odd, he thought, that he could hear *that* sound but not recognize Graham's knock on the door. Graham had used his hard rubber hand, too, because he had been holding his suitcase in his real hand. Neal Carey was out of shape and he knew it.

He also knew it was useless trying to explain to Graham that the books on the floor *were* "work work," so he settled for, "Last time we talked, I was 'suspended,' remember?"

"That was just to cool you out."

"I take it I'm cooled?"

"Ice."

Yeah, Neal thought, that's me. Ice. Cold to the touch and easy to melt. The last job almost chilled me permanently.

"I don't know, Dad," Neal said. "I think I've retired."

"You're twenty-four years old."

"You know what I mean."

Graham started to laugh. His eyes squinted into little slits. He looked like an Irish Buddha without the belly.

"You still have most of the money, don't you?" he said. "How long do you think you can live on that?"

"A long time."

"Who taught you how to do that—stretch a dollar?"

"You did."

You taught me a lot more than that, Neal thought. How to follow a mark without getting made, how to slip in and out of an apartment, how to get inside a locked file cabinet, how to search a room. Also how to make three basic, cheap meals a day, how to keep a place clean and livable, and how to have some respect for myself. Everything a private cop needs to know.

Neal had been ten years old the day he met Graham, the day he tried to pick Graham's pocket, got caught, and ended up working for him. Neal's mother was a hooker and his father was an absentee voter, so he didn't have what you'd call a glowing self-image. He also didn't have any money, any food, or any idea what the hell he was doing. Joe Graham had given him all that.

"You're welcome," Graham said, interrupting Neal's reverie.

"Thanks," said Neal, feeling like an ingrate, which was exactly how Graham wanted him to feel. Joe Graham was a major-league talent.

"I mean, you want to go back to gradu-ass school anyway, right?" Graham asked.

He must have talked to my professor already, Neal thought. Joe Graham rarely asked a question to which he didn't already know the answer.

"You've talked with Dr. Boskin?" Neal asked.

Graham nodded cheerfully.

"And?"

"And he says the same thing we do. 'Come home, darling, everything is forgiven.' "

Forgiven?! Neal thought. I only did what they asked me to do. For my troubles I got a bundle of money and a stretch in exile. Well, exile's fine with me, thank you. It only cost me the love of my life and a year of my education. But Diane would have left me anyway, and I needed the time for research.

Graham didn't want to give him too much time to think, so he said, "You can't live like a monkey forever, right?"

"You mean a monk."

"I know what I mean."

Actually, Graham, Neal thought, I *could* live like a monk forever and be very happy.

It was true. It had taken some getting used to, but Neal was happy pumping his own water, heating it on the stove, and taking lukewarm baths in the tub outside. He was happy with his twice-weekly hikes down to the village to do the shopping, have a quick pint and maybe lose a game of darts, then lug his supplies back up the hill.

His routine rarely varied, and he liked that. He got up at dawn, put the coffee on, and bathed while it perked. Then he would sit down outside with his first cup and watch the sun rise. He'd go inside and make his breakfast—toast and two eggs over hard—and then read until lunch, which was usually cheese, bread, and fruit. He'd go for a walk over the other side of the moor after lunch, and then settle back in for more studying. Hardin and his dog would usually turn up about four, and the three of them would have a sip of whiskey, the shepherd and the sheepdog each having a touch of arthritis, don't you know. After an hour or so, Hardin would finish telling his fishing lies, and Neal would look over the notes he had made during the day and then crank up the generator. He'd fix himself some canned soup or stew for dinner, read for a while, and go to bed.

It was a lonely life, but it suited him. He was making progress on his long-delayed master's thesis, and he actually liked being alone. Maybe it was a monk's life, but maybe he was a monk.

Sure, Graham, I could do this forever, he thought.

Instead, he asked, "What's the job?"

"It's chickenshit."

"Right. You didn't come all the way over here from New York for a chickenshit job."

Graham was loving it. His filthy little harp face shone like the visage of a cherub whom God had just patted on the back.

"No, son, it really is about chickenshit."

That's when Neal made his next major mistake: he believed him.

Graham opened his suitcase and took out a thick file folder. He handed it to Neal.

"Meet Dr. Robert Pendleton."

Pendleton's photo looked as if it had been taken for a company newsletter, one of those head-and-shoulders shots that sit above a caption reading, MEET OUR NEW VICE-PRESIDENT IN CHARGE OF DEVELOPMENT. He had a face you could cut yourself on: sharp nose, sharp chin, and sharp eyes. His short black hair was thinning on top. His gallant effort at smiling looked like an unnatural act. His necktie could have landed airplanes on a foggy night.

"Dr. Pendleton is a research scientist at a company called AgriTech in Raleigh, North Carolina," Graham said. "Six weeks ago, Pendleton packed up his research notes, computer disks, and toothbrush, and left to attend some sort of dork conference at Stanford University, which is near—"

"I know."

"—San Francisco, where he stayed at the Mark Hopkins Hotel. The conference lasted a week. Pendleton never came back."

"What do the police have to say?"

"Haven't talked to them."

"Isn't that sort of SOP in a missing-person case?"

Graham grinned a grin custom-made to hack Neal off. "Who said he was missing?"

7

"You did."

"No, I didn't. I said he didn't come back. There's a difference. We know where he is. He just won't come home."

All right, Neal thought, I'll play.

"Why not?"

"Why not what?"

"Why won't he come home?"

"I'm pleased to see that you're asking some better questions, son."

"So answer it."

"He's got himself a China doll."

"By which you mean," Neal asked, "that he's in the company of an Oriental lady of hired affections?"

"A China doll."

"So what's the problem and why are we involved?"

"Another good question."

Graham got up from the chair and walked into the kitchen. He opened the middle cabinet of three, reached to the top shelf, and pulled down Neal's bottle of scotch.

"A place for everything, and everything in its place," he said cheerfully. "Another thing I taught you."

He came back into the sitting room, reached into his case, and came out with a small plastic travel cup, the kind that telescopes out from a disk into a regular old drinking vessel. He poured three fingers of whiskey and then offered Neal the bottle.

"Damp in here," Graham said.

Neal took the bottle and set it on the table. He didn't want to end up half in the bag and take this job out of sentiment.

Graham lifted his cup and said, "To the queen and all his family."

He knocked back two fingers of the scotch and let the warmth spread through him. If he had been a cat he would have purred, but being a cretin, he just leered. Braced against the chill, he continued, "Pendleton is the world's greatest authority on chickenshit. AgriTech has millions of dollars sunk into chickenshit."

"Let me guess," Neal said. "Does the Bank have millions of dollars sunk into AgriTech?"

Graham's sudden appearance was starting to make sense to Neal.

"That's my boy," Graham said.

That says it, too, Neal thought. I'm Graham's boy, I'm Levine's boy, but most of all, I'm the Bank's boy.

The Bank was a quiet little financial institute in Providence, Rhode Island, that promised its wealthy clients two things: absolute privacy from the prying eyes of the press, the public, and the prosecutors; and discreet help on the side with those little problems of life that couldn't be settled with just plain cash.

That was where Neal came in. He and Graham worked for a secret branch of the bank called "Friends of the Family." There was no sign on the door, but anybody who had the necessary portfolio knew that he could come into the back office if he had a problem and talk to Ethan Kitteredge, and that Ethan Kitteredge would find a way to work things out, free of charge.

Usually Kitteredge, known to his employees as "the Man," would work things out by buzzing for Ed Levine, who would phone down to New York for Joe Graham, who would fetch Neal Carey. Neal would then trundle off to find somebody's daughter, or take a picture of somebody's wife playing Hide-the-Hot-Dog in the Plaza Hotel, or break into somebody's apartment to find that all-important second set of books.

In exchange, Friends had sent him to a toney private school, paid his rent, and picked up his college bills.

"So," Neal said, "The Bank has a humongous loan out to AgriTech, and one of its star scientists has taken a sabbatical. So what?"

"Chickenshit."

"Yeah, right. What's the big deal about chickenshit?"

"Not *any* chickenshit. *Pendleton's* chickenshit. Chickenshit is fertilizer, right? You spread it on stuff to make it grow, which sounds pretty fucking gross to me, but hey. . . . Anyway, Pendleton's been working for umptedy-zumptedy years on a way to squeeze more growing juice out of chickenshit by mixing it with water treated with certain bacteria. This, by the way, is called an 'enhancing process.'

"Now it used to be that you couldn't mix chickenshit in water because it would lose its juice, but with Pendleton's process, not only can you mix it with water, but you get something like triple the effect.

"Naturally, this would make a nice little item on AgriTech's shelf. I might even buy you some for Christmas. You could rub it on your dick, although I doubt the stuff could be *that* good."

9

"Thank you."

"But don't get your hopes up, because just when Doc Guano gets *this close,*" said Graham, holding his thumb and forefinger a sliver apart, "to inventing Supershit, he goes off to this conference and meets Miss Wong."

"Is that really her name?"

"Do I know? Wong, Wang, Ching, Chang, what's the difference?"

"Yeah, so? Doctor This, Doctor That, what's the difference? I'll bet you AgriTech has more than one biochemist."

"Not like Pendleton, they don't. Besides, he took his notes with him."

Neal could see it coming and he didn't want this job. Maybe Robert Pendleton didn't want to finish *his* research, he thought, but I want to finish mine. Get my master's and go on for the old Ph.D. Find a job in some little state college somewhere and spend the rest of my life reading books instead of running dirty errands for the Man.

"Have the cops pick him up for theft, then. The notes are AgriTech's property," Neal said.

Graham shook his head. "Then maybe he'd be too unhappy to play with his test tubes anymore. The AgriTech people don't want their professor in the slammer; they want their chickenshit in the pot."

Graham took the bottle off the table and poured himself another drink. He was enjoying himself immensely. Aggravating Neal was almost worth the terrifying flight over, the endless trip to Yorkshire, and the hike up that damn hill. It was good to see the little shit again.

"If he doesn't want to come back, he doesn't want to come back," Neal said.

Graham tossed back the whiskey.

"You have to *make* him want to," he said.

"You mean 'you' in the collective sense, right? As in 'one would have to make him want to.' "

"I mean 'you' in the sense of *you,* Neal Carey."

All of a sudden, Neal Carey felt a lot of sympathy for Dr. Robert Pendleton. Each of them was shacked up with something he loved— Pendleton with his woman and Neal with his books—and now they were each being pulled back, kicking and screaming, to the chickenshit.

Because of him, they get me, Neal thought, and because of me they'll get him. It's all done with mirrors. He reached for the bottle and poured a healthy drink into his coffee cup.

"What if I don't want to?" he asked.

Graham started rubbing his fake hand into his real one. It was a habit he had when he was worried or had something unpleasant to say.

Neal saved him the trouble. "Then you'll have to *make* me want to?"

Graham was really working on the hand now. Pissing Neal off was fun, but extorting him wasn't. However, the Man, Levine, and Graham had agreed that Neal had been shut up with his books too long, and if they didn't get him back into some kind of action, they would lose him. That happened sometimes; a first-class UC—an undercover guy— would be put on R-and-R after a tough job and never come back. Or, worse, the guy would come back dull and rusty and do something stupid and get hurt. Happened all the time, but Graham wasn't going to let it happen to Neal. So he had come to fetch him for this dumb, chicken-shit job.

"You been away from Columbia for what, a year now?" Graham asked.

"About that. You sent me on a job, remember?"

Neal sure as hell remembered. They had sent him to London on a hopeless search for the runaway daughter of a big-time politico—just to keep his wife content and quiet—and he had screwed up and actually found her. She was hooking and hooked, and he had wrenched her off her pimp and the junk and delivered her to her mother. Which was what the Man wanted him to do, but the politician was sure as hell pissed off, so Friends had to pretend that Neal had screwed them over, too. And so he had "disappeared." Happily.

"Can you do that?" Graham asked. "Just take off from gradu-ass school like that?"

"No, Graham, you can't. Friends of the Family fixed it. What am I telling you for? You're the one who fixed it."

Graham smiled. "And now we're asking you for a little favor."

"Or you'll *un*fix it?"

Graham shrugged a that's-life shrug.

"Why me?" Neal whined. "Why not you? Or Levine?"

"The Man wants you."

"Why?"

Because, Graham thought, we ain't going to sit around with our hooters in our hands while you turn yourself into a hermit. I know you, son. You like to be alone so you can brood on things and get happily

11

miserable. You need to get back to work and back to school—back with some *people*. Get your feet back on concrete.

"You and Pendleton are both eggheads," Graham said. "The Man figures he's been paying for your expensive education for jobs just like this one."

Neal took a hit of scotch. He could feel Graham pulling in the line.

"Pendleton's some sort of biochemist. I study eighteenth-century English Lit!" Neal said. *Tobias Smollett: The Outsider in Eighteenth-Century Literature:* Neal's thesis title and a sure cure for insomnia. Except, that is, for eighteenth-century buffs. Both of them would love it.

"I guess all eggheads look alike to the Man."

Neal tried a different tack.

"I'm out of shape, Graham. Very rusty. I've worked maybe two cases in the last two years and I screwed *both* of them up. You don't want me."

"You brought Allie Chase home."

"Not before I botched it up and almost got us both killed. I'm no good at it anymore, Dad, I—"

"Stop being such a crybaby! What are we asking here? You go to San Francisco and find the happy couple, which shouldn't be too difficult even for you, seeing as they're in the Chinatown Holiday Inn, Room ten-sixteen, right there in your file. You get the broad alone, you slip her some cash, and she dumps him. She's no dope. She knows that money for nothing is better than money for something.

"Then you buddy up to Pendleton, have a few shooters with him, listen to his sob story, and pour him onto a plane. What'll it take? Three, four days?"

Neal walked over to the window. The rain had let up a little bit, but the fog was heavier than ever.

"I'm glad you have this all figured out, Graham. Are you going to do my research for me, too?"

"Just do the job and come back. You can spend the whole summer here at the Mildew Hilton if you want. You have to be back at school September ninth, though."

He reached into his case and pulled out a large manila envelope.

"The schedules and book lists for your—what do you call them?—your seminars. I worked it out with Boskin."

Graham is so damned good, Neal thought. Old Graham brings the prizes with him and dangles them in front of my nose: seminars, book lists. . . . You have to hand it to him—he knows his whores.

"You're too good to me, Dad."

"Tell me about it."

So there it is, Neal thought. A few days of sleazy work in California, then back to my happy monk's cell on the moor. Finish my reading, then back to graduate school. Jesus, this double life of mine. Sometimes I feel like my own twin brother. Who's insane.

"Yeah, okay," Neal said.

"I'm telling you," Graham said, "this one is a grounder, easy throw to first, out of the inning."

"Right."

So maybe it's time to come down from the hill, Neal thought. Ease myself back into the world with this sleazy little job. Maybe it's too easy up here, where I don't have to deal with anything or anyone except writers who've been dead for a couple hundred years.

He looked out the window and couldn't tell whether he was looking at rain or fog. Both, he guessed.

"Have you heard from Diane?" Graham asked.

Neal thought about the letter that had sat unopened on the table for six months. He'd been afraid to read it.

"I never answered her letter," Neal said.

"You're a stooge."

"Tell me about it."

"Did you think she was just going to wait around for you?"

"No. I didn't think that."

He had left her with no explanation, just that he had to go do a job, and he'd been gone now for almost a year. Graham had contacted her, told her something, and forwarded her letter. But Neal couldn't bring himself to open it. He'd rather let the thing die than read that she was killing it. But she wasn't the one who had killed it, he thought. She was just the one who had the guts to write the obituary.

Graham wouldn't let it drop. "She left the apartment."

"Diane wouldn't be the kind to stay."

"She found a place on 104th, between Broadway and West End. She has a roommate. A woman."

"What did you do? Follow her?!"

"Sure. I thought you'd want to know."

"Thanks."

"Maybe look her up when you get back to the city."

"What are you, my mother?"

Graham shook his head and poured himself another shot. "Way I look at it," he said, "she's a friend of the family." He never should have opened the door.

2

She was a looker, all right, this Lila.

That was her name, or the name she used working conventions, anyway. Neal learned this from the file Graham had given him, which he had ample time to peruse on the endless trip to San Francisco. It included a Polaroid taken at dinner by one of Pendleton's AgriTech buddies, which showed Pendleton sitting at a banquet table with a striking Oriental woman. The buddy had scrawled "Robert and Lila" along the bottom.

Looking at the photo, Neal couldn't blame Pendleton for preferring Lila to his Bunsen burners. Her face was heart-shaped, her hair was long, straight, and satin black, swept up on the left by a blue cloisonné comb. She had beautiful, slanted eyes that gazed on Pendleton with what looked like affection as he struggled with his chopsticks. She was smiling at him. If she was a pro, Neal thought, she was a classy pro, and he liked her just from looking at her picture.

He had no feel for Pendleton yet. The book on him was pretty simple. Forty-three years old, single, married to his work. Born in Chicago, B.S. from Colorado, M.S. from Illinois, Ph.D. from MIT. Taught for a couple of years at Kansas State and then went for the corporate bucks. First for Ciba-Geigy, then for Archer, Daniels Midland, and then AgriTech. Had been there for ten years before he ran into Lila. Lived in a condo, played a little tennis, drove a Volvo. No financial problems, credit hassles, debts. In fact, when you compared his salary and bonuses with his expenses, the guy should have a bunch of money in the bank. Drinks a beer on weekends. Friendly enough, but no close buddies. No women. No boys, either. Fertilizer was his life.

Jesus, Neal thought, no wonder the guy went off the deep end when he discovered sex with a gorgeous, exotic woman in a city as beautiful as San Francisco.

Neal had first gone to San Francisco back in 1970, seven years earlier, when the city was the counterculture capital. Sporting longish hair, denim, one tasteful strand of beads, and the hungry look of the fugitive, Neal was working point for Graham on your basic Haight-Ashbury runaway job. He located their particular flower child in an urban commune on Turk Street. She was the daughter of a Boston banker, and was trying hard to live down her capitalist heritage. Neal had shared a bowl of brown rice and a floor with her, gained her trust, and then ratted her out to Graham. Graham did the rest and Neal heard later that she ended up at Harvard. All betrayals should end so happily.

His next trip to the city was even easier. He was a mature twenty then, and one of the Bank's clients wanted to film a television commercial in front of a sculpture in Battery Park. Turned out the sculpture was the work of a San Francisco artist who didn't like to open his mail or answer his phone. Neal found A. Brian Crowe at a coffee house on Columbus. The artist dressed all in black, of course, and hid behind his cape when Neal approached him. The two thousand dollars in cash persuaded him to come out, though, and they sealed the deal over two iced espressos. A. Brian Crowe left happy. Neal hung around the city for a week, and *he* left happy, which made this an unusual assignment all around.

Neal figured you'd have to be a fool not to love San Francisco, and whatever else Dr. Robert Pendleton was or wasn't, he was no fool. He was probably a man getting a little romance for the first time in his life and not wanting to let go of it, one of the lucky few who found a hooker who was also a courtesan, a true lady of the evening. She probably took presents instead of cash, or maybe a discreet check had been deposited in her account.

So Neal would write her another check, and that would be that.

Neal closed the file and cracked *Fathom* open. He fell asleep after a couple of chapters. The flight attendant woke him up to put his seat upright for the approach to San Francisco.

Neal had never liked the Mark Hopkins Hotel. The bill was always as large as the room was small, and the Snob Hill address didn't impress him. But it always helps a bribery deal to look like money, and he wanted to ask Lila to a quiet drink at the Top of the Mark and have quick access to a room where he could hand her some money in privacy, so he swallowed his distaste and checked in.

He handed the Bank's gold card to the precious clerk, confessed to having only one small bag, and found his own way to the sixth-floor room, which occupied a corner, so you could actually turn around in it without folding your arms across your chest. The windows allowed a view of the Oakland Bay Bridge and some nicely restored Victorian houses on Pine Street. Neal didn't care much about the view, as he didn't plan to spend a lot of time there. He wanted a slow shower and a quick meal before getting down to work.

He called down to room service and ordered a Swiss cheese omelet with a plain, toasted bagel, a pot of coffee, and a *Chronicle.* Then he stripped off his airline-grody clothes and stepped into the shower. After months of heating his own water for barely tepid outdoor baths, the steaming spray felt great. He stayed in a little too long and was still shaving when the doorbell rang.

He signed for the bill and the tip, poured a cup of black coffee, and sipped at it while he finished shaving. Then he sat down at the small table by the window to devour the food and the newspaper.

Neal was a print junkie, which he figured came with being a native New Yorker. He bypassed the front page of the *Chronicle* in favor of Herb Caen's column, enjoyed that, and then turned to the sports section. The baseball season was about to start, and the Yankees looked pretty good for '77. That's one of the great things about spring, he thought. All the home teams look like they have a shot. It's only in the sere days of summer that hopes begin to wilt, then wither and die in fall. Unless, of course, you have relief pitching.

After a thorough perusal of the sports pages, he turned to the front section to catch up on the news. Jimmy Carter really was President, wearing Ward Cleaver sweaters and treating the country like a collective

Beaver. Mao was still dead, and his successors were squabbling over the remains. Brezhnev was ill. The same old same old.

Which reminded him that he had the same old job to do: find some miscreant and bring him home. He used his third cup of coffee to come up with a plan.

It wasn't much of a plan. All he had to do was amble down to the Holiday Inn, trail them until he could find a way to contact her alone, and make his pitch. Then pick up the pieces of Pendleton's shattered heart and check them through to Raleigh. Almost as easy as giving money to a starving artist.

That's when he got the bright idea to let his fingers do the walking. Why drag his ass all the way down the hill and waste time following them around? Call their room instead. If he answers, hang up. If she answers, say something like, "You don't know me, but I have a thousand bucks in cash sitting under your water glass at a table at the Top of the Mark. The name is Neal Carey. One o'clock. Come alone." There wasn't a hooker in the world, no matter how classy, who wouldn't make that appointment.

Safe, simple and civilized, he thought. No point making this any harder than it has to be.

He found the hotel number in the file and dialed the phone.

"Room ten-sixteen, please," he said.

"I'll transfer you to the operator."

He took a sip of coffee.

"Operator. May I help you?"

"Room ten-sixteen, please."

"Thank you. One moment."

It was more than a moment. More like ten moments.

"What party are you trying to reach, sir?"

Uh-oh.

"Dr. Robert Pendleton."

"Thank you. One moment."

Ten more moments. Long ones.

"I'm sorry, sir. Dr. Pendleton has checked out."

Swell.

"Uuuhh . . . when?"

"This morning, sir."

While I was showering, filling my face, and lounging over the spring training reports, Neal thought.

"Did he leave a forwarding address?"

"One moment."

Did he leave a forwarding address? Your basic desperation effort.

"I'm sorry, sir. Dr. Pendleton left no forwarding address. Would you like to leave a message in case he calls in?"

"No, thank you, and thanks for your help."

"Have a nice day."

"Right."

Neal poured another cup of coffee in the time it took to call himself an asshole. All right, think, he told himself. Pendleton's checked out. Why? Maybe money. Hotels are expensive and he's found himself a pad somewhere. Or maybe AgriTech kept bugging him, so he changed hotels. Or maybe the party is over and he's on his way back to Raleigh. That's the best maybe, but you can't afford to count on it. So back to work.

Pendleton isn't a pro, so chances are he won't think about covering his traces. He probably doesn't know that anyone is on his trail. And there's only one place to pick up his trail.

Neal hustled to get dressed. He put on a powder blue button-down shirt, khaki slacks, and black loafers, slipped on a red-and-blue rep tie but left the knot open, and dumped half the stuff out of his canvas shoulder bag, leaving enough in to give it some weight. Sticking his airline ticket jacket into the pocket of his all-purpose, guaranteed-not-to-wrinkle blue blazer and shoving a ten-dollar bill in his pants pocket, he hoofed it to the elevator, which seemed to take forever to get there. He figured he was ten minutes away from his only shot at tracking Pendleton and he didn't know if he had the ten minutes.

The Holiday Inn was on Kearny Street, a straight shot down California Street from the Hopkins. Normally he would have walked there, but the cable car was pulling up just as he hit the sidewalk, so he bought a ticket and hopped on, hanging on the side like he'd seen in the movies. It was sunny and cool out, but he was already sweating. He was in a race with the maids at the Chinatown Holiday Inn.

He got off on the corner of Kearny and California, three blocks south of the Holiday Inn. He didn't run but he didn't exactly walk, either, and he did the three blocks in about two minutes. Avoiding the doorman's eyes, he headed straight for the bank of elevators, and there was one waiting for him. He caught his breath on the way up. Or almost caught it. He wanted to look a little breathless for the show.

The doors slid open and he looked at the sign—1001–1030—with an arrow pointing to the left. He trotted down the hallway and, sure enough, there were two maids' carts sitting between rooms 1001 and 1012. So, Neal thought, it all depends on where they started.

He tried to look worried, hassled, and in a hurry. None of this required any serious level of method acting.

"I'm going to miss my flight," he said to the maid who was just stepping out of 1012. "Did you find a ticket?"

She gave him a blank look. She was young and unsure. He stepped around her to 1016 and jiggled the handle. It was locked.

"Did you find a ticket in this room? Airline ticket?"

The other made came out of 1011. "What you lose?"

She was an older woman. The boss.

"My plane ticket."

"What room?" she asked, checking him out.

He knew he couldn't give her time to connect Pendleton to the room. He hoped the good doctor hadn't been a big tipper.

"Could you let me in, please? I have to catch a flight to Atlanta in forty-five minutes."

"I call manager."

"I don't have the time," Neal said as he pulled the ten-dollar bill out of his pocket and laid it on the edge of her cart. "Please?"

She took her key ring and slipped the key in the lock. The younger one started to speak rapidly in Chinese, but the older one shut her up with a hard glance.

"Quick," she said to Neal. She stood in the doorway as she ushered him in. The younger one joined her, in case Neal swiped an ashtray or a TV or something.

Neal had tossed a lot of rooms in his life, but never in front of an audience with the clock running, unless he counted the endless practice sessions with Graham. This was like some sort of private cop game show, where if he passed round one he got to go on for cash and prizes. It would have helped if he knew what he was looking for, but he was just looking, and that took time.

The bed was unmade, but otherwise the room was neat. They hadn't left in a hurry. They had even left their wet towels in the bathtub and thrown their trash in the cans.

Neal started with the bureau drawers. Nothing.

"Shit," he said, just to give the scene realism.

He checked the nightstand beside the bed. There was one of those little hotel notepads beside the phone book and the Bible. He turned his back to the audience and stuck it in his pocket.

"I'll never make it," he said.

"Under bed?" the older maid suggested.

He humored her and got down on all fours and looked under the bed. There wasn't even any dust, not to mention a bachelor sock, or a note telling him where they had gone.

"Maybe I threw it away," he said as he got up. "Stupid."

The maids nodded enthusiastically in agreement.

The trashcan was full, as if they'd straightened up before leaving. Polite, thoughtful people. Three empty cans of Diet Pepsi sat on some pieces of cardboard, the kind you get with your laundered shirts. A pocket map of San Francisco and a bunch of ticket stubs at the bottom.

"Jesus, how could I be so stupid?" Neal said as he bent over and reached into the trashcan. He showed his audience his butt as he slipped his airline ticket out of his pocket and into the can. Then he put the map and the ticket stubs under the ticket envelope, straightened up and showed them the ticket, then stuffed the whole mess into his lapel pocket.

"Thank you so much," he said.

"Hurry, hurry," said the older one.

Hurry, hurry, indeed, thought Neal.

Security picked him up in the lobby.

Security in this case was represented by a young Chinese guy who was both larger and more muscular than Neal would have preferred. His chest looked uncomfortably stuffed into his gray uniform blazer, and he had big, thick arms. He had clearly spent some quality time on the old bench-presses. Neal, who didn't have to worry about leaving space in his jacket for his muscles, knew the guy would have no trouble pinning him up against a wall and keeping him there. The guy's white shirt was rumpled around a waist that was beginning to go to fat, and he had a two-way radio hooked to his belt. There was probably a nightstick stuck into the belt somewhere, Neal thought, probably at the small of his back. Except nothing about this guy was small. And he seemed to want to talk.

"Excuse me, sir," he said. There was no trace of a Chinese accent. "May I ask what you were doing in Room ten-sixteen?"

The younger maid hadn't wasted any time calling down. So much for her five bucks, Neal thought.

"I left my—"

"Save it. That wasn't your room."

Neal nodded at the other guests in the lobby. "Can we do this outside?"

"Sure."

He opened the door for Neal and let him get a good feel for his bulk. Neal knew that his next move would be to get in front of him and maneuver him to the wall. Which would be the end of the game, so it just wouldn't do to let Benchpress here make that next move.

Neal looked off to his left as soon as he cleared the doorway, held up his hand, and yelled, "Taxi!"

The front cab in line started to edge forward on the curb as a bellhop hustled over to open the cab door.

"No, no, no," Benchpress said, waving his arms as he quick-shuffled between Neal and the cab.

This was okay with Neal, who didn't want to take a cab anyway. He wanted to take a nice long walk up a long, steep hill to see just how badly Benchpress wanted to carry all those big muscles and that belly up a pitch to talk. With Benchpress off to his left, Neal had his whole right side open to move, and he knew where a right turn would take him: through North Beach and then up Telegraph Hill, which was plenty long and steep enough for what he had in mind. He took a hard right and headed out.

Benchpress wasted two seconds standing by the cab wondering how embarrassed he should be, and then another second trying to decide if the chase was going to be worth it.

He decided it was.

Neal wasn't happy to look over his shoulder and see Benchpress coming after him, but he wasn't too worried either. The guy wasn't going to cause a scene—not near his hotel, anyway—and he wasn't going to call the city police over this kind of crap. Nevertheless, it wouldn't hurt to make sure this thing became real personal, so Neal wasted a second of his own to turn on his heels and grin at Benchpress. Then he inserted his middle finger in his mouth, twisted it around, popped it out, and displayed it to Benchpress.

Benchpress took it personally. He nodded, put his head down, and started forward.

Okay, Neal thought, come on. I've spent six months hiking up and down a steep Yorkshire moor carrying packs of supplies. No overweight, pumped-up rent-a-cop can catch me on a hill.

Neal led him up Kearny and took another right on Broadway, which was a little flatter then he remembered. He picked up the pace past the strip joints and sex shops that were just opening to catch the early trade. Benchpress wasn't distracted by the tired barkers who were sipping on Styrofoam cups of coffee, or by the sleepy dancers who were just arriving with their dancing togs in gym bags slung over their shoulders. He didn't trip over any of the empty beer or wine bottles, or slip on any of the wax-paper sandwich wrappers or any of the trash that littered the North Beach strip. A sharp, cool wind was blowing off the Bay and into their faces, but that didn't slow Benchpress down much either.

Reduced to cheap tricks, Neal crossed Broadway in mid-traffic, inspiring some aggravated honking but no apparent concern in Benchpress, who swatted a Renault out of his way and kept coming.

Jesus, Neal thought, what a day. First I screw up and let Pendleton take off, next I find the only house detective in America with an overdeveloped sense of duty.

He swung a left onto Sansome Street, which gave him the incline he was looking for. Like a sparkling brook that flows into a polluted river, Sansome Street seemed a world apart from Broadway. Its street-level garages led up to to white and pastel apartments and houses that featured large sun rooms overlooking the Bay. A lot of their windows had those security-service decals plastered on them, the kind that let prospective burglars know that they shouldn't mess around here unless they wanted police academy dropouts with nightsticks, rottweilers, and inferiority complexes coming down on their sorry asses.

Sansome Street was pretty, trendy, and expensive looking, and Neal wondered where the money came from. Maybe it came from streets like Broadway, money that slipped through the fingers of the strippers and the whores, money that got away from the junkies and the porn addicts, from the sad drunks who paid six bucks a shot to peek over their grimy glasses of cheap bourbon at the bitter shake-and-jiggle of somebody's baby girl. Maybe it was the angry neon glare of the strip that paid for the warm, bright sun rooms with the view of the Bay.

His class-war reverie took his mind off the pain that was starting to shoot through his legs, pain that reminded him to take Sansome Street for what it was, a steep route up Telegraph Hill. He sucked it up and shifted into high gear. There's a trick to climbing a hill: you keep your knees slightly bent as you walk, like Groucho Marx going up a staircase. Every three or four steps you rock back on your heels. The technique saves wear and tear on the knees and ankles, and it moves you up a hill faster. Fast enough to leave a musclebound, beer-bellied badge from Woolworth's stretched out on the pavement sucking air.

After punishing his pursuer for a couple of minutes, Neal looked back over his shoulder and saw that Benchpress was huffing, puffing, muttering, sweating . . . and gaining on him.

Neal didn't know where Benchpress had learned Carey's Own Special Hill-Climbing Technique, but figured his patent was in jeopardy. Also his ass, because his legs started to do one of those reverse Pinocchio numbers and turn to wood. The pot of coffee and the cheese omelet he had consumed started to make some serious complaints in the form of an excruciating cramp, and his lungs began to ask if all this was such a good idea.

He looked around for some boulders or something to roll down on Benchpress like they do in the movies, but didn't see any. So he took a nice, deep gasp and plunged a little faster up the hill. Plan A, the Leave-the-Fat-Boy-on-the-Slope Maneuver, hadn't worked, so he tried to come up with a better Plan B. The wit and wisdom of Joe Graham came to him.

"If you can't beat em," Graham had once intoned, "bribe 'em."

He had about a ten-second lead on Benchpress and figured he'd need at least fifteen. His current tactic wasn't getting it done—in fact, he'd be really lucky to reach the park at Coit Tower with a five-second cushion, and five seconds weren't going to be enough for what he had in mind, so he broke into a run.

"Run" was a grandiose word for the shuffling jog he managed. His heart went into its Buddy-Rich-on-Speed imitation, the pleasant cramp in his stomach reached down into his groin, and his lungs issued a strong protest in the form of a wheezing gasp. But his legs kept moving. They ran up to the corner of Filbert Street and turned right, then hopped over to the north side of the street. While his legs were busy running, his right hand reached into his jacket, lifted out his wallet, and put it in his left hand. The two hands cooperated to take out one of the Bank's crisp one-hundred-dollar bills and put the wallet back. Then they tore the bill in half, the left hand putting its half in the left pants pocket, and the right hand gripping its prize in its sweaty palm.

He looked back quickly and saw that Benchpress hadn't hit the corner of Filbert yet, so it looked like he'd get his fifteen ticks. He hit the bottom of Coit Tower park, found a bowling-ball-sized rock at the base of a tree, and put the half-hundred under it. Then he sprinted as fast as he could up the walkway to the observation tower and marked the location of the tree. He leaned against the railing next to one of the coin-operated binoculars to catch what was left of his breath. As he sucked for air, he took off his left loafer and put the hotel notepad and the ticket stubs inside it before he put the shoe back on. People who search you, even after they've beaten you unconscious, often forget to look in your shoes.

He took in a fresh gulp of air as he checked out the view from the observation terrace, which was as stunning as he remembered. The whole bay stretched out in front of him. Off to his left he could make out a small section of the Golden Gate Bridge as it touched Marin County, and above that he could see the southern slope of Mount Tamalpais. Down and to the right of Mount Tam he could see Sausalito, and scanning farther to the right he saw small sailboats dancing on the sapphire blue water around the plump, notorious little island of Alcatraz. To his right he could see the whole span of the Bay Bridge as it led to Oakland. A huge freighter was plying its way up the bay toward San Mateo.

He had about five seconds to enjoy all this splendor before he turned to see Benchpress shuffling to the base of the walkway. Neal saw a homicidal look in the security guard's eye and wondered if he was about to get beaten to the proverbial pulp.

This is no big deal on television, where the private eye hero gets trashed by three guys twice his size, because when you see him after the commercial he has some beautiful woman tending his wounds and he's up and about, so to speak, one roll-cut later. But real-life beatings hurt.

Worse, they injure, and the injuries take a long time to heal, if they ever do. Neal just wanted to avoid the whole experience.

He put his back up against the railing and one of the binoculars on his left side as Benchpress reached the observation terrace and began to move toward him.

"Are you going to make me chase you *down* the hill now?" Benchpress asked as he edged along the railing toward Neal. He was breathing hard, stalling to catch his breath.

"I don't know, would it work?"

"You're an asshole. You know where I live? Chinatown. Sacramento Street? Clay Street? California Street? You know what they are?"

I'm an asshole all right, Neal thought.

"Hills," Neal said. "They're big hills."

"I've been walking up and down those streets since I was a kid. You think you're going to shake me on a hill? Get real."

"You're right. I apologize."

"That's okay. Now what's your story? What did you steal?"

"Nothing."

Benchpress was taking his air through his nose now, timing his breathing and slowing it down. He shifted his eyes around to see if they were alone. They were.

He pulled his security guard's badge out and held it up for Neal to see.

"Let's make this easy now," he said.

"I was looking for something."

"PI?"

"Yeah, okay."

"ID?"

Neal couldn't handle any more initials, so he held out the torn hundred-dollar bill.

"You can relax," he said. "You did your job. I didn't steal anything. You ran me down. Take the prize."

He stuck the bill behind the coin slot of the binoculars and started to back away.

"You're offering me a bribe?"

"Yeah."

"I don't have anything against the concept, I'm just checking it out."

"Basically, I'm paying you not to beat me up to defend your honor."

He smiled, accepting Neal's craven surrender graciously.

"Where's the other half?" he asked.

"It's under a tree down there somewhere."

He was one quick fat man. His right foot shot out and kicked the air twice, face-high, before Neal could even break into tears.

"I'm not playing hide-and-seek for half a bill that probably doesn't exist."

Neal edged farther along the railing away from Benchpress as he said, "Here's how it's going to work. You take the half-bill here and start walking down the path. I stay right here where you can see me. The tree is within sight. When you're, oh, let's say twenty steps away, I'll start giving you directions—you know, 'you're getting warmer, you're getting colder'—until you find the other half."

Benchpress thought about it for a few seconds.

"There are only two paths down from here," he warned Neal.

"I know."

"If you try to screw me, I can catch you."

"I know that, too."

"If I have to do that, I'll break your ribs."

Enough is enough, thought Neal, even for a devoted coward like me. This gig might bring me back onto this guy's turf again, and I'd need *some* status to make a deal. We have to get on a more equal footing here.

"Maybe," Neal said. "I'm carrying, Bruce Lee."

That stopped Benchpress for a second. He hadn't considered the possibility of this goofball having a gun.

"Are you?" he asked, studying the contours of Neal's jacket.

"Naaah."

But you're not sure, Benchpress, are you? Neal thought. That's okay. That's just fine.

"Do we have a deal?" Neal asked.

"I think we can work something out," Benchpress said. He reached out slowly and took the bill from the coin slot. Then he fixed Neal with a hard-guy stare and started to back away.

Neal counted to twenty, slowly and loudly, and then started to give Benchpress directions. The game went on about a minute before Neal saw him reach under the rock and come up with the other half of the bill.

"Okay?" Neal shouted.

"Wait a minute! I'm checking the serial numbers!"

Smart guy, thought Neal. Next time I come back, he'll have an office job.

"Okay!" hollered Benchpress. "Now what?"

"I don't know! I've never done this before! You have any ideas?"

"Why don't I just walk away?"

"How do I know you won't be waiting for me at the bottom?"

"You have an ugly and suspicious mind!"

"Tell me about it!"

Neal was debating with himself whether to trust him, when Benchpress yelled, "Do you have a dime?"

What the hell?

"Yeah!"

"Okay! I'll go to Pier Thirty-nine! You wait fifteen minutes and then put the dime in the binoculars. Look down to Pier Thirty-nine and I'll be standing there waving at you."

Interesting concept, Neal thought. He shouted, "Right! That gives you a good ten minutes to sneak up the other side and then kick my head into the Bay!"

"You don't trust me?"

No, Neal thought, but I don't have a choice, do I? Unless I want to stand on this hill for a few days.

"You can't walk to Pier Thirty-nine in fifteen minutes!" Neal shouted.

"I'm going to take a cab, asshole!"

There was always that.

"Okay, okay. Just get going!"

"It's been nice chasing you!"

"Nice being chased!"

Neal watched as Benchpress disappeared beneath the trees. He checked his watch. It was ten-forty-five, but felt to him like it should be a lot later. He spent the time catching his breath, slowing his heartbeat, and enjoying the view. He waited twelve minutes and then put his dime in the binoculars and focused in on the pier. Benchpress must have found himself a hell of a cabbie, because it was not quite eleven when Neal saw him standing on the pier, looking up toward Telegraph Hill, smiling and waving.

I love a man who takes an honest bribe, Neal thought.

Neal took his time getting down Telegraph Hill. He strolled down Greenwich Street onto Columbus Avenue, stopped to admire the Cathedral of Saints Peter and Paul's terra-cotta towers, and took a seat on a bench in Columbus Square. He shared the bench with two old men who were chatting amiably in Italian. The seat gave him a nice view of the park, where he saw young mothers pushing baby carriages, older Chinese people doing t'ai chi, and still older Italian women, dressed in black, tossing bread crumbs to pigeons. He liked what he saw, but he liked what he didn't see even better: no Benchpress, no small groups of Benchpress's friends and associates searching for a young white guy in a blue blazer and khaki slacks. Trust is one thing, he thought, stupidity is another.

He gave it five minutes on the bench before moving on down Columbus toward the corner of Broadway. Bypassing a half-dozen Italian cafés, bakeries, and espresso bars—there would be time for those later—he headed straight for the City Lights Bookstore.

Neal had known about the City Lights Bookstore long before he had ever visited it. What Shakespeare and Company was to the Lost Generation, City Lights was to the Beat Generation. It was a literary candle in the window that showed the way back from Kesey to Kerouac, and in a sense back to Smollett and Johnson and old Lazarillo des Tormes.

Mostly it was just a goddamn good bookstore that had tables and chairs downstairs where people were encouraged to sit down and actually read books. There were no smarmy signs about its being a business and not a library. Consequently, it was both a pleasure and a privilege to buy a book from City Lights, and that was part of what Neal had in mind.

He stepped through the narrow doorway, nodded a greeting to the clerk at the counter, and headed down the rickety wooden stairs to the basement. Several other pilgrims were browsing the shelves, rapt in their perusal of sections labeled "Counterculture," which held treasures not easily found in Cleveland, Montgomery, or New York.

He did a little browsing himself, settled on a paperback copy of Edward Abbey's *Desert Solitaire,* and sat down at a table. He spent a few minutes enjoying Abbey and then discovered an itch that required scratching on the sole of his left foot. He took off his loafer, removed the notepad and ticket stubs, and put them on the table. One of the great things about City Lights was that nobody cared what you spent your time looking at.

He started with the notepad, which didn't take much time because there was nothing written on it, nor were there any impressions on the top or second pages. So far, no good.

The ticket stubs were more interesting, each being proof of purchase of a $3.50 round-trip fare from Blue Line Transportation on the Number four bus. Six of them, each from last week. Neal didn't know where the Number four bus went, but it couldn't be that far at $3.50. Where the hell could Pendleton have been commuting to? Or was it Lila? A commuting hooker?

Neal stuck the tickets and pad back in his pocket, bought the Bank the copy of *Desert Solitaire*, and headed back up Columbus. He knew exactly what he needed to follow up the lead, and found it at a sidewalk café called La Figaro, where he ordered a double iced espresso and a slice of chocolate cake. Sugar, caffeine, and carbohydrates were exactly the brain food he needed to inspire him, and he was sitting outside reveling in self-indulgence and Edward Abbey when he felt a shadow looming over his shoulder and heard a voice ask, "So, you have any more money for me?"

Neal looked up at him and smiled.

A. Brian Crowe hadn't changed much. He still hung out in the same cafés. He was still tall and skinny, still sported shoulder-length blond hair, and still dressed all in black. Even carried the same black satin cape draped over his shoulder.

"Are there more corporate giants wanting to film their obscenities in front of my art?" Crow asked.

"I'm afraid not."

"Then you could at least offer me an espresso."

"It's the least I could do."

Crowe signaled the waitress, who headed straight for the espresso machine. Crowe was obviously no stranger to cadging drinks at La Figaro.

"How's the life of a starving artist?" Neal asked when the coffee had been served.

"Fat," Crowe answered. He swirled half the espresso around in his mouth, then jerked his head back suddenly and swallowed. He savored the aftertaste, then jerked his thumb back over his shoulder at a skyscraper down in the Financial District. "They wanted a sculpture for their lobby. They commissioned Crowe, who charged them an unconscionable fee, which they foolishly paid. Crowe bought his apartment."

"You *bought* an apartment?"

"It was a very large sculpture," he explained. He tilted the cup into his mouth again and knocked the coffee back. His prominent Adam's apple bobbed, and he looked like a turkey swallowing raindrops. "It occupies a prominent place in a traffic pattern trod by the sensually enslaved but socially ambitious, some of whom have decided to attempt their climb up the social ladder clutching their very own Crowe. The monetary expression of their undying gratitude allows Crowe to live in the manner to which he has become accustomed."

"Sun room? View of the bay?"

"In short, I am *in,* and therefore in the money. Buy me another espresso." His long fingers whipped a card from his pocket.

"C'mon, Crowe! *Business cards?*"

"You know a lot of corporate types, don't you?"

"I guess the Sixties are really over."

Crowe raised an eyebrow at the waitress, who quickly came over with two espressos. Crowe leaned over his cup and looked sadly at Neal. He dropped the artsy pose and said, "My three-piece-suit clients are always asking me to get them acid. *Acid!* I haven't done acid since the first Monterey Festival."

"So you're off the bus?"

"And on the gravy train. The Sixties are over, the Seventies are on the downslide, and the Eighties are almost upon us. You want to be carrying some money into the Eighties. Remember that, young Neal. It's about making money now."

Neal took the card. "My clients don't usually come to me looking for art, but . . ."

"Networking, you know? Networking gets the right people together with the right people."

"The 'right people,' Crowe? You joining the country club next? You were a *communist,* for crying out loud!"

"I turned in my card. I'm thirty-eight years old, young Neal. I can't work for rice and beans and dope anymore. One day I looked in the mirror and saw my happy hippie face differently. It looked pathetic. I was a tourist attraction, local color for the tourists who hadn't figured out the hippie thing was already dead.

"So I quit doing art for art's sake and started doing it for A. Brian Crowe's sake. I learned some interesting things, like the fact that a corporation won't even look at a piece that costs a thousand bucks, but will fight over the same piece when it costs ten thousand bucks. I just started adding zeros to my price tags. I got myself an agent and started going to parties and sipping white wine with the right people. You can call it selling out. . . . I call it *selling*."

Neal avoided his gaze. Crowe looked older. The fire in his eyes had become embers.

"It's okay with me, Crowe."

The artist snapped back into his role. He stood up, whirled his cape around his shoulders, and said, "Crowe's address and phone number are on the card. Give Crowe a call. We'll do dinner."

Neal watched him stride out the door. A. Brian Crowe, flamboyant artist, counterculture hero, Gold Card member.

That's all right, Neal thought. Every one of us is at least two people.

3

Neal got back to the Hopkins, found Blue Line Transportation in the Yellow Pages, dialed the number, and found out that the old Number four plied a route from downtown San Francisco to Mill Valley, where it dropped its passengers at "the Terminal Bookstore." Neal wondered if the Terminal Bookstore specialized in texts for morticians, but was generally willing to ride any bus that ended its journey at a bookstore. He had an hour and a half to catch the two-twenty from Montgomery Street in the Financial District.

He went down to the gift shop in the hotel basement and picked up a guidebook to the Bay Area. The index told him that he could read about Mill Valley on page sixty-four, where he learned that Mill Valley was a charming little village in Marin County, nestled on the southern base of Mount Tamalpais, just a few minutes' drive from the Golden Gate Bridge.

Neal bought a copy of the book and a bright blue vinyl tube bag that proclaimed "I Left My ♡ in San Francisco," and headed back to his room.

He ordered a cheeseburger from room service and started to pack the tube bag. The last bus back from Mill Valley left at 9:00 P.M. and seeing as he didn't have any idea what he was going to do, he didn't know if he'd be done doing it by then, so he packed for an overnight: a black sweater, black jeans, black tennis shoes, gloves, burglary kit, and two thousand dollars in cash. He took a quick shower, changed into a fresh shirt, and put his khaki slacks and all-purpose blue blazer, rep tie, and loafers back on.

The costume made him more forgettable than he was already. With his medium build, medium height, brown hair, and brown eyes, he could have been the poster boy for Anonymous Anonymous.

He wolfed down the eight-dollar cheeseburger, then took his tube bag, his paperback copy of *Ferdinand Count Fathom,* and his unremarkable looks and headed out to catch the two-twenty.

Like a lot of voyages, this one was born of desperation. There was no reason for him to expect that Pendleton and Lila should be in Mill Valley, and no way for him to locate them even if they were. But the tickets to Mill Valley were the only leads he had, so he might as well pursue them. The only other option was to put a call in to Friends and tell them he had blown it, and that was no option at all.

So he figured he'd just take the ride to Mill Valley, snoop around a little, and see what he could see. Maybe he'd have one of those rare instances of dumb luck and run into Pendleton on the bus. Maybe find him at the Terminal Bookstore, poring over the the latest issue of *Chickenshit Illustrated.* Maybe he'd waste an afternoon chasing a wild goose.

But there were worse fates than cruising across the Golden Gate Bridge on a sunny California afternoon. After six months in the rain and fog of a Yorkshire moor, the blue sky and open vista made Neal a little giddy. His cynical heart raced a bit, his jaded New York eyes widened, and his sardonic agent-for-hire leer opened into a smile as he rolled across the bridge, the Pacific on the left, the Bay on the right.

Just a natural-born tourist on an outing, he thought as the bus pulled into Mill Valley. A chameleon, a mere ripple in the shadows: the unobserved observer.

He stood out like a hard-on in a harem.

Nobody in Mill Valley wore a tie, Neal saw, and if anyone wore a jacket, it had leather fringe on it. Everyone was wearing plaid cotton shirts with denim overalls, or denim workshirts and painter's pants, or actual robes. And a lot of sandals, running shoes, and biker boots.

Neal, on the other hand, looked like a Young Republican in need of an enema. Like a Ronald Reagan delegate at a communist party meeting. Like a rookie insurance agent going to sell term-life to Abbie Hoffman. As he stepped off the bus, the locals gathered around the Terminal Bookstore actually stared at him. He couldn't have been any more conspicuous if he had been wearing a sandwich board reading, UPTIGHT, UNCOOL, NON-JOGGING, MEAT-EATING, EAST COAST, URBAN NEOFASCIST WHO DOESN'T MEDITATE. Even the mellow dogs lying under the benches pricked up their ears and started to whine with unaccustomed anxiety, as if expecting Neal to slip a leash on them or otherwise impede their freedom to revel the oneness of nature.

The intellectuals playing chess at the outdoor wooden tables paused in their deliberations to stare at Neal's neckwear. A couple of the older, kinder ones shook their heads in the sadness of a dim memory when they themselves had been similarly encumbered. Three teenagers who were sharing a joint suddenly developed a need to scamper to the trash barrel, which was painted a deep forest green. A winsome young lady playing a wooden flute stopped her warbling and hugged her instrument tightly to her breasts, as if afraid that Neal might snatch it out of her hand and use it to beat a kitten to death.

Neal wished he were naked—he would have felt less self-conscious. But there he stood, fully clad, in beautiful Mill Valley.

And it was beautiful, set in a hollow edged by steep hills made green with pines, cedars and redwoods. Houses built from these native woods blended into the slopes, and their cantilevered decks kept watch over the village. Coffee shops, restaurants, and art studios framed the main square, which was actually a triangle, the apex of which was occupied by the Terminal Bookstore.

The fast-running brook that bordered the west side of the village provided a natural air-conditioning effect; the air was cool and crisp— even cold in the shadows—and people found spots in the sunshine to sit and consider the world. The world seemed a pretty nice place from Mill Valley, as if its citizens had gotten the Sixties right, frozen the best parts of it here, and made them work. The world seemed pretty nice, that is, unless you were wearing a button-down oxford shirt, blue blazer, and polished black loafers.

Neal sought cover in a coffee shop across the street. It had floor-to-ceiling picture windows on three sides. The walls, floors, and counters were made of polished pine, and wooden stools were set by the wrap-around bar. A middle-aged blond women smiled at him as he walked in, attractive wrinkles of laughter and sunshine crinkling around her brown eyes. She was wearing a fire-engine red chamois shirt over faded denims.

"What would you like?" she asked.

"One black coffee to go,"

She stared at him sympathetically.

"What kind?" she asked.

"Black."

She pointed at a blackboard behind her on which about a dozen brands of coffee were written.

"Uuuuhhh," said Neal, "Mozambique Mocha."

"Decaf?"

He felt a sudden burst of courage and defiance.

"Caf," he said. "Double caf, if you have any."

She came back a few moments later and handed him a Styrofoam cup.

"You really should drink decaf," she said as she looked pointedly at his attire. "Really. You looked wired."

"I *am* wired."

"See?"

"I *like* being wired."

"It's an addiction."

"It is."

"Try herbal," she said with great sincerity. It was clear to Neal that she was convinced he was dying.

"Herbal *coffee?*" he asked.

"It's so good."

"And so good for you?"

"You should meditate," she said as she poured him his poison. "Unwind."

"Nah, then I'd just have to get all wound up again."

He took his black, caffeinated Mozambique Mocha and sat on a bench in the square. He sipped at his coffee and wondered what to do next. He had been in Mill Valley for at least five minutes and neither Pendleton nor Lila had shown up yet. Didn't they realize he was on a tight schedule? Oh, well, he thought, when in Mill Valley. . . . He loosened his tie, unbuttoned his collar, set his coffee down, and leaned back, raising his face to the late-afternoon sunshine. Maybe I *should* meditate, he thought. Maybe if I meditate hard enough I can make Pendleton appear. Better yet, Lila.

Her name wasn't Lila, it was Li Lan. She wasn't a prostitute, she was a painter. And she wasn't as beautiful as she was in the snapshot. She was far more beautiful.

Neal stared at the two photographs of her on a poster at the Terminal Bookstore. The poster promoted a showing of her paintings at a local gallery called Illyria. "Shan Shui by Li Lan," it read, and included black-and-white photos of several paintings: large, sprawling landscapes featuring mountains mirrored in rivers and lakes. The photos of Li Lan were arranged so that in one she appeared to be contemplating her work, while in the other she stared out at the viewer. It was this image that captivated Neal. Her face was open and unprotected. All the lines of sorrow and happiness were there for him to read. Gentleness lit her eyes.

We never learn, he thought. We assumed she was a hooker because of who *we* are.

He had only seen the poster because he had quickly become bored with meditating and wandered over to the bookstore to entertain himself. The bookstore turned out to be also a café and cabaret and who knows what else, and it had a bulletin board announcing local events, one of which was Li Lan's show.

The Illyria Gallery was right across the street, three doors down from the coffee shop. He had been looking right at it as he sat on the bench.

He didn't dick around browsing for books or consuming java or eating. Instead, he bought a copy of Shakespeare's *Twelfth Night,* found a phone booth with a directory, and called the Asian Art Museum in San Francisco. He got put on hold several times before he got a staffer who was willing to have a phone conversation with a student doing a research paper.

The bleached wooden door to Illyria was set back between two plate-glass display windows that featured large acrylic landscapes by Li Lan. The interior was a large, whitewashed, open room in which canvas partitions had been hung at strategic angles to display paintings and prints. A few bleached wood stands held small sculptures, and brightly colored printed textiles hung from the high ceiling like sails in a low breeze. A larger version of the poster he had seen was set on an easel just inside the door.

A woman sat behind a desk writing in a ledger book.

" 'And what should I do in Illyria?' " Neal asked her.

"Buy something, I hope," she answered. She was small and maybe in her early forties, with thick, shiny black hair pulled back severely from her face. Her blue eyes were also shiny; she had a small, aquiline nose and thin lips. She wore a black jersey dress and black ballet shoes.

Neal couldn't tell whether she was impressed with his erudition, but she sure did notice the "I Left My ♡ in San Francisco" bag.

"Can I show you something?" she asked.

Like the door, maybe?

"Are you the owner?"

"I am. Olivia Kendall."

"Olivia . . . hence the gallery's name."

"Not many people who walk in here make the connection."

"*Twelfth Night* might be my favorite Shakespeare. Let me see. . . . 'When my eyes did see Olivia first—Methought she purged the air of pestilence. . . .' How's that?"

She stepped out from behind the desk.

"That's pretty good. What can I do for you?"

"I came to see the Li Lans."

"Are you a dealer?"

"No, I just have a strong interest in Chinese painting."

Since about an hour ago.

"Good for you. We've sold several. Tomorrow is the last day of the show."

"I'm not sure I'm buying."

"You'll wish you had. Two of the purchases were museum buys."

"May I look at them?"

"Please."

Neal didn't know a lot about art. He had been to the Met twice, one on a school trip and once on a date with Diane. He didn't hate art, he just didn't care about it.

Until he saw Li Lan's paintings.

They were all mirror images. Steep, dramatic cliffs reflected in water. Swirling pools in rushing rivers that showed distorted images of the mountains above. Their colors were bright and dramatic—almost fierce,

Neal thought, as if the paints were passions fighting to escape . . . something.

"Shan Shui," he said. " 'Mountains and Water,' a reference to the Sung Dynasty form of landscape painting?"

Like the nice lady at the museum told me?

Olivia Kendall's face lit up with surprise. "Who *are* you?" she asked.

I don't know, Mrs. Kendall.

"And she certainly shows a *southern* Sung—*Mi Fei*—influence," Neal continued. He felt like he was back in a seminar, discussing a book he hadn't read. "Very impressionistic, but still within the broader frame of the northern Sung polychromatic tradition."

"Yes, yes!" Olivia nodded enthusiastically. "But the wonderful thing about Li Lan's work is that she has pushed the ancient technique almost to its breaking point by using modern paints and Western colors. The duality of the mirror images reflects—literally—both the conflict and harmony between the ancient and the modern. That's her metaphor, really."

"China's metaphor, as well, I think," Neal said, grateful that Joe Graham wasn't there to hear him.

Neal and Olivia slowly examined the paintings, Olivia translating the titles from Chinese: *Black and White Streams Meet; Pool With Ice Melting; On Silkworm's Eyebrow*—this last showing a narrow trail up a steep slope beneath the reflection of a rainbow.

Then they came to *the* painting. A gigantic precipice was shown reflected in what seemed to be the fog and mist of the bottomless chasm below. On the edge of the cliff sat a painter, a young woman with a blue ribbon in her hair, looking down into the chasm, and her mirror image—the saddest face Neal had ever seen—stared back up from the mists. It was Li Lan's metaphor: a woman sitting serenely with her art and at the same time also lost in an abyss.

The face in the mists was the focal point, and it drew Neal's eye down and in, down and in, falling off the precipice until he felt as if he were trapped in the abyss, looking back up at the face of the painter, up the impossibly steep cliff. In the cool of the northern California dusk his hands began to sweat.

"What's this one called?" he asked.

"The Buddha's Mirror."

"It's incredible."

"Li Lan is incredible."

"How well do you know her?"

Yeah, lady, how well? Well enough to tell me where she is? Who she's with?

"She stays with us when she's in the States."

Careful, Neal, he told himself. Let's be nice and careful.

"She's not a local, then?"

"To Hong Kong, she is. I'd say she comes over here every couple of years or so."

"Is she here now?" he heard himself ask, wondering as he said it if he was moving too quickly.

He felt more than saw Olivia Kendall's curious stare and kept his eyes focused on the painting.

"Yes, she is," Olivia said carefully.

What the hell, he decided, let's roll the big dice.

"I have a great idea," Neal said. "Let me take all of us out to dinner. Mr. Kendall, as well. *Is* there a Mr. Kendall?"

Olivia looked at him real hard for a second and then started to laugh.

"Yes, there is definitely a Mr. Kendall. There is also a Mr. Li, so to speak."

"I'm afraid I don't catch your drift."

Okay, okay. Just tell me that she's otherwise engaged, all right?

"Are you interested in her paintings or in *her*? Not that I blame you—she's drop-dead gorgeous." She reached out and patted his arm. "Sorry. You're a little young, and she's very involved."

Bingo.

Okay, Neal, he told himself—think. How about *The Book of Joe Graham*, Chapter Three, Verse Fifteen: "Tell people what they want to hear, and they'll believe it. Most people aren't naturally suspicious like you and me. They only see one layer deep. You make that top layer look real, you're home free."

He looked Olivia Kendall right in the eyes, always a useful thing to do when you're lying.

"Ms. Kendall," he said, "these are the most beautiful paintings I've ever seen. Meeting their creator would make me very happy."

She was an art lover, and he was counting on that. She wanted to believe that a young man could find art so moving that he had to meet the artist. He knew it had far less to do with her perception of him than with her perception of herself.

"You're very sweet," she said, "but I'm afraid we have plans. In fact, Lan is making dinner tonight. Some Chinese home cooking."

"I'll bring my own chopsticks. . . ."

"Seriously, who are you?"

"That's a complicated question."

"Shall we begin with an easy one? What's your name?"

That's not as easy as you might think, Olivia. My mother gave me the "Neal," and we just sort of settled on the "Carey."

"Neal Carey."

"Now that wasn't so hard. And what do you do, Neal Carey, when you aren't inviting yourself to dinner?"

"I'm a graduate student at Columbia University."

"In . . ."

"New York."

"I meant what's your major?"

"Art history," he said, and regretted it as soon as the syllables were out of his mouth. That was a really stupid mistake, he thought, seeing as everything you know about art history is scribbled on a spiral pad in your pocket. Joe Graham would be ashamed of you. Oh, well, too late now. "I'm writing my thesis on the anti-Manchu messages encoded in Qing Dynasty paintings."

Oh, God, was it Qing or Ming? Or neither, or all of the above?

"You're kidding."

Oh, please, don't let that be "You're kidding" as in, "You're kidding, that's what I did *my* thesis on."

"No."

"That's hopelessly remote."

"People often say the same thing about me."

"How *did* you come to be interested in something so obscure?"

"I revel in the obscure."

Which is true, he thought. My real thesis is on the themes of social alienation in Smollett's novels. So feel sorry for me and invite me to dinner.

"Listen," Olivia said, "tonight really is a private sort of evening. But I'm sure Lan will come in tomorrow to help close the show down. Could you come back then? Maybe we could have lunch."

41

Yeah, and maybe you'll tell Li Lan and Dr. Bob about the interesting visitor you had in the shop and they'll take off. Maybe you've already seen through my act.

"I'm going home tomorrow morning."

"Sorry," she said. Then, as if offering a consolation prize, she warbled, "Did I give you a brochure? It has photos of the paintings."

She reached over to one of the pedestals and handed him one of the slick, four-color catalogs.

"Thank you. Do you think you could ask Li Lan to sign this for me?"

"You can ask her yourself. Here she is."

I didn't even hear the door, I'm so out of shape, Neal thought.

Then he stopped thinking altogether and fell in love and it was just like falling off the edge of a cliff into the clouds. Falling toward Li Lan in the mists.

Olivia said, "Li Lan, Neal Carey. Neal Carey, Li Lan. Neal is a big fan of your work."

It took her a moment to work out the slang, then she flushed slightly, struggling to set down the two grocery bags she was holding. She put them down on the the floor and then bowed her head ever so slightly to Neal. "Thank you."

Neal was surprised to feel himself also blushing, and more surprised to notice that he bowed back. "Your paintings are beautiful."

She was small, and a little thinner than he would have thought from her pictures. She was wearing a paint-stained T-shirt and black jeans, and still looked elegant. Her hair was pulled back into a single ponytail tied with a blue ribbon. Those gentle brown eyes sparkled like sunshine on autumn leaves.

"I went to the city," she told Olivia, "to do some special shopping for dinner tonight."

"You should have had Tom or Bob bring you. I'll call Tom to come pick you up."

"I can walk," she said. "It is a beautiful day. And they are busy speaking about garden."

"I'm calling them."

Li Lan nodded her head. "According to your thought."

"Neal is a student of Chinese art history," Olivia said.

Oh, shit. Shit, shit, shit. Shit.

"Truly?" asked Li Lan.

Well, no.

"He is doing research on Qing Dynasty painting. Something political."

Had he been alert, had he been in true working shape, he might have noticed Li's slight wince on the word *political.* She turned those eyes to him as she said, "Ah, yes . . . Chinese paintings can mean many different things at same time. Picture of single flower is picture of single flower but also picture about loneliness. Qing picture of—what is word?— goldfish . . . shows just fish, not fish in water. Perhaps is about Chinese people with no country. Perhaps is about just goldfish."

"Do your paintings mean many different things?" Neal asked. His voice sounded funny to him, thin and hollow.

She laughed. "No, they are merely pictures."

"Of real places?"

"To me." She smiled shyly and then turned stone-serious and looked down at the floor.

No wonder he loves her, Neal thought. Run away, Doctor Bob, run away. Take her with you or follow her where she goes, but don't let her go.

Suddenly he was desperate to keep the conversation going. "Are you speaking about the reality of the mind?"

She looked up at him and said, "It is the *only* reality, truly."

"You two have so much to discuss," Olivia said. It was one of those unspoken questions women are so good at asking each other. Do you want to invite this guy to the dinner? Would Bob mind? It's okay with me if it's okay with you.

"I think then he must join us for dinner," Li Lan said. "Is that all right?"

"What a good idea!" Olivia said, as if the thought had never occurred to her or to Neal, even though all three of them knew exactly what had transpired.

"I must warn you, *I* do the cooking. Is it still all right?"

"It sounds wonderful."

"It is not, but I would be delighted."

"Eight o'clock?" Olivia asked them both.

"Great," Neal said.

"Very good," said Li Lan. "Now I better be going, get busy."

"I'll call Tom."

43

"No, please. I can walk."

"The bags look heavy," Neal said.

"Not very heavy."

Olivia shook her head and said to Neal, "She's a tough lady."

Li Lan flexed her biceps and made a ferocious face. "Oh, yes. Very tough." Then she dissolved into seemingly helpless laughter.

Neal knew all about helpless right then.

So he did something he knew how to do. He went to the library. Maybe it would settle him down, and God only knew he needed to bone up on Chinese art. Jesus, he thought, why did I have to come up with that stupid lie? I know better than to overreach like that.

Settle down, he told himself. So Li Lan is beautiful, so what? You knew that coming in. So she's an artist instead of a hooker? So what? You know some nasty artists and some pretty nice hookers, so don't jump to conclusions. So she did a painting that sucked your soul into a vortex, so what? It's not much of a soul to begin with.

So why are you so obsessed with Li Lan? Pendleton is the subject. So shake it off. Cool out. This is just another job, another gig, and the endgame is to send Pendleton home, stop his California dreaming, and get him back to the lab. Then you can go back to your own desk. So do it.

So do what? What now? You can't hand her two K and tell her her to dump him. That plan is out the old window. Maybe she'd like to go to North Carolina with him. Yeah, right. Maybe he'd like to go to Hong Kong with her. Maybe . . . maybe you should actually talk to them before forming any opinions. Just lay it out to Pendleton and see what happens. Keep your head and do your goddamn job.

He found the Asian arts section in the subject card catalog, then went to the stacks and tried to concentrate on Qing Dynasty landscape painting. That's what he started with, anyway. He ended up staring at the photo of Li Lan in the brochure.

He grabbed a cab at Terminal Square and gave the driver Kendall's address.

Olivia answered the door. She had changed into a white silk brocade jacket over black silk trousers. "In honor of the occasion," she said, brushing the backs of her fingers across the jacket.

"Stunning," Neal said.

"A gift from Li Lan. Please come in."

The house seemed built for magic evenings. The large, open living room was dominated by windows that stretched from the floor to the cathedral ceilings. The floors were made of wide hardwood planks brought to a high polyurethane shine. Broad cedar crossbeams spanned the width of the room. The eggshell-white walls highlighted black-and-white photographs as well as prints and paintings.

Outside the window a pine deck wrapped itself around a steep slope. Steps led from the deck onto a flagstone patio surrounded by a cedar fence that provided privacy from the scattered houses on the facing hills. Potted shrubs, flowers, and bonsai trees sat on the deck around a sunken hot tub.

A large jute sofa sat in front of a glass coffee table and faced the picture window. Two cushioned chairs were set off at angles to the sofa to create a sitting area. To the left of that was a dining-room table, and farther to the left, behind a breakfast bar, was a spacious kitchen centered by a large butcher's block.

The table was set with black dishes, glasses, and a black tea set. A large white lily in a black vase was the centerpiece.

Li Lan was standing in the kitchen, carefully stirring something in a sizzling electric wok. Dr. Robert Pendleton stood beside her, holding a platter full of diced tofu.

"Okay . . . now," Li Lan told him, and he dumped the tofu into the wok.

"Two more minutes," she said.

"That will give you time to meet our guest," Olivia said. "Neal, this is Bob Pendleton."

"Nice to meet you," Neal said. Yeah, right.

Pendleton wiped his hands on a towel, pushed his glasses back up on his nose, then reached across the breakfast counter and shook Neal's hand.

"Pleasure," he said.

Not so fast, Doc.

"Now, where did Tom get to?" Olivia asked no one in particular.

"He went to fire up the hot tub," Pendleton said. "Can I offer you a drink, Neal?"

"A beer?"

"Dos Equis or Bud?"

"Bud, please."

"Bud it is."

Neal watched him as he went to the refrigerator and looked for the beer. He was even thinner than he looked in his photograph, with a body that looked like it had never met a quart of chocolate ice cream. He was wearing a bright green chamois shirt and baggy khaki trousers, with a pair of brown moccasins that someone must have bought for him; they were much too laid back for a biochemist. His hair was a trace longer than it had been in the photo, and he looked older. Neal was surprised at his voice—it was low and gravelly—but didn't know why he should be. Preconceptions again, he guessed.

Pendleton set a bottle of beer on the counter.

"Do you want a mug?" he asked.

"The bottle is great, thanks."

"Get ready with sauce," Li said. "Hello, Neal."

She was preoccupied with preparing the meal, which was okay with Neal because it gave him a chance to stare at her. Her hair hung long and straight—the blue cloisonné comb had only a decorative function. She had put on light eyeshadow and red lipstick. Her black western shirt had red piping and red roses on the shoulders, and her black, pointed-toe cowboy boots were etched with blue designs. It was one of those outfits that could look either ridiculous or wonderful. It looked wonderful.

Neal was in the midst of this observation when Tom Kendall came in. He was short and plump, with prematurely white hair and a white beard. He was sporting a green chamois shirt that looked identical to Pendleton's, and jeans with sandals. He had light blue eyes and a ruddy complexion.

What's the bit with the lookalike shirts? Neal wondered. Who is Pendleton supposed to be in love with, anyway? Li Lan or Tom Kendall?

"The tub," Kendall said in a soft, reedy voice, "will be *hot* by the time we're ready. Neal—I assume you are Neal—when you are a Marin County shrink married to a woman who owns an art gallery, you are expected to have a hot tub. It wouldn't do to violate an archetype."

He smiled broadly and shook Neal's hand. "I'm Tom Kendall."

"Neal Carey."

"I see you have a beer, which prompts the question: why don't *I* have a beer? Why don't I have a beer, Olivia?"

46

"I don't know, sweetie."

"You'll have to get it yourself," Pendleton said. "I'm in big trouble if I miss my sauce cue."

"*Big* trouble," Lan said.

"Some bartender. Bob and Lan are the official host and hostess tonight," Kendall explained to Neal. "Bob can't cook, so the deal was he would tend the bar."

"Now with the sauce," Li Lan said, and Pendleton poured a small bowl of red sauce into the wok. The sizzling stopped with a whoosh.

Olivia said, "Neal, please have a seat." She gestured toward the sofa.

"Actually, I'd rather watch the cooking."

"No, please sit," said Li Lan. "Dinner should be surprises."

Dinner was surprises.

The first round of drinks was a surprise. Having consumed his share of straight scotch in his time, Neal didn't figure any little Chinese wine in a tiny black cup could get to him, but the clear, fiery liquid scorched his throat and smoked his brain. He didn't quite manage to utter the salutation, *"Yi lu shun feng,"* offered by the rest of the party. Instead he choked out, "Jesus, what the hell is this?"

"Ludao shaojiu," Lan said. "White wine, very strong."

"Uh-huh," Neal answered.

Then she set a plate of appetizers on the table. They were pastries—translucently thin dough filled with red bean paste. The pastries were very sweet, which was just fine with Neal as they put out the flames in his mouth.

"These are *won*derful!" Olivia said.

"Xie xie ni," Li Lan answered. Thank you.

"So good they deserve a toast," Tom Kendall said, and he filled everyone's cup with more wine. "What's a good toast in Chinese?"

Li lifted her cup. *"Gan bei*—empty cup."

"Gan bei!" they responded.

Neal managed the toast this time and threw back the wine. He was surprised that it went down easily. Something like fighting fire with fire, he thought.

Li had gone back into the kitchen, and she came back with the next course, individual bowls of cold noodles in sesame sauce. She noticed Neal's discomfiture as everyone started to dig in with their chopsticks.

Smiling at him, she said, "Put bowl to mouth, use chopsticks to push in."

"Slurp," Pendleton said. "Just get them up near your mouth and slurp."

Neal slurped, and the noodles seemed to jump out of the bowl into his mouth. He wiped a drop of sesame sauce off his chin and felt a twinge of guilt. What are you waiting for? he asked himself. Pull the trigger. Pendleton's sitting right across the table from you, so just say something like, "Dr. Bob, the folks at AgriTech want you to punch in now, so what are you going to do?" Why don't you say that, Neal? Tell him you're here to hound him until he goes home? Because you're not ready to have them despise you yet. Because you like these people. Because Li Lan is smiling at you. He opened his mouth to speak and then filled it with more noodles. There'd be time for betrayal later. Maybe after the next course.

The next course was pot stickers, small, pan-fried dumplings. Li Lan had made three for each of them. "One shrimp, one pork, one vegetable," she said, and then laid three small bowls in the center of the table. "Mustard, sweet sauce, peppercorn sauce, very hot," she said.

She walked around the table, stood behind Neal, picked up his pair of the black enamel chopsticks, and put them in his right hand. Then she laid one of the sticks between his thumb and index finger, and the other under his forefinger. Then she lifted his hand, squeezed so that the sticks seized one of the pot stickers, and then guided his hand to dip the pastry into the mustard. Then she brought the food to his mouth. "See?" she asked. "Easy."

Neal could barely swallow.

"Lan," Olivia scolded, "you've hardly eaten a thing!"

Lan sat down, effortlessly stabbed a pot sticker, swished it in a generous amount of peppercorn sauce, and popped it into her mouth.

"It is very bad," she said, and then devoured another one.

"Is very good," Pendleton told her. "Uhhh . . . *hen hao.*"

"Very good!" she said. "You are learning Chinese."

Neal watched Pendleton blush—actually blush—with pleasure. This guy is in love, he thought, major league.

"More beer," Pendleton said awkwardly, aware that the Kendalls were beaming at him. He brought back two handfuls of Tsingtao bottles and passed them around.

The beer was ice cold and tasted great along with the hot mustard and the hotter peppercorn. Neal drank it in long draughts and practiced with his chopsticks as Tom Kendall and Bob Pendleton talked about feeding the roses in the garden out back. Li Lan popped back into the kitchen and emerged with another dish: a whole smoked sea bass on a platter. She showed them how to use their chopsticks to pry the white flesh off the bones, and it took a long time, another beer, and another round of *ludao* to finish off the fish.

As they were celebrating their conquest with more cups of wine, Olivia Kendall said, "So, Neal, tell us about your work."

Well, Olivia, I'm a rent-a-rat who has lied his way into your house in order to threaten your friends.

"It's very boring, really," he said.

"Not at all."

"Well," he said, reaching through the haze of wine, beer and food to try to recall his notes, "primarily I'm interested in the political subtext contained in Qing Dynasty paintings as an effort to subvert the ruling foreign Manchus."

Okay?

"And how do you pursue this research? What are the sources?" Tom Kendall asked.

Et tu, Tom?

"Museums mostly," he said. "Some books, doctoral dissertations . . . the usual."

He wondered if he sounded as stupid to them as he did to himself. Come on, Neal, end this. Just tell them that you wouldn't know a Qing Dynasty painting if it was tattooed on your left testicle. Get it over with.

"You have looked at the pictures at the De Young Museum?" Lan asked.

The De Young Museum . . . San Francisco.

"Oh, yes," he answered. "Superb."

He looked at Pendleton and asked, "Now, what do you do?"

A pathetic desperation effort, Neal thought.

"I'm a biochemist," Pendleton said.

"Where?"

Pendleton pushed his glasses up on the bridge of his nose. His lips edged into a small smile as he answered, "I'm between jobs right now. So I'm abusing the hospitality of these good people."

"Nonsense," Tom said quickly. "Bob is the official Kendall Household Adviser on Rose Fertilization."

"You've done a wonderful job," Sylvia said. "Now if you could just think of a way to kill the weeds . . ."

"Not my line, I'm afraid. I only know how to make stuff grow."

"You can keep your present position for as long as you want," said Kendall.

"The pay isn't so hot," Pendleton said, "but the food is great, the beer is cold, and the company . . ."

Pull the trigger, Neal. Pull it now.

"The company is sublime," Neal said.

Yeah, it is, he thought as he finished off his cup of wine. You cultivate loneliness like a flower in your garden, you treat people like weeds that need to be torn away, and here is a world where people love eating together, talking together . . . love being with each other. A world you've imagined but never experienced. Until now. Until this evening. Talk about abusing the hospitality of good people. . . .

"Chicken with peanuts and dried red peppers," he heard Li Lan saying, and he looked up to see her set down a steaming plate.

"The peppers are not for eating," she continued, "just for flavor."

The chicken dish stoked the dormant flames in Neal's throat and brought tears to his eyes. Every bite was hotter and more delicious than the last and made the wine taste sweeter and cooler.

He watched Li Lan gracefully take the half-peanuts with her chopsticks and feed them to Pendleton, and he felt simultaneously touched and jealous. Let him go, he thought. Let him go and let yourself go. You can start over. Take the rest of your money out of the bank and stay here. Apply to Berkeley. Or Stanford. Or become the Official Kendall Household Adviser on Eighteenth-Century English Literature. You must be getting drunk. *Getting* drunk? You *are* drunk. With wine, with beer, with great food, with soft lights, with . . . you're drunk.

"Oh, God, *more?*" he heard Olivia groan in mock despair as Li Lan brought out a plate of broccoli, bamboo shoots, water chestnuts, and mushrooms in bean sauce.

"Your show ends tomorrow?" he asked Lan as he munched on a crisp stem of brocolli.

"Yes," she answered sadly.

"It was very successful," said Olivia.

"Then where do you go?" Neal asked.

She didn't answer. You could cut the tension with a chopstick, Neal thought.

"Home," she said quietly.

"Hong Kong?" Neal asked.

She looked straight at him. "Yes. Home. Hong Kong."

"Let's not talk about it," Olivia said. "It makes me sad."

What about you, Dr. Bob? thought Neal. Does this mean you're going home, too?

"I have a toast to propose!" said Tom. "Fill up your cups!"

Olivia poured out the wine.

Tom lifted his cup and scanned the table, looking each of them in the eye, then said, "To beauty—the beauty of Lan's art, the beauty of the crops that grow through Robert's knowledge, and the beauty of friendship."

Neal drained his cup as a stupid question came to him: Had Judas liked the wine at the Last Supper?

Neal had never liked being naked. People didn't get naked in New York, not outdoors, anyway, and they sure as hell didn't shuck their clothes in public in England. But it was hot-tub time, and his hosts insisted that he join them. They didn't use bathing suits in Marin County, and he was undercover—so to speak—so he surrendered his clothing in exchange for a promised towel and robe and then slid into the deepest part of the hot tub. He was grateful for the dim blue lighting on the deck, and more grateful that it was only Pendleton who joined him at first.

"I'm not a hot-tub kind of guy," Neal said.

"Neither am I."

"Then what are we doing here?"

"I wanted to talk with you and know I'm not being recorded."

Great, Neal thought. You sure fooled them.

"So, did the company send you?" Pendleton asked.

Neal thought about saying something clever like "What company?" or "Huh?" but decided that the old game was up and he might as well get it over with.

"Yeah."

"That's what I thought. Lan says that you don't know anything about Chinese painting."

"I just know what I like."

If Pendleton thought the joke was funny, he disguised it pretty well. "What does the company want?" he asked.

"They want you back."

Jesus, this is stupid, Neal thought. Sitting here up to my chin in steaming water, half in the bag, trying to persuade another naked man to go back to work. I *have* to get a real job.

"I'm not going back," Pendleton said. His thin chest puffed out in determination.

"What's the problem?"

Perspiration had slid Pendleton's glasses down his nose, and he pushed them back up again. Then he said, "You've seen her."

Yeah, Doc. I've seen her all right. I wish I hadn't.

"Look, Doc, they allow love in North Carolina."

"To a Chinese woman?"

Come on, Doc, Neal thought. Lighten up. Join us in the 1970s. What's the big deal?

"Sure, why not?"

Pendleton snorted sarcastically and shook his head. "I'm going with her," he said.

"Yeah, well, there's a problem with that."

"Yeah? What problem?" Pendleton asked.

Neal saw that he was getting pissed off.

"You have a contract that has a year and change left. They'll sue you."

"Let them try to get to my money in Hong Kong."

The hot water was starting to get to Neal. The wine didn't exactly help, either. He felt enervated, tired.

"Doc, you don't want to do that. Look, if it's really love, it'll last a year and a half. She can visit you, you can visit her. . . . I'll bet AgriTech would even spring for the air fare. Finish out your time and then you'll be free and clear."

It's been about a year since I left Diane, Neal thought, and I don't think it's going to last. And who am I to talk about being free and clear? I haven't been either free or clear in my whole life. If I were, I wouldn't be sitting here.

"You're never free from those people," Pendleton said bitterly. "Once they have you, they think they own you forever."

I know the feeling, Doc.

"It's a free country, Dr. Pendleton. If you don't want to sign the *next* contract, don't sign it. But the harsh fact is that you have to honor the one you have." Or love the one you're with, or something like that, and why did I have to drink all those toasts?

"Honor?" Pendleton said with a chortle. "I don't know."

They sank into a sullen silence. It didn't last long, because Li Lan came out wearing a black robe and carrying a tray with a teapot and three cups. She set the tray down by the edge of the tub and then straightened up and undid the belt of the robe.

Just then Neal couldn't quite figure out whether Li Lan dropping her robe would be the best thing in the world or the worst thing in the world, and when she opened the robe around her shoulders and then let it slide to the deck, it turned out to be both. His heart stopped, his throat tightened, and he tried not to stare as she slipped into the hot water beside Pendleton. She rested one hand on his shoulder.

"Now we are all undressed," she said to Neal.

"He *is* from the company," said Pendleton.

Lan nodded.

"They sent him to bring me back," Pendleton continued.

"To talk to you," Neal said. "I can't bring you back against your will. I can't throw cuffs on you and haul you onto a plane."

"You're damned right you can't," Pendleton said. He looked like an angry bird.

"Robert . . ." said Lan quietly, stroking his shoulder, calming him down.

"Just go back and talk to them," Neal offered. "You owe them that, don't you? At least go back and tell them you're quitting, see if you can work things out."

He kept talking, laying out the whole thing: It was no big deal, everything was forgiven, Pendleton wasn't the first guy to fall in love and lose his head for a while, no sense in destroying a distinguished career. Why, Neal himself would even help Pendleton negotiate some sort of visiting arrangement. Swept away with his own eloquence, he pushed on: North Carolina is beautiful; a change of scene would help Lan grow as an artist; there is, in fact, a large Oriental community in the Research

Triangle. He was so convincing he convinced himself: their life would be great, *his* life would be great, they would visit each other for magic evenings.

Lan turned around and started to pour three cups of tea. The movement of her shoulder blades sent another pang shooting through Neal. When she turned back and leaned over to hand Neal a cup he could see the tops of her breasts, but it was still her eyes that drew him. She seemed to be looking into his mind, maybe into his soul. She handed Pendleton a cup and then leaned back to sip her own tea.

"Maybe Neal Carey's thought is correct," she said.

"I'm not leaving you," Pendleton said quickly. He sounded like a twelve-year-old.

"Will Robert have much trouble if he does not return?"

"His research is very important."

"Yes, it is." She smiled at Pendleton warmly, and Neal would have donated his *live* body to science to see that smile sent his way.

"You're *more* important," said Pendleton thickly, and Neal had the sudden impression that Pendleton was going to start crying.

"It's not an either/or situation," Neal said.

" 'Either/or'? " Lan asked.

"One thing or the other."

She took another sip of tea, set the cup down, and took Pendleton's face gently in her hands. She leaned toward him until her face was an inch from his.

"*Wo ai ni,*" she said softly. I love you.

It was such an intimate moment that Neal wanted to turn away. His Chinese was pretty much confined to Column A or Column B, but he knew that she had told Pendleton that she loved him.

"*Wo ai ni,*" Pendleton answered.

Li Lan reached out under the water and took Neal's hand, gently folding his fingers into hers.

His heart started to race.

She let his hand go.

"We will go with you tomorrow," she said. "Both of us."

Pendleton's head whipped around like he'd been jerked on a choke chain and he started to protest, but Li Lan's hand on his stopped him.

"Your work is important," she said.

She closed her eyes and settled into the water—the image of perfect repose.

Pendleton couldn't let it go as easily. "Tomorrow—"

She cut him off without opening her eyes, "—is a dream. Tom and Olivia wish to speak with you now."

It was one of those don't-I-hear-your-mother-calling-you bits, and Neal watched as Pendleton dutifully got out of the water, wrapped a towel around his waist, and stomped into the house. So much for the submissive Oriental woman, Neal thought. Then he realized he was alone with Li Lan, and he stopped thinking altogether. They sat there for at least five excruciating minutes before she spoke.

"You will not let them hurt him?" she asked.

Hurt him?! What the fuck?

"Nobody wants to hurt him, Lan. They just want him to come back to work." I mean, we're talking about a research lab here, right? not the Gambino family.

"Please do not let them hurt him," she implored.

"Okay." Look at me like that, Li Lan, and I won't even let them hurt his feelings.

"Promise."

"I promise." Should be an easy enough request to fill. They want him back so bad they'll probably give him a raise and a bonus. Monogrammed test tubes. Fur-lined eyepiece on the microscope.

Li Lan stood up. She stood in front of Neal as if inviting him to look her over, as if she were in a lineup at a cathouse. He tried to look away, tried as hard as the booze, the steam of the tub, and his own feelings for her would let him. He felt himself swallowing hard and staring, first at her body and then at her eyes.

"I will go to speak with him," she said.

Neal looked around for a towel but didn't see one. "Yeah, it's about time to get going."

She shook her head. "No. Wait for me, please. I will come back."

"Uhhh, would you bring a towel, please?"

"You are shy."

"Yeah."

She put her robe on. The silk stuck to her wet skin.

"There is no reason to be shy. I will come back to thank you."

"Aww, shucks, m'am. You don't need to thank me . . . jes' doin' my job."

He was pretty surprised when she leaned over and kissed him, quickly and softly, on the lips. "I will be back in a moment . . . to thank you."

It was a whisper of a promise.

"No," he said, more reluctantly than he felt real good about.

She looked at him quizzically.

"You don't understand," Neal said. "That's not the way it works. You don't need to buy . . . insurance."

Of course, if you want to leave him and run away with me and live happily ever after, that's another story.

"It's not insurance. You have been very nice."

Right. She's not buying it. She's still scared for him, and she's ready to give it up to get a little added protection. Where does a painter learn about that?

"Really, Lan. No thanks."

But please don't ask again, Lan, because I think I'm out of no-thank-yous.

She looked confused for the smallest part of a second, then smiled and shrugged. The robe came off her shoulders with the shrug and she gave him another long look, a think-about-what-you're-passing-up pose, and it shook him. Backlit by the light coming through the picture window, she looked unreal, unearthly—divorced from the mundane world of reality, and jobs to do, and boring ethics. She became part of a magical evening, of a different kind of life—a world in which he wanted to lose himself, float with her in the mirror mists. He told himself to get up, get out, but she froze him in place, held him in the whirlpool, trapped him in the vortex.

He leaned over to splash some water on his face and barely heard the whine of the bullet that just missed his head and smacked into the wall of the house.

He sank into the water.

4

品

Terror has a way of clearing the mind.

You can cloud the brain with exotic booze and plain old-fashioned lust, but then shoot a little terror at it, and it will clean right up. Adrenaline is a wonderful thing.

So Neal was already thinking hard as he sank under the water. It was noisy down there, with the filters and bubblers and all, but he could hear Li Lan's footsteps running, not walking away, and he could hear a car pull out of the driveway and screech down the street. He figured it was either his hosts or his would-be executioners, or both at the same time.

He was in no hurry to surface, though, just in case the shooter still had an eye to the crosshairs and was was waiting for him. It took an act of great will for Neal to let himself rise to the surface, dead-man's-float style, and show the back of his head on the water. He lay there holding his breath and trying not to think about that second bullet smashing into his skull, spattering bone, blood, and brains.

He hadn't heard the bullet leave the gun, so it must have been silenced, but he sure as hell had heard it smack the wall. You can't silence that. So he didn't think the shooter would hang around too long, or even come check on the body. But you never knew . . . the shooter could be moving on him now, coming up slowly and carefully, with a pistol this time, to deliver the coup de grace. Neal knew he'd never hear him in the noise of the hot tub, never hear the shot that would kill him.

He lay as still in the water as he could, hoping that if the shooter was still there, he was watching him through the scope of a rifle from a distance, where he wouldn't be able to see if there was blood in the water or not. He held his breath, trying for one more minute, just one more minute, and then he'd make the break.

She set me up, he thought as pain started to shoot through his lungs. Literally set me up. Put me on my feet, up nice and straight where I'd be a perfect target and she'd be safe. But why? I guess I'll have to find her and ask her.

He sank his head back under the water and then lunged up, diving for the edge of the pool. He rolled twice in the direction the shot had come from and pressed himself against the fence. Forcing himself to count slowly to five, he caught his breath and then scrambled on all fours to the sliding glass door, reached up to open it, and dove behind the sofa.

His skin pricked with the pins and needles of fear.

The house was quiet. Of course it would be, wouldn't it, he thought, if someone were waiting with a gun. While I crouch here, naked and dripping and just wanting to lie down and cry. Okay, okay, get on with it. Get dry, get some clothes on, and get going. First things first. Let's make sure we're all alone in the house.

The first couple of steps were the hardest. He straightened up and walked past the big picture window. He checked behind the breakfast bar, then walked down the hallway and looked into the bedrooms and the baths. He was alone in the house. Where had all his new little friends gone? Off somewhere waiting for all the nasty blood to drain out of the filter system? Pretty damn smart, shooting him in a hot tub. So little to clean up.

They were so damn confident they had left his clothes right there in the guest bedroom where he had shucked them. His vinyl bag also. That struck him as odd. Why hadn't they taken his belongings along with them and dumped them? Maybe they were waiting to get rid of them along with his corpse.

He checked his bag. They had clearly gone through it, but hadn't taken anything. All his nice burglar stuff, his book, even the two grand in cash were all there. Strange, but true.

He took a towel from the bathroom rack and dried himself. Now what would Graham tell me to do in this situation, he asked himself. Easy. He'd tell me to get the fuck out of here, lay low, and call in for help. "No job is so important," the gremlin had told him more than once, "it's worth dying for. Believe me, son, the client wouldn't do it for you." None of the usual jokes or insults, just a straightforward command: Save your ass.

So, according to the Gospel According to Graham, Book One, Chapter One, Verse One, he should waste no time and haul his butt out of there. But he was beginning to get past the fear into something else: anger. He was starting to get goddamned good and pissed off that they had tried to kill him—*would* have killed him if he hadn't leaned over to splash a little water on his face—and he wanted to get a little of his own back. They had made the worst kind of fool of him, set him up in the worst kind of way. Betrayed him.

The absurdity hit him. How could *they* betray *me*, he thought? It would be like Christ pulling a pistol on Judas after the kiss.

Nevertheless, he was angry. And scared. Someone had tried to kill him and he didn't know why and that was a dangerous situation. He put on the black sweatshirt, jeans, and tennis shoes he had packed in the bag, then smeared some black greasepaint on his face. If they were out there somewhere wanting to put a bullet in him, he could at least make it a little harder on them. Then he opened the window and threw his bag out, put both hands on the top of the sill, and swung through, falling gently into some shrubs. It took him ten minutes to find just the right tree, a tall, thick cedar with a low-hanging limb. He hauled himself up on the limb and climbed as high as his fear of heights would let him: about another ten feet.

His perch gave him a nice view of the Kendall household, which was what he wanted. He especially wanted to see what would happen when someone came to dispose of a body that had disposed of itself.

Three hours is a long time on surveillance, but particularly long when you're literally up a tree. Neal cursed everyone he could think of, starting with Joe Graham, the Man, Levine, Pendleton, the Kendalls, and concluding with one Li Lan, a true artist in every sense of the word. She painted some pretty pictures, all right.

He was still thinking about her when the car—a dumb Saab, naturally—pulled into the driveway, and the Kendalls got out. If they were shaken up with guilt, or hyped with blood lust, or even enervated from a rather special evening, they showed no signs of it. Olivia went straight into the house as Tom went around to the deck. Neal watched as he pulled the blue plastic cover over the tub and then turned the lights out. If there was supposed to be a dead Neal Carey in there, this guy sure didn't know about it.

Maybe I imagined the whole damned thing, he thought. Then he remembered the sight of Li Lan standing naked on the deck wearing only that smile, and he could hear the sound of that bullet like it was through a headset, and he knew he hadn't imagined anything. Someone had tried to take him out of the game permanently, and he didn't have a clue who or why. He waited for another half hour to see if anything more interesting developed. It didn't, so he let himself down from the tree.

Well, he thought, they suckered me with the oldest combination known to man, booze and a woman. I guess I put one over on them: They wasted their money on the booze.

He moved cautiously but at a steady pace, using the sides of the streets to walk from tree to tree. He knew it would get trickier as he got closer to town, and standing at a phone booth would be the riskiest part, but that was a chance he had to take. He remembered that there was a convenience store on the other side of town, and he headed there. His route would take him through Terminal Square and right past the bookstore and the gallery. It was too much open ground, so he cut north of the square and worked his way toward the sound of running water. He let himself down into the creekbed and followed it south. There was more creek than bed, so he spent most of the walk sloshing through ankle-deep running water—or falling into ankle-deep running water—and it took him an hour to make it to where he thought the convenience store was. He crawled to the edge of the creekbed and peeked out. He had overshot the store by about a quarter of a mile, but there, glistening in the modest parking lot, was a phone booth.

Neal walked back up along the bed, came up to the lip again, checked that the road was empty, and crossed over to the telephone.

He dialed the number he had found in his wallet.

A grumpy voice answered on the eighth ring. "What!"

"Crowe?"

"Who else?"

"It's Neal Carey. I need your help."

"Are you having an aesthetic crisis?"

"Sort of."

Crowe's Porsche 911—black, of course—rolled into the parking lot just before sunrise. Neal, huddled and shivering in the wet grass on the edge of the creekbank, scrambled across the road and jumped into the passenger seat.

"Drive," said Neal, "and turn the heat on."

Crowe put the car in gear, pumped up the heat, and glanced at Neal's black clothes and black face.

"I can understand a philistine like you trying to emulate Crowe, but do you think you have perhaps taken it a bit too far?"

"Crowe, how do you feel about harboring a fugitive?"

"Are you in trouble with the law?"

"The cops are probably looking for me."

Crowe's face broke into a huge grin as he shifted the car into high gear. "A fugitive from the law seeking refuge in the Crowe's nest! And we thought the Sixties were over! What are you doing?"

Neal crouched down on the car floor. "Hiding. At least until we get over the bridge."

"Far out."

Crowe's Nest occupied the top floor of a three-story house overlooking the Bay from Telegraph Hill.

"A pleasant stroll," the artist explained, "for Crowe to visit the cafés, bistros, dim-sum places and Italian restaurants that contribute to the overall splendor of Crowe's existence."

Neal sat down in a canvas deck chair beside a gigantic sculpture created from the remains of a 1962 Plymouth Valiant, the tailpipe of which was positioned in a fairly impressive phallic display. The walls were decorated with masks—African masks, Chinese opera masks, harlequin masks, even hockey goaltenders' masks. The walls, the carpet, and all the furniture were stark white.

"The monochromatic color scheme makes Crowe stand out all the more," said Crowe. "Now please go and cleanse yourself lest you sully the snow-white purity of your present and, may I add, exalted, surroundings."

Neal took a wonderful, hot shower, scrubbing away all traces of black pancake makeup, mud, and sweat. Then he wrapped himself in one of Crowe's huge white towels and found that Crowe had laid a white terrycloth robe out for him.

He was further surprised to find that Crowe had used the time to start making breakfast: Texas-style French toast, grapefruit, coffee, and champagne. Crowe motioned Neal to sit down at the table beside the picture window. White tablecloth, white linen napkins.

"I didn't know you could cook," Neal said.

"Neither did you know that Rubens could paint."

"Makes a great sandwich, though. Interesting table."

"Of course. Nineteen fifty-five Renault drive shaft and windshield glass."

"Do you always have champagne with breakfast?"

"Every day, since corporate America began to recognize Crowe's surpassing genius."

"The French toast is wonderful."

"When Crowe creates, he creates wonder."

"What do you want to know about my situation, Crowe?"

"Only how I can help."

"You're doing it."

"Then that's what I need to know."

After breakfast, Neal took a cab to the Hopkins. He figured that whoever had tried to shoot him didn't have a way to connect him to the hotel and, in any case, wouldn't try to take him out there. Besides, he needed to make a private phone call and pack his stuff.

What he needed to do was talk to Graham. He dialed his number, let it ring three times, and then hung up. He waited thirty seconds and dialed it again.

But Graham didn't answer. Ed Levine did.

"Where's Graham?" Neal asked.

"Neal Carey, my favorite fuck-up!"

"Where's Graham?"

"In the old country, probably slumped over a table in some dirty pub. I'm handling his caseload."

"I only talk to Graham."

"I'm sure he'll be touched to hear that, asswipe, but he's on vacation. You'll talk to me."

Vacation? Neal had known Graham for ten-plus years and had never known the man to take a day off. "Are you kidding?" Graham had asked him. "My job is lying, stealing, and cheating. How much more fun could I have?"

"Neal? Neal, sweetheart?" Levine was saying. "What are you calling for? Have you fucked up the job yet? Maybe paid Pendleton to stay in Frisco and put the hooker on a plane to AgriTech, something like that?"

Something is wrong here, Neal thought. Something is very strange. Careful now.

"I haven't even found him yet," Neal said. "He's not where you guys said he would be."

"Neal, you couldn't find your arm in your sleeve."

Witty, Ed. This was the guy who had once given Joe Graham one glove for Christmas.

"Where is Graham?" Neal asked again.

"Jesus, cut the cord, will you? What is he, your mommy? Seeing as how he had to go to England to change your diaper, he decided to take the ferry ride to Ireland and visit the home of his ancestors. He's probably at the Dublin Zoo, all right?"

No, it's not all right. Graham had told him a hundred times that he never wanted to go to Ireland: "We got rain and whiskey right here in New York."

"Yeah, all right," Neal said.

"Lighten up, college boy," Levine said. It was a continuing source of resentment: Friends had put Neal through Columbia, Levine had put himself through night school at City. "Come home. The job is over. Pendleton came back all by himself. Called a little while ago from Raleigh airport, and he's on his way in to the lab."

"Swell."

You lying sack of shit.

"So go back to your little cottage, pack up your shit, and get your ass back to New York. We might just decide to make you work for a living."

"Yeah, okay."

"What's the matter, Neal? Pissed off because the job ended before you could be a big hero? Cheer up. At least you didn't kill this one."

Levine laughed and hung up. Neal dialed another number.

"AgriTech. May I transfer your call?"

"Dr. Robert Pendleton, please."

"One moment."

Here we go again.

Another voice, a harsh male voice, came on the line. "Who is this?"

"Who is *this*?"

"Why are you inquiring about Dr. Pendleton?"

"Why are you inquiring why I'm inquiring?"

"Please identify yourself or I will have to terminate this call."

Terminate this call?! What the hell is going on with this stupid case? Who says stuff like "terminate this call"? Security types, that's who.

"This is the assistant manager at the Chinatown Holiday Inn," Neal said. "Dr. Pendleton left some medication behind when he checked out, and I wanted to know if I should FedEx it, or whether regular mail would do."

"One moment."

They must all go to the same school, Neal thought.

"Dr. Pendleton says that regular mail will be sufficient."

"May I confirm that with him personally, please? Company rules."

"He's very busy at the moment."

"I'm sure he is. Thank you."

Neal packed in a hurry. Suddenly he didn't want to be in the hotel, where anyone could find him. There were too many contradictions. Joe Graham never takes vacations and hates Ireland, but he's on vacation in Ireland. Ed Levine says that Bob Pendleton is back at work, but he isn't, because AgriTech security relays a message from him about medication that doesn't exist. And someone tries to kill me because I found Pendleton.

Whoever was diddling the door was doing it well, because it barely made a sound. But Neal Carey had done a lot of doors and he heard it like it was an alarm bell. Which it was.

Someone had picked up his trail and was planning something nasty in the ever-so-nice Mark Hopkins, and there was no way out of the tiny room.

Which was maybe okay, he thought.

Neal grabbed the letter opener off the desk and waited behind the door. He was scared as hell, but he was also getting a little tired of being jerked around, and whoever was coming through the door was going to get a little surprise in the form of a letter opener swung fast and hard.

Neal's heart raced like the ball on a roulette wheel as he heard the lock click and watched the door handle come up. If the guy had a gun, he had to beat him to the punch, so to speak—put him down hard and keep him down so he could ask him a few questions.

The door came open slowly and Neal let loose. The point of the opener stuck into the intruder's arm and quivered.

"What's the matter? You got a babe in there, you don't want me to come in?"

Joe Graham was staring at him curiously.

"Come in."

Graham plucked the letter opener from his rubber arm. He looked disgustedly at the sleeve of his shirt. "This is a new shirt, Neal. I just bought it."

Neal's heart slowed to a mere gallop. He slammed the door shut behind Graham. Looking at the purple shirt, he said, "I did you a favor."

Neal plunked himself down on the bed and let out a long sigh.

"You're not happy to see me," said Graham.

"I thought you were on vacation in Ireland."

"Funny thing about that, son. I finished prying you out of your cave and called in. All of a sudden, Levine is nagging me about all this vacation time I got built up. Says I have to take it right now. I say okay, but then get to thinking maybe there's a reason they don't want me around just when they send you on a job. I get thinking maybe I should come back on the sly and check on my dearly beloved son, who might fuck up and get himself hurt without his dear old dad there to help him out. So, son, how have you fucked up and what kind of trouble are you in?"

Neal started at the top and told Graham the whole story, taking him through the search of Room 1016, his dance with Benchpress, the trip to Mill Valley, dinner at the Kendalls, Li Lan's seductive offer, and the shot that nearly killed him. Graham sat silent for the whole monologue, except for a few tongue-cluckings and mutterings of "Shame" at some of Neal's more egregious errors.

When Neal finished the long story, Graham asked, "So what did she look like naked?"

"What?"

"The babe. The China doll. What did she look like in the flesh?"

"Jesus, Graham."

Graham went over to the courtesy bar and removed two of the little bottles of scotch. He wiped the hotel's glass with a handkerchief, poured himself a double, and sipped contentedly.

"Tell me again. From the hot-tub part."

"Graham, if you think I'm going to sit here and indulge your prurient—"

"Indulge *this*," Graham said, showing him precisely. "Now tell your old dad. And don't skip a single juicy detail."

When Neal had finished the reprise, Graham smiled, shook his head, and said, "She never was going to do you, you idiot. She was just stalling you so Pendleton could get in the car without your getting wise. She doesn't know you like I do."

"What do you mean?"

"She told you to wait, remember? Then, when you weren't buying—you're an asshole, by the way—she gave you something to keep your, uh, mind on until everyone got nice and comfy in the car. Then she ran off, leaving you holding, shall I say, the bag?"

Neal wondered if he looked as stupid as he felt.

"You don't think she really wanted to have sex with me?"

"Well, you were naked. She probably got a good look at you."

"What about the shot? She was setting me up!"

Graham went back to the refrigerator, found a six-dollar can of smoked almonds, and poured them on a plate. He popped the nuts in his mouth as he talked.

"Maybe she was, maybe she wasn't. Could be none of them knew anything about any shot."

"She ran away!"

"Good idea when shooting breaks out. What did you want her to do, cover you with her body? Oh, that's right, that's exactly what you wanted her to do."

"Pass me an almond."

"Get your own food."

"That *is* my food."

"Not anymore."

Neal found a Swiss chocolate bar priced like a silver ingot.

Graham continued, "You ask me, I don't think she even heard the shot. I think she was just running from you because that was part of the plan. Get you all hot and bothered so you weren't thinking straight—again, they don't know you like I do—and leave you wet and naked in the tub. No clothes, no towel. Very bright of you, by the way, son. You also ask me, I don't think the bullet was meant for you, as appealing an idea as that might be."

"Why not?" Neal asked, realizing he sounded almost indignant, as if suddenly he wasn't important enough to be shot at.

"They could have whacked you anytime. The broad didn't have to show you her stuff to do that. They could have popped you when you first got in the tub."

"So who—" Neal started, but stopped because he couldn't talk and think at the same time. Why had AgriTech told him Pendleton was there when he wasn't? Maybe because they thought Pendleton was dead?

"I called Ed," Neal said. "He told me Pendleton came back and told me to do the same."

"So?"

"So I called AgriTech and they told me the same thing."

"So Ed is right for a change. These things happen."

"But Pendleton isn't there, Dad." He related his ruse involving the medication, then sat silently while Graham rubbed his rubber fist into his palm.

"I think," Graham said finally, "we have to find out a little more about AgriTech."

Something about AgriTech was wrong.

The library said so. One of the things that Neal loved about libraries was that they were all the same—not the layout or the architecture or the carpeting, of course, but the system. Once you learned the system, every library was known ground. Hunting ground.

He started with the usual suspects—*Standard and Poor's, Moody's, Dun & Bradstreet*—and found out that AgriTech was a much smaller company than he thought it would be, a lowly sixteenth ranking in the agrichemical category.

The bigger surprise, though, was that it was privately held. That didn't make sense. Companies engaging in large, long-term research projects usually need the capital they can get on the public market.

They're attractive investments, and the initial investors usually like to roll them over early.

But private firms are just that—private. Harder to get data on, less responsible to watchdog agencies. Neal found a copy of *Ward's Directory*, which specialized in private companies. He found out that AgriTech employed 317 people—not many for a research company—and had a narrow market base, mostly in the development of pesticides for the tobacco industry.

Pesticides? Neal thought. What happened to fertilizer? To the old chickenshit?

He took a look at the directors and principal officers. The president was one Leslie P. Little, Ph.D. Chemistry degrees from Nebraska, Illinois, and MIT. Impressive resumé of employment at several large agrichemical firms. Vice-President Harold D. Innes very similar. Dull stuff. But Secretary/Treasurer Paul R. Knox—even the title was an anomaly—was a little more interesting. Pretty standard management education, including a Columbia M.B.A. and a long list of prior employment—but it looked fuzzy, out of focus. Knox had worked for Trans Pax, an import-export firm in San Diego, before moving to something called the Council for Swedish-American Trade. He had stayed there for two years and then taken a position in Stockholm with Sverigenet, an American computer consulting firm. After three years at Internet he had split for Hong Kong as executive director of a telecommunications equipment importer called Dawson and Sons, Ltd. Two years there, and he'd left for Directions in Social Inquiry, apparently a polling operation, in Silver Springs, Maryland. Then on to the board of AgriTech, where he was also the comptroller.

By the record, Neal thought, this guy knows less about chemicals than any junior high school student on the West Side.

Neal scanned the board of directors. None of the names meant anything to him until he came to the fourth entry: Ethan Kitteredge, the Man himself. So the Bank had come across with the big loan and bought itself a seat on the board. But for what?

Follow the money. Or, in this case, the money man. Somewhere along the line, Ethan Kitteredge had handed a packet of bucks to Paul Knox, who had a pinball background.

Neal went across the street, grabbed a quick cup of coffee and a toasted bagel, and headed back into the library. It was already noon, and he would have to repeat the process he had used in AgriTech with all of Knox's former companies. He figured it would take him at least another three hours. It didn't; none of the companies existed.

He looked in every source that he knew, but couldn't find any entry for Trans Pax, Internet International, or Directions in Social Inquiry. Dawson and Sons wouldn't have been listed anyway, but Neal suspected it was another cardboard company.

So how about the Council for Swedish-American Trade? Was it a nonprofit agency to stimulate business, a government-sponsored agency, or a private concern that put itself in the middle of any potential deal and took its ten points?

Neal found the Washington, D.C., phone book on microfilm, but couldn't find any listing for the Council. Ditto when he called information. He got the number for the Department of Commerce, and a half-dozen transfers and holds got him to somebody at the International Trade Administration's Export Counseling Center who at least pretended to be interested in Neal's brilliant plan to market high-efficiency electric space heaters to the Swedish consumer. This helpful person forwarded Neal's call to the Administration's desk officer for Sweden, who politely feigned fascination and advised Neal to contact the Swedish consulate, board of trade, and interior affairs bureau, but who never mentioned the Council for Swedish-American Trade.

"What about the Council for Swedish-American Trade?" Neal asked finally.

He could almost hear the chuckle that preceded the answer, "They're not really in your field."

"How come?"

"They tend to handle more high-tech, larger-volume sorts of things."

"I'm planning real high volume," Neal said with a trace of belligerence.

"And when you get there, I'm sure they'll be glad to talk to you. In the meantime, I really recommend you give the consulate a call. . . ."

Okay, okay, Neal thought. What do we have here? A guy on the board of an agrichemical company who has no background or education in agriculture or chemistry. The same guy has worked for a bunch of companies that can't be traced and for a council on Swedish-American trade that isn't interested in talking to someone about trade between America and Sweden.

We have a company that should be public that's private—a company that makes pesticides and is desperate to get back a biochemist whose specialty is fertilizer. We have the Bank writing a big loan to this company to develop not a new pesticide, but a new fertilizer, and then taking a seat on the board of the company. And we have the Man at the Bank sending me to get the scientist back. Then someone tries to shoot me when I do.

We have Levine lying about Pendleton's return, and AgriTech security backing up the lie. We have Levine telling me to come home and forget about it. Why would they say Pendleton's back when he isn't? Why isn't Levine jumping up and down and screaming at me to do my fucking job and bring him back?

Unless all of a sudden they don't want him back.

Unless they want to make sure he doesn't come back.

Ever.

Paranoia is like a seatbelt—it's when you don't put it on that you get in an accident.

So thought Neal Carey as professional paranoia gripped him around the middle. Graham would never let anything happen to me while he's on the job, so they take him off. They make a big show out of sending their golden boy retriever, me, to find the absent professor. Good old dog that I am, I go on point, and someone shoots . . . not me, but what they think is Pendleton. Dark night, dimly lit deck, the back of my head to the hill, where the shot came from. It's possible.

So someone goes out and picks up my poor corpse and makes the sad announcement that Robert Pendleton is dead. Murdered. The investigation fizzles and is forgotten.

But who has the swag to carry that kind of load? The same people who have the swag to set up dummy companies, phony histories, and multimillion-dollar insider loans.

He reran his conversation with Pendleton in his head. *Meeting in a hot tub to make sure he wasn't wired. "So did the company send you?" No, idiot, not the company, but the Company. The Company.*

Paranoia. Pure fucking paranoia, Neal thought. The CIA? What would a dorky biochemist be doing for the CIA? Get real.

But the bullet was real. Very real, so pay attention here. Suppose they did try to whack Pendleton? That presents some problems for one Neal Carey. If they still think they killed Pendleton, they have to deal with me somehow. And if they know by now that they missed Pendleton, they'll be looking for both of us. They'll know where to look for Pendleton. He's with Li Lan.

And they sure as hell know where to find me, don't they? I have a return ticket to my isolated cottage in the moors.

Except I'm not going to be there. There's only one thing to do when paranoia hits this bad—run with it.

First he had to get to Crowe, because Friends and their new CIA buddies could connect Crowe to him with a quick cross-referencing of the files just by pushing a couple of buttons and asking for Neal Carey cases in San Francisco. So he had unwittingly put the artist in some danger.

Crowe answered on the first ring.

"Crowe."

"It's Neal."

"You are taking me to an expensive dinner, aren't you?"

"Crowe, has anyone been around asking for me?"

"No."

"Anything unusual? Repairmen you didn't expect? Pollsters? Jehovah's Witnesses?"

"No! I'm in the mood for French cuisine, I think."

"Just shut up and listen. I won't be back. Thanks for all the help. If anyone comes around asking questions, you haven't seen me or heard from me in years, okay?"

"Where are you going?"

"It's too long a story."

"Where are you now? Neal, are you in trouble?"

Well, sort of, Crowe. I have this creepy feeling that the CIA and my own employers want to kill me, but other than that . . .

"I just need to disappear for a while, Crowe."

"Let me help, Neal."

"You already have. Thanks, Crowe, and 'bye."

Neal met Graham outside the Chinese Crafts Center on Grant Avenue. Groups of tourists from Grey Line bus tours were prowling Chinatown, gawking in store windows and choosing restaurants as night fell and the neon came up.

"Let's take a walk," Neal said. He told Graham about his research and his suspicions about AgriTech.

"And the Man is on their board?" Graham asked when Neal was finished.

"Yeah."

"So what is AgriTech to the CIA or the CIA to AgriTech?"

"I don't know. But I'm going to find out."

Graham grabbed him by the elbow. "Are you crazy? You're not going to do shit. What you're going to do is what I'm going to do."

Neal wrenched his arm away. "Which is what?"

Graham started walking again and gestured for Neal to come with him. As they were walking, Graham started to lecture.

"Neal, listen. I don't know if you're right or not about this CIA thing. Sounds crazy to me. But whatever is going on here, it is very serious. With this kind of stuff, we don't fuck around. So what we're going to do, we're going to catch the next plane to Providence, we're going to walk into the Man's office and say, 'Mr. Kitteredge, please tell anyone you may or may not know that Joe Graham and Neal Carey don't know anything and care less.' Then we're going to ask him what he wants us to do. He's going to tell us in polite terms to keep our fucking mouths shut and forget about Dr. Robert Pendleton, and Neal—that's what we're going to do."

"They're going to kill her!"

"You mean *him*."

"I mean both of them."

Graham looked at him real funny. "You mean *her*."

"All right. Her."

Graham slammed his rubber hand into a lamppost. "Fuck! What is it with this babe, everyone falls in love with her?"

"I'm not in love with her."

"Yes, you are."

Yes, you are, Graham thought. I know you, kid, you're in love with the heartache.

"Look, Neal . . . say you find them, say you warn them. What then? Are you going to save them? How? You won't save them, dickhead, you'll join them. You'll be in the wrong place at the wrong time, and this time the bullet won't miss. Son, you don't know these people, what Pendleton did, what the China doll did. Maybe they deserve it."

"Her name is Li Lan. She has a name."

"A little while ago you thought she set you up for a bullet in the head, now you want to rescue her. What next, you want to fuck her? Listen, Neal, if you want a little Chinese pussy, I'll buy you some, it's all over the place."

Neal's fists clenched. For a moment he thought he might punch Graham.

Am I in love with her? he wondered. I must be, because the thought of her hurts, the thought of her dead . . . and I don't give a rat's ass about Pendleton and haven't since I saw her. And the thought of never seeing her again . . .

"See you, Dad."

Neal turned and started walking away. Graham is always telling me that he taught me everything I know, let's see if he taught me everything *he* knows, he thought. Graham may be the best street man ever born, but I may be the best ever made.

He was right, but he was right on both counts. Graham hung on his tail like a burr on a dog. Neal couldn't get the space he needed to break the connection. He took the older man along Grant, then up Clay to Stockton. He passed through crowds and crossed the street, doubled back, went into a store through one door and left through another, took it fast, took it slow, and still Graham stayed with him. It was all right, though. In this game, like baseball, the tie goes to the runner, and Neal knew that time was on his side. Graham couldn't stop to call in for backup, so he wasn't able to drive Neal into a tightening net. And once Neal shook him, that would be it.

Mark Chin had kept the net loose all day and was glad it was finally time to jerk it shut. He'd let the *kweilo* sit around the Hopkins hotel, had let the one-armed guy come in, had waited while the *kweilo* did his thing in the library, and finally saw his spot as the two *kweilos* had an argument. About fucking time. It had taken the efforts of seven of his best boys to keep this Neal Carey person in an invisible net. Now the mark was running hard, trying to shake his partner. The opportunity was at hand.

He fell in behind him and let himself be seen as the mark turned to check on his partner.

* * *

73

Neal saw Benchpress come out of a doorway behind him, and this time Benchpress looked like an opportunity. Graham was coming up about fifty feet behind them. Neal turned on his heel and bumped straight into Benchpress.

"A hundred bucks for taking that guy out without hurting him. Another bill for meeting me, giving me some help."

Benchpress mumbled an address and turned back toward Graham.

Graham saw the guy coming, but it was too late. The fucker was huge, and Graham felt himself wrapped in a bear hug that choked his breath and obliterated his view. In two seconds there were three more Chinese guys around him.

"Don't hurt him," Chin told his assistants.

"I'll beat whatever he paid you," Graham said.

"This isn't an auction."

And Neal was going, going, gone.

Neal checked the address on the doorway under a yellow neon sign with XXX on it in black letters. A tired-looking black man behind the raised counter nodded to him. There were three or four customers in the shop, but none of them looked up from the porno magazines.

"You can shop, you can buy, you can get tokens from me. You can't read. This isn't a library," the counterman said to Neal.

"I'm meeting a guy."

"Gay stuff back and to the left."

Benchpress came in just then and handed a five-dollar bill to the clerk, who handed back a plastic sleeve full of tokens. He jerked his head to Neal and pointed to a swinging door at the rear of the shop.

"Step into my office."

Chin selected a booth, gestured Neal in, and shut the door behind him. There was a pull-down bench just large enough for one person to sit on. A box of Kleenex completed the furnishings. Chin dropped two tokens into a coin slot, then glanced at the channel selector.

"Any preferences?"

Neal shook his head.

Chin pushed a button and the porn video started.

"Sit down. Make yourself at home."

"Thanks."

Neal handed him another fifty.

"I get the idea," Chin said over the sound track of groans of phony passion, "that you got more than a fifty-dollar problem."

Neal could hear similar groans from the next booth.

"Turn up the volume," he said.

Mark Chin cranked it up to full. The tinny rock music vibrated on the cheap walls.

"So?" Chin asked.

"I need a place to hide."

"No big deal."

"In Hong Kong."

Cries of "Fuck me, fuck me, fuck me!" seemed to be coming out of Mark Chin's chest, as if he were the dummy in an obscene ventriloquist's act.

"No big deal," he said.

"Great."

The video rose to an ear-shattering crescendo of passion as Chin asked, "It's about the woman, isn't it?"

"What woman?"

"Room ten-sixteen, the incredibly gorgeous Chinese woman."

The video shut off in mid-climax. Chin stuck another token in the slot and changed channels. Two women in a steam room were making tentative advances. Their quiet conversation was a welcome relief.

"That Pendleton is a lucky guy," Chin continued. "Me, I would not mind a piece of that luck."

Neal felt himself flush with anger. What is this, he thought, jealousy?

"So what is he?" Chin asked. "The chemist?"

Now how the hell would you know that? Neal wondered. He didn't answer, but let the soft sighs coming from the video fill the silence.

Chin said, "Pendleton tests the heroin? Tells the boss, 'This is good, this is not so good'? He makes a nice salary, plus benefits? She's one of the bennies? You don't want to mess with that, that's tong business. Big time."

"I have to find her."

Yeah, I do. Find her to warn her. Find her to ask her some questions. Find out what the hell is going on. Find out how to come out of this alive.

"What, you're in love?"

Why is this so obvious to everybody but me?

"Yeah, okay."

Chin shook his head disgustedly. The two women on the video began a fresh erotic encounter.

"It's your funeral," Chin said. "When are you leaving?"

"As soon as possible."

"Before your friend finds you?"

"How hard is it to disappear in Hong Kong?" Neal asked.

"It can't be too hard. People disappear in Hong Kong every day."

Neal opened his bag and came out with a package of cash. He counted ten hundred dollar bills out and handed them to Chin.

"Disappear me."

Chin folded the money into his pants pocket. The old saying was right, he thought—it's amazing how lucky you get when you work hard. But he wasn't that interested in old sayings. His metaphor of preference was western chess, and he knew that to capture the opponent's queen, you had to move a pawn forward. He pointed both open palms toward Neal, closed his fingers, and snapped them open again.

"Presto!"

As he and Neal left, the warm ripple of a woman's laughter followed them.

5

Xao Xiyang took the lid off the mug and sipped at the green tea. His neck ached, his eyes hurt, and even the fine quality of this particular tea did nothing to change the stacks of figures on his desk.

He sat back in his chair and lit a cigarette. The acrid taste of the cheap tobacco burned his mouth. His lesser colleagues teased him—as regional party secretary he could easily have used the "back door" to procure as many Marlboros as they could bring from Hong Kong—but the habit of caution was still with him. He had known men to be imprisoned during the Great Proletarian Cultural Revolution for far lesser "crimes" than smoking American cigarettes.

He took off his glasses and wiped them on the short sleeve of his cheap cotton shirt. He could smell his own stale perspiration in his armpits. He glanced at his watch and realized that he had been poring over the agricultural statistics for seven hours. And still they didn't change.

Ninety-seven million people in this province, Xao thought. More than in the entire Han Dynasty at its height, more than the Ming, more than Rome. I am responsible for ninety-seven million people. And I don't know how to feed them. Here, in the so-called Rice Bowl of China, we can no longer feed ourselves. A cultural revolution indeed.

His assistant, Peng, currying favor, had repeated to him the flattering play on words that was being repeated in the teahouses: "If you want to eat, go see Xao Xiyang." And it was true that he had made some reforms, throwing out some of the ideologues who were so badly mismanaging some of the production teams. But "some" was not good enough. The reforms had to be systemic.

And the system was so idiotic, Xao thought as he took another long drag on his cigarette. Insane, really. And I blame you, old friend, he thought, looking at the Chairman's portrait that hung on the office wall, as it did on all office walls.

They had begun as *tongmen-jr*—comrades—although the Party cliché was a curse on his tongue now. He had looked up to the Chairman then, almost as an older brother. He had joined the Party, fought the Kuomintang, lost, and joined the Chairman on the Long March. How clear things seemed in those days, how clear and pure in the crystalline air of the mountains, when he and the Chairman and all the rest were fighting to build a new China in a new world.

And the fighting. Fighting the Kuomintang, and then the Japanese, and then the Kuomingtang again. Fighting with the Chairman's guidance, under his precepts of guerrilla war. Like fish swimming in the sea of the people. And as they fought, they liberated, came to control vast areas of the country. And they threw out the landlords and gave the land to the peasants, then recruited the peasants for the army. And he remembered that when they retreated from a village, the Kuomingtang would come back in and shoot all the peasants who had been left behind.

What fighting he had seen! Bodies stacked like rice hulls along the side of the road. Entire villages beheaded by the Japanese. He remembered the Japanese patrol they had pinned down in the mountain pass—they had picked them off one by one over the course of three days. When finally they went to loot the bodies, they saw that some of the Japanese had not been shot at all, but had frozen to death, their bodies stuck to the rocks by ice, their fingers frozen to their rifle triggers.

And in those same mountains he had met her. She was a courier, a message runner . . . a spy. She risked torture at the hands of the Japanese, but she never flinched, and he had heard of her before he met her. He chuckled at the memory. They hadn't called it "love," that would have been too romantic and decadent. No, they had called it a "oneness of spirit in revolutionary fervor"—but it was love. Such beauty . . . such soul . . .

They married in a high mountain meadow and honeymooned in a tent under tall cedars. Then they went back to their separate duties. He was terrified for her, terrified for himself that she might never return from her dangerous missions. For five years they made infrequent, brief rendezvouses—passionate couplings in peasant huts or tents, even caves. And when the Japanese had been beaten, and the Kuomintang destroyed, they met in the joyous celebration in Tiananmen Square and never separated again. Started a life and raised a family and never separated again until . . .

Xao Xiyang lit another cigarette. I must be getting old, he thought. I seem given to the old man's habit of living in the past, in the realm of memory. But you, old friend, he thought as he looked again at the portrait, you are now in the realm of the shadows. Thank you. The last, best thing you could do for us was to die. It is only a shame you didn't do it sooner. You should have died on the day of victory, when we all stood on Tiananmen Gate and proclaimed the republic. The New China.

Before you decided to become an emperor.

Xao took another sip of the green tea and pronounced another curse on the head of his old friend. He pronounced it in the name of twenty million of the dead. Twenty million peasants, twenty million of "the people," who had starved in the Chairman's Great Leap Forward. "Great Leap," indeed—the great leap from this world to the next. The next world, he thought. Good Marxist that I am, I don't believe in the next world. But I will see you in hell, old friend.

The Chairman's Great Leap Forward started in 1957, after an unusually fine harvest. But the Chairman wasn't satisfied with the mere production of food; society had to be recorded along less "individualistic" and "selfish" lines. Collectivization of all the land was accelerated. The entire rural population was organized into production teams. No peasant dared own so much individual property as a chicken. Worse still, by year's end, over 300,000 "stinking intellectuals," including the best economists and scientists, had been labeled "rightists" and shipped off to prison camps.

So when the crisis hit, all the experts who might have controlled it were gone, and no one else dared speak. The Chairman set quotas for grain production, and the new commune managers met them all—on paper. The Chairman looked at the figures and boasted that the new order—the new China—was working just as he said it would, and commanded in the name of "the people" that collectivization be speeded up. Then he set higher quotas, and the people met them—on paper.

Figures may not lie, but the people who write them do, and the Party cadres who reported the figures did just that. They were afraid to be labeled "defeatists," so they reported victory. They ordered fields to lie fallow to avoid a glut of grain. They took peasants from the fields and set them to building warehouses to hold all the grain that would be harvested. On paper.

But in the fields and the paddies it was a different story, for less than half the grain the figures claimed was actually harvested, and even less was processed. Crops rotted in the fields while the peasants built useless warehouses, fields were not tended while the peasants were sent to work in "backyard steel mills" to help with industrialization. Collectivization was chaos. Urban cadres who knew nothing about agriculture gave idiotic and contradictory orders to the peasants. The already fragile transportation system broke down completely, and precious farm tools and invaluable fertilizers sat in stalled railroad cars or were "lost" entirely. Grain production dropped over sixty percent, and while the cadres dutifully checked nonexistent grain into nonexistent warehouses, the Chairman shipped the real grain to the Soviets to repay the debts of industrialization.

The experts who might have helped—the Western-trained agronomists, economists, statisticians, and biochemists—were in prison for the very crime of being Western-trained experts. The few who had escaped that fate were silenced the moment they spoke the truth that the Great Leap Forward was a sham, a tragic fiasco launched by a madman. The emperor had no clothes and the people had no food.

The people starved. Twenty million people starved to death in three years. Many more died of malnutrition-related diseases in the years following. And more than half of the dead were children.

That was our "New China," Xao thought, a land where we starved our children.

He could never shut his eyes without the sights coming back to him. His nightmares were not of the war with all its various horrors, but of *those* years, of the emaciated mothers—too weak to walk—who lay beside the road, trying to feed rice husks to babies who were already dead. Or of the children begging him for food, staggering toward his staff car on spindly legs, their rheumy eyes asking him questions for which he had no answers. *If you want to eat, go see Xao Xiyang.*

I will see you in hell, old friend. You and I will both be there, because I, too, posed for the cameras in the "model villages," those sham communes that received the money, the fertilizers, and the pesticides. I, too, posed beside the huge piles of grain, the fattened hogs, and the smiling peasants with fat and rosy-cheeked children. I, too, congratulated their leaders and held them up as an example to the rest, even though I also knew that their figures were lies. Even with all their resources, they had to lie. And the rest of the country had to live up to the lie, and send out more grain, and starve all the more. Oh, I will join you in hell, old friend.

Finally the slaughter became too much for some of the higher Party members, who braved the Chairman's wrath and forced him to put a check on the insanity. Collectivization was modified and slowed down. Some land was freed up to private agriculture. A few of the experts who had survived the purge were returned to their posts. A slow, painful recovery began as the professionals took over from the politicians and pragmatism took precedence over idealogy. By 1965, food production reached its normal levels. There was still hunger, but starvation disappeared. And the Chairman sulked and bided his time.

You gave us barely a year, old friend. One year of peace and prosperity and you started it off again. Chaos: the Great Proletarian Cultural Revolution.

Xao chuckled at the sheer insidious brilliance of it. The Chairman succeeded in defining success as treason. The experts, the careful planners, the scientists, the intellectuals, the prudent small farmers were all condemned as "capitalist roaders." The proof? Their very success! The wonderful inverted logic! As if to say that it was impossible to succeed within the system, and that therefore those who did succeed did so outside the system, via the "capitalist road." They were traitors, and it was their treason that sabotaged the system and made it not work! It was an argument only a child could accept, and it was to children that the Chairman argued it.

In doing so he released a torrent of pent-up adolescent rage. In a society in which repressed youth were taught to respect their elders, the

Chairman urged them to overthrow those same elders. With the un-canny radar of the psychopath, he targeted the teachers first. Those Confucian demigods, so long used to blind obedience, awoke one morn-ing to find themselves ridiculed in "big-character posters," confronted by formerly docile students demanding a voice in the classroom. Granted that voice, the students denounced their teachers for not being "pure" enough, for not being "red" enough, for not loving the Chair-man enough. In the end, the teachers were accused of being educated, and once that lunacy was accepted, the floodgates opened.

Officials were denounced for planning, scientists for doing research, journalists for writing, intellectuals for thinking . . . farmers for growing food. In the "permanent revolution," everything by definition was to be turned upside down. The only thing that mattered was political fervor. Fervor for what? For the Chairman's thought. And what did the Chair-man think? He thought there should be political fervor.

So success became sabotage, planning became plotting, education became ignorance. In this upside-down world, children denounced their parents, agricultural experts carried buckets of shit, illiterate peasants "wrote" railroad timetables.

And you, old friend, became an emperor. "All is chaos under the heavens," you wrote, "and the situation is excellent." The Emperor of Chaos.

Xao lit another cigarette. He remembered when the children had come for him. Those Red Guards, swollen with pride, waving their red banners and carrying the red books. They had come to denounce him as a reactionary.

His immediate superior had opened the door to the mob and wel-comed them in, praising them, and thanking them for their true insights into "Mao Thought." It wasn't unusual; many of the officials had agreed to denounce and be denounced. Betray your subordinates to buy time, betray your superiors to move up. Anything to buy time, anything to survive, because this time they knew that they must survive. How-ever many didn't make it—and many didn't—some of the professionals must survive to rebuild. So he had felt no anger when his friend and trusted superior had denounced him to the mob as a Western-influenced capitalist-roader. He was sitting calmly in his office, smoking a cigarette, when the local Red Guard burst in and tied his hands behind his back. They put a huge dunce cap on his head and marched him through the streets, where the mob threw rotten vegetables at him, spat on him, and screamed insults in his face.

They grilled him for five days, privately in a cell and in public "struggle sessions." He wrote self-criticism after self-criticism, always giving them enough to feed on but not enough to bury him. He denounced other officials, particularly those he knew to be rabid ideologues, as co-conspirators. The same patron who had denounced him arranged for his exile to Xinxiang instead of imprisonment or slow death in the countryside.

The exile lasted for eight years. Eight years of patience, planning—and plotting. Painstakingly and quietly he rebuilt contacts, sent and received messages from like thinkers. There were hundreds of patriotic officials left who had found a quiet harbor and were waiting for the storm to peak. It finally did, in near civil war, when the army acted to quell the internecine fighting between rival groups of Red Guards.

But the economy was once again ruined. The professional class had been virtually eliminated. Millions of disaffected Red Guards wandered the countryside, and the lunatics were still in charge of the asylum. And this time she did not come back.

And you, old friend, you finally expired.

Xao stared down again at this quarter's grain production figures from the communes. Doubtless more lies. More inflation of the truth. No one wants to look bad. Still afraid to be denounced. Old habits die hard.

The best farmers denounced as rightists and killed or thrown into prison. A generation of our best scientists lost, their research—bought so dearly, so painstakingly, so patiently—lost in a blaze of idiotic, insane adolescent fury unleashed by you, old friend.

But slowly Xao's true comrades began to emerge from their hiding places. Deng himself, his own patron, came out of hiding in Canton to manuever once again to the fore, and was now engaged with Hua in a struggle for control. Deng, who even recently was denounced for advocating the use of foreign experts, was patient. The stakes were too high to be rash, Deng had warned him—they were playing for the very soul of China.

Xao turned his chair around and looked out the window at his driver standing beside the car. He buzzed for his assistant, the ever-dour Peng. "Tell my driver I will not be leaving for at least two more hours. Ask him to go around to the Hibiscus and get himself some food, and ask him to bring something back for me."

"Yes, Comrade Secretary." Peng smirked. Comrade Xao had sent the driver to the Hibiscus restaurant every evening this whole week. He must eat four *yuan* a day!

"And see if you can get someone in here to work on this ceiling fan!" Xao continued. "It's stifling in here!"

Xao went back to the statistics. Even taken at face value, they were dismal. Allow for exaggeration, and they approached disastrous. He reached into the bottom left-hand drawer of his desk and pulled out a blue folder labeled, PRELIMINARY STATISTICS ON PRODUCTION FROM PRIVATE HOLDINGS. It was the only copy. Best not to let the bastards in Beijing see this stuff quite yet.

He delved into it yet again. It was tantalizing: the only production statistics in his province that were actually on the rise. And these farmers had every reason to lie on the downside, since they owed a percentage of all their production to the commune. And still . . . and still . . . Oh, old friend, I wish I could stoke the flames of hell with these papers for you. Make you burn a little more.

He was involved with his statistics when his driver came back with a covered dish of bean curd and vegetables and a large tureen of fish soup. The driver set it on his desk in front of him.

"Thank you," Xao said. "Did you eat?"

"Yes, Comrade Secretary."

Xao offered the pack of cigarettes. His driver, a tall, well-built young soldier he had brought with him from Henan, shyly took one cigarette. Xao struck a match, lit a fresh cigarette for himself, and used it to light the soldier's.

"And?" Xao asked.

"There was a message."

"Good."

" 'The doll is in the hallway,' " the driver recited.

Xao inhaled the smoke, which tasted better than it had all day. He was suddenly ravenously hungry.

"Tell her to wait."

"Yes, Comrade Secretary."

The driver saluted and left the room.

84

Xao took a pair of chopsticks from the top desk drawer and wiped them on the hem of his shirt.

" 'The doll is in the hallway,' " he repeated to himself. "Good."

The food was delicious.

PART TWO
The Unpredictable Ghost

6

Kipling had it wrong with that bit about East and West never meeting. East and West meet in Hong Kong.

Hong Kong usually gets called an island, which is true as far as it goes. The *island* of Hong Kong meets the basic requirement, being surrounded by water, but the *colony* of Hong Kong includes more than 230 islands. However, the largest chunk of the colony sits on the mainland, which is to say it isn't surrounded by water at all. It's surrounded by China.

The colony of Hong Kong is more correctly called the Crown Colony of Hong Kong, which is a way of letting you know it's one of those pieces of real estate the British stole when they were still capable of doing that kind of thing. They grabbed Hong Kong Island itself back in 1841 as compensation for a few warehouses of their opium that the Chinese burned. Seems that the Chinese government had some objections to the British trying to turn Chinese citizens into junkies, and interfered with the sacred principles of free trade by confiscating the dope. So Queen Victoria lent the Royal Navy to her drug dealers and showed the cheeky mandarins that British merchants would peddle dope to anyone they damn well pleased, thank you very much. The navy shelled a few forts, killed a few chinks, and took an empty little island called Hong Kong as reimbursement for the out-of-pocket expenses. The Queen was pissed, though, because she thought she should have gotten a lot more for her money than one stinking rock with no potential customers on it, and fired the guy who inked the contract. That's the thing about pushers—they're never satisfied.

Sure enough, the British spent the rest of the century asserting the sacred right-to-deal, teaching the yellow heathen a lesson, and collecting more land as a tutorial fee, and that's how the Crown Colony of Hong Kong came to occupy some 366 square miles, and the Chinese came to wish that Kipling had been right.

The West had the nifty high-tech weaponry, but the East had something better: population. Lots of it. You can plant any flag you want, but if it waves over a place that has a few thousand Brits and five million Chinese, you don't need a rocket scientist to figure out that the place is more Chinese than British. And it took the Chinese about five minutes back in old '41 to decide that there was some serious money to be made by getting in the middle between the West and the East, and that Hong Kong was just the place to do it. Hong Kong became the back door to China, a place from which to sneak stuff in and sneak stuff out, and any time you have a lot of sneaking going on, you have a lot of money going with it. Nothing sweet moved in either direction without Hong Kong getting a taste, and the place became a paradise for people with an aptitude for your basic capitalism with the gloves off.

The Chinese moved there in droves. They walked, they took boats, they swam. They still do. No one really knows the population of Hong Kong, especially since 1949, when Mao took over and made things hot for people with an aptitude for your basic capitalism with the gloves off, and inspired several hundred thousand of them to go for a moonlight swim in the South China Sea.

So Hong Kong is crowded. Now, arithmetic will tell you that five million or so people in 366 square miles isn't that bad, but long division doesn't tell you that most of those 366 square miles go up and down. Most of Hong Kong is made up of steep hills, many of them uninhabitable, so the population is crammed into relatively small segments of the colony. When you get a lot of people in a small area where lots of money changes hands, what you also get is great extremes of wealth and poverty, because the fingers on some of those hands are pretty sticky.

The rich tend to live on the tops of the hills, of course, especially on "the Peak," more properly called Victoria Peak, the oh-so-exclusive neighborhood founded by the early Western drug lords but later dominated by Chinese financiers. Your status on the Peak is determined by your altitude; the goal is to literally look down on your neighbor. In many ways, the Peak is a little piece of England. It has the cultural airs of the English aristocracy fortunately modified by Chinese love of life. The Peak's inhabitants send their children off to Oxford or Cambridge for college, take four-o'clock tea, play croquet, and complain that the servants get cheekier every year. At the same time, they drive pink Rolls-Royces, the tea tends to be jasmine, they light incense to Buddhist saints to ensure good luck in gambling, and the servants are a part of a hugely extended family.

The poor have hugely extended families, too, and most of them would be thrilled to get a job pouring tea in a mansion on the Peak. That would mean they could get enough to eat and maybe a place to sleep where they could stretch their legs out. A lot of the poor live on the mainland section called Kowloon, where there's a person for every nine square feet and where the real-estate moguls plowed some of the hills into the ocean and put up huge blocks of high-rise tenements.

Kowloon has a lot of people and a lot of everything else, too, especially neon. The neon proclaims the sale of cameras, watches, radios, suits, dresses, food, booze, and naked ladies dancing for your pleasure. The main street is called Nathan Road—the "Golden Mile"—and walking down Nathan Road at night is like having an acid flashback, a trip through a tunnel of bright, flashing lights with surround sound.

Walking up Nathan Road, on the other hand, is like walking from Europe into Asia, and in the old days that was at least symbolically the case, because the Orient Express began down near the Star Ferry Pier at the bottom of Nathan Road. If you walk north up the road from there, you're pointed for China proper: the People's Republic of China, the PRC, the Middle Kingdom. Where East and West don't meet. So you don't want to walk too far up the Nathan Road. You get too far up the Nathan Road and you're not necessarily coming back.

Unless you're Chinese, that is, which makes all kinds of sense when you think about it. As crowded as Hong Kong is, as rough and tumble in its unbridled, unchecked, unregulated commercial competition, the Chinese keep going there. Sometimes the gatekeepers at the PRC border simply open the gates, and the flood is unstoppable. Other times those agrarian reformers on the mainland lock their people in, so the people sneak down the Pearl River from Canton, or crawl under the fence up by the New Territories, or wade across the Shumchun River, or paddle rafts across Deep Bay.

They come for a lot of reasons: opportunity, freedom, refuge, asylum. But the reason that most of them come can be summed up in one simple, uncomplicated word.

Rice.

Neal Carey didn't crawl under a fence or wade a river or paddle a raft. He came in a Boeing 747 wide-body on which the Singaporean stewardess handed him steaming hot towels to wipe his face and wake him up. He came on the overnight flight from San Francisco. Mark Chin and his associates had driven him to the airport, and Chin had given him instructions on what to do when he landed at Hong Kong's Kai Tak Airport.

"My cousin Ben will be there to meet you, right outside of immigration," Chin had told him.

"How will I know him?" Neal asked.

Chin had smiled broadly. "You'll know him."

It didn't take long for the efficient and unsmiling immigration officials to handle the incoming crowd. Neal told them that he was there as a tourist, and they asked him how much money he had brought with him. His answer matched the number he had put down on the immigration form, and they let him right in. He didn't tell them he was going to put the Bank's gold card away for the duration, though, lest he be tracked down via the paper trail.

He didn't have any trouble recognizing Ben Chin. He had the same thick chest, the same block-of-granite face, and the same short black hair. He sported a silk lavender shirt, white denims, and black tassled loafers. His wraparound reflective sunglasses were pushed up on his head.

Ben Chin didn't have any trouble recognizing Neal, either.

"Mark said to hide you out and help you find some babe, right?" he asked as he grabbed Neal by the shoulder.

"Close enough."

"So maybe I should get you out of a crowded airport," Chin said. "Where's your luggage?"

Neal hefted his shoulder bag. "You're looking at it."

Chin led him through the terminal and out into the parking lot.

"Kai Tak Airport is a very sad place, you know. According to legend, this is where the Boy Emperor, the last ruler of the Sung Dynasty, jumped off a cliff into the ocean and drowned."

"Why did he do that?"

"He lost a war with the Mongols or something, I don't know. Anyway, he didn't want to be captured."

"I don't see a cliff or an ocean."

"Bulldozers. We'd rather have an airport than a suicide launch pad."

Chin unlocked the trunk of a '72 Pinto and threw Neal's bag in. Then he opened the left-side passenger door for Neal. He gestured for Neal to get in and then walked around to the right side of the car and squeezed himself behind the steering wheel. As they pulled out of the lot, he asked, "Aren't you going to tell me how good my English is?"

"I hadn't planned on it."

"I did a year at UCLA."

"Yeah?"

"Yeah, but I flunked out." He patted his belly. "I clean-jerked a few too many brews, you know what I mean?"

"I've had those nights."

"Did you go Greek?"

"Hmm?"

"Which frat?" Ben asked.

"I lived at home."

"Oh," said Ben.

He sounded so disappointed that Neal added, "In an apartment. By myself."

"Cool."

Help me, baby Jesus, Neal pleaded. Less than a week ago I was happily burrowed in my little hill, now I'm trapped in a '72 deathmobile in Hong Kong with a failed frat rat. Life is a strange and wonderful carnival of experiential delights.

"So what do you do now?" Neal asked, trying to avoid a discussion of those good old college days of keggers, mixers, and coeds.

"I'm a security guard at the Banyan Tree Hotel."

Please, baby Jesus, come down now. I'm off the midway and headed for the sideshow tents.

93

"It's the family trade. Besides, it gives me access to a gym. And a place where I can conduct a couple of sidelines, if you know what I mean."

Yeah, I think I know what you mean.

"The security work?" Ben continued. "I have it dicked. The place was a mess when I took the job. Thieves . . . beggars . . . little kids swiping handbags. The tourists were really put off. And vandalism that you wouldn't believe. I came in and brought some of my boys with me. We cleaned it up, you know what I mean?" He showed Neal his enormous fist. "Now the word is out. We don't have to work much, and the owners are happy to pay us, feed us, let us use the gym—an empty room now and then when the need comes up, if you know what I mean."

Yeah, I know what you mean. You organize the thieves, the beggars, and the pickpockets. You commit the vandalism. Then you make it stop. It works the same way in Chinatown in New York, or in Little Italy. People pay you to protect them against yourself. It works the same way on Wall Street, on Capitol Hill. On the street it's called "protection," in the halls of power they call it "lunch."

"I think I know what you mean, Ben."

"I think you do, too."

Ben Chin eased his way skillfully into the flow of slow-moving early-morning traffic. He stayed in the mainstream moving down Chatham Road for about twenty minutes, then manuevered into a turn lane and onto Tung Tau Tsuen Street.

Chin pointed out the window to a patch of decrepit, filthy, high-rise tenements about the size of two football fields.

"You don't ever want to go in there, Neal."

"No?"

"No. That's the Walled City. You go in there, you don't come back out. It's like a maze."

Neal said, "I don't see any walls."

"Torn down. It was a Sung fort. Even the British didn't want it when they took over in Kowloon. You're looking at one of the worst slums in the world. No government, no law. It's the end of the road."

Ben sped up again and turned back onto Chatham Road.

"Speaking of the end of the road," Neal said, "where are we going?"

"To the hotel. We got you a nice room."

Any time now, baby Jesus.

94

"Ben, didn't your cousin explain to you that some people might be looking for me?"

"Sure."

"So, a hotel?" Neal asked. No wonder you flunked out.

"Not a hotel, Neal. *My* hotel. You don't sign the register, and you have a room we can keep an eye on. Nobody will get to you."

"Who's 'we'?"

"My boys at the hotel."

"The other guards that you supervise."

Ben Chin chuckled. "Sure. We pride ourselves on keeping our guests safe and secure."

Chin took a left off Chatham onto Austin Road.

"Hey, Ben?"

"Yeah, Neal?"

"Let's cut the happy-Buddha, Hop Sing routine, and get down to it. You're mobbed up, right?"

"I don't know what you mean by 'mobbed up.'"

The idea sure didn't make him mad, though. He was grinning with glee.

"You're a junior executive with one of the Triads. In the management training program, so to speak."

"Oooohh, 'Triad' . . . the man thinks he knows the lingo."

Yeah, the man thinks he does. You'd have to be deaf, dumb, and stupid to do my kind of work in any major city in America and not know about the crime syndicates that controlled so much of daily life in every Chinatown. Neal knew that the Triads' high-ticket item was heroin, but the protection racket provided a big slice of the daily bread, and the Triad bosses used this extortion as a training ground for its thugs and up-and-comers. The Triads had spread their fingers over the Asian communities worldwide, but their home offices were in Hong Kong.

"Quit running a number on me, Ben."

"So you're from New York, Neal? You've had some Peking Duck on Mott Street and you think you're an expert on the inscrutable world of the Orient? Let me tell you, something, Neal—you know shit."

He took a left off Austin onto Nathan Road.

"So tell me what I need to know," Neal said.

"You need to know that you're in good hands and leave it at that."

"*Am* I in good hands?"

"The best."

The Banyan Tree Hotel occupies a block on the east side of Nathan Road in the Kowloon District called Tsimshatsui—the Peninsula. It's the major tourist area in Hong Kong, with its "Golden Mile" shopper's paradise, restaurants, and bars.

"You'll blend right in here," Chin assured Neal as they climbed the back staircase, not bothering to check in. "And you're prepaid."

They walked up to the second floor and then grabbed the elevator to the ninth. Neal's room, 967, was large and anonymous. Its furniture and decor could have been in any hotel room in New Jersey, except that the large picture window looked out over Kowloon Park, across from Nathan Road. The banyan trees that lined the park were survivors from the days when Major Nathan first surveyed the lines for the dirt track that at the time led to nowhere and hence got the name "Nathan's Folly." The park appeared to be filled mostly with old people and kids. A deformed beggar, his legs bent underneath him, was crawling along the sidewalk, feebly chasing passersby.

"Welcome to Kowloon," Chin said. "The real Hong Kong."

Neal sat down on the bed and began to go through the papers in his briefcase. "What does 'Kowloon' mean?"

"Nine dragons," Chin answered as he lit up a Marlboro. He almost looked like a dragon himself, a big, dangerous beast puffing smoke. "The old people thought that the eight hills here were each dragons, and they were going to call the place Eight Dragons. Then the Sung Emperor came, and the Emperor is a dragon, so that made nine. Nine Dragons— Kowloon."

"It looks pretty flat to me."

"It is. Most of the hills were 'dozed to make room."

Neal took the brochure advertising Li Lan's paintings from his briefcase and handed it to Chin. "Where is that address?"

"Is this the babe?"

"Yeah. Is it far from here?"

"Good looking. No, not far. Kansu Street is just up the Nathan Road. Yaumatei District. You get some sleep, then I'll take you there."

"I'm not tired."

"She's a painter?"

"Yeah."

"Maybe she'd like to paint my picture. What do you think?"

"I think you should tell me how to get to two-thirty-seven Kansu Street."

The beggar across the street scored some coins from a young woman tourist. Chin offered the pack of cigarettes to Neal, who shook his head.

"I think," Chin said, "that I better take you there."

"Why? Is it a dangerous neighborhood?"

"It's not the neighborhood, it's the situation."

"What situation?"

"You tell me."

Neal got up and looked out the window. The beggar would have been tall if had been able to stand up. He was certainly thin. He moved by supporting himself on his hands as he swung his torso like a gymnast on the bars of the horse. The crowds of pedestrians surged around him, creating an eddy in the stream of traffic.

The situation is, Neal thought, that I'm a renegade from my own company, which may or may not join the CIA in wanting me dead. The situation is that this woman set me up, maybe even set me up to be killed. The situation is that somehow I'm in love with her anyway and I need to warn her that she's in danger. The situation is that I have to find her to get some answers before I can get on with my life.

"The situation is," Neal said without turning away from the window, "that I need to talk to the woman at two-thirty-seven Kansu Street. That's the situation."

"Mark told me to take care of you."

"And you have."

"He said there are people looking for you."

"There are."

"So you need protection."

Neal turned back from the window. If I boot him, he thought, he'll lose face with his cousin and with his own boys. Besides, this is his turf and I couldn't lose him if I tried. All I can do is make it harder on each of us.

"I'll need to speak with her alone," Neal said.

"Sure."

"Let's go."

* * *

97

One thing you have to say for Ben Chin, Neal thought: he's organized. As soon as they hit the street, three teenage boys fell in behind them. They all had that lean and hungry look that Caesar was so worried about, and they all wore white shirts over shiny black trousers and loafers. They dropped their cigarettes as soon as they saw Chin, and wordlessly arranged themselves in a fan formation about thirty feet behind Chin and Neal. A bucktoothed boy, smaller and skinnier than the others, ranged ahead of them, rarely looking back but figuring out their intended path anyway.

"Who do we have to look out for?" Chin asked him. "White guys?"

"Probably."

Chin grimaced, then said, "Okay, no problem."

"You have a scout ahead of us."

"You have a good eye. But he's not a scout. He's a doorman. If we have to run, he opens a 'door' in the crowd for us and shuts it when we're through."

Neal knew what he meant. A doorman in a street operation is like a downfield blocker in a football game. When he sees his players running his way, he clobbers a civilian or two to open a hole. Once his own guys make it through the hole, he throws himself in the way of the pursuit. That's the way it usually works, but if the doorman sees that it's the opposition in the way instead of bystanders, he uses a knife or a gun or his hands to open the hole. When that happens the doorman is usually a goner unless the sweepers can get up to the action real fast. A doorman is expendable.

So Ben Chin sure knew what he was doing. Having a doorman ready is about the only way out of a net. Which was one of those good-news-bad-news jokes to Neal: good that Chin was ready for a trap, bad that he thought he had to be.

Chin himself seemed relaxed. He moved easily through the crowd, glancing at the store windows and checking out the women. To the casual observer he looked like a Kowloon tough on a leisurely search for some fun. But Neal saw the alertness in his eyes and recognized that each scan of a portable radio or an approachable woman screened a search for potential trouble. Chin was watching out for something, and Neal had the feeling that he wasn't looking for some white guys. The various *kweilo* tourists that passed by didn't earn a second glance.

Neal felt his paranoia come back on him like a stale shirt. Or maybe it was the fact that he had been on all-night flight and hadn't bothered to shower, shave, or get a meal. It felt like a mistake, but then he remembered that the last time he had stopped to indulge in such human comforts, he had let Pendleton and Li Lan skip out to Mill Valley. He wasn't going to give them the chance this time.

Chin was staring up and to the left, and Neal braced himself for some action. He turned to follow Chin's gaze, and saw that it led to a movie marquee. Chin was staring at the poster advertising the current feature. The three sweeps stopped in their tracks, and one of them turned around to cover the rear. The Doorman used the pause to cross over to the west side of Nathan Road, then he stopped on the corner to turn and watch his boss.

Chin didn't see any of it, but then again, he didn't have to. He had a well-trained team and he knew it, and this gave him little luxuries like freedom to check out a movie.

The marquee said that the theater was called the Astor, but that was the end of the English; everything else was in Chinese ideograms. The posters showed a brightly dressed Chinese couple in period costume gazing fondly at each other, and another still of the same couple bravely wielding gigantic swords against what looked like an army of grinning villains.

"This place has the latest flicks from China," Ben Chin explained. He looked at his watch. "Maybe we can go this afternoon."

The Book of Joe Graham, Chapter Seven, Verse Three: "Everyone has a weakness."

"Yeah," Neal said. "Let's see how it goes."

The Doorman was doing a quick shuffle-step across the street, like a puppy whose master is taking too long to open the door for a walk. Neal didn't blame him; the Doorman's job was a lonely one, especially when he was cut off from his team by a broad and busy avenue. The doorman had a lot of responsibility here. It was his job to give the "Walk/Don't Walk" signal.

Street crossings are tricky in this kind of work. You have to time it so the traffic flow doesn't cut the sweepers off from the people they're protecting. You also have to keep a sharp eye on all the cars that are coming and going. One car might cut off the sweepers while the crew in a second car takes out the target. A street crossing is a vulnerable moment.

They did it flawlessly, the Doorman using subtle hand gestures to call the signals, and the rest of the team coming across in one smooth flow. It was as nifty a job as Neal had ever seen, and he thought he could detect a small look of relief on the Doorman's face as he led them west on Kansu Street.

Tenement buildings with cheap-looking ground-floor flats made up most of Kansu Street. You couldn't really call the buildings slums, but they were dirty and in need of a paint job. One of the main landlords must have gotten a great deal on pastel green paint, because the color dominated several buildings on one block. Narrow balconies, open to the street but roofed with corrugated metal, edged most of the buildings. Television antennae poked out over the balcony railings and made a convenient place from which to hang laundry. Beds and hammocks also filled a lot of the balconies, and here and there the tenants had nailed up sheets of tin to provide a little privacy for the family members who lived out there.

Hong Kong couldn't stretch out, so it stretched *up*. Everywhere you looked, the older, lower tenements were giving way to massive, block-long high-rises that had the unmistakable anonymity of government housing projects. The private sector was on the move, too; when the existing buildings had overflowed, people had simply moved themselves and their belongings out into the side streets and jerry-rigged shacks out of tin, old sheets, and cardboard. A few of these pioneers with a little more cash or some connections had scored some precious wood and built actual walls.

Neal felt as if he had stepped off Nathan Road into a Malthusian scenario in which the eye could never rest. The landscape was literally crawling; there was motion everywhere he looked. Children scampered along the balconies and played the same games played by kids everywhere, but their games of hide-and-seek seemed to encompass hundreds of contestants, and there was no place to hide. Merchants lined the sidewalks hawking an infinite variety of goods. Old women stood at windows or balconies shaking out sheets and towels, while their husbands leaned over the railing and smoked cigarettes or spat out sunflower seeds while they talked with their neighbors.

The noise was incredible: a din of conversation, banter, argument, negotiation, advertisement, and protest all conducted in the singsong but rapid-fire Cantonese dialect. Old women expressed outrage over the price of a fish while their sisters moaned in triumph or despair over the clackety-clack of mah-jongg tiles. Men trumpeted the virtues of bolts of cheap cloth or the undoubted tenderness of a particular chicken, while their less ambitious brothers argued over the chances of a two-year-old filly at Happy Valley that afternoon. Children squealed with unrestrained joy, or giggled at some private joke, or wailed in misery as a mother hauled them by the hand back into a building.

Then Neal noticed the smell—or, more accurately, the smells. The aroma of cooking predominated. Neal could distinguish the smell of fish and rice, and it seemed to him there were dozens of odors that he didn't recognize, smells that rose from steaming woks in the street shacks and hung over the area like a permanent cloud. There was also the smell of a sewage system that couldn't begin to cope with the demands placed on it, and the underlying stink of standing human waste permeated the air. The acrid smoke of charcoal braziers, masses of burning cigarettes, and building power plants made the air thick and hazy, and competed with the salt air of the nearby sea.

Yaumatei was a total crowding of the senses. Neal, after spending the last six months as the only occupant of an open moor, could only imagine what it might be like to to inhabit a world where, from the moment of birth to the moment of death, one never experienced a single moment alone.

Chin and his crew moved through the crowd like sharks through the ocean, constantly in motion and serenely calm. Their eyes never seemed to move from a straight-ahead gaze, and yet they seemed to take in everything. Neal noticed that people in the crowd would spot them and then quickly find something fascinating to look at on the sidewalk until the gang passed by. No hawkers or loiterers or curious kids approached Neal, even thought they were several blocks off the main *kweilo* tourist route. He was sealed off.

It took them about ten minutes to find number 346, which looked pretty much like 344 or 345. The building was mustard yellow and only five stories tall. The typical balconies stuck out like guardian parapets, the colorful laundry resembling pennants.

"You have a flat number?" Chin asked Neal.

The Doorman stood in the building's foyer, looking up the staircase. An ancient woman, clad entirely in black from her skullcap to her shoes, sat on a stool staring nervously at him between puffs of a cigarette.

"No."

Chin laughed. "I'll bet now you're glad I came with you."

He approached the old woman and spoke roughly to her in Cantonese. She spoke back just as roughly, and Neal felt relief when Chin laughed, reached into his pocket, and handed her a cigarette. Her eyes showed pleased surprise when she saw the Marlboro.

"Give me the picture," Chin said.

Neal handed him the brochure, and Chin showed it to the old woman. She stared at it for a few seconds and gave a brief response.

"She knows her," Chin explained to Neal, "but she wants more cigs to tell us."

Neal felt a rush of excitement in his stomach. Li Lan might be just upstairs, a few seconds away.

"Ask her if she's with a white man."

"This old bag?"

"Li Lan."

Chin's face crinkled up in a broad smile as he looked at Neal and said, "I think I get it. You want the guy beat up?"

"No."

"Suit yourself."

Chin turned back to the woman and handed her three more Marlboros. She snatched them, then snarled at him and stuck her hand out.

"Gau la!" Chin answered. ("Enough!")

"Hou!" ("Yes!")

Chin gave her one more cigarette.

"Do jeh." ("Thank you.") She shoved the cigarettes in her jacket pocket and then pointed upstairs and gave directions.

"Mgoi," Chin said sarcastically. ("Thanks for the help.") "Upstairs, fourth floor."

The doorman went ahead of them and two of the crew followed. The third stayed at the lobby door.

When they reached the apartment, Neal said, "I want to talk to her alone."

"We'll wait out here," Chin agreed.

Neal felt his heart racing as he knocked on the door. There was no answer, no scuffling of feet, no cease in conversation. He knocked again. Still no answer. The third time wasn't a charm. The locked door presented only a momentary inconvenience, and Ben Chin nodded approvingly at Neal's dexterity with his AmEx card.

"Fuck!" Neal yelled.

The apartment was empty. Not merely unoccupied, but empty. No clothes, no cooking utensils, dishes, pictures, old magazines, toilet paper, toothbrushes. . . . A bare bed and an old rattan chair were the sole occupants of the one-room apartment.

Neal looked out the window at the balcony. Nothing. He turned around to see Ben Chin standing in the open doorway. Chin looked angry, a lot angrier than he should have been, but Neal didn't notice it. He was too pissed off.

"Go get the Old Mother," Chin said to the Doorman in Cantonese. Then he turned back to Neal and said, "It looks like you missed her."

"No kidding."

"She must have just left. Apartments don't stay empty long around here."

"She took the time to clean it."

Chin laughed. "Maybe. It's more likely, though, that the neighbors stripped it the second she walked out the door."

Pretty goddamn inconsiderate of the neighbors. Didn't they know I'd want to search for clues?

Neal heard the old woman squawking in the staircase. The Doorman brought her into the room. At Chin's signal he shut the door behind them.

"Are you a ghost?" Chin said to her in Cantonese. He walked across the room and opened the window. *"Can you fly?"*

Neal didn't understand the words, but the threat was fairly clear. A thug is a thug is a thug, and his techniques vary little from culture to culture.

"Come on, Ben," Neal said, feeling more tired than he had for years. Chin ignored him.

"Answer me," he said to the old woman. *"Are you a ghost? Can you fly?"*

She glared at him with a look that spoke more contempt than fear. She didn't say anything.

"Why did you make me climb four flights of stairs for nothing? Huh? Why didn't you tell me she had left?"

Her answer was a variation on the "you didn't ask" theme.

"Where did she go?"

"How would I know?"

"Let's see if you can fly."

The Doorman grabbed her from behind and put his hand over her mouth to stifle her shriek. Neal stepped in front of the window.

"Tell him to let her go," he said.

"Stay out of it."

"I'm paying the bill, I give the orders," Neal answered.

"I'll give you a refund. Now get out of the way."

Neal slammed the window shut. He realized his knees were trembling and he knew that if Chin wanted to throw the woman out the window he could do it. Shit, he thought, if he wants to throw *me* out the window he can do it.

No real witty, intimidating threats came to him, so he settled for, "What could she tell us anyway?"

"Everything," Chin said. "The old bag has probably been sitting downstairs for forty years. She sees everyone who goes up and everyone who comes down. If she hears someone fart, she knows what he ate for lunch."

Chin stepped up to the woman and poked her in the chest. *"Tell me."*

She broke into a long monologue.

"What man? What kind of man?" Chin asked.

The question inspired another soliloquy. When she was finished, Chin signaled the Doorman to release her. She sank to her knees on the floor and gasped for air, looking up at Neal with an expression of unmitigated hatred.

Chin wasn't much friendlier when he said, "Okay, Mr. Gandhi. Old Woman Know-Nothing says your babe was here with a *kweilo*—a white guy—for just one day. Do you think this old hag wouldn't notice that? Do you think that anybody on this whole block wouldn't notice that? She says another guy came to visit both days. A Chinese. She says the three of them left together this morning, but she doesn't know where they were going, and she had better be telling the truth."

Neal plunked himself down on the windowsill. He was tired and angry and he didn't like the smug look on Chin's face.

"Okay," Neal said, "so you got out of her that they were here, and now they're not, and they left with a Chinese man. Hell, they should be easy to find now. All we have to do is find a Chinese man."

Chin looked at him like he was thinking about the window again. Neal looked at the Doorman and pointed to the door. Chin nodded his okay and the Doorman left.

"And something else," Neal said to Chin. "I don't like the way you work. You're on a job with me, there are certain things you don't do—I don't care if it's your turf and your language. One of the biggest things you don't do is you don't rough up old women, or any women, or any*body* unless you have to. And by 'have to' I mean only if we're in actual, physical danger. Now if you can't deal with that, fine—walk away right now and I'll finish the job myself."

The silence that followed was about as long as a "Gilligan's Island" rerun.

"You don't know how things work here," Chin said quietly.

"I know how *I* work."

"If you had talked to me that way in front of my crew, I would have had to kill you."

Neal recognized a peace offering when he heard one. He had to give Chin back some face.

"I know. That's why I sent him out of the room. To tell you the truth, I was pretty scared." He gave Chin his most self-deprecating laugh.

Chin laughed back and the deal was done.

"Okay," Chin said. "Your checkbook, your rules."

"Okay. Now what?"

Chin thought for a second.

"Tea," he said.

"Tea?"

"Helps you think."

"Then tea it is. I need all the help I can get."

Chin pulled a money roll out of his pants pocket, peeled a $10HK bill off, and handed it to the old woman.

"*Deui mjyuh,*" he said. ("I'm sorry.")

She stuffed the bill inside her blouse and scowled at him.

"*Cigarette!*" she demanded.

He gave her the pack.

The teashop was more like an aviary. It seemed to Neal that every other customer in the place was carrying at least one cage with a bird in it.

105

"I feel so underdressed," Neal said to Chin as they sat down at the small round table. The Doorman had gone in before them, secured the table, and left. The rest of the crew waited outside, patrolling the sidewalk and observing every customer who came in.

"Local color," Chin answered. "I thought you might enjoy it."

Neal looked around the large room. The customers were all men, mostly older, most of them accompanied by brightly colored songbirds in bamboo cages. Some of the cages looked like they cost a small fortune. They featured sloping rooflines with carved dragons painted in shiny colors. Some had swinging perches with gilded chains and ivory bars. A few of the really old men had their pets perched proudly on their wrists. The birds—and it seemed to Neal that were hundreds of them— sang to each other, every warbling tremolo inspiring a choral response. As the birds exchanged tunes, the old men chatted happily with each other, doubtless swapping bird anecdotes and heredities. The men seemed to know each other as well as the birds did, and all parties were enjoying their social outing. The teashop was a riot of sound and color, but Neal noticed that it wasn't really noisy.

"Quite a place," Neal said.

"They used to be all over Hong Kong," Ben said, "but keeping birds is dying out with the old people. Now there are only a few Bird Teahouses."

A waiter came over, wiped the table with a wet towel, and set out two handleless cups.

"What kind of tea do you want?" Chin asked Neal.

"You order for me," answered Neal, who drank at least one cup of tea a year and was only vaguely aware that there was more than one kind.

"Let me see . . . you are tired but need to concentrate, so I think maybe a Chiu Chou tea." He said to the waiter, *"Ti' kuan yin cha."*

"Houde."

"I ordered a very strong Oolong tea. It will keep you awake. Alert."

"That would be a refreshing change. So what do we do now?"

"Give up."

"Can't."

"Why not?"

Neal listened to the cacophony of birdsong, chatter, and rattling cups for few moments before he answered.

"There are other people looking for her and her friend. I think the same people might have reason to be looking for me. These other people do not have kind intentions—they'll kill her, her friend, and me if they have to. I don't know why. I do know that I have to find her, warn her, and find out what this is all about before I can get back to a normal life."

A normal life. Right.

"How did you get involved in this?"

Neal shook his head.

Chin tried again. "Mark told me it's a drug thing."

"I don't think so."

The waiter came back and set a pot of tea on the table. Chin took the lid off, sniffed the pot, and put the lid back on. He filled Neal's cup and then his own.

Neal sipped the tea. It was strong all right, slightly smoky and bitter. But it felt good going down, warm and soothing. It occured to him that he hadn't really stopped moving since the bullet had buzzed past his head, that he was wandering in the dark without a plan, moving for the sake of motion, making assumptions based on himself, not on the subject.

He took a long draught of the tea. So what do you know? he asked himself. You know that Li Lan and Pendleton have skipped out on you again. Back up. Skipped out on *you*? Why do you think you have anything to do with it? Maybe they already know about the danger and that's what they're running from. Running? Maybe they're not running at all. Maybe they came to Hong Kong and simply changed living quarters. The one-room apartment was small even for lovers.

So how do you find them? They've taken off in the most densely populated area of the most densely populated city in the world, so how do you find them?

You don't.

You let them find you.

He looked up from his cup and saw that Chin was also sitting back and relaxing. He didn't seem to mind Neal's silence or be bothered by it. He was just drinking tea.

You let them find you, Neal told himself. Why would they want to do that? Depends on who "they" are. If "they" are Li and Pendleton, maybe they find you because you're making such a pain in the ass of yourself that they have to deal with you. If "they" are the same people who almost canceled your reservation in Mill Valley, maybe they find you because they *can* find you, and they tie up a loose end.

That's me, Neal thought, the quintessential loose end.

He poured another cup of tea for himself and Chin, then sat back in his chair. He was sitting in a place where old men combined their pleasures by taking their pet birds to tea. He could take a few moments to enjoy it. Besides, the game had changed. The second cup of tea was much stronger, the third stronger yet, and then the pot was empty. Chin turned the lid upside down on the pot and the waiter picked it up and returned a minute later with a fresh pot.

"Maybe I can't find her," Neal said. "But I can look for her."

"True."

Neal poured the tea.

"Maybe I can make a big show of looking for her."

Chin took some tea and swilled it around in his mouth. Then he tilted his head back and swallowed. "Then maybe the unfriendly people who are looking for you will find you."

"That's the idea."

If they missed me once, they can miss me again. But *I* won't miss *them* this time.

"That's a crazy game."

"Do you want to play?"

"Absolutely."

Chin got up and signaled for the check.

"You ready?" he asked Neal.

"Not yet."

"You need something?"

"I need to sit here and finish the tea and listen to the birds sing."

The birds must have heard him because they launched into an avian symphony of particular virtuosity. Even the old men stopped their conversations to listen and to enjoy the moment. When the crescendo died down, everyone laughed, not in derision but in the joy of a shared pleasure.

Neal Carey was dog-tired, jet-lagged, culture-shocked, and snakebit, but at least he knew what to do next.

7

He checked into the Banyan Tree properly this time, via the lobby and the registration desk. He whipped out the Bank's plastic—so what if they tracked him down?—tipped the bellhop, and settled right back into his room. He poured himself a neat scotch, left a wake-up call for seven o'clock, and read two chapters of *Fathom* before dropping off.

Angels watched over him in his sleep. The angels in this case were not the winged spirits that one Father O'Connell used to tell him about when a younger Neal would help him find his way back to the rectory from the Dublin House Pub. Neal would listen patiently, if skeptically, to the old priest's description of a guardian angel that followed you everywhere, as he relieved Father O'Connell of all his pocket money and decided that maybe these angels existed after all. The angels now were a bunch of Hong Kong Triad thugs who had thrown a loose protective net around Neal, and who prowled the hotel corridor, watched the entrances and the sidewalks, blocked the stairway leading to Neal's floor, and did it all without being noticed.

Neal had insisted on that as the price for accepting protection at all.

"This won't work if I'm traveling in a mob," he had told Ben Chin. "I have to look like an easy target."

"A slam-dunk," agreed Ben, who after all, had attended UCLA. "Don't worry. My boys will lay back."

So Neal slept soundly until the phone rang at seven. He showered and dressed—white shirt, khaki slacks, indestructible blue blazer, no tie—and went downstairs to the dining room. He stopped off in the gift shop and picked up the *South China Daily* and the *International Herald Tribune.* The latter provided him with sports news to read as he tossed down four cups of coffee, two pieces of white toast, and three scrambled eggs.

He went back up to his room and the package was waiting on his bed, just as he had arranged. He didn't know how Chin had managed to get all of it done in one afternoon and evening, but it was all there: five hundred flyers with the photo of Pendleton and Li Lan at dinner, and a message in Chinese and English reading, IF YOU HAVE SEEN THESE PEOPLE, CONTACT MR. CAREY, and going on to give his hotel number and extension. There was also a neatly typed list of all the art galleries that might handle Li Lan's sort of work. There were about three dozen listings with addresses and phone numbers.

Chin had even grouped the galleries geographically, starting in Yaumatei and working down the Golden Mile, and then across the Hong Kong Island.

The first gallery was in the hotel and looked unlikely, but it was a good place try out a new lie.

"Good morning," Neal said to the clerk behind the glass counter.

"Good morning. Are you enjoying your stay in Hong Kong?"

She was a Chinese woman, in her mid-forties, Neal guessed, and she was wearing an elaborately embroidered padded jacket that looked more like a uniform than her own clothing. The gallery sold a lot of jewelry and cloisonné and exhibited some large oil paintings of Hong Kong subjects: the view from Victoria Peak, Kowloon at night, sampans in the harbor. They seemed more like expensive souvenirs than artistic expressions.

"Very much," Neal answered. "I'm hoping you can help me."

"That is what I am here for."

"I'm a private investigator from the United States, and I am looking for this woman," he said, handing her a flyer.

She looked at it nervously. "Oh, my."

"The woman, Li Lan, is an artist. A painter, to be precise."

"Is she in some kind of trouble?"

Some kind.

"Oh, no, quite to the contrary. You see, I represent the Humboldt-Schmeer Gallery in Fort Worth. We would like to discuss a *major* showing of Miss Li's work, but she seems to have changed her place of residence and we cannot seem to locate her through normal channels. Hence the reason for my disturbing you. Would you, by any chance, happen to know her?"

"There are so many artists in Hong Kong, Mr. Carey. . . ."

"As there should be in a place of such beauty."

"I am afraid I do not know this one, and I am sure we do not sell her work."

"Thank you for your time. May I leave this flyer with you, in case you should remember something?"

"Yes, of course."

"My telephone number is right there."

"In the hotel . . . very convenient."

"There is of course a modest reward, and a healthy sum of money in it for Miss Li, if we can locate her."

"I understand."

So will Miss Li, if she gets the word. The name Neal Carey will ring a clanging bell. *Hi, remember me? Last time you saw me I was dead.*

He hit three more galleries in the next hour, working his way north up Nathan Road. None of them sold Li Lan's paintings, nor had the staffs ever heard of her. Neal made a turn south and headed back down, picking up four more galleries on side streets before he got back to the hotel. The first clerk dismissed him perfunctorily as unlikely to buy anything, the second was a polite young Chinese man who displayed great interest but offered no useful information. The third was an avant-garde place where the young owner thought she might have met Li Lan at a gallery showing on the island once, and the fourth spoke no English at all, but took a flyer. During this entire walk, Neal caught a glimpse of Ben Chin only once, and another time he thought he saw the Doorman in a crowd of people in front of him.

Neal stopped at the hotel desk to check for messages. There weren't any, so he headed south down Nathan Road, into the heart of the expensive tourist district of Tsimshatsui. The day had turned hot and sunny. Tourists, shoppers, and the regular denizens crowded the sidewalks. Neal visited three galleries within the next six blocks. Nobody in any of them had ever heard of an artist named Li Lan, and nobody recognized the woman in the photograph. Neal left the flyers behind.

Two hours and four more shops found him down at Star Ferry Pier, the southernmost point of Kowloon. He could see the gray skyscrapers of Hong Kong Island ahead of him across Kowloon Bay. Victoria Peak loomed above the high-rises like a watchful landlady. Neal spotted the Doorman ahead of him on the runway to the ferry. The Doorman glanced at him nervously, his eyes flicking ahead to the ferry and behind Neal to his boss. Neal read the gesture: Was he planning to board the ferry and cross over to Hong Kong Island? That would take special arrangements. Neal pivoted back toward Nathan Road and strode away from the pier. He could feel rather than see Chin's net shifting northward, and knew that the Doorman would be running to retake the lead position. Neal slowed down to make his job a little easier in the midday heat.

Neal decided that he would hit the galleries on Hong Kong Island the next day. It was time to become a slower prey and let the predator catch his scent. If anyone was out there sniffing the air, they could hardly miss it. Just to make sure, he turned east along Salisbury Road and headed for the Peninsula Hotel. If there was a place to see and be seen in Kowloon, it was the Peninsula.

The Peninsula Hotel had once been the end of the road, a place where weary travelers stayed before boarding the Orient Express for the long trip back to the West. Its architecture was classic British colonial: a broad veranda, large columns, and white paint. The veranda, now enclosed in modern glass, sheltered a tearoom and featured a view of the bay and Hong Kong Island. The locals who were jaded to that panorama came for a vantage point from which they could observe just who was taking tea with whom, and what romantic liaisons or commercial conspiracies could be inferred from the comings and goings in the Peninsula lobby.

Neal paused halfway up the broad steps to the Peninsula and stood gawking at the view, which was his way of announcing to Chin, the boys, and whoever else was interested, "Hello! I'm going into the Peninsula Hotel now!"

The waiter sat him at a single table in the middle of the enormous tearoom. Neal ordered a pot of coffee, an iced tea, and a chicken sandwich and then settled in to do what everybody else was doing, surreptitiously checking each other out.

It was a well-heeled crowd, the prices at the Peninsula being somewhat steep, and the room had a self-congratulatory air that added to the incestuous feeling. The customers were mostly white, with a sizable minority of conservatively dressed Chinese who had yet to lose the slightly defensive expression inherited from the days when they had been welcomed only as waiters. A large tourist contingent, mostly gray-haired Europeans, rounded out the crowd. The chatter was subdued and desultory; people were too busy looking over their companions' shoulders to engage in any really direct conversation.

Neal could just make out the Doorman loitering in the outer lobby, and he didn't so much as lift an eyebrow when Mark Chin took a single table nearby and began to ogle every woman in the room who looked like she might be under eighty years of age.

Neal polished off the meal, paid the exorbitant check, and took his sweet time getting up and leaving. He hit five more shops on his way back to the Banyan Tree. Li Lan's name didn't ring a bell in any of them, not a tinkle or a chime.

He worked his way back to the Banyan Tree. He wasn't surprised to see the Doorman lurking in the hallway outside his room.

"How are you doing?" Neal asked him.

The Doorman nodded and smiled shyly.

"Okay," he said, trying out the word.

"Okay."

Jesus, Neal thought, he looks about twelve years old.

Then it occurred to him that he had been younger than that when he started working the streets for Friends.

The Doorman was still standing there, as if he wanted to say something but was afraid.

"You want to come in?" Neal asked.

The Doorman smiled. He didn't understand a word.

"A drink? Uhhh . . . Coca-Cola?"

The Doorman tapped his wrist and then pointed at Neal's. Neal looked at the inexpensive Timex watch he had bought at least three years ago.

"The watch? You like the watch?"

The Doorman nodded enthusiastically.

Neal took it off his wrist and handed it to the Doorman. Apparently the Doorman didn't rate a watch in the peculiar pecking order of the gang. The Doorman strapped it to his wrist and held it up to his face to admire it.

Shit, why not?

"Listen," Neal said. "I need it now. I'll buy one tomorrow and you can have this one. Or you can have the new one, okay?"

He held out his hand for the watch. The Doorman took it off his wrist and put it in Neal's hand. He looked fucking heartbroken.

"Tomorrow," Neal said. Hell, how do I explain? He traced his index finger along the dial of the watch and moved it in a circle twelve times. "Tomorrow?"

The Doorman grinned and nodded.

Neal pointed at the Doorman's wrist. "Tomorrow it's yours. Okay?"

"Okay."

"Okay. I'm going to grab some sleep."

The Doorman bowed and backed off around the corner. Neal went into the room and made himself a scotch. He sipped at it while he tried to read some *Fathom* and then gave up and flopped down on the bed. He was beat.

The phone woke him up. The digital clock on the radio said it was four-twenty in the afternoon.

"Hello," he said.

"Stop it."

"I haven't even started, Lan."

"Stop it. You do not know what you are doing."

"Why don't you come here and tell me?"

There was one of those long silences he was getting so used to on this gig.

"Please," she said. "Please leave us alone."

"Where are you?"

"Someone will get hurt."

"That's why I've been trying to find you. At first I thought you set me up for a bullet in the old hot tub the other night. Now I think maybe the shot was meant for Pendleton."

He didn't get quite the reaction he expected, a gasp of horror or a gush of gratitude. It was almost a laugh.

"Is that what you think?" she asked.

"Maybe it's what I hope."

"I am asking you again—please leave us alone. You are only helping them."

"Helping who?"

"Stop this stupid searching you are doing. It is too dangerous."

If he hadn't been half asleep, he could have mumbled something really slick like, "Danger is my business, baby," but instead he asked, "Dangerous for who?"

"All of us."

"Where are you? I want to talk to you."

"You *are* talking with me."

Oh, yeah.

"I want to see you."

"Please forget us. Forget me."

No, Li Lan, I can't do either of those things.

"Lan, I'm going to start again tomorrow. I'm going to hit every gallery and shop in Hong Kong. I'm going to pass your picture around the entire city and I'm going to make a spectacle of myself doing it unless you agree to meet me tonight."

Pause, pause, pause.

"Wait one moment," she said.

He waited. He could hear her speaking, but could not make out the words. He wondered if she was talking to Pendleton.

"The observatory on Victoria Peak at eight o'clock. Can you be there?"

"Yes."

"Okay."

"Aren't you going to tell me to come alone?"

"You are foolish with me. Yes, come alone."

She hung up.

Neal felt his heart racing. If this is love, he thought, the poets can keep it. But three and a half hours sure seems like a long time.

He ordered a wake-up call for six o'clock and lay awake until the phone rang.

*   *   *

115

Getting to Victoria Peak wouldn't be too tough, Neal thought. Getting there alone would be impossible. That's what Ben Chin had told him, anyway.

"No way," Chin had said, with a firm shake of the head. He knocked back a hit of Neal's scotch with equal firmness.

"My checkbook, my rules, remember?"

"That was different."

"How?"

Neal had a scotch of his own sweating on the side table, untouched after the first sip.

"You weren't putting your butt on the line. Cousin Mark would be really pissed if I let you get killed."

"I'm not going to get killed."

"Why does she want to meet you at the Peak? Why not here at the hotel?"

"She's afraid and she doesn't trust me. She wants to meet in a public place."

"Let her meet you on the ferry, then."

"You can't run away on a ferry."

"That's what I mean."

Neal sat down on the bed and slipped into his loafers.

"I'm not going up there trailing your whole crew."

"You'll never know we're there."

"I told her I'd be alone."

"Did she tell you she'd be alone?"

Good point.

"No, I think she'll be with her friend."

"I think she'll be with a whole bunch of friends. You should be, too."

Neal stood up and put on his jacket.

"No."

"Okay. Just me."

"No."

"How are you going to stop me from following you?"

There was always that.

"Okay, just you."

Chin smiled and polished off his drink.

"But," Neal said, "you stay in the background, out of sight and out of earshot. I want to talk to her alone. Once we make the meet and you see that it's safe, you back off. Way off."

"Whatever you say."

"So are you ready to go?"

"It's only six-thirty. We have plenty of time."

"I want to get there early."

"Love is a many-splendored thing."

"I don't want to be set up again."

The rush onto the Star Ferry made a New York subway look like a spring cotillion. The same crowd that had been standing patiently and passively on the ramp moments earlier turned into an aggressive mob as soon as the entrance chain was dropped. Splitting into gangs, trios, couples, and the odd loner, the mob spilled onto the double-decked, double-ended old green-and-white vessel, flipping the backs across the benches to face forward.

Neal, a survivor of the Broadway Local, just managed to stay on his feet as the crowd shot off the ramp and pushed him forward. He claimed an apparently scorned seat toward the rear of the boat and wondered how Ben Chin was going to stay with him. The boat filled up quickly and took off quickly. There was no time for lollygagging; the Star Ferry made the nine-minute crossing 455 times a day.

It was some nine minutes. From sea level, Hong Kong's skyscrapers loomed like castle keeps, their gray steel and glass standing in sharp contrast to the green hills above. A staggering array of boat traffic jammed the waters of the bay. Private water taxis zipped back and forth while old junks lumbered across. Sampan pilots struggled with their sculling oars to maneuver through the chop left by the motorboats. A tugboat guided a gigantic ocean liner into a dock on the Kowloon side.

Lights began to glow in the early dusk, and neon reflections started to appear on the water, casting faint red, blue, and yellow shades on the bay, the boats, and even the ferry passengers. Neal's arm dangled out the window, and he watched it change color as the neon sign proclaiming Tudor Whiskey flashed.

Most of the passengers seemed unaffected by the scene. Only a handful of scattered tourists were paying any attention at all. The regular commuters talked or read newspapers or loudly spat sunflower-seed hulls onto the deck. Ben Chin was just sitting, staring impassively ahead, three rows behind Neal.

Neal leaned out to get a view of the Peak. His chest tightened. *She'll be there*, he thought. *What will she look like? What will she be wearing? What will she say? Will she be holding Pendleton's hand?* A fierce pang of jealousy ripped through him.

Jesus, Neal, he told himself. At least try to remember the job, the gig. The job is about Pendleton, not Li Lan. Yeah, but you took yourself off the job, remember? There is no job. There won't be any job. There's only her.

The crowd began to stir in anticipation of the docking. Neal stood up and resisted the impulse to look behind him. Chin would doubtless pick him up. The crew dropped the chains and the mob surged off the boat.

Neal had studied his guidebook and knew where to go. He came off the dock and crossed wide, busy Connaught Road and headed up past City Hall to Des Voeux Road, where he took a left and found the tramway station on the bottom of Garden Road.

He waited about five minutes for the small green-and-white funicular car to arrive, then found a window seat on the right side toward the front. Chin sat down on the left-side aisle toward the rear. Neal didn't see any of Chin's crew, and figured that the gang leader had kept his word.

The tram started with a jerk and began to pull up the steep slope of the peak. Most of the commuters got off on the lower two stops at Kennedy Road and Macdonnell Road. Thick vegetation of bamboo and fir trees flanked the narrow tram line on both sides, and sheer rock ledges showed where the line had been blasted through. At times the grade was so steep that the tram car seemed to defy gravity, and Neal felt that it would pitch over backward, tumbling them down on top of the tall commercial buildings that seemed to stand directly beneath and behind. He had an image of the steel cable snapping from the strain and the car hurtling backward through the air, end over end, until it finally crashed into the concrete and steel of the city below. Neal was afraid of heights.

The tram finally pulled into the Upper Peak Station. Neal got off on shaky legs. She had told him to meet her at the observatory. It wasn't hard to find, being only a few feet to the left of the station. He was forty minutes early for the meet, but he took a quick look around to make sure she wasn't there. She wasn't, and he turned his attention to the scene beneath him.

The view stretched out in the distance to the New Territories and the Chinese border, hidden in the brown hills that were going gray in the late dusk. Neal could see the entire Kowloon peninsula laid out in front of the hills, its concrete tenements, rows of docks, hotels, and bars beginning to glow with the lights that were blinking on as night came and people arrived back at their homes. The Star Ferry pier glowed in bright neon, and boats in the bay turned on their navigation lights. Directly beneath him, Neal watched the commercial towers of Hong Kong turn into giant pillars of light in the gathering darkness.

Neal stood on the observation deck watching day turn to night. It was like seeing a bland watercolor landscape change into a garish movie screen filled with electric greens, hot reds, cool blues, and shimmering golds. Hong Kong was a glimmering jewel necklace on a black dress, an invitation to explore a woman's secrets, a fantasy that tiptoed on the knife edge between a nightmare and a dream.

He forced himself to turn away from the panorama and reconnoiter the area. He took a right on the narrow paved walkway called Lugard Road, which led around the edge of the peak through the thick forests and gardens. A low stone wall bordered the downhill side of the trail, and informal footpaths led off into the woods on the uphill side. There were frequent turnoffs with benches where one could enjoy different perspectives of the stunning view below, but most of the tourists went no farther than the observatory, and the trail was almost deserted save for a few young lovers and a couple of joggers. Neal walked along the trail for about ten minutes and then turned around and went back to the observatory. He hadn't seen anything suspicious, nothing that looked like a trap or an ambush. He checked his watch: twenty minutes. He walked down to the tram station and waited.

What am I actually going to do? Neal wondered. Just tell her that someone is trying to grease the good doctor? She seems to know that already. Tell her that I think the CIA has a serious grudge against Bobby-baby and may want to waste both of them? Ask her if she tried to kill me back in groovy Mill Valley? Would she tell me if she did? Tell her I'm in love with her, that I've dumped my job and my education to follow her, that I can't live without her? What will she do? Dump

Pendleton on the spot and take the tram down with me? Hold my hand? Run away with me? Just what the hell am I doing here, anyway?

He looked around and saw Chin loitering on the hill above him. They exchanged a quick time-to-get-going look, and Neal started himself up toward the observatory. Maybe it's just another dodge, he thought. Maybe she won't be here at all.

She was there. Right on time and alone. Neal felt a twinge of guilt as he looked at her. She stood on the observatory deck where it joined Lugard Road. She looked splendid. She was wearing a loose black blouse over jeans and tennis shoes. Her hair hung long and straight, parted in the middle, and her blue comb was fastened to the left of the part. The view behind her turned to mere background. She looked directly at Neal and gestured quickly for him to follow her up Lugard Road.

Pendleton was standing by a bench at the first turnout. He was looking at the view. He wore a white shirt and baggy gray trousers, and he was fidgeting with a key chain in his right hand. Li Lan took him by the elbow and turned him to face Neal.

Neal was twenty feet from them when Pendleton asked, "What do you want?"

"Just to talk."

"So talk."

"I'm trying to warn you—"

The look in Li Lan's eyes cut him off. She was looking over his shoulder, and her face showed fear and anger.

"Bastard," she hissed at Neal. She grabbed Pendleton by the arm and pushed him up the path in front of her. They started to run.

Neal turned around to look behind him and saw Ben Chin standing there. He didn't take the time to bitch him out, but started running after Li and Pendleton, who were disappearing around a sharp curve beneath a huge banyan tree. No problem, Neal thought, he could catch them easily. He hit his stride quickly and was gaining on them when he reached the curve. He could hear Ben Chin pounding along behind him.

Li Lan hadn't come alone. There were three of them, and they stepped between Neal and his quarry. They were ten feet in front of him and they looked like they all had the same favorite movie—each wore a white T-shirt, jeans, and a black leather jacket, and each was carrying a chopper, a Chinese hybrid between a carving knife and a cleaver. Neal could just see Lan and Pendleton fading into the darkness behind their human screen. He looked at the Leather Boy in the middle: a large, solid youth who stood there shaking his head. Neal stopped cold and stood as still as he could. He raised his hands in the universal gesture of surrender and began to back up gently.

"Okay . . . okay . . . you win," he said. "I'll just go back the way I came." I'll go all the way back to Yorkshire, if you want. Walking. Backwards.

He heard movement in the bushes above him. Maybe it was Ben Chin. Maybe he had broken their deal and hidden his whole vicious crew in the woods. Please. . . . Neal slowly turned his head to see three more armed men come down through the woods to block the path behind him. Wrong crew.

Oh shit, oh dear. Okay, Ben Chin, where are you? Nowhere to be seen. You're pretty tough with old ladies, Ben, but when it comes to your peer group . . .

Neal risked a glance to his right. Maybe, just maybe he could make it to the low stone wall and jump over the edge. The problem was that he didn't know what was over the edge, a nice soft fir tree or a fifty-foot precipice culminating on a rock.

Leather Boy One raised his chopper and made a crisscross motion in front of his chest. Neal heard the fighters behind him close in another couple of feet. Then the line in front of him did the same thing.

The fifty-foot-drop option didn't seem so bad. Being smashed on a rock seemed preferable to being chopped to pieces. His Eighteenth Century Lit friends would call that a Hobson's choice.

Leather Boy One raised his chopper.

The Doorman dropped from the limb of the banyan tree right on top of Leather Boy One. They crashed to the ground and the Doorman reached out and grabbed the ankle of another one of the gang and pulled his feet out from under him. The Doorman was no match for Leather Boy One but held him down long enough to look up at Neal and gesture with his eyes to jump over the tangled mass—he had opened the door.

Neal heard a mass of running footsteps from behind and then in front, and Chin's crew filled the path in both directions. One of them sliced the third Leather Boy across the arm with a chopper while the other reached out and pulled Neal over the top of the Doorman and Leather Boy One, who were still grappling on the ground. Then he pushed Neal along the path.

121

"Run!" he yelled.

Leather Boy One got a leg behind the Doorman's ankle and flipped him over. He brought his chopper down on the back of the Doorman's knee. The Doorman screamed in pain and grabbed Leather Boy One's ankles and held on. The chopper came down again, on the other knee.

Chin's assistant was pushing Neal away from the scene.

"Go, go, go!" he yelled.

"We have to help him!"

"He's dead!"

Neal looked behind him and saw that both gangs were fighting. Screams of rage and the clang of metal on metal hit his ears, and the flashes of steel under the streetlamps dazzled his eyes. He felt more arms pulling on him now, moving him away from the fight, away from where the Doorman lay bleeding and whimpering, away from the danger. He could run now and make it, and Chin's assistant and the others would protect his back. He felt the cool, clean air of safety.

He tore himself away fom the arms and headed back toward the Doorman, who lay in the middle of the fight. Neal grabbed one of the Leather Boys by the back of his jacket and ran him over the side of the wall. Another one was leaning over the Doorman, searching for money. Neal grabbed the back hem of his jacket and pulled it over his head, trapping his arms. He hauled back and hit him in the face four times and the boy dropped. Neal reached under the Doorman's arms and began to drag him back along the path, where Chin's assistant and two of the others stood watching in disgust and confusion. They were outnumbered, they had just enough manpower to get Neal out, not fight a pitched battle, and the *kweilo* had fucked it up, and wasted a good doorman in the bargain.

"Help me!" Neal yelled to them.

The rest of Chin's gang were now backing off in the opposite direction, back toward the observatory, flashing their choppers in front of them to hold off their advancing enemies. Leather Boy One and two of his comrades placed themselves squarely between Neal and Chin's assistant, who began to back down the trail. Neal was surrounded again.

Fuck it, he thought, and knelt down over the Doorman. He had never seen so much blood. It was all over them. He took off his jacket, ripped off a sleeve, and wrapped it around the Doorman's leg above the wound, trying to remember how to tie a proper tourniquet. The leg was almost severed, the tendons cut through. The Doorman had lost a lot of blood. His face was gray and his eyes were faint. He looked at Neal with reproach, an expression Neal read to mean, "You have wasted my sacrifice."

Neal looked up at Leather Boy One.

"Get a doctor."

Leather Boy One stepped over to them and kicked the Doorman in the leg, right on the wound. The Doorman howled. Neal held him as tightly as he could and stared up at Leather Boy One, memorizing his face. If I ever get out of this, he thought. Leather Boy One smiled broadly at him and raised his big knife over Neal's face. Neal summoned up every bit of courage and rage he had to stare him in the face. Leather Boy One prepared to bring the chopper down in a smooth backhand stroke into Neal's throat. Leather Boy One was smiling.

The bullet hit him squarely between the eyes. He crumpled to the ground with the smile still on what was left of his face. Two more silenced shots whooshed in the air and the rest of the Leather Boys scattered into the woods.

The man lowered the pistol and stepped into the light of a streetlamp. He was a white guy in a khaki suit.

"Mr. Carey," he said. "You have fucked things up, but good."

"Call an ambulance."

The man stepped over and took a cursory look at the Doorman.

"It's too late."

"Call a fucking ambulance!"

The man spoke in a mild Southern accent. "The tendons are cut. Have you ever seen the life of a cripple in Kowloon? You're not doing him any favors."

The image of the beggar across the street from the hotel came back to Neal. He stroked the Doorman's head and then felt along the side of his neck. There was no pulse.

"Believe me, he's better off," the man said. "Now it's time to go."

"What about the bodies?"

"They'll be taken care of."

Neal took off his watch and put it on the Doorman's wrist. Then he looked up at the man.

"Who the hell are you?" he asked.

"You might say I'm a friend of the family."

123

*   *   *

Neal figured that the house was somewhere on the Peak, because they hadn't driven more than five minutes before they were let in through a guarded gate to a long driveway. Neal couldn't see very well through the heavily tinted windows in the back of the car, but he could tell that the house was large and secluded. The man ushered him in through a downstairs door and led him down a hallway past a large study and into a bathroom.

"I'll see if we can scare up some clean clothes," the man said.

"Who—"

"I'll answer all your questions later. Right now I don't want you getting bloodstains all over these people's nice furniture. Why don't you get washed up and then join me in the study?"

The man left and Neal stripped off his clothes. His slacks and his shirt were sticky with blood. He bundled them up and threw them in a trashcan. The he ran some hot water into the sink, took a washcloth and soap, and scrubbed himself. His hands were trembling. He looked at himself in the mirror, and the man who looked back seemed a lot older than he remembered.

Then he heard a timid knock on the door. He opened to see an old Chinese man in servant's livery. The man handed him a white short-sleeved shirt, some baggy black cotton trousers, and a pair of black cloth rubber-soled shoes, then shuffled away. Neal put the clothes on. The shoes were a little too large, but they would do. He padded down the hallway into the study.

Thick red drapes masked wall-to-ceiling windows, and a rich Oriental carpet covered the floor. The effect was one of tremendous quietude. An enormous black enameled desk took up most of one wall, and a smaller black enameled coffee table flanked by a sofa and two straight-backed chairs occupied another. The man was sitting in one of the chairs. His tie was unknotted, his shoes were off, and he was sipping from a nearly transluscent cup.

"You want some tea?" he asked Neal.

"Fuck you and your tea. Who are you?"

"Sorry about the coolie clothing. It's all we had around."

Neal didn't answer.

"My name is Simms," the man said. He had thick blond hair cut very short, and blue eyes. He looked about thirty plus.

124

"Are you with Friends?"

"I'm not against them."

"I'm not in the fucking mood—"

Simms set his cup down. "See, I really don't care what you're in the fucking mood for. I just had to kill someone because of you, because you just couldn't do what you were told. So let's forget about your mood, all right? Have some tea."

Neal took the other chair. He poured himself a cup from the teapot that was set on the table.

"And please don't trouble yourself to thank me for saving your ass. I'm just a public servant doing my job," Simms said.

"Thank you."

"You're just barely welcome. Believe me, Carey, if I didn't need you, I just might have let them chop you up, I'm that pissed off at you."

The Book of Joe Graham, Chapter Eight, Verse Fifteen: Don't give the bastards anything, not when you're right, and especially not when you're wrong.

"Boo-hoo, boo-hoo," Neal said. "And by the way, fuck you. I've been doing this shit for half my life and I've never seen anyone killed before. Now I see a kid get his legs half hacked off and another get his face blown away and I've got blood all over me, literally and figuratively, and I figure you're involved in all of it. So don't give me this guilt trip, you preppie fuck. I have plenty already."

Simms smiled and nodded his head.

"Can I have a real drink instead of this goddamned tea?" Neal asked.

Simms went to the sidebar and poured Neal a healthy scotch.

So you have a file on me, Neal thought. And you're not with Friends. Which leaves alphabet soup.

"CIA?" Neal asked.

"If you say so."

"So AgriTech is just a paper corporation."

"AgriTech is real, all right. It has laboratories, offices, a lunchroom, company picnics, the whole nine yards."

The whiskey burned pleasantly in Neal's stomach. He wished he could just go out and get drunk.

Instead he said, "Yeah, AgriTech also has a treasurer named Paul Knox, who has a—how shall I put this—'fantastic' employment record."

"Paul's a good man."

"Yeah, I'm sure he's a credit to his race and a terrific fourth if you're caught short at tee-off time, but I want to know why one AgriTech research scientist is worth all this killing."

Simms held his teacup gently in both hands and inhaled the smell, as if the answer were in the tea's aroma.

"AgriTech," Simms explained in a slow, soft drawl, "is what we call a 'bench company.' It's a place to put players you can't use on the field at the moment but who you want around in case you need them. In the good old days before Watergate and Jimmy 'I'll never lie to you' Carter, we had a lot more money to keep people on our full-time payroll. As it is now, anytime we want to hire a janitor, we have to appear before a Senate subcommittee and explain to some alcoholic wazoo why we can't clean the toilets ourselves.

"So we took some of the monies that were sitting around in nooks and crannies and invested it in businesses that perhaps needed a little help. We even created companies out of whole cloth. These companies are expected to conduct actual business, turn a profit, meet a payroll—"

"The whole nine yards."

"—and in return they employ some people we can't keep on our lists but might want to use from time to time. Naturally, we need to have understanding people in executive positions in these companies, because, as you have demonstrated, the books do not always bear the closest of scrutinies."

"And these execs might have to okay some frequent and lengthy leaves of absence."

"That too."

"But Pendleton isn't on an authorized leave."

"Not hardly."

"So what happened?"

"So what happened is we got greedy. See, we had ourselves this bench company called AgriTech. AgriTech makes pesticides. At the same time, we found it a little difficult to obtain appropriations for research funds. So it seemed like a natural solution to ask AgriTech to carry a little bit of that load for us."

Neal finished his drink. He didn't feel any better.

"So you funneled illegal money into AgriTech to conduct unauthorized chemical experiments."

126

"Which is another way of putting it."

"Under the watchful eye of Paul Knox."

"Probably."

"And Robert Pendleton was conducting the actual research."

"Can I freshen that drink for you?"

"So that whole story I was given about chickenshit—"

"*Was* chickenshit. For all I know, Pendleton might have been working on some sort of superfertilizer for AgriTech, but for us he was working on herbicides."

Neal took the fresh glass from Simms. Well, well, well, Doctor Bob, he thought. This does put a different light on things. Good old, kind old Doctor Bob doesn't make things grow, boys and girls—he makes them die.

"You see," Simms continued, "if you know how to make something grow, you have a pretty good shot at knowing how to make it *not* grow. Killing it when it's still in the ground is a whole lot nicer for all concerned than spraying it with, for example, Agent Orange."

"It's real humanitarian work, all right."

"It is, in fact. Especially if the plant you're thinking about killing is the poppy plant."

The next shot of scotch still didn't provide Neal the soothing warmth he was after. "Okay, so Pendleton gets the Nobel Peace Prize. What's your beef with him?"

"The woman, of course."

Of course.

"You're an art critic?" Neal asked.

"She's a spy."

"Oh, come on!"

This is getting too fucking ridiculous, Neal thought. Li Lan a spy? Next thing you know he'll tell me A. Brian Crowe is an FBI agent.

"She's a Chinese operative," Simms insisted. "Look, Pendleton went to this conference of biochemists at Stanford. The opposition covers those things as SOP. We do the same with their meetings. Li Lan—and let's call her that for convenience, who knows what her real name is—is assigned to snuggle up to one of the scientists. Share a little pillow talk, you know: 'Who are you? Where do you work? Gee, that's fascinating, tell me all about it.' It just gives the opposition an idea about who's up to what. Usually it doesn't go beyond that, but little Li hits a home run. The mark falls in love with her.

"She contacts her bosses, who do a little research of their own. Let's face it, Carey, if a half-baked rent-a-cop like you can tumble AgriTech, Beijing can do the same. They tell her to stick with him, do do that voodoo, etcetera, until he's so pussy-whipped he'll follow her anywhere."

"Like to Hong Kong."

"Like to Hong Kong, where he's just a midnight boat ride from the PRC. Maybe they grab him, maybe they've already turned him and he goes willingly, but whichever ... Li Lan gets a promotion and Pendleton gets an eight-by-ten hospitality suite in some Beijing basement and an opportunity to answer all kinds of interesting questions on a daily basis."

Dinner should be surprises.

"Where did I fit in?" Neal asked.

"No offense, but we used you like a springer spaniel. Your job was to flush them from the bushes and make them run. You did a great job, by the way, Fido."

Okay, except Fido here went on point and the hunter didn't let them run, he took his best shot. What's wrong with this metaphor?

"Thanks, but why did you want them to run? Why not arrest them in the States? Wouldn't that have been easier?"

"Sure. The only problem is that the old boys in the Congress won't allow us to conduct operations within the States. That's why we used Friends of the Family instead of sending one of our own pups. If we had picked up Li Lan in the States, we'd have had to turn her over to the FBI, and that would have been a damn shame. They'd have just had a big old trial and chucked her lovely ass into prison, which is not the best and highest use of that particular piece of flesh."

"What are you talking about?"

"Li Lan wants to turn Pendleton. We want to turn Li Lan."

Neal settled back into the rich red velvet of the seat cushion. This was getting interesting. Maybe there was a way everybody could survive this thing, although Simms's explanation was still one bullet shy of a load.

"See," Simms went on, warming to his subject, "we don't take these things personally. We harbor no ill will toward Li Lan or Pendleton. Hell, we have so many Russians defecting we can't keep the safe houses stocked in vodka. We turn them away. But a Chinese defector? A rare bird, my friend. A rare bird who could sing some interesting songs.

"We knew she'd run to Hong Kong to cover the trail before she took him into the PRC. If we could trap her here and explain her options . . . well, we think she'd choose air conditioning, ice cubes, color television, and the good old U.S.A. over a Hong Kong jail cell. Hell, she'd probably prefer that over the pure numbing blandness of the PRC. A lot of the comrades will defect just to go shopping."

"And if you take her in Hong Kong you don't have to deal with the FBI."

"Exactly."

"Or any bothersome defense attorneys or judges or that shit."

Simms sighed. "Try to be professional about this, Carey. Her options aren't all that rosy. If she came with us, we'd debrief her for a year or two and set her loose with a nice new identity and a bank account. For a Third World baby like Li Lan, that's like winning the lottery."

Yeah, maybe it is, Neal thought. She could stay with Pendleton, paint her paintings, go to the supermarket and shop for elaborate Chinese dinners. There are worse lives.

"What would you do to Pendleton?"

"Nothing. Frankly, his brains and his knowledge protect him. We'd rather have him working for us than for the Chinese. Of course, you've fucked all this up, Carey, with your heroic chase up Austin Road. When you first slipped your leash in San Francisco and bolted over here, I was ready to have you busted. But then you actually came up with a half-bright plan, so I thought, let's go with it. Mind you, we've had you followed since day one.

"I figured that you weren't coming up to Victoria Peak just for the view, so I was all nice and ready to make contact with our little friend. But you spooked them and they called out the troops and I lost them. Mostly because I had to save your worthless butt. Thanks."

Neal contemplated the red hue of the room reflecting in the golden color of the scotch. Maybe it's all true, he thought. In which case I *was* the target in the hot tub, just like I was a candidate for the slice-and-dice treatment tonight. But then why would she want to meet with me at all? Just to set me up? Sure, so the track is a little colder for the next guy. And if she thought *I* was the CIA hound, that's exactly what she would do. Come on, Neal, face it. How many times do you have to dodge the bullet, so to speak, before you face the facts? She's a killer. A spy and a whore and a killer. A triple threat.

"So what's next?" Neal asked.

"Well, I'm going to have the staff bring in some food and we're going to have a nice long chat. You're going to tell me everything—and I mean everything—you can remember about your friend and mine, Li Lan. What she wore, what she said, what she did—everything. Then I'll have the driver drop you off at the ferry and you go back to your hotel and stay there until the next flight out."

"And what about Li and Pendleton?"

"If I can find her before she bolts to the PRC, I'll offer her the deal. She'll take it."

"What if she won't talk to you? What if she bolts?"

Simms poured a cup of tea and savored the smell.

"Well," he said, "I can't let her take Pendleton to China." He slipped the lapel of his jacket back to show the butt of his automatic pistol. "More tea?"

8

卐

Neal shuffled down the hotel hallway in his Chinese clothing. He was
played out. The debriefing had taken over two hours, and he had told
Simms everything. He had told him about the bus tickets, about the art
gallery, about the dinner. He had even told him about the seduction in
the hot tub. Told him about everything except the shot that had almost
killed him.

He wasn't sure why he had held that back, except that he suspected
Simms knew about it anyway, and he had wanted to see if the CIA man
brought it up. He hadn't.

The hallway was empty. No protective net, no Doorman. Obviously
Chin was through protecting him. Good, he thought. I've had all the
protection I can stand. He fished his room key out of his pocket and
opened the door.

Ben Chin was sitting on his bed.

"You were great back there on the Peak," Neal said. "Too bad there
weren't any old ladies for you to push around."

"You're alive, aren't you?"

"The Doorman isn't."

Chin shrugged. "He did his job."

"That's right. Where were *you?*"

"Doing *my* job. I followed your friends."

"Bullshit."

"True. I went up into the gardens and picked up their trail."

"Where are they?"

Chin looked down at the bedcover. "I lost them coming off the ferry."

"Kowloon side?"

"Sure."

Neal went into the bathroom and splashed cold water on his face. He was as tired as he could ever remember being. His chest ached from the old shotgun wound he'd taken the last time he'd stepped in between predator and prey, and he just wanted to fall asleep in a steaming bath. He brushed his teeth, rinsed his mouth out, and then ran hot water to shave. When he was finished he stood in the bathroom doorway and said to Ben Chin, "You're fired. Get out."

"You're the one who fucked up, not me."

"You lied to me. You brought your crew along when you promised me you wouldn't."

"If I hadn't, you'd be dead."

"So the Doorman's dead instead."

"It was his job to die so you could escape." Chin's jaw tightened and his eyes narrowed. "Would you rather be dead instead of him? Tell the truth."

The truth. What the hell does the truth have to do with anything?

"No," Neal said. "No. I wouldn't."

Chin smiled triumphantly—one of those smiles that says, *That settles it, then.*

"Where's your crew now?"

"They don't want to work with you anymore."

Okay, Neal thought. Which means you know what happened up there. You know your boys left me for dead. Why were you waiting for me here, then? Why weren't you surprised to see me walk in?

Okay, you can't give Chin the chance to realize he just screwed up.

"So," Neal said. "You couldn't stay on their tails, huh?"

"It's hard to do without help."

Right, Neal thought. He peeled off the Chinese clothes and changed into the black pullover, jeans, and tennis shoes he had last worn in Mill Valley. Then he took two glasses off the bar, poured two fingers of scotch into each, and handed one to Chin. It gave him a chance to look right into Chin's eyes.

"It's okay," Neal said. "I know where they are."

Oh, yeah, Neal thought as he saw Ben's eyes widen ever so slightly, you're interested. But why? Because she was responsible for killing one of your boys? Job satisfaction?

"Where?" Chin asked.

"They're at the Y."

"How do you know?"

"Bob Pendleton may be a hell of a biochemist, but he makes a lousy fugitive. He was fiddling with a key chain when I saw him. I got a quick look at the thing. It had the YMCA symbol on it."

"There are two in Kowloon. One right by the ferry, the other up Nathan Road."

"The second one is in Yaumatei?"

"Yes."

"Let's go."

"I thought I was fired."

"You're rehired. I need someone who speaks Chinese and who can bribe a desk clerk. With money, not muscle, right?"

"Right."

Right.

It was two in the morning and there were still people on the street. The lost souls of the small hours lingered on the edges of the light pools thrown by the streetlamps, or hovered around the fires set in trashcans. Vagrants slept on cardboard sheets in the middle of the wide sidewalks or crouched in the doorways of closed shops. Most of the night clubs and gambling joints were still open, their neon lights reflecting brightly off the puddles in the gutters. A few prostitutes too old or too ugly for the tourist trade farther down the road stood stoically outside the gambling halls, hoping to rent a celebration to the winners or solace to the losers. Here and there a slice of darkness broke the neon glow, and each niche was like a cave that sheltered a human being—a scraggly kid too weak to join a gang, a dull-eyed opium addict lost in his private dream, a psychotic woman babbling her outrage at omnipresent enemies, a hungry mugger waiting for the improvident drunk to stumble by at the right moment—each a player in the slow game of musical chairs that makes up the urban food chain.

The YMCA was on Waterloo Road, two blocks west of Nathan. Neal waited on the steps while Ben talked to the nervous night clerk. The place reeked of good intentions and bad bank statements. Metal screens shielded the broken glass in windows and doors. The pea-green high-gloss paint was cheap and easily cleaned, and the smell of disinfectant overpowered the aroma of the musty mud-brown carpet.

It was the sort of place that offered anonymity and Neal knew that Li Lan or her handlers must have chosen it quite deliberately.

Chin's conversation didn't take long.

"Room three-forty-three," he said to Neal, as if it were an offering.

"Thanks. See you tomorrow."

"I'll wait down here."

"No."

"Dangerous neighborhood this time of night."

"Go home."

Chin shrugged. "Whatever you say, boss."

"That's what I say."

Chin turned around and went out the door. Neal watched until he had turned the corner on Nathan Road.

Neal was surprised that the elevator had an operator, an old man with withered legs and a grotesquely distorted face. Neal held up three fingers and the man leaned forward on his stool and used a lever to shut the door. The elevator whined with age as it crawled up the three floors.

The third-floor corridor was narrow, and covered in old green carpeting. Neal stood outside of 343 for a full two minutes and listened. He couldn't hear anything. It's just another gig, he told himself as he took his AmEx card from his wallet and slipped it behind the bolt. The lock gave up quicker than a French general, and Neal was in the room just as quickly.

A shaft of light from a streetlamp pierced the thin curtain and outlined her in a golden glow where she lay sleeping on the bed. Pendleton lay beside her, his back toward the door. Neal shut the door behind him, just the way Graham had taught him to, keeping the knob open until the bolt was aligned and then slowly letting the knob turn shut. Then he squatted next to the bed, brought his right arm over her head, and clapped his hand over her mouth as his thumb and index finger pinched her nostrils shut. He put his left hand under her jaw and pressed his thumb and index finger under the two joints. Her eyes popped open and she stared at him in fright. He slowly shook his head back and forth, and she accepted this warning to keep quiet. He stood up slowly and lifted her by the jaw. She grabbed his wrist and he squeezed harder. Her eyes widened in pain. He lifted until she was perched on her toes and then walked her to the bathroom door and set her down on the edge of the bathtub. He closed the door behind them, then turned on the light.

"Hi," he whispered. "Bet you didn't think you'd see me again, huh?"

She didn't answer.

"The CIA is looking for you, but I guess you already know that."

She shook her head.

"Right. Anyway, they have a pretty good deal to offer you. I think you should take it. We can wake up Bobby baby in a minute and use the phone. I'll make the call for you, but I want you to answer a few questions for me first."

She was staring at him. Just staring, and it was making him mad.

"What was that all about back in California? The little striptease that ended with a bang? That's a lousy way to set somebody up, and why set me up anyway? Why did you think you had to kill me?"

She kept on staring. He tried to look back into her eyes and ignore the fact that the T-shirt was all she was wearing.

"Goddamn it, I deserve an answer!"

"I didn't try to kill you. Someone was trying to kill Robert."

"What the fuck are you talking about?"

"I only wanted to make sure you would stay there, in the hot tub, while we had a chance to escape. Then I heard the shot . . . I became afraid . . . I ran away."

"You thought I was dead."

"Yes, until you began leaving those messages everywhere. I was happy you were alive, but I wanted to warn you of the very big danger. So I wanted to have a meeting with you, but you came with that man."

"What man?"

"The man who was hunting us in California. The very big Chinese man."

"I came with a Hong Kong man."

"No. I saw him at hotel in San Francisco."

135

"Mark Chin?"

"I do not know his name."

Mark Chin and Ben Chin, who looked so much alike . . . she thought Ben was Mark, figured she'd been tricked, and called out the troops.

"Are you with CIA?" she asked.

"No, I'm a private cop."

"I do not understand."

Neither do I. "Did you think I had come to the Peak to kill you? To set you up?"

She nodded.

"Do you think that's why I'm here now?"

She nodded again.

"Because you think I'm CIA?"

"No."

"Who, then?"

"White Tiger."

White Tiger? What the hell is a White Tiger.?

White Tiger, she told him, was one of the most powerful of the Hong Kong Triads. It had been shattered during a government crackdown in the early Seventies, and its leaders had fled to Taiwan, where they found a warm welcome in the form of shelter, money, and sage leadership. Reorganized and refinanced, White Tiger reinfiltrated Hong Kong and recolonized outposts in New York, London, Amsterdam, and San Francisco. It was involved in the usual gang enterprises of loansharking, drug dealing, prostitution, and extortion, but it also took out subcontracts from the Taiwanese secret service for surveillance jobs, kidnappings, and hits. Its primary role in Hong Kong was to serve as a counterbalance to the procommunist Triads, such as the 14K.

"And you think Chin is White Tiger?"

"Of course."

Of course. I was set up from jump street, or at least from Kearny Street, at the good old Chinatown Holiday Inn. Mark Chin was on the same trail I was, and let me bird-dog for him. He took my hundred bucks at Coit Tower, walked down to a phone booth on his way to Pier Thirty-nine, and called in some troops, who put such a good tail on me I didn't catch it. He must have been cracking up when I came to him and asked him to hide me in Hong Kong. He passed me right along to cousin Ben, who I brought up the Peak with me as protection. And who I also brought right here. Shit.

He asked Lan, "What does Taiwan have against the good doctor?"

Pendleton answered as he opened the bathroom door.

"They don't want me to go to China," he said. "What the hell is going on here?"

Neal stood up slowly and raised his hands in front of his chest. "That's what I'm trying to figure out, and I don't think I have a lot of time to do it."

"You got that right," Pendleton said. "Can you at least let her get dressed?"

"Yeah."

Lan got up and went back into the bedroom. Neal could hear her opening drawers. He wondered if she was going to come back in with a gun. He wondered why he trusted her not to.

"You were telling me about Taiwan," Neal said as if they'd been interrupted during polite chatter at a cocktail party.

"The Taiwanese want me dead."

"Why?"

"They're AgriTech's biggest customer."

"I had a long talk with a guy named Simms last night."

"Who's he?"

"He works with Paul Knox."

"Oh."

"Oh. And he told me about the stuff you create in your test tubes, Doc. Why should Taiwan give a shit?"

"We were developing it for sale to Taiwan."

"Why does Taiwan want an herbicide that kills the poppy?"

"Because heroin is power. Because they want to control the warlords of northern Thailand, Laos, and Burma. The border countries. And they sure as hell don't want the PRC to have it, because the PRC would use it. Heroin is one of Taiwan's biggest businesses. They're scared shitless of the PRC getting that kind of hammer over them."

So it was the Taiwanese, using their White Tiger subcontractors, who had taken a whack at what they thought was Pendleton in the Marin County hot tub. The Taiwanese want him croaked, the CIA want him alive, and they're both using me to nail him. But what does Pendleton want?

137

"And you're planning to take your product to the PRC?"

"I'm planning to go with Lan."

Lan appeared in the doorway. She had put on a pair of blue jeans, a black pullover jersey, and sandals.

"She doesn't love you," Neal said. "Don't you know that? She's a Chinese spy. They sent her to sleep with you. It was in her job description."

"I know all that. She told me."

"Can we get out of the bathroom?" Neal asked. "It's starting to feel like the stateroom scene in *A Night at the Opera.*"

Lan and Pendleton sat on the bed, which seemed appropriate enough to Neal, and he sat down in the old overstuffed wingback in the corner, by the window.

"So it's true love, right?"

Right. They told him the story, sharing the narrative like newlyweds telling a stranger how they met. She was a spy of sorts. It was her ticket out, the price for a life of relative freedom in Hong Kong and America. She really was a painter, and that was her cover in the States. Her handlers approved because it gave her access to culture, which in the States meant money, which meant power. She made it a point to attend all the cocktail parties, all the receptions, all the corporate bashes. Usually her bosses required nothing more than simple reports on who was who, who was doing what, and who might be sympathetic toward a struggling nation of communist reformers.

Then Pendleton's conference had come along. She'd picked him up in an expensive restaurant—charmed him, flattered him with the simple gift of attention. She'd led him into leading her to bed, taught him the things that her trainers had taught her, talked to him, listened to him.

In the morning she reported back, in the afternoon received her orders, and that night went back to his bed. She took him to the clouds and the rain, and then lay still in his arms as he told her about his life, his work, his secret dreams. They went on a long, early-morning walk in Chinatown, watched the old ones do t'ai chi, shopped in the markets, went for dim-sum and tea, and then back to bed. She had to go to Mill Valley for her show, and he visited her there and met her friends, and went there every day.

Then *he* came: the White Tiger soldier, Mark Chin. Their escape was narrow, they needed somewhere to hide, and Li Lan talked to her good friend Olivia Kendall. In the quiet of the Kendall house, Lan and Pendleton talked for hours, told each other the heretofore covert parts of their lives, wondered what to do. Pendleton knew that AgriTech would come looking for him, maybe send a Company errand boy to fetch him, and sure enough, Neal had turned up. They weren't sure whether he was CIA or a rent-a-cop hired by AgriTech, but they had to get free of him. Along with dinner, they cooked up a plan to give him the slip: get him drunk, get him unclothed in the hot tub, and give him a good reason to sit there and wait for Li Lan to come back. Only, of course, Li Lan wasn't coming back. They were going to run to Hong Kong, where she would play along with her bosses and their 14K allies to hide long enough to figure out what to do. She was as surprised as Neal when the shot whooshed through the air. Scared, she had run all the faster, and they'd caught the next flight to Hong Kong.

According to plan, she should have just turned him over to her handlers, but she hedged. They were in love, truly in love, and she knew full well what was in store for him in the PRC. And her life of freedom would be over. Her cover blown, she could not return to the West. She would be given some drab bureaucratic job, and there would be no more decadent painting. So she made up stories, said she was having difficulty persuading him, she needed more time, more space. Besides, their trail was still too hot. She urged patience.

"Then I turned up again," Neal prompted.

She nodded. "You were telling everyone where we were."

So she had to stop him. He was bringing the world down around them. Her bosses were getting nervous, White Tiger might pick up the trail, the CIA was surely sniffing around. He was putting them in great danger. Himself as well: Her bosses wanted to have him killed. So she had to stop him, had to meet with him to persuade him to stop this crazy search.

"That's when you called me to set up the meeting at Victoria Peak. But you still weren't exactly sure who I was, so you brought backup along, just in case," said Neal.

"Her people insisted," Pendleton said. "These 14K goons trailed along. And it was a good thing they did."

Because she spotted Ben Chin, whom she mistook for his cousin. Not that it made any difference, he was still a White Tiger Triad member assigned to kill them. She thought that she had made a terible mistake, that Neal was not a private detective or a government agent, but a White Tiger hireling paid to set them up. She ran him right into the ambush, the ambush that Ben Chin was too smart to fall into. He went right for his target, but couldn't catch them in a spot where he could gun them down and hope to get away. They shook him off and came back to their hideout, the obscure YMCA.

"And now you have come again," Lan said. "But alone."

Not quite, Lan. But he skipped that part for the moment, and told them about Friends of the Family, about his assignment, about being duped by the Chins. He told them about Simms's rescue, about the debriefing, and about the deal that Simms would offer if he had the chance.

"I don't know," Pendleton said. "Can we trust them?"

"It's not a matter of trust. You have something they want."

"Li Lan, you mean."

"There's a wicked kind of symmetry in this situation. You can go to China, where she turns you over, or back to the States, where you turn her. The issue is simple. Which is better? You go to China, you're a prisoner for life and so is she. You go back to the States, she's a prisoner for a while and you're a free man. They'll even let you stay together, as long as you're a good boy."

"What's in it for you?"

Good question, Doc. What *is* in it for me? I lose Li Lan, but then again, I never had her. And maybe if I bring you back, the powers that be will let me come back too, back to my comfortable cell. Maybe that's the best you can expect in this world, a comfortable cell.

So he explained his deal to them. If he could bring them in, he could go back to school, back to his own research.

"We can have it all," he said. "You can play with your test tubes, you can paint, I can muck around with eighteenth-century literature. It's what I'd call a happy ending."

"Except Li has to betray her country," Pendleton said, although it was more like a question.

She stared at the floor. "It is not a country. It is a prison."

"What about family?" Neal asked.

"Dead."

He wanted to hold her. Throw his arms around her and tell her that

140

it was all right, that there were all kinds of families and that she had found herself a new one. She looked tired and hurt and played out.

"Shall I make the call?" he asked.

Pendleton looked at Lan. It was her decision to make.

"Please," she said.

Neal picked up the phone and dialed the number Simms had given him. It took a couple of minutes to clear for Simms to come to the phone.

"Did you forget something?" asked Simms.

"Your order's ready. You want to pick it up or you want me to deliver?"

"Jesus H. Christ. Where are you?"

"A YMCA on Waterloo, near Nathan Road."

"Stay put! I'll be there in an hour."

"Hurry up."

Simms's voice took on an edge. "Is there a problem?"

"There could be," Neal said, wondering where Ben Chin was, "but I don't think the problem will happen as long as I'm here."

"I'll get someone right there."

"How will I know him?"

"Ask him the subject of your would-be master's thesis. He'll know."

"You guys think of everything."

"We try."

"I'm only turning them over to you personally. Deal?"

"Deal."

"See ya."

So that's that, Neal thought. An hour or so and it's over. And I'll never see her again.

That's when he heard the awful screech of the elevator, heard the doors slamming shut on the third floor, and stopped wondering where Ben Chin was.

Neal met him in the hallway.

"What are you doing here?"

Ben Chin raised his hands into a fighting position. "The game's over, Neal. I'm here to get them."

"You've been trumped."

"What do you mean?"

141

"I mean that they represent some valuable assets to the CIA, who are not going to be happy with you if you waste them. So let's not fuck around, okay?"

Chin dropped his hands and smiled. Then his right hand came up and it had an automatic pistol in it. He pointed the silenced muzzle at Neal's face.

"I don't give a shit about the CIA. I don't work for the CIA. I don't want to hurt you, but I don't care very much one way or the other. So you walk away and we both forget we ever met. Or I do you right here. Either way, they die. So let's not fuck around, okay?"

Either way they die. Simms's second choice. And Pendleton and Lan didn't care about *you* getting killed, Neal. They figured it was better you than them. Well, better them than me.

"Okay."

"That's what I thought. Door locked?"

"Not anymore."

"You get out of here, Neal. You're too far up Nathan Road. Way too far."

Neal walked past him down the hallway. Chin turned the doorknob with his left hand and slowly opened the door. Pendleton was sitting on the bed. Lan was standing by the window. Chin dropped into the shooter's position—knees bent, both hands on the pistol's grip—and brought the barrel down until it was pointed at Li Lan's heart. She looked at his eyes.

Neal barrel-rolled him from behind, taking him in the back of the knees and sending him flying onto his ass. Neal jumped on top of him and grabbed his wrist.

Chin was fast. He used his free hand to punch Neal in the side of the head and then he threw him off. He kicked Neal in the ribs, and the force of the blow crashed Neal into the hallway wall. This took about a second and a half, and neither Li nor Pendleton moved an inch. Neal slumped against the wall. His head was spinning and he couldn't catch his breath to move. The pain in his ribs doubled him over.

"Asshole," Chin said. He raised the gun to finish him off.

Li Lan flew, or at least it seemed that way to Neal. One second she was standing against the wall and the next instant she was flying through the air, her legs curled beneath her. She flew until she was even with

142

Chin's head, and then her right leg shot out like a snake striking. The foot hit him on the underside of his jaw and his head snapped backward. He was unconscious even before the back of his head hit the wall and he slid to the floor.

He woke up hearing Li Lan urging him, "Come, come. We must go."

He was lying on the bed in their room. He felt like throwing up, and his rib cage felt as if somebody had stuck burning matches into it. She would have looked like an angel to him if he hadn't just seen her kick a man's head about off. Maybe she looked like an angel anyway.

"Come on. We must go," she said.

He shook his head. That was a mistake—Quasimodo crawled in and started ringing the bells. "We have to stay put. Simms will be here soon."

Pendleton pointed to Chin. "He won't be out forever."

"He might be dead," Neal said.

"Yes, he may be," said Li Lan. "We must go now."

Pendleton jerked him to his feet. The corridor wasn't spinning. It was lurching like a broken carny ride with a drunken operator at the controls.

"Where are we going?" Neal asked.

"I know a place to hide until we can call your Mr. Simms," Li Lan said. "Now come, please."

"We should take the stairs. Elevators are traps," Neal said. He leaned over painfully and picked up Chin's gun. "I suppose you know how to use one of these things?"

"Yes." Li Lan took the pistol, unscrewed the silencer and dropped it to the floor, then stuck the pistol in the front of her jeans, under the jersey. "Can you walk down the stairs?"

"If you're absolutely sure I can't just lie here and take a nap."

"Where we are going you can rest."

"Where *are* we going?"

"To see Kuan Yin."

"Naturally."

Elevators may have been traps, but the stairs were murder. Each step drove a jolt of pain through Neal's ribs and up into his head. He was beginning to wish Li Lan had let Chin shoot him.

When they reached the door to the lobby he said, "You'd better let me go first. Chin may have friends down here."

He didn't. He was so fucking arrogant he had come alone. Neal signaled his new friends and he, Li, and Pendleton strolled right out the front door onto the street.

Chin's crew stood across the street, leaning against a parked car.

"Hi!" Neal shouted as he waved. "Boy, I'll bet you never thought you'd see me again, huh?"

The three thugs straightened up and started for him, spreading out as they did. Neal walked slowly toward them as Lan and Pendleton moved sideways behind Neal's screen, getting ready to run up Waterloo to Nathan.

"Yeah, I beat the crap out of those guys back on the Peak! Thanks for leaving us back there, by the way! Now don't come any closer! The lady has a gun! Show the boys the gun, Lan!"

Li Lan showed the gun.

A boy inside the parked car stuck the barrel of an M-16 out the window.

Li grabbed Pendleton's hand and ran. The sniper in the car couldn't sweep fire without hitting his own guys, and was about to pop off a single round into Neal's chest when the car took off after the runners. The car doors swung open and the other punks scrambled into it as it headed up Waterloo Road. Neal ran after them and saw Li lead Pendleton into an alley. The car screeched to a stop, and three of the hunters got out. The car went on to circle the block, probably to cut off the other end of the alley. They were setting up a classic block-and-sweep operation wherein the three "sweepers" would drive their quarry into the "block"—in this case bursts of fire from an M-16. Li and Pendleton were trapped.

Neal flattened himself against the wall of the building. He looked up and saw a fire escape. Jesus loves me, he thought, this I know. . . . Hong Kong or no Hong Kong, a city is a city, and nobody does a city better than your friend Neal Carey.

Pulling himself up onto the fire escape, he climbed to the roof of the building, then crawled to the edge and peered down through seven stories of darkness into the alley. He could just make out Li and Pendleton, who were working their way along the near wall, trying to make it out to the other side. Shit, didn't they realize they were caught in a trap? He could also see the three hunters spread out across the alley, moving steadily and confidently.

Well, maybe he could worry them a little bit.

It took him maybe thirty seconds to find something. A concrete block had been set near the door of the stairway, probably to prop it open in the heat of the day. He carried it to the edge of the roof, tiptoeing along until he was even with the line of sweepers. He hefted the block up to his waist and flung it over the side.

It missed the end sweeper by a good foot, but the sound was like an explosion, and fragments of concrete flew everywhere. The three men dropped to the ground. One of them held a hand over his eye and screamed.

Lan and Pendleton stopped and looked up.

"Don't go out the alley!" Neal yelled.

They squatted behind some garbage cans and froze.

Ah, rooftops, Neal thought. Tar Beach. The last refuge and repository of the cityscape. The final storage place. He found a cardboard carton overflowing with beer and wine bottles, evidence of some husband's secret tippling. He carried it over to the edge of the roof and looked down to see the two unwounded sweepers get up carefully and slowly begin moving up the alley.

Neal was impressed with the aerodynamics of the wine bottle as it plummeted through the night sky. He had given it a slight backflip, so it revolved end over end in a gentle arc before smashing on the concrete of the alley floor. The sound was spectacular. The two sweepers dove for cover on either side of the alley. He aimed his second one at the sweeper on the far side and scored a direct hit on his back. The sweeper yelped and rolled backward to the near side. Neal launched another one, and then another, and then risked a long peek over the edge. The two sweepers had their faces pressed up against the near wall.

Your basic standoff.

A burst of machine-gun fire raked the edge of the roof and sent Neal sprawling. Lying flat along the edge, he risked opening one eye, and saw the boy with the M-16 advancing from the other end of the alley, gun held at his hip. He was shouting to his comrades. You didn't have to speak any Cantonese to understand that he was asking them what the fuck was going on, or to comprehend that they were trying, as quickly as possible, to tell him to shut the fuck up. The boy stopped and just stood there in the alley, rifle on hip, finger on the trigger, waiting for something to happen.

Nothing happened. Li Lan was either too scared or too smart or both to go against an M-16 with a pistol, although the boy made a perfect target standing for a one-shot deal. Maybe, Neal thought, she can't see him from where she is. That must be it. Maybe I'm the only one who can see him, which really stinks. Why me?

Neal reached out and pulled the carton away from the edge. Crawling on his belly, he pushed the box in front of him. It seemed to take forever to reach the point where he figured he'd be about even with Machine Gun Kelly. He inched the carton to the roof's edge and peeked over. The boy was starting a cautious advance, moving sideways, close to the near edge of the wall so as to give Li Lan as small a silhouette as possible.

Neal wished he had paid even a little bit of attention in Mr. Litton's physics classes back in high school. Litton had always been hauling the students up to the roof to drop shit off and then perform calculations, but Neal was goddamned if he could remember what the calculations were or what they were intended to prove except the fact that he was the dumbest kid in physics class. So he just shoved the carton off the edge of the roof and hoped for the best.

One of the sweepers must have seen it go, because he shouted a warning to the gunner, who had a natural but stupid response: He looked up.

That cost him the two precious seconds in which he might have ducked, or run, or even just covered his head with his hands. But he didn't do any of those things. He just looked up into the darkness, not seeing anything at all until the whole sky was filled with one massive, empty beer bottle hurtling straight toward his face.

Then the alley became a cacophony of shattering glass, thumping bodies, trashcans tipping over, and the clatter of a rifle hitting concrete.

And pistol shots.

The two sweepers hit the dirt as soon as their buddy with the rifle went down, and Li Lan popped a couple off above their heads to make sure they stayed down as she and Pendleton came back up the alley toward Waterloo Road.

Neal got up and ran across the roof. Shit, he wasn't going to lose them again. He hit the fire escape and scurried down as fast as his legs and his ribs would let him.

"Hurry!" Li Lan yelled.

She and Pendleton were standing on the sidewalk waiting for him.

"Why didn't you grab the rifle?" he asked her as he hit the street. "Come on!"

They ran after her down Waterloo onto Nathan and followed her as she turned right onto the broad street. She hailed a taxi on the corner and they all got in.

"*Wong Tai Sin,*" she told the driver.

"*Haude.*"

The driver took a right and headed north, up the Nathan Road. Way up, through the sprawling tenements of Mongkok, past Argyle and Prince Edward Street and into Kowloon City, a nest of shiny skyscrapers that literally towered over the surrounding slums. The driver turned onto Lung Shung Road and stopped in front of a massive building with red columns and a garishly yellow roof.

Li Lan paid the driver and gestured for the men to get out.

"Where are we?" Neal asked.

"Wong Tai Sin Temple," Li answered. "We are coming to thank Kuan Yin."

"Who's Kuan Yin? Your case officer?"

She shook her head and laughed. "Kuan Yin is goddess of mercy. She has been very kind to us tonight."

"Goddess? What kind of communist are you?"

"A Buddhist communist."

"And this is a twenty-four-hour temple?"

"Gods do not sleep."

"Mao wouldn't like hearing this."

"The Chairman is dead. He has met the Unpredictable Ghost."

"Who's that?"

"The Unpredictable Ghost guards the next world. He guides souls to the next world."

"Which next world? Heaven or hell?"

"You don't know. That is why he is called unpredictable. I will show him to you in the temple."

"No thanks."

She laughed again. "Sooner or later you will meet him. Better to know him sooner."

"Better later."

"As you think. Come. First we get our fortunes told."

"You really do make a shitty Marxist."

She led to them to where an old man sat behind a tiny, ramshackle booth on the outside of the temple. She handed him some coins and he handed her a bright red cup with holes in its cover. She held the cup up to her ear, tipped it upside down, and shook it. A stick fell out. She caught it in her other hand and gave it to the old man, who studied it intensely and then began to talk to her in rapid Chinese. She smiled broadly and answered. Then she bought another cup and handed it to Pendleton.

"Do one, Robert. Prayer stick. It will tell you your fortune."

"I know my fortune. I'm going to live happily ever after with a beautiful woman whom I love very much."

"Thank you, Robert."

Neal thought he might throw up, and it wasn't his ribs.

"What's your fortune?" he asked.

"To go inside the temple."

"Listen, we have to get hold of Simms. He's probably at the Y right now, going nuts."

"Just quickly thank Kuan Yin."

"Quickly."

They went up the steps past elaborately carved railings. A large screen was set in the middle of the entrance, leaving a narrow passage on either side.

"What's this for?" Neal asked.

"Bad spirits can only move in straight lines," Li Lan explained. "Therefore they cannot get into the temple."

Every bad spirit I know is absolutely incapable of moving in a straight line, but never mind, Neal thought.

They stepped around the screen, presumably leaving any bad spirits behind, and into an enormous chamber. Dozens of shrines lined the two side walls, each shrine an altar presided over by a statue of its particular spirit. Even at this hour of the day, some pilgrims knelt at the altars, praying, and other devotees had left burning sticks of incense, small piles of apples and oranges, or coins as offerings or invocations. Rich red fabrics hung from the walls and large rectangular lamps hung from the ceilings, which, combined with the burning candles and sticks of incense, cast the room in a dark golden light.

The shrine at the front wall dominated the room. A large statue of a young woman sitting in the full lotus position occupied a broad platform. Her face was alabaster white, her eyes almond-shaped, her smile beatific. She wore a diaphanous gown slung over one shoulder, a headpiece of gold laminate, and black-lacquer hair piled high on her head. The effect was a strange combination of garishness and benevolence.

"Kuan Yin," whispered Li Lan.

Li Lan knelt at the railing below the platform. She touched her head to the floor three times, then repeated the series twice more. She stayed hunched over, and Neal could see her lips moving. She was speaking to her goddess. Neal and Pendleton stood awkwardly behind her.

When she got up, she went to Neal and said, "We must see to your injuries."

"We must call Simms."

"How can we call him if he is at the Y, going nuts?"

"We call the Y and have him paged."

"I am not waiting out in the open for your Simms to arrive. Too dangerous."

She had a point. A five-year-old kid can keep a secret better than a cabdriver who's offered cash, and it was a safe bet that Chin's gang, and maybe Ben Chin himself, were strongarming the neighborhood to find the cabbie that had driven off with Li and the two *kweilo.* And it wasn't exactly rush hour—the cabbie wouldn't be that hard to find.

"Where do you want to go?" Neal asked.

"It is arranged."

It's arranged. Swell.

"By your handlers. No way."

"Not by my handlers. By *them.*" She waved her arm impatiently around the temple.

"By who?"

"By the monks. Do you really think I stopped to get our fortunes told? Do you think I am a superstitious idiot? I stopped to arrange a hiding place."

"You know these people?"

"These people are all the same every place." She looked at him stubbornly. "Long before there was a communist party, there was Kuan Yin. Now . . . let's go!"

"I don't know."

Pendleton grabbed his elbow. "I do. I don't want to hang around here waiting to get blasted to bits by a machine gun. You can trust Li Lan with your life. I have."

Terrific, Doc. Every time I've trusted Li Lan, I've just barely gotten away with my frigging stupid inane life. Nevertheless, the good doctor has a point, and I don't much fancy going back out on the street.

"So let's get going," said Neal.

"Finally."

She knew just where she was going. She strode to the corner of the room and knelt down at the shrine, beneath the statue of an old man wearing a torn robe, a hideously mocking grin, and carrying what looked to Neal like a gold ingot. She performed the nine bows, and then took a small bell from the altar railing and rang it just once. Then she turned to Neal.

"Neal Carey," she said, pointing at the statue, "meet Unpredictable Ghost. Unpredictable Ghost, Neal Carey."

"Pleasure," Neal muttered.

A monk appeared from behind the shrine. He was tall and thin. His head was shaved and he wore a plain brown robe and sandals. He returned Li Lan's bow and motioned for them to follow him.

There was a red curtain behind the shrine, and behind the curtain was a wooden door. It opened to a stairway that took them down to a basement, which looked like a maintenance shop for the temple. Wooden lathes, jars of paint, brushes, candles, and parts of lanterns lay scattered about in no discernible order. Here and there a head or a hand or a trunk from a statue was set on a small worktable. Body Shop of the Gods, Neal thought. The monk led them through this room into a boiler room, through a plain, functional metal door, and into a corridor. Down two more steps and they entered a corrugated metal tube.

It was as narrow and dark as a walkway in a submarine. Every thirty feet a naked light bulb dangled from the low ceiling. Moisture dripped from the seams in the sides and tops of the tube. Neal could hear traffic noises above them and realized they were going underneath the street.

"Are we in the goddamn sewer?" he asked Li Lan.

"Quiet."

He turned around to Pendleton. "Are we in the goddamn sewer?"

"Looks like a goddamn sewer to me."

"Christ, I didn't like *reading* Victor Hugo, never mind *living* it."

"Quiet."

They went up two steps and then through another door. They were in a basement of sorts, a small, musty, dirt-floored chamber. The monk stepped onto a short ladder and unlocked a hatch. Then he stood at the bottom and gestured for them to climb up. This was as far as he went.

Li Lan went up, then Pendleton. He took his sweet time about it, Neal thought, impatient to get above ground again. He followed Pendleton up the ladder and was instantly sorry.

He was in hell.

It was an alley, maybe four feet wide, maybe a little less. A sliver of daylight revealed filth-encrusted walls, on which moss, urine stains, and dirt competed for space. The ground beneath him was a mix of mud, shit, broken glass, and some cracked and broken planking.

Neal covered his mouth and nose with his hands, but the stench was overwhelming. His eyes teared and he fought back retching.

Tenements loomed above him, so high and close they looked as if they were about to topple over. Homemade bridges crossed the alley, veritable villages of hammocks were strung from one side to the other, tangles of wires and cables looked like jungle vines.

Here and there holes had been punched in the lower walls, and people were burrowed into them. Neal could see them peeking out at him through iron grilles and bamboo screens.

He heard Pendleton mutter, "Jesus. Jesus Christ."

And the sounds, the sounds were horrible. Amid the din of thousands of voices just talking, Neal heard babies crying, children screaming, old people moaning. In the distance ahead he could hear a pack of dogs growling, and from inside the walls around him he could make out the scurrying feet of rats.

Neal reached ahead and grabbed Li by the shoulder.

"Where are we?"

"The Walled City."

"What is it?"

"It is what you see."

She brushed his hand off and started ahead. He pushed Pendleton aside, grabbed her by the collarbone, and spun her around.

"What is it?" he asked again.

"It is the Walled City!" she screamed at him. "People—you would call 'squatters'—live here. The gangs rule it. It is drugs, it is prostitutes, it is sweatshops. It is rats, it is packs of rabid dogs. It is children

151

gang-raped and sold as slaves, it is people living in holes! It is filth. It is when nobody cares!"

"I never knew a place like this existed."

"Now you know. So what?"

"What are we doing here?"

"We are hiding."

"For how long?"

"Don't you like it here?"

"For how long?"

She calmed down. He hadn't seen rage in her before, and it scared him. Pendleton stood aside like a frightened, overgrown child.

"Until you can phone your Simms."

"Can he get in here?"

"With the people he knows."

"Gang people, Triad people?"

"Of course."

"Are there telephones here?"

"There is everything here."

She turned around and went ahead. She turned left into a slightly wider alley where people sat slumped against the walls in a doped-out haze. Then she turned right into a concrete tunnel, where they walked through muck, stepped over sleeping bodies, and ducked under dangling light bulbs and power cords. They stepped into another alley, narrower and filthier than the last.

"Jesus!" Pendleton gasped.

A pack of rats was feeding on the bare feet of a human corpse. Neal hunched over and finally vomited, trying hard not to touch the walls.

"Come on," Li Lan hissed. "We are there soon. It is better."

The alley led to a T-junction. They went to the left, then through a series of zigzags, then straight on and made two more rights.

We're in a goddamn maze, Neal thought, and we can hardly see the sky. He suddenly realized that he wouldn't stand a chance of finding his way out of there. Not a chance.

They came onto a small circular patch of bare dirt that formed a hub for five alleys.

Four teenage boys, dressed in sleeveless white T-shirts, baggy khaki slacks, and rubber sandals squatted in a circle, smoking cigarettes and rolling dice. It was clearly their turf. The boys stared at the newly arrived trio with amazement. An unexpected bonanza of rape and pillage had been dropped in their midst. The biggest one, the leader, rose to his feet and approached Li Lan. He gazed at her with frank sexual interest, stretched his face into an exaggerated leer, and made a comment to his buddies. They chirped with amusement and got to their feet. The leader pulled a knife from his pants pocket and held it up to Li's face.

Pull the gun, Lan, Neal thought. This is no time to be a Buddhist.

She didn't pull the gun, but said what sounded to Neal like two words. The boy's grin crumbled into a frown of concern and his hand dropped to his side. He barked an order to the others and they took off running down one of the alleys. Then he launched into a monologue of obsequious friendliness. Neal didn't understand a word, but knew shuffling when he heard it, and this kid was tapdancing for his ass. Li wasn't buying it. She stood looking at him sternly, not throwing him as much as a crumb. The kid started to shuffle harder.

Ten minutes later, Neal saw why. The two errand boys came back escorting a guy who had "honcho" written all over him. He was older, maybe in his early twenties, and sported a gray pinstriped suit, a blue shirt, a plum tie, and a charcoal fedora. A lit cigarette was jammed in the corner of his mouth. He didn't show any fear toward Li, but he was polite and respectful, bowing slightly to her as he approached and then nodding to Neal and Pendleton.

He listened to Li for a minute, nodded again, and quietly issued orders. The three boys started to run off, but he stopped the leader, then gave him a vicious backhand to the face. The boy fell into the dirt, picked himself up, bowed to Li Lan, and ran off. The honcho shook his head, then reached into his jacket and produced a pack of Kool Lights. He offered one to Neal and Pendleton, who declined with polite smiles and shakes of the head.

"He's a stupid boy," he suddenly said. "Useless. I will kill him if you wish."

"Thank you for the courtesy, but no," Li answered.

He's a clever bugger, Neal thought. Making the offer in English to give Li tremendous face in front of her guests.

He turned to Neal. "Don't worry about White Tiber. They are big men in Kowloon. This is not Kowloon."

This isn't Kowloon, thought Neal. This isn't even the fucking earth. The honcho's appearance had attracted an audience. The local kids were gathered around them in a wide circle, and Neal looked up to see people looking out the windows of the ratty concrete and wooden buildings that surrounded the circle. The alleys were filling with wishful gawkers.

"Mr. Carey will need to use a telephone," Li said. Neal got the idea she said it just to fill a silence.

"Sure . . . anything," the honcho said casually.

Yeah, okay, how about a helicopter?

The honcho's acolytes pushed their way through the crowd and apparently announced that they had accomplished their mission.

"Will you come with me, please?" Honcho asked Li. The crowd parted in front of him as he led them up one of the alleys, into a courtyard ringed by shacks full of sewing machines, through one of the shacks and out a back door into another alley, and then into a cul-de-sac.

At least it looked like a cul-de-sac. When Honcho led them down a stairway into what appeared to be a basement building entrance, the steps ended in a concrete wall. Just to the right, however, there was a narrow crack in the wall. Honcho turned sideways and squeezed through, motioning his guests to follow.

Neal could just fit through the crack, and he shuffled along sideways for about ten feet, trying not to scrape himself on the walls, which pressed against his back and his nose. The walls were home to about ten thousand strains of exotic bacteria, and Neal figured that one open wound would be good for about twenty-five different blood tests. He could feel slime rubbing off on his shirt and pants, and was grateful for once that he couldn't see up or down. He didn't want to know.

This alley, if you could call it that, ended in another wall. This time the crack led off to the left, and Neal endured another twenty feet of rising claustrophobia before they reached their apparent destination. He had to hand it to old Li Lan: She couldn't have found a better place to hide.

Some jerry-rigged wooden steps rose straight up from the alley into a dark hallway. They passed by two closed doors before knocking on the third.

Neal followed them in through Door Number Three, not really thinking he'd find Monty Hall, the patio set, and the trip to Hawaii. What he did find was a bare, low-ceilinged eight-by-eight room. In the right corner a homemade ladder provided shaky access to a primitive loft that had been literally carved out of a wall. The loft was just large enough for a stool and, incredibly, a telephone. Maybe it was for running a book, maybe for taking drug orders, maybe it was for calling up local shops and asking them if they had Prince Albert in a can, but there it was. A stubby black rotary telephone. Neal wasn't sure he had ever seen anything so beautiful in his whole life.

An old man and a boy squatted on the floor of the main room. They held rice bowls to their lips, and their chopsticks were flashing furiously, scooping the dirty white rice into their mouths. The old man wore a sleeveless T-shirt that may have been white sometime during the Sung Dynasty, and a pair of khaki shorts that came down to his calves. His white hair had been shaved close to the scalp, and he had a wispy white beard. His eyes were dull and yellow and showed the resentment he felt at being interrupted in his meal.

The kid, on the other hand, was delighted. He stared unabashedly at Neal, and dropped two or three grains of rice onto the black sports shirt he wore over denim cutoff and rubber sandals. His grin showed bad, crooked teeth, and his eyes looked milky and runny. Infected. Neal figured the kid to be maybe twelve, the old man about a hundred and twelve.

The kid reached under his shirt and came out with a comic book, which he held up to Neal's face.

"Hulk!" he screamed, then screwed his face up and hunched over, growling and showing teeth. "Hulk! Hulk!"

"That's pretty good," Neal said, trying to be friendly.

He reached for the comic book to express admiration, but the kid snatched it back. Then he pulled himself up, threw out his chest, put his hands on his hip, and flashed a confident, macho smile.

"Superman?" Neal asked.

The kid shook his head, then hit him with the smile again.

"*Bat*man," Neal said.

"Batman! Da-da-da-da-da-da-da-da . . . Batman!"

"You're good."

"Marvel Comics. *Ding hao!* Marvel!"

Honcho pointed to the horizontal telephone booth above them with deliberate nonchalance. "Ma Bell," he said. "Knock yourself out."

Pendleton had flopped down in a corner, head in hands. He was done in. Li Lan stood in the center of the room, looking at nothing, expressionless, waiting for the next thing to happen. Neal knew that the next

155

thing was to call Simms and arrange to get the hell out of here. Wherever here was.

"Are you guys ready to do this?" he asked Li and Pendleton.

Tough shit if you're not, he thought, because we are definitely doing this.

Pendleton kept his head in his hands, but nodded.

Li Lan said, "Yes, we are ready."

"It's a local call," Neal said to Honcho as he climbed the ladder.

"Doesn't matter," Honcho answered. "We don't pay."

The loft was the size of a baker's oven and about as hot. There was no room to stand up, and Neal had to bend over, even sitting on the stool. The phone cord came through a small hole that had been drilled in the wall.

It's a nice scam they have going here, Neal thought. Stealing phone service. Wonder how much they charge the locals to make a call. He dug in his pocket for Simms's number.

Great. There was no fucking dial tone.

"I think I'm not doing this right," he said.

Li Lan came up the ladder and leaned into the loft. Even in this sewer she looks gorgeous, Neal thought. Absolutely killer. And she was looking into his eyes so deeply he thought for a moment that he actually might die.

"I'm sorry," she said.

"Don't be sorry. Just show me how to use the phone."

She reached over and gently pulled the cord. It fell out of the hole.

"Is not real," she said.

A dummy phone for the dummy.

"Why?" he asked.

This time the eyes were angry. As cold and hard as ice.

"You can see all this," she said, sweeping her arm around to indicate the neighborhood, "and ask why? Why I am a communist? Why I fight for the people? The question you should ask is why you are not, why you do not. You created all this, you made it. Now you can live in it."

He couldn't breathe. His chest felt like it was in a vise. Live in it? Live in it?! She can't mean what I think she means. Jesus God, please, no.

He could barely make himself ask the question, and it came out in a hoarse whisper. "Are you leaving me here?"

"Yes."

156

Not even a hint of regret. Cold, hard, and straight.

She started down the ladder. He grabbed the top of it and held on, then twisted himself onto the ladder. He stopped when he felt the blade press against the tendons of his knee. He looked down to see the boy, all of his bad teeth showing in an immense and joyful grin, holding the chopper to his leg. The message was clear: Make a run and you'll be hobbling for life. And anyway, where would you run? Neal climbed back into the cave. The boy pulled down the ladder, then reached up and took away the stool.

Honcho, Pendleton, and Li were gone.

9

꒐

Joe Graham hated Providence, a sentiment that united him in at least a small sense with the rest of the world. Providence is a town for insiders, for third-generation harp politicians, Quebecois priests with a gift for gab and a glad hand at charity breakfasts, and mafioso smart guys who run sand and gravel companies and therefore know where the bodies are buried.

It was also a town for a bank that knows where the money is buried, and Ethan Kitteredge was sort of the ace archaeologist of bankers. He could make old money look new, new money look old, and lots of money look gone, and he did it in layers. Ethan Kitteredge was so good at taking care of other people's money that he had even started a side operation to take care of his investors' very lives. Friends of the Family looked out for the family friends—that is, the people who put enough money in the Kitteredge family bank to allow the Kitteredge family to live in the quiet splendor to which it had become accustomed. And AgriTech had run a whole lot of money through Ethan Kitteredge's bank.

This fact made Joe Graham hate Providence even more than usual on this particular day, because Joe Graham had been summoned to a rare meeting at Kitteredge's office to discuss the AgriTech file. The office looked like a captain's cabin on a whaling ship. Nautical models plied the grain of expensive wooden bookcases filled with navigation texts and sailors' memoirs. Kitteredge's enormous mahogany desk was about as old as the ocean, and had on it a model of the Man's pride and joy, his schooner *Haridan*. The place reeked of the sea, which further irritated Joe Graham, who thought the ocean was one gigantic waste of space. He had been to the beach once and hated it: too much sand. So he sat in one of those hard New England chairs, staring pointedly at Ed Levine, while Kitteredge and some preppie cracker discussed the finer points of government policy over a pot of tea. Joe Graham couldn't give a rat's ass or a hamster's dick about government policy. He only wanted to know what had happened to Neal Carey.

So while this Simms yokel was mumbling something about the Chinese tradition of quid pro quo, Graham interrupted him to ask, "So where is Neal Carey?"

Levine shot him a dirty look, but Levine could go fuck himself, maybe eat a couple more steaks and drop fucking dead of a heart attack. Levine was his supervisor, but Graham had known Levine when he was nothing more than hired street muscle. He was one tough Jew—big, fast, smart, and mean—and Graham wasn't scared of him one bit. Right now he was so angry he'd stick his rubber arm up Levine's ass and twirl him.

The cracker, Simms, sighed at the interruption but condescended to answer, "He's gone."

"What do you mean?"

"Which word didn't you understand, Mr. Graham?"

"Listen, you mealy-mouthed fuck—"

"That will be enough, Joe—" Kitteredge said.

Graham saw the Man turn pale with anger. The Man believed in maintaining a tone of immaculate courtesy. Which he can afford to do, Graham thought, because he's got me to do the nasty shit. Me and Neal.

"No, sir, excuse me, but that's not enough," Graham said. He'd thrown the "excuse me" and the "sir" in there in an attempt to save his job and his pension. "Neal Carey gets sent on a job and doesn't get told what it's really about. Nobody tells him that Pendleton's cooped up with a commie spy. Okay, Neal goes off the deep end and boings a major hard-on for this slash—"

"Pardon me?" Kiteredge asked.

"He develops a romantic obsession for the woman," Levine explained as he drilled Graham with a shut-the-fuck-up glare that didn't shut him the fuck up.

"So," Graham continued, "Blue Suit over here knows free labor when he sees it and stands back while Neal gets deeper and deeper into the shit, and now he shows up here and tells us Neal is gone. So, Mr. Simms, the word I don't understand is 'gone.' Maybe you can explain that?"

Simms looked to Kitteredge as if he expected him to intervene.

Kitteredge did. "Yes, Mr. Simms, perhaps you could explain?"

"Neal Carey telephoned me from the YMCA in Kowloon and said he had Pendleton and Li Lan and please come and get him. I of course said I would, and sent the nearest available resources over. When they got there, perhaps forty-five minutes later, Carey, Pendleton, and the woman were gone. When I got there in another hour, they were still gone. That was six weeks ago. We have since managed to track them as far as a temple near the Walled City."

"What's that?" Levine asked.

"It is the eighth circle of hell. It is an area only about the size of three football fields, yet perhaps the densest maze in the urban cosmography."

Kitteredge leaned over his desk. "Mr. Simms, please spare us any further demonstrations of your . . . erudition. We all acknowledge that you are intelligent. You may take that as a stipulation, and please begin to speak in English."

Simms flushed. He didn't particularly care for Yankees, or Irishmen, or for that matter Jews, and he was having to put up with an especially unpleasant combination of all three.

"The Walled City is a no-man's-land. It had its beginnings as a fort that became a haven for squatters during the early days of British colonization. Neither the Chinese nor the British attempt to administrate it, so it is controlled by an uneasy confederation of tongs. Tongs, or Triads, are gangs—"

"We have them in New York," Graham said.

"How nice for you. Anyway, the original walls have long since crumbled, but the area is actually an impenetrable maze, a hovel of the worst kind of crime: Drugs, extortion, slavery, and child prostitution flourish there. The police rarely venture inside, and tourists are warned that even to step into the Walled City is a risky proposition. People simply disappear."

Gone, Graham thought.

"If Carey was lured into the Walled City, I'm afraid he is in desperate trouble."

"He's a tough kid," Levine said, but Graham could hear the fear in his voice. Ed Levine always said that he hated Neal Carey, but Graham knew better. Besides, Neal was Ed's employee, one of his people, and Ed Levine was fiercely protective of his people.

"That won't do him much good, I'm afraid," Simms answered. "If he's in there, he's in one of the most vicious slums in the world. A place without law, ethics, or morals. A jungle."

"What will happen to him?" asked Kitteredge, who had a banker's way of cutting to the bottom line.

"I doubt they'd murder him outright, unless the Li woman ordered it."

"Why not?"

"Because he's much more valuable alive."

"To whom? As what?"

Simms smiled tightly. "A white youth would be an oddity there, to say the least. A commodity. They will probably auction him off to the highest bidder. This really is excellent tea. What is it?"

Simms's hand reached for the teapot but never made it. A hard rubber artificial arm slammed it to the table and held it there.

"Go in and get him," Graham said.

"Impossible. Now remove your arm, please."

"Go in and get him."

"I don't want to have to hurt you."

Graham pressed down hard. "Yeah. Do some of your fancy CIA shit on me. Terrify me."

"Ease up, Joe," Levine said. Graham could feel that the big man was getting ready to move, to peel him off Simms.

"I'll break his fucking wrist, Ed."

"Have you all considered the possibility that your Carey isn't in the Walled City at all? That perhaps he is cashing a check in Peking, or on a nice beach in Indonesia somewhere, laughing at all of us?"

Simms was trying to maintain his cool, but the voice betrayed pain.

"Mr. Graham," said Kitteredge, "please release your . . . hold . . . on our guest's arm."

Graham pressed down a little harder before letting up. He looked Simms in the eye and repeated, "Go in and get him."

161

Simms ignored him and turned to Kitteredge. He was red in the face and rubbing his wrist as he asked, "What do you want me to do, Mr. Kitteredge?"

"Mr. Simms, I want you to go in and get him."

"Look, Carey has disobeyed every single directive we've issued. He's blown a major operation. And, frankly, I don't know whether (A) we can find him, and (B), if we do, whether we could get him out."

Levine came from around the desk, leaving his usual position on the right hand of God. He leaned against the Man's desk and looked down at Simms. "In that case, I don't know whether (A) we can continue our current financial relationship with AgriTech, or (B) we may have to call in our paper."

Simms blew his cool. "You don't fuck with the government."

"Watch us."

"You think you can take on the CIA? You don't know what you're dealing with."

"We know enough to launder your goddamn money for the past ten years," Levine said.

Kitteredge raised a hand to object. "I'm not sure I would call it 'laundering.'"

"Taking their slush fund, running it through the Bank, and then loaning it back to to their pet corporation to pay for research? Come on, Mr. Kitteredge, what would you call it?"

"Patriotism."

Nobody answered that one.

Kitteredge smoothed back the unruly lock of ash-blond hair that fell across his forehead. "For an . . . organization . . . such as ours, it is our duty and our privilege to support our country. Because we are who we are, that support often takes a covert form. So be it. We do what we can do. However, gentlemen, in this particular case we have erred grievously. We have—albeit unwittingly, and I am very angry about that, Mr. Simms, very angry—sent our colleague, Neal Carey, into dangerous waters without the proper navigational aids. Thus, sailing in the dark on uncharted waters, he has foundered. If he has indeed . . . drowned . . . we must mourn him. But if he is marooned, we must rescue him. We will use—and you will use, Mr. Simms—all our resources to do so. Am I understood, gentlemen?"

Ed Levine and Joe Graham nodded.

"Mr. Simms?"

Simms nodded.

"The tea is black gunpowder. Many of my ancestors invested in the China trade," Kitteredge said.

"Tea traders?"

"Uhhmm. And opium, of course."

Right, thought Graham. Opium in and tea out. Sounds like money in the bank. Make that money in the Bank.

"Take some with you, Mr. Simms. I'll have my secretary make up a package," Kitteredge added.

The abruptness of the dismissal startled Simms. Just who the unholy hell did these people think they were? Nobody wanted to find young Neal Carey more than he did. He shook Kitteredge's hand, nodded to Levine, and ignored Joe Graham as he left the room.

Kitteredge sat back in his chair and touched his fingertips together at his lips. He looked like he was praying, but Graham knew it was a habit he had when he was in deep thought. So Graham just shut up, something he thought he maybe should have done earlier, because maybe the Man was searching for just the right words to fire him.

Finally he spoke. "Ed?"

"I think we have to assume that Carey's been the subject of hostile action," Levine said. "Carey's an arrogant, undisciplined, unreliable fuck-up, but he's no traitor."

"For the right woman?" Kitteredge asked.

"In Carey's case, there is no right woman. He's psychologically incapable of that depth of feeling."

Kitteredge turned to Graham. "Do you concur?"

"If Ed means that Neal is generally pissed off at women and doesn't trust them, sure," Graham answered. "Is this what they teach you in night school, Ed?"

Levine was on a roll. "It's more than not trusting them. Neal expects betrayal. His mother was an addict and a prostitute, and worse than that, she left him—"

"We kicked her out of town."

"Nevertheless, deep down, Neal knows that any woman he loves will eventually leave him, betray him. When she does, she validates his view of life. If she doesn't, he'll do something to make her leave. If that

163

doesn't work, he'll leave and be pissed off when she doesn't follow him. So—"

Graham slammed his fist on the table. "If Doctor Fraud here is finished, I'd like to start looking for Neal."

"That's what I'm trying to do, Graham. Keep your arm on. What I'm saying, so that even Graham can understand it, is that it's just not possible that Neal is living happily in China somewhere with this broad."

"So you believe he's a prisoner, Ed," asked Kitteredge.

Ed got quiet for a minute, which made Graham nervous. Ed being quiet was never good news.

"Yes," Ed answered. "Or he's dead."

"He's not dead," Graham replied.

"How do you know?"

"I just know."

"Terrific."

"Either way, gentlemen," Kitteredge said, "we have to find him."

"How are your connections in Chinatown?" Levine asked Graham.

"Not so good anymore. Things have changed, the old guys are dying out. It's all kids now, and they're all crazy. Gun-happy. But I'll ask around, see if anyone can do some digging in Hong Kong."

"With your permission" Ed said to Kitteredge, "I'll head over there, keep the heat on our friend Simms."

"Good," Kitteredge said. "I'll make the appropriate calls to Washington to apprise certain people of our . . . sentiments in this matter."

Swell, Graham thought. Maybe if we hadn't been dicking around with certain people in Washington, we wouldn't have to have any sentiments in this matter. Well, the Man can make the phone calls, but in the end it's going to come down to somebody putting his feet on the ground and walking in and getting him. And guess who that's going to be.

"Shall we be about it, gentlemen? Time seems to be an issue here."

Joe Graham headed back to the train station and only had to wait about an hour before catching the Colonial back to New York. He'd visit a couple of the old boys on Mott Street, but he knew exactly what would happen. They would look somber, give him a bunch of assurances, and then do exactly nothing. He didn't blame them; it wasn't their problem, and the Chinese didn't usually go around borrowing trouble.

They had plenty of their own. No, Graham would go through the motions to make the Man happy. But then he was going to hop on a plane to Hong Kong and go find his kid. Walled City, hell . . . Joe Graham was from Delancey Street.

10

Neal thought about escaping at first.

It should have been easy—his guards were a lunatic boy and an ancient man. Neal came up with clever nicknames for them. He called the boy "Marvel" and the old man "Old Man." Neal almost tried to bolt when they stripped him, when Marvel stood close by with the chopper raised as Old Man took Neal's shirt, pants, socks, and shoes. Neal thought maybe he could grab the chopper, overpower Marvel, and make his break. But he didn't expect that the old man would be that quick and he also didn't expect the handcuffs—rusty bracelets that were comically large and looked like props from an old vaudeville bit. And he didn't know that handcuffs could be so heavy. Cuffed, weighted down, and stark naked, he knew he wouldn't stand a chance, so he went docilely back to the cave as the boy nudged him up the ladder.

He thought maybe he could wait it out. Simms must be poring over the city for him, tracking his steps, figuring out that he was somewhere in this no-man's-land. Surely, any minute, the door would come crashing in, and Simms, leading a band of efficient killers, would rescue him. Any minute now . . .

Any minute turned to any hour turned to any day now as Neal tried to keep track of the time. It must have been during the second week when he got so sick. He had taken to counting the days by the rice bowl, because they gave him one a day. It wasn't exactly rice, either, but more like rice gruel, a runny, dirty little mixture with some rice grains and God only knew what else floating in it. He had always had trouble with chopsticks, and with the handcuffs on it was a lot worse, especially since his wrists were raw from the weight of the rusty metal. But he forced himself to raise the bowl to his mouth and shove the food down. And he made himself use the bucket they gave him as a lavatory, the bucket that Marvel emptied once a day for him when he remembered.

So by counting rice bowls, he figured it was the second week when his guts turned to napalm and the violent, uncontrollable emissions of the green, watery shit started. He couldn't stop it, all he could do was double over from the fierce cramps, and after a while he couldn't even do that. All he could do was writhe in it, then lie exhausted until the next spasm hit.

Marvel thought it was funny, but Old Man got pissed off, yelled at him, and took away the bucket on the old "use it or lose it" theory, Neal supposed. And he supposed that the stench he made was his only form of vengeance, and maybe it would provoke them into killing him, which seemed like a decent option by the end of the second week. Because by the end of the second week he had given up all hope of escape or rescue.

He tried to fight it at first, tried to make himself eat, even though every mouthful meant another spasm of dysentery. He tried to make himself at least sip on the weak tea they gave him, because he knew that he was getting dehydrated and that was what would kill him first, but each sip was like liquid flame, and there was that day—which day was it? how many rice bowls?—when he soiled himself and just lay there sobbing while Marvel danced around beneath him mimicking his sobs between peals of laughter and cries of "Red Kryptonite! Red Kryptonite!" and Old Man screamed at him. That was when Neal stopped eating, and the next day he stopped even trying to drink, and started the conscious process of dying. He thought about Li Lan, and Kuan Yin, the goddess of mercy, and where were they now? He thought about Simms, the incompetent son of a bitch, and then about Joe Graham.

Then he started crying again. Please, Dad, come get me. Dad. Come get me. Please.

The diarrhea stopped, because there was nothing left, and the cramps became worse. The dry fire in his stomach wrenched him upward like an inchworm crawling. The fevers came and hit him hard, twice a day. He shook with cold, the chain between his hands rattling like Marley's Ghost, his teeth chattering. He felt as if he were being poked with thousands of icy needles. Then the fever would suddenly stop, and he would be rewarded with unconsciousness. The dry heaves and cramps were his alarm clocks, and the cycle would begin again, and after a while he lost track of time because there were no rice bowls to count anymore.

So he wasn't sure when it was that Honcho showed up and threw the fit. Neal was lying in the cave, racked by cramps, when he opened his eyes and saw Honcho standing on the ladder peering at him intently. Honcho grunted with disgust, got off the ladder, and began screaming at Old Man, punctuating his major points with kicks at Marvel, who scrambled into a corner and huddled up. Honcho kept putting the boot into him as he argued with Old Man, who didn't take the diatribe passively, but also came over and started kicking the kid.

Honcho came back up the ladder, grabbed Neal by the back of the neck, and lifted him into a sitting position. Then he launched into what seemed to Neal like a critique. He jabbed his finger at Neal's ribs, pointed at his eyes, and then pinched his own nostrils and made an exaggerated snorting sound. He let Neal drop, came back down the ladder, and pointed back up at him and asked what sounded like a single question.

Neal didn't need to be a Chinese language scholar to know what the question was: Who'd want to buy a piece of shit like this?

I would, Neal murmured. I have at least eight thousand pounds sterling in a bank in London, boys, and if you'll take me back to my hotel, I'll write you a check. And I won't stop payment, I won't. I promise. We can go the bank together and cash it. You can have it all, guys.

But Honcho went on like he didn't even hear him, like Neal was just moving his lips and babbling. Honcho pointed to Marvel, and then back to Neal and asked another question, something like: Maybe you'd like to trade places with him?

Honcho leaned over and slapped Marvel in the face a couple of times and then issued a general order: Take care of the merchandise!

He slammed the door on his way out. Old Man started to grumble, relieved his frustration by slapping Marvel, and then sent the boy out. Marvel came back a few minutes later with a large bowl of water and a rag. It took him a long time to wipe the encrusted filth off Neal. He was careful about it, turning Neal over as gently as he could and wiping Neal's forehead when the cramps hit.

In the meantime, the old man swung into action. He dug around under his *kang* and came out with a lamp that looked like a large sterno stove, a long-stemmed pipe, and a tin cigarette case. He lit the lamp, and when he had a nice glow going, he used a long needle to spear a tiny ball of opium, a blackish green nugget. He held it over the burning lamp.

Fondue, Neal thought. Hell of a time for fondue.

The old man screamed at Marvel, who scrambled down the ladder and stood in waiting. The old man ignited the opium, stuck it into the pipe, and handed it to Marvel, who climbed back into the loft and held the pipe to Neal's lips.

"Kryptonite?" Neal mumbled. He brushed the pipe away.

"Kryptonite," Marvel said, and pushed the pipe back to Neal's lips.

"Red Kryptonite or Green Kryptonite?"

"Green."

"Okay, then."

Neal took a short draw on the pipe as the old man fried another ball of opium. Marvel went back down and fetched in the pipe and went back up to Neal.

"Flash," said Marvel.

Neal didn't fight the pipe this time or the next. The fourth time Marvel came with the pipe, Neal reached up for it and held it to his own lips.

Neal floated to the ceiling and then through the roof. He drifted up over the Walled City into the blue sky and then he flew right into Li Lan's painting, the one on the mountainside above the abyss. He sat down with Li Lan on the precipice and looked down at the other Li Lan in the canyon beneath them.

"I found you," he said.

She set her brushes down and took his hand. "No," she said gently, "I led you here."

"Why did you leave me?"

"I knew you could fly."

He felt the tears well up in his eyes and then spill over onto his cheeks. It felt good, so good to cry, and he let the tears pour into his open mouth and they tasted sweet, and she must have known that because she took a single tear with her tongue, swallowed it, and smiled.

He recognized her then.

"Kuan Yin," he said. "You are Kuan Yin."

His eyes flooded with more tears and she lapped them off his face. She opened his mouth with her tongue and drank more tears as the sky became a brilliant blue and she took him inside her and gently rocked him. She wrapped her hands around the back of his head and pushed his mouth to her nipple and fed him. She softly chanted his name and the pain receded and then it was only pleasure, only pleasure, only pleasure, and then she was weeping and he soothed her straining neck with his lips as the wet and warmth of her moved on him. And then her reflection floated up from the abyss and reached out her hand and Li Lan took it and held it tightly and drew her reflection into herself and Neal saw his own reflection in the mists below—his eyes sunken, his face pale with pain and hunger—and he reached out and took it and drew it into himself and then they were all together, all inside each other, and they fell off the edge of the cliff and into the mists.

11

Xao Xiyang toook a deep drag of the cigarette, stubbed the butt out in the full ashtray, and lit another one. It was a deep character flaw, he knew, that anxiety made him chain-smoke. He should meditate instead, or do t'ai chi, but he lacked the patience. Another character flaw.

Besides, his smoking made the interior of the limousine smell bad. His late wife had complained about it constantly—it had been one of the many running jokes they shared—and he felt a quick stab of sorrow that she was not there to nag him about it.

He looked out the window at the wide boulevard. His was one of the few automobiles among the thousands of bicycles, their bells jingling like an immense flock of chirping birds. The car came to a stop at a four-way intersection in front of a traffic island on which a white-uniformed policeman waved his arms and did a showy pirouette to face a new stream of traffic. Behind the officer loomed a gigantic billboard picturing a young couple beaming at their baby. Their single baby. It was a boy, Xao Xiyang observed. In the birth-control propaganda, the one child was always a boy. Not so in life, thought Xao, whose wife had given him two beloved daughters, no sons.

The officer spotted the official limousine and hurriedly stopped the other traffic and waved it through. Normally, Xao would have told his driver to wait, but today he was in a hurry. On most other days he loved to linger on Chengdu's wide, tree-lined streets, to get out of the car and walk the sidewalks, look over the shoulders at the many artists who painted the flowers, the trees, and the pretty old buildings. Or perhaps stop in at one of the many small restaurants and sample some noodles in bean paste, or tofu in the fiery pepper sauce that was the city's specialty. Sometimes he would stand and chat with the crowd that inevitably formed around him, listen to their concerns, their complaints, or maybe just share the latest joke.

But there was no time for joking today, he had no appetite for noodles or tofu, and the only painter that concerned him was the one he had code-named China Doll. She had—unwittingly—left a mess behind her in Hong Kong, a mess that threatened to ruin his entire plan, the one he had worked on for so many years. Ah, well, he remineded himself, she was still something of an amateur, and amateurs will make mistakes. But still their mistakes must be made right.

She had done well, however. She had made her way through and brought her package with her to Guangzhou, where his secret ally controlled the security police. Despite his eagerness to see her, and finally to meet the scientist she had brought with her, he had let them sit hidden in Guangzhou until it was safe to bring them into Sichuan.

He had thought that would be a matter of a few weeks, but then the trouble started in Hong Kong. Who would ever have thought there would be so much commotion over one young man? So many people looking for him, making so much noise. If that noise reached certain ears in Beijing . . . well, he wouldn't let it, that was all. He would take the necessary steps, had taken the necessary steps, and that, after all, was the best way to set one's anxieties to rest.

He looked out the tinted windows at the neat row of mulberry trees that lined the road. Soon the pavement would end, and the road would turn to that deep red earth so distinctive of Sichuan. Already he was seeing the signs of the countryside: peasants laboring beneath shoulder poles, cyclists maneuvering bicycles heavily laden with bamboo mats or cages of chickens—even one with a pig tied across the rear hub, children riding on the necks of their buffaloes, urging them off the road toward the rice paddies.

The sights raised his spirits, reminding him of the ultimate aim of all his planning and plotting. Beijing would doubtless call it treason, would

172

give him the bullet or the rope if they caught him, but Xao knew that his treachery was the most patriotic act of a patriotic lifetime. May the god we don't believe exists bless Li Lan, he thought. She has brought us the scientist—the expert—and with his help these children riding so happily to their chores will never know the suffering their parents did. They will never be hungry.

If you want to eat, go see Xao Xiyang, he thought, mocking himself. Well, the great Xao Xiyang had better clean up this mess in Hong Kong, clean it up before those red ideologue bastards in Beijing use it to gain the upper hand again. Use his disgrace to embarrass Deng and tie his hands.

He used the cigarette butt to light a fresh one. He told his driver to speed up and then sat back to think.

It took an hour to get to the production team headquarters. His car had been spotted and the word of his arrival had preceded him. Old Zhu was standing in the circular gravel driveway to greet him. Old Zhu, the production team leader, was only thirty-three, but he looked old. Xao suspected that even his schoolmates had called him Old Zhu. Old Zhu was impossibly earnest. He cared about only one thing: growing rice. And in China, Xao mused, that *would* tend to make one old before one's time.

Xao got out of the car and greeted Zhu warmly, trying to head off the rapid-fire bows that were Zhu's habit.

"Have you had rice today?" he asked Zhu. It was the traditional Chinese greeting, asking if the person had eaten. It was not always a rhetorical question.

"I am full, thank you. And you?" asked Zhu, managing to get three bows into his answer.

"I can never get enough of the rice grown by the Dwaizhou Production Brigade."

Zhu flushed with pleasure and led Xao into a two-story stone building that served as a meeting hall, recreation center, and hospitality suite. They went into a large room that had several large round tables and bamboo chairs. On one of the tables were a pot of tea, two cups, two glasses of orange drink, four cigarettes, and a small stack of wrapped hard candies. Zhu pulled out a chair for Xao and waited until he was seated before taking a chair himself. Then he poured tea into the two cups and waited to hear the purpose of the chairman's visit.

173

Xao sipped his tea and politely nodded his approval, provoking another blush.

"Your figures for this quarter," he said, "are excellent."

"Thank you. Yes. I also think that the brigade has done well."

"Of particular satisfaction are the figures from the privatized land."

Zhu nodded seriously. "Yes, yes. Especially in pigs, a bit less so in rice, but overall we are very pleased."

"As well you should be."

Xao took a swallow of the hideously sweet orange drink and forced himself to smile. He lit two cigarettes and handed one to Zhu.

"I think," Xao said, "that we shall be making further advances soon."

Zhu stared at the floor, but Xao could see the excitement in his eyes. "Even so?" Zhu asked.

"So . . . if I were able to give you a certain rare resource, you feel you would be able to make good use of it."

Zhu didn't hesitate. "Yes. Oh, yes."

Xao was surprised to feel his heart pounding. Such was the state of paranoia in their people's republic that he even hesitated to trust Zhu, Old Zhu, the ultimate farmer, the man he had watched repair tractors as if he were operating on his own children, the man he had seen thigh-deep in the paddies teaching the old ones better ways to harvest, the man he had seen weep over the arrival of a shipment of fertilizer.

"And you understand," Xao continued, "that this resource must be kept a secret, even from the authorities of the government?"

Zhu nodded. He looked Xao squarely in the eyes and nodded.

Done, Xao thought. He inhaled the smoke deeply, held it in his lungs, and let it out along with his sigh of relief. He sat quietly with Zhu, drinking tea and smoking cigarettes, as they both thought about the step they were going to take and dreamed their individual dreams.

After a few minutes Zhu asked, "Do you wish to see her?"

"Yes."

"Do you wish an escort?"

"I know the way."

Zhu stood up. "Will you be joining us for dinner?"

"I am afraid I do not have the time."

"I shall have the cooks prepare something for you. You can eat on the way back to the city."

"You are very kind."

"And for your driver, of course."

Zhu left, and Xao finished his cigarette before walking outside. The late afternoon was pleasantly warm, and he enjoyed walking along the dike between the broad rice paddies. Dwaizhou was an ordered miracle of neat fields, fishponds, and mulberry trees stretching along the broad Sichuan plain seemingly forever, or at least up to the mountain range that rose faint purple on the western horizon. Maybe when it was all over, when he had completed his work, he could retire here and spend his days raising carp and playing checkers. A dream, he thought. My work will not be finished in a thousand thousand years.

He walked two *li* before coming to the small concrete building on the edge of the wood that Zhu had let stand to harbor rabbits for hunting. The building had a corrugated tin roof, a metal door, and a single barred window. The guard stood at attention in front of the door, and Xao realized that Zhu must have sent a runner, some fleet child, ahead of him, to warn the guard.

He motioned for the guard to unlock the door, then gave the nervous young man a cigarette and told him to take a walk, out of earshot but within sight. When the guard was far enough away, Xao ordered the prisoner to step outside.

She never changes, he thought. How long had it been? Ten years? Eleven? She still wore the Maoist clothes, the baggy green fatigues and the cap. But no red armband—those were gone with the Red Guard. Her hair was tied in two pigtails held with red ribbon—her sole affectation. She was still lovely.

She bowed deeply.

He did not return the bow.

He said it before he could lose his nerve. "I am going to release you soon."

He saw her eyes widen in surprise. Or was it dismay?

"You cannot release me."

"It is within my power."

"I mean that I am a prisoner of my own crimes. No one can release me from them."

Perhaps that is true, he thought. Indeed, I have tried and tried, and I have been unable to forgive you. And it is eleven years, not ten. How could I have forgotten?

175

"Your release does not come from my mercy, it comes from my need."

"Then I am grateful to serve your need."

"How long have you been a prisoner?"

"Eight years."

"A long time."

"You have been gracious enough to visit often."

Gracious, he thought. No, not gracious. I have visited you to struggle with my own soul. To see if I could overcome my own hatred. I have kept you as a mirror in which to view myself.

"My needs may require you to exercise some of your former skills. Can you?"

"If it serves you."

"It is dangerous."

"I owe you a life."

Yes, he thought, you do. He studied her closely, studied her as he had so often. He wanted to reach out to her, to share the pain, but instead he stiffened and said, "Be ready, then. I shall call."

She bowed. He turned on his heel and signaled the guard to lock her back up, lock up this woman who had killed his wife.

12

Ben Chin watched the gorgeous Shaolin nun beat up on the evil mandarin and then got up from his seat. He would have watched more of the film, but his neck still hurt from when that bitch had tried to kick his head off, and besides, it was time to get back to work.

He didn't have to look behind him to know that his new crew was following him up the aisle. His old crew, the useless old women, had been demoted to running errands, and now the Triad bosses had sent him a sleek, new gang of stone killers straight from Taiwan. They'd also given him an assignment: Go into the Walled City and do the job right this time. Do what you have to do. Use money, drugs, fists, knives, or guns, but get it done.

Fine. He was looking forward to the reunion. And it was close, so close. Almost two months of hard work—two months of well-placed bribes, of threats, of dangerous reconnaissance missions into the Walled City—had finally yielded a reward. Getting in was another problem, getting out a bigger one yet. But the job itself would only take a minute: have one of his new boys make the buy, then take the merchandise into an alley somewhere and put one in the back of his head. It wouldn't be as good as slicing up the bitch, but still . . .

His crew was following him as he hit the street and the goofy little kid got in his way.

"*Superman* twenty-fifth anniversary issue? Very cheap?" the kid asked, holding some raggedy-looking comic books in Chin's face.

"What the—?"

The kid threw himself to the sidewalk, and Chin saw the car across the street a half-second before the rounds from the AK drilled through his chest.

His body toppled to the pavement. The neon of the theater marquee flashed on his blood soaking into the covers of *Superman, Batman,* and *The Green Hornet.*

Simms shook the cylindrical can until a prayer stick fell out. He took the stick, wrapped a crisp American hundred-dollar bill around it, and handed it back to the old monk in the booth.

It was costing him a hell of a lot of money to locate Neal Carey, but it was worth it. There was no telling what could happen if somebody else got to him first and heard the story he had to tell. Simms didn't know what Neal did or did not know, and he wanted to be the first to ask him. Then he would make sure Carey disappeared for good, and report his sad demise to those white-trash Yankee sons of bitches in Providence.

The monk came out of the booth and led Simms into the temple, to a statue of a grotesque old man carrying a bar of silver. The monk pointed to the silver bar and then pointed to Simms.

Simms didn't tell the monk that he spoke perfect Chinese, thank you very much, he just reached into his wallet and pulled out another C-note. The damn Buddhists were worse than the Catholics for soaking you for money.

The monk took the bill, disappeared briefly into the booth, then came back in a few minutes and led Simms through a door and down into some sort of tunnel. Simms was glad he had the piece with him, even though he had no intention of going all the way into the Walled City. The deal was that they would bring Carey halfway into the tunnel and turn him over as soon as they counted the cash.

Honcho stepped into the hovel, poured himself a cup of tea, and sat down to strip the AK. The old man glared at him.

"Where have you been?" the old man asked.

"To the movies," Honcho answered. He looked up into the cage at Neal. "He still in the clouds?"

"Where is the boy? I need help here, you know."

"I don't think he's coming back. The last time I saw him he was chasing a car. He didn't catch it."

That much was true. One of Chin's shooters had woken up enough to pop a couple into the kid as he was running up Nathan Road.

"Not much help anyway," the old man said.

"Not much of a boy."

"How longer will the *kweilo* be here? If much longer, I want a new boy."

"Not much longer."

"You found a buyer?"

Honcho pulled a wad of bills from his pocket.

"Four buyers," he said. "Well, *three* now."

"How do you sell something three times?" the old man asked.

"Practice."

Simms waited in the tunnel. He figured he was underneath Lion Rock Road, which made sense if they were going to bring Carey out from the Walled City. He wished they'd hurry the hell up, though. Water was dripping from the ceiling onto his suit and the tunnel was like a steambath. Why couldn't they behave like white people and just deliver Carey to a civilized hotel room?

He heard footsteps coming down the tunnel. Four sets. He made out the faces through the steam. Not a pair of round eyes to be seen.

Simms edged his back up against the wall and waited for their leader to get closer. The leader was easy to pick out—slick dresser, sly leer.

"Did you forget something?" Simms asked.

"Maybe you'd like a nice Chinese boy," Honcho answered.

"Maybe I'd like what I paid for."

"Vietnamese? I have a ten-year-old you'd like."

"I want the American," Simms said, more out of principle than anything. He knew when a deal had gone south. Now it was matter of getting out.

"Sorry," Honcho said. He didn't have to worry about a *kweilo* faggot stupid enough to walk into a tunnel all by himself.

179

Simms just smiled as two of the lads edged up alongside of him. The third stood behind the leader's shoulder.

"Then give me my money."

"No cash refunds. Only merchandise."

"I'll take my money."

Simms knew he wasn't going to get any cash. But he needed a negotiating point. Something along the order of "You let me out of here and I'll forget about it."

Honcho pointed his chin at the two guys who were pressing in on Simms.

"Talk to the complaint department."

The kid on Simms's left pulled a switchblade, flicked it open, and waved it in front of Simms's face. Simms pulled a silenced pistol from his pocket, stuck it into the side of the kid's knee, and squeezed the trigger.

"I don't think so," Simms said.

He stepped over the kid, who was flopping around like a fish in the bottom of a boat.

"I'll be leaving now," said Simms.

13

品

Joe Graham stood impatiently on a narrow, cracked sidewalk on Lion Rock Road, outside one of the tenement buildings that ringed the Walled City like giant barricades. He shivered a little as he watched a "dentist" in a ground-floor stall dig into the tooth of one of his patients with a hand-powered drill.

Graham was nervous for a lot of reasons. He was dangerously close to the infamous ghetto into which Neal Carey had disappeared; he didn't have a gun; he was there without orders from the Man. But most of all he was nervous because the smart-ass Chinese kid was late for their appointment to trade the rest of the cash for Neal Carey.

A couple of minutes later the guy showed up. He had a couple of buddies with him, but no Neal.

What's the scam, Graham wondered. What now?

"So?" he asked the guy.

"The deal's off," Honcho answered flatly. Fuck it. Let the *kweilo* work it out.

The words hit Graham like a shot in the chest and he didn't even flinch as the two helpers patted him down. He wasn't carrying, anyway.

"What do you mean?" Graham asked.

Honcho shrugged. "What's the difference?"

"I want to know."

Of course. All the losers did.

"You were outbid."

"I didn't know I was in an auction."

"Now you know."

Graham felt himself getting hot all over. Maybe it was the wiseguy smirk—it was the same old smirk the wiseguys always had, didn't matter what country you were in. Maybe it was the barrels of the pistols his two escorts were showing him. More likely it was the fact that he had lost Neal again.

"I'll top the highest bid."

"You must be awfully horny."

"I'll double it."

"Sorry."

"How much? Name it!"

"Too late."

Graham grabbed him by his silk lapel and pulled him in tight, trapping the guy's right arm under his own artificial one and pressing hard. He saw a glimmer of pain and fear appear in the punk's eyes and held him tighter. See if the fuckers want to shoot now.

"Listen, asshole," Graham hissed. "This isn't over. It'll never be over until I get that kid back safe."

"Let go of me."

"I'll bring an army in there."

"You do that."

Graham shoved him hard and the punk fell against his buddies. One of them leveled his pistol at Graham.

"Do it, chickenshit. Do it."

Honcho grabbed his boy's wrist and started to back away.

"Go home, old man," he said.

They left Graham standing there. He didn't stand there for long. He went off to get an army.

The *kweilo* pushed the rice bowl away and pointed to the opium pipe. Old Man sighed—it was the same argument every day. The *kweilo* wouldn't eat unless you gave him some opium, and when you gave him the opium, he didn't want to eat. Old Man signaled the usual compromise, holding up the index finger of each hand. One serving of rice for

182

one rock of opium. The *kweilo* nodded and wolfed down half a bowl of rice.

Neal sucked his reward down and grabbed his chopsticks to get the next mouthfuls of rice over with. He did this four more times and then he was flying out of the room again. The pain, the cramps, the aching loneliness, the fear, the godawful boredom stayed on the ground with his body as his mind flew to join Li Lan in her paintings. It never lasted long, never long enough, but it was a little bit of heaven in a whole lot of hell.

So he was real pissed off when the door came swinging open and Honcho walked in. Honcho was always a pain. Honcho didn't want him to do too much opium. Honcho wanted him complacent, not completely stoned. Neal wanted to be completely stoned.

Honcho had his clothes.

A shaft of pure fear penetrated Neal's opium haze.

I've been sold.

He saw the buyer come through the door.

"Oh, God," Neal murmured. "You've come to get me."

Then he broke down into racking, uncontrollable sobs. He was still crying as they took the pipe from him, got him dressed, and took him to the door.

Neal stopped at the doorway and stuck his stoned, teary face into Old Man's.

"You are," Neal said, "the Unpredictable Ghost."

The old man nodded happily as Honcho hauled Neal out the door.

Sergeant Eddie Chang stood aside as two of his men kicked in the door. He had ten other officers with drawn guns backing him up, so he leaned against the wall and lit a cigarette.

He was pissed off. He'd spent half his life scrambling around to get out of the Walled City, and he didn't like coming back for any reason. Especially business.

But the word had been sent from New York. And the word had come from a former Hong Kong police sergeant who had skipped out ahead of the prosecutors with only the clothes on his back and six million dollars in cash. And this old cop had bought himself a couple of new suits and the entire New York City Triad organization, so if he gave the word to give this one-armed guy anything he asked for, that's what

Eddie Chang was going to do, even if it meant paying a vsit to the old neighborhood.

The old neighborhood was giving him some pretty dirty looks, too. He could feel them coming down from the tenement windows, from the alleys, and especially from the young stud who was lying face down in the dirt with his hands behind his neck and a machine-gun barrel jammed against his head.

"Pick him up," Chang ordered.

The officer hauled the kid to his feet. Chang lit another cigarette and stuck it into the kid's mouth.

"You're pretty far from your turf," Honcho said.

"I'm here from Big-Ear Fu, so shut your mouth."

The door gave way and the two cops burst inside. The little one-armed round-eye was right behind them.

"He's not there," Honcho said to Eddie.

"Where is he?" Graham asked the old man who was huddled in the corner. "Where is he?!"

Graham looked around in disbelief. The place was impossibly filthy and it stank to high heavens. He looked up at the hollowed-out loft and saw the handcuffs.

It was a bad moment for Eddie Chang to bring Honcho in, because Joe Graham was going nuts. He grabbed the cuffs and swung them in a wide arc that ended abruptly at Honcho's neck.

"Where is he?!"

"He's gone."

"Where?!" The cuffs hit Honcho's face.

Eddie Chang stepped in and moved Graham away.

"He told me your friend's an addict. Opium."

"That's impossible."

"Nothing's impossible here."

Graham broke away and got himself a little space. Neal smoking opium? Neal a junkie like his old lady?

"Where is he?" Graham repeated.

"They sold him to some Chinese," Chang said.

"When?" Graham asked.

Honcho smiled. "You just missed him."

184

Graham grabbed Chang by the elbow. "Let's get going. We can catch them.

"There's no way," said Chang. "He could be anywhere in the world by now."

"You know junkies," said Honcho. "Maybe he just flew away."

Chang threw Honcho to the floor, then pulled his pistol from its holster and pointed it at Honcho's head.

"Yes?" Chang asked, looking at Graham.

Graham thought about Neal Carey being held a prisoner here, being force-fed dope, being sold off to some Asian brothel. He looked down at Honcho.

"No," Graham said. He had enough blood on his conscience and other things to do. Like look all over the world for Neal Carey.

PART THREE
The Buddha's Mirror

14

Neal woke to the rattle of the cup on the tray. The waiter made the noise intentionally as he set the breakfast on the side table by the bed.

"Good morning, Mr. Frazier. Breakfast," the waiter said before padding softly out of the room.

Neal rolled over under the starched white sheets and turned toward the sound. He could smell the strong coffee in the pot, the scrambled eggs under the platter, and the warm *mantou*—a large roll of steamed bread. The dish of pickled vegetables that he never ate made its stubborn appearance on the plate, along with a small bowl of shelled peanuts. There was also a glass of orange juice, a bowl of sugar, and a small pitcher of milk. It was the same breakfast they had served him for the past two weeks, and the same breakfast he had relished each morning, eating it slowly and savoring every taste, texture, and smell.

For the first . . . what had it been, a week? . . . they hadn't given him any solid food, just herbal tea and later some weak soup. And they had jammed needles into his unresisting body. Not hypodermics, but those acupuncture needles he'd always thought were purest bullshit until the dysentery started to get better. The cramps stopped, the horrendous diarrhea didn't return, and pretty soon he was eating solid food again, including the more-or-less American breakfast that they went to such pains to cook him.

189

He sat up, propped himself against the heavy wooden headboard, and poured a cup of coffee. Jesus, he thought, the heady joy of simple pleasures, such as pouring yourself a damn cup of coffee. The first sip—and he sipped carefully, experience having taught him that they served their coffee *hot*—brought almost overwhelming pleasure. He swished the coffee around in his mouth for a moment before swallowing. Then he got up, tested his shaky legs on the floor, and wobbled to the bathroom. He was still weak, still thin, but he enjoyed the ten-foot trip enormously. It represented great progress in his self-sufficiency.

The bathroom was immaculate. Neal figured that even Joe Graham would approve of its shining porcelain and gleaming tiles. Neal used the john—no small joy after his months of shackles and buckets—then let the water run from the tap until it was steamy hot and scrubbed his hands.

Am I becoming a clean freak, he wondered, like Graham?

He likewise let the shower run while he sat on the closed toilet seat and drank coffee. When he saw steam rise over the shower curtain, he stripped off the silk pajamas and stepped in. He winced as the water stung the raw skin on his wrists, which had been bandaged until just the day before. He spent at least ten minutes scrubbing himself with the sandalwood soap and shampoo before carefully stepping out. He had to sit down for a few minutes before he was strong enough to dry himself off. Then he put his robe back on, carried his tray to the round table by the window, and sat down to eat.

Food seemed like a miracle to him. It all seemed like a miracle.

At first he thought she had come in a dream like all the other dreams. He knew that when he came to, he would still be lying in his cave, handcuffed in his own filth and misery. But this dream was different.

He became terrified when they blindfolded him, even though it was her hand leading him through the maze of the Walled City. He had settled down when he felt himself being eased into a car, and it seemed like a short trip before he was being led along what felt like a gently rocking dock and onto a boat. He realized vaguely that he was being taken below, and then she took the blindfold off.

It was Li Lan, of course. She had come for him, and he didn't ask why—he didn't *care* why. All he knew was that she was his Kuan Yin, his goddess of mercy, and she had taken him out of hell, and now she was giving him another bowl of opium.

He drifted in and out of sleep as the boat eased along the coast. They gave him another pipe before putting the blindfold on, and he had only the haziest memory of being carried onto land and lifted into the back of a truck. She took the blindfold off again when the truck was all closed up, and it seemed as if they drove for days, and it also seemed as if the pipes were smaller and fewer.

He remembered being taken out of the truck in the middle of the night, remembered seeing soldiers, remembered seeing her face, lined with concern, as he felt a sharp jab in his arm.

"I will see you again," she said.

Then he remembered nothing until he woke up in the clean bed with the stiff, white sheets.

And she was gone again.

In her place were doctors and nurses, murmuring in the careful, professional tones that they affect everywhere. They murmured over him, made him sip tea, massaged his sore back, rubbed salve on his wrists and bandaged them, then made him into a human porcupine.

As the days went by, he needed less attention, until he was down to the daily ministrations of the waiter, a masseuse, and one visit from the doctor.

His curiosity rose with his strength. As he emerged from the fog of illness, malnutrition, fear, and opium, the large questions began to strike him: Where am I? Who's in charge here? What happens next?

Nobody would tell him anything. In fact, so far he hadn't met anyone who spoke English, expect for the waiter's obviously rehearsed "Good morning. Breakfast." From his ground-floor window he could see only a rectangular, gravel-surfaced parking lot cut off from the street by a tall gate. A ten-foot high fence, topped by strands of barbed wire and delicately screened by shrubs, stretched to the left into a copse of trees. To the right, it ran into another wing of the building.

Neal knew he was in a city because he could hear traffic noises, although it took him several days to recognize the late-afternoon ca-cophony as the jingling of thousands of bicycle bells. He heard few cars but more trucks, and occasionally the uniformed guard at the gate would swing it open for a delivery truck or an official-looking car.

So, as for where he was, he knew he was in a city somewhere in China.

Who was in charge? Who had him? He tried to put it together. If Li

Lan was, as it seemed, a Chinese spy, then it must be the Chinese intelligence service. But why? Why dump him in the Walled City and then come back for him? Why all the TLC and the first-class treatment—silk pajamas, for Christ's sake? Why did the door lock behind the waiter, the nurse, and the doctor? Why was he in this luxurious solitary confinement?

These musings led to the not-unrelated question of what would happen next. What the hell did they want from him? What did they want him to do? The pleasant thought that they were cleaning him up to send him home occurred to him, but he didn't allow himself to dwell on it. Better to concentrate on getting well, and just see what happened. Besides, what choice did he have?

And there was still another question: Where was Li Lan?

He pushed that thought from his head and dug into his eggs. They really weren't bad at all, almost as if the cook were used to making Western breakfasts, although they had been fried in some kind of oil he couldn't identify. And he had grown quite fond of the *mantou,* the fist-sized steamed bun they served in place of toast. He was chewing on it when the first nonmaterial need he had felt since he could remember hit him: a newspaper.

God, how he suddenly yearned to have a newspaper. Hell, it was a natural. Newsprint went with breakfast like bacon with eggs, and he longed—*longed*—to find out what was happening in the world, and maybe read a little sports news. Sports. Was it still baseball season? Or football? Or that fantastic time of the American calendar when both were in full swing, so to speak?

I must be getting healthy, he thought.

The opium jones had been tough, but not that tough, he considered. Maybe it was because he didn't do enough for long enough to get really addicted, or maybe it was because the Chinese know how to treat it, but he hadn't felt the agonies of withdrawal he had observed in others, including his own sainted mother. Every once in a while, particularly as he recovered enough to feel actual boredom, a pang of need—no, it was more like *want*—struck him, and he would muse on how nice it would be to drift off on an opium cloud. But he was enjoying the real pleasures of real food and real comfort too much to become seriously obsessed with the smoke and mirrors of a dope high. He'd take a good cup of coffee any day, thank you. Now if he could just get a newspaper.

Of course, a newspaper couldn't answer some of the other small questions that niggled at him during his wealth of spare time. Why did everyone call him Mr. Frazier? Why was the closet full of clothes for Mr. Frazier? Why did these clothes have labels from Montreal, Toronto, and New York? Why did they all fit him perfectly? Who was this Mr. Frazier, who had the same size shirts, the same size shoes, the same inseam as his? Neal was strictly an off-the-rack guy, but Mr. Frazier obviously had a close relationship with a pretty good tailor. Neal had never dressed so well in his life.

All dressed up and nowhere to go, Neal thought.

Silk pajamas.

He tried to work up a little indignation about the whole thing, but he was just too tired. He took another sip of coffee, pushed back his chair, and slipped back to bed. He needed more sleep, his head was getting fuzzy, and somewhere in the back of a still-muddled brain, he knew he would need more rest to handle . . . what? He let himself drop into sleep. The waiter would wake him with lunch.

It was a setting for two, and it came early.

Neal knew a hint when he saw one, and changed from his robe into some of the clothes made for the mysterious Mr. Frazier: tan slacks, a light blue sports shirt, and cordovans. He shaved carefully, his shaky hand nicking him only once, and brushed his hair. He had just finished when he heard a timid knock.

A young man stuck his head in the door.

"May I come in?" he asked. His English had only a slight accent.

"Yes. Please."

He was in his early twenties, about five-seven, maybe 120 pounds if he had a lot of change in his pockets. He wore gray trousers that looked like polyester, a stiff white shirt, and a dark brown jacket. He had thick glasses with heavy brown frames. His black hair was thick, parted at the side, and just touched the tops of his ears. His smile looked nervous but warm, and he blushed with shyness.

"My name is Xiao Wu," he said. He stuck his hand out, a gesture that looked as if it had been learned in a class.

Neal shook his hand. "Neal Carey."

Wu's blush turned to scarlet and he dropped his eyes to the floor.

"Frazier," he mumbled.

"Excuse me?"

"Your name is Frazier."

"Okay."

Wu brightened considerably when he saw the heavily laden tray on the table.

"We are having lunch!"

"Please sit down."

"Thank you!" He bowed slightly and took a chair.

"May I examine the food?" he asked.

"Please."

Wu lifted the covers off the four dishes and issued *oohs* and *aahs* and other sighs of satisfaction. Neal decided that this guy didn't get too many business lunches, if indeed that was what this was.

Wu remembered the protocol.

"Are you comfortable?" he asked.

"Very comfortable."

"Thank you!"

Oh, you're very welcome, Xiao Wu.

"Would you like to eat lunch?"

I live for lunch these days, Xiao Wu.

"You bet."

Wu looked puzzled. "Was that a colloquialism?"

Neal nodded.

"Slang?" Xiao smiled broadly.

"Slang."

"I am very interested in American language . . . as distinct from English language," Wu said quietly.

"You and me both."

"Especially American abusive language."

"You've come to the right place, Xiao Wu."

"You will teach me some?"

"Fuck yes."

Wu giggled with unabashed enthusiasm, and repeated "Fuck yes" several times as if to memorize it. Then he uncovered a platter of hot noodles and filled Neal's plate before he filled his own. He didn't wait for Neal to start, however, but started right in on the noodles with his chopsticks, shoveling them down in a few smooth motions.

"I am also very interested," he said when he was done, "in Mark

Twain. Do you know Mark Twain? *Huckleberry Finn?* It is no longer banned, we are allowed to read it in school now."

Swell. *We're* not.

"He's a wonderful writer."

"Aaah. Fish."

"Xiao Wu, who are you and what are you doing here?"

Wu's supply of blushes held up. Direct questions are considered quite rude in China.

"I am to be your translator."

"What for?"

"Would you like some fish?"

Okay, I'll play.

"Sure, why not?"

"No reasons."

"That was slang."

" 'Sure, why not'? That means you would like to eat fish?"

"Fuck yes."

"Fuck yes."

Wu used his chopsticks to place some bits of flesh on Neal's plate, and then spooned bean sauce on top. He then helped himself and concentrated on eating. Then he asked, "You would be ready to accept an important guest this afternoon?"

"Fuck yes."

Wu started to laugh and then stopped himself and frowned. "You must not say that, though, in front of important guest."

"Say what?"

"Fuck."

"Okay."

"It is very funny, though."

"Who's the important guest?"

"Vegetables?"

"You bet your ass."

Wu looked startled, looked at Neal sideways, and said, "More slang."

Neal nodded and Wu dished out the steamed vegetables—broccoli, pea pods, bamboo shoots, and water chestnuts. He ate with the dedication of a true artist.

"Wu, where are we?"

"I am authorized to tell you that."

"Shoot."

Wu chuckled again. "You are in Chengdu," Wu said proudly.

Chengdu . . . Chengdu . . . Chengdu . . .

"Not to offend you, but where is Chengdu?"

Wu's face clouded slightly. "Chengdu is the capital city of Sichuan Province, which is in southwest China."

Southwest China? My, my my . . .

"What day is it?"

Wu quickly checked his mental list of what he was authorized to say. "June the twenty-sixth."

Jesus H. Christ! June twenty-sixth?

"How long have I been here?"

"Two weeks," Wu answered, then added proudly, "and change."

Neal did some mental arithmatic. God, he thought, that means I was in that Hong Kong hellhole for over two months. Two and a half.

"And what am I doing here?"

"Soup?"

"You're not authorized to tell me that."

"I am not," Wu said sadly. "And I don't know."

"But the important guest does?"

"This is why he is important."

"May I have some soup, please?"

"I am honored."

The soup was a delicate chicken broth with some vegetables. Wu pretended not to notice that Neal's hand trembled and that he had a hard time getting the soup into his mouth.

"No fortune cookie?" Neal asked when they were finished with the meal.

"You must not make jokes in front of—"

"Important guest. Don't worry, I won't. It's just that I'm enjoying speaking English. Thank you."

"You are welcome," Wu said. He added shyly, "And I am honored. Perhaps we can later discuss Mark Twain?"

"I would enjoy that very much."

"You must rest now."

"That's all I do."

"Your guest will be here in"—he made a show of looking at his watch—"one and one half an hour."

196

"An hour and a half."

"Yes. Thank you."

Wu stood up and stuck his hand out again. They shook hands and Wu left the room. Neal heard the lock click.

Okay, he thought, I am the mysterious Mr. Frazier. It's possible. Maybe they know something I don't, such as my father's name; maybe it *is* Frazier. You're getting giddy. Settle down. Half an hour of conversation and you're losing your head. Mark Twain. Fuck yes.

Okay, so you know a little more than you did this morning. You're in Chengdu, the capital of Sichuan, southwestern China. You're way up Nathan Road now. So? So they probably wouldn't bring you all this way if they were just going to clean you up and turn you back. And if you've been taken by the intelligence service, why aren't you in Beijing? I mean, does the CIA take defectors to Arizona? I don't know, maybe they do. And they've assigned you a translator, which means they want you to talk to somebody. Or they want somebody to talk to you.

Okay, but what do you have to tell them? They already know more about Li Lan than you do, ditto with Pendleton by now. . . .

Simms.

You can tell them about Simms.

Which brings up an interesting moral dilemma.

The important guest was right on time, almost as if he had been standing in the hallway looking at the second hand on his watch. Neal heard the same timid knock, then the door opened and Wu's head popped in. He looked nervous.

"May we come in?"

"Of course."

Wu held the door open for the important visitor. The important visitor was short, somewhere in his late forties, and was a few noodles shy of being chubby. The fat was really starting to show in heavy circles under his eyes. His hair was greased and combed straight back on his head. He wore a gray business suit, white shirt, red tie, and black shoes. He carried an expensive-looking attaché case. His whole affect screamed "bureaucrat."

"This is Mr. Peng," Wu said. "Mr. Peng, this is Mr. Frazier."

Is this where we toss a coin and I choose to receive?

"Please sit down," Neal said.

Peng sat in one of the chairs and gestured for Neal to take the other. Wu stood behind Peng.

So much for the classless society, Neal thought.

Peng took a pack of cigarettes from his shirt pocket and offered one to Neal. Neal shook his head and Peng lit his cigarette, then looked over his shoulder at Wu and said, *"Cha."*

Wu hustled out into the hallway. Neal heard him talking to somebody, and a minute later he returned with a waiter who carried a tray with tea, coffee, and cups.

"Mr. Peng understands that you prefer coffee to tea," Wu said.

"Mr. Peng's understanding is correct."

"Mr. Peng suggests that we be informal and 'help ourselves.' "

"Absolutely."

Wu poured cups of tea for Peng and himself as Neal took a cup of coffee. Wu tentatively sat down on the corner of the bed and seemed visibly relieved when Peng didn't object. Peng nodded to him, and Wu launched into their prepared opening.

"Mr. Peng is the assistant to Provincial Party Secretary Xao Xiyang."

Neal saw Peng smile with self-satisfaction and wished that he knew a little more about Chinese politics.

"I am honored by his visit," Neal said. "The coffee, by the way, is very, very good."

Wu translated the remarks. Peng smiled again and responded.

"The coffee is from Yunnan," Wu translated, "and he is very happy that you like it."

Neal decided to get things going.

"Please express to Assistant Provincial Party Secretary Peng my gratitude for rescuing me from my dire situation and for taking such wonderful care in bringing me back to health."

Wu translated, listened to the response, and returned Peng's answer. "Mr. Peng says that he is not Assistant Provincial Party Secretary but assistant *to* the Provincial Party Secretary and says that he is merely a humble representative of greater powers, who, he is sure, are honored to be of service to you and would thank you for your gratitude."

Wu let out a sigh of relief at getting the entire answer.

Neal smiled and nodded at Peng.

"Now tell him I want to leave."

Wu thought for a moment, and then said in Chinese, *"He says that his sense of decorum does not allow him to accept any more hospitality from the People's Republic, and he does not wish to be of any more trouble."*

Peng took a drag on his cigarette. *"Bu shr."*

No.

"Mr. Peng says he is afraid that you are not ready to undertake a long journey at this time."

"I know I am in Chengdu, but what is the building, and why am I being held?"

The translation ensued, and Wu said, "You are in the Jinjiang Guest House. It is a hotel."

A hotel? A hotel?!

"Why is the door locked?"

A thin film of sweat started to appear on Wu's forehead as he translated.

Peng smiled and uttered a one-word answer.

"Security," Wu said.

"It is locked from the outside."

Neal wasn't sure, but he saw a flicker of annoyance pass over Peng's face and wondered if he understood the question. Maybe it's just a natural sequence, or the tone.

Wu was quite pleased with the answer. "We are very thorough in the People's Republic of China, especially in regard to the safety of foreign guests."

So that's what I am—a foreign guest.

"I was under the impression," Neal said, "that crime is virtually nonexistent in the People's Republic."

Wu gave him a dirty look and then translated, "Mr. Peng understands that crime is virtually omnipresent in the United States."

"Once again, Mr. Peng's understanding is correct."

Peng smiled broadly at the answer, inhaled some smoke, and then drank some tea. Neal picked up his coffee, sipped at it, and stared over the cup at Peng. Peng stared back. Wu sweated.

"Ask him," Neal said, "if we can cut the shit and get to the point."

He saw Peng flinch slightly at "shit."

"Mr. Frazier suggests that we dispense with polite introductory conversation and commence substantive discussions."

" 'Shit'? He said 'shit'?"

199

"Yes."

Peng made no effort to mask his frown. He puffed on his cigarette and barked a brusque answer.

"Mr. Peng understands that your fatigue and ill health prevent you from exercising proper courtesy."

"He called me an asshole, right?"

"Close."

"Please tell him that I am eager to listen to his wise counsel, and hope that I can learn from his comments."

Neal stared at Peng as Wu translated.

You know you're being bullshitted, Neal thought, and you don't care. All you want is the outward appearance of compliance, not to be shown up.

Peng started to speak in measured bursts, giving Wu time to translate as he went along.

"Mr. Peng's superiors understand that your life has been in some danger, danger from which—as you acknowledge—the People's Republic has rescued you. They further understand that this danger is, to a large degree, of your own making, due to your unfortunate interference in matters that do not concern you."

On the contrary, Mr. Peng. They concern me greatly.

"They also understand that you do not represent the intelligence agencies of your country. If it was felt that you did, the situation would be quite different."

Here it comes, Neal thought. He's about to hit me with Simms.

Peng paused for a drink of tea, then continued.

"The People's Republic wishes to return you to your home as quickly as possible."

As possible.

"This, however, requires certain security procedures."

About which you are very thorough, especially in regard to the safety of foreign guests.

"Such as cleansing your identity."

Cleansing my identity? What the hell does that mean? Does my identity need to make a sincere act of contrition and do fifty-eight Hail Marys?

"Why?" Neal asked.

"Mr. Peng would prefer that you do not interrupt."

"Why?"

Peng sighed and passed the happy word on to Wu, who passed it along to Neal. It was like a game at a dull party.

"Mr. Neal Carey has caused an uproar," Wu explained hesitantly, "and we cannot allow that uproar to be traced in or out of the People's Republic. It would be inconvenient for us and dangerous for you, as certain enemies you have made would find it easier to track you down and do you harm. However, Mr. William Frazier has caused no such uproar."

He's a convenient guy, that Mr. Frazier.

"Okay . . . so?"

"Perhaps, then, it is better to allow people to believe that Mr. Carey died in the treacherous slums of capitalist Hong Kong. Therefore, you will assume the identity of Mr. Frazier. Mr. Frazier is a Canadian in the travel business who is doing research for his company about the many potentials for tourism in Sichuan."

Yeah, right.

"Then what?"

"After completing your research, you will go home."

"Where is 'home'?"

"We have purchased an air ticket to Vancouver. After that, it is up to you."

This is the most chickenshit story I have heard yet in this chickenshit job. The pick of the litter, the best of show . . .

"Why not just fly me out tomorrow? Why go touring?"

Peng was good. Peng didn't miss a beat.

"We wish to establish a strong identity for you. It is more safe."

Boys, boys, boys. I've been running scams on people most of my life, so I know one when it's run across my nose. What is it you need from me? What is there in Sichuan that I have to see? Or that has to see me?

"How long will it take me to complete my research?" Neal asked.

"Perhaps a month."

A month on display, Neal thought. Okay, pick your metaphor. They're going fishing and you're the bait. They're going birdhunting and you're the dog. Well, you owe them one, and anyway, what choice do you have? Besides, maybe it's not a "what" they want you to see. Maybe it's a "who."

Maybe it's Li Lan.

201

"When do I start?" he asked.

Wu's face broke into a relieved grin. Peng was satisfied with a narrow smile and another drag on his cigarette. Then he spoke to Wu.

"Would you feel well enough to start tomorrow?" Wu asked.

"Fuck yes."

"He says his health is much improved."

Fuck yes.

15

Chengdu is the New Orleans of China.

In the States, you go to New York if you want to work. But if you want to play, you go to New Orleans. In China, you go to Beijing if you want to get something done. But if you want to do nothing, you go to Chengdu.

The people of Chengdu have the easy bonhomie common to southerners worldwide, and, like the denizens of New Orleans, they consider their city not so much a municipality within a country as a land of its own. There is considerable justification for this sentiment in Chengdu, which was the capital of the ancient land of Shu some four hundred years before the unification of China. The state of Shu rose again after the fall of the Tang Dynasty, leaving Chengdu and the whole province of Sichuan with an attitude of autonomy considerably frustrating to its would-be rulers in Beijing.

Chengdu has always attracted poets, painters, and artisans. Maybe it's the warm weather or the sunshine. Maybe it's the lush bamboo, or the hibiscus, or the surrounding countryside of fertile rice paddies and wheatfields. Maybe it's the broad boulevards or the black-tiled houses with the carved wood balconies, or the wide sidewalks or the promenades that flank the river called the Silk Brocade. Maybe it's all those things combined with a spirit of independence, but Chengdu loves its artists with a ferocious pride.

And its food. Like New Orleans, people go there to eat, and the natives are always eager to take you places that serve the "real thing." In Chengdu that means outdoor stands that dish up hot noodles, a crowded restaurant that serves bean curd in forty-two different sauces, or a place on the outskirts that makes a hot chicken with peanuts that has inspired poets.

And tea. Before the Cultural Revolution pronounced them decadent, tea pavilions dotted the city. Often in the open air, or under bamboo leave roofs, the teahouses were neighborhood places where the locals gathered to consume vast quantities of green tea, play some mah-jongg, and carry on the exuberant conversations for which Chengdu was famous. They were places where poets sat in corners to write, and where artists sketched and painted. Here in the tea pavilions the natives escaped the summer's afternoon rains and listened to the great storytellers hold forth for hours with much-loved tales from the golden past, stories about flying dragons, or runaway princesses, or the flight of the emperor Tang Hsuan Tsung into the vast wilderness of the western Sichuan mountains.

Of course, Chengdu changed with the revolution, and many of the city's older neighborhoods were sacrificed to the new god of industrialization. A new generation of artists arrived, but their sketches became not paintings but blueprints, and their poetry could only be found in the dull symmetry of utilitarian factories and exhibition halls. The population swelled to a million workers, with three million more laboring in the surrounding industrial suburbs. The city that had once been famous for its silk became renowned for its metals, and the silky softness of the Chengdu spirit was muted with factory soot.

The new regime collectivized the surrounding countryside, replacing the efficient, highly productive estates and small family farms with huge, unwieldy communes. For the first time within memory or legend, the province knew hunger. During the Great Leap Forward the city itself avoided mass famine, but, ironically, the roads to the countryside were clogged with starving refugees from the Rice Bowl districts outside the city. Mao himself visited in 1957 to discuss his economic strategy with local agricultural experts. He told them to meet their quotas.

After a brief respite of normality, the Cultural Revolution erupted, first in Beijing, then in Shanghai, and then in Guangzhou, as Mao sought to destroy his government and replace it with the "permanent revolution." It seemed to happen overnight in Chengdu; its urbane, insouciant people awoke one morning to find the "big character posters" in the schools, then in the streets, and then in government hallways. A Chengdu unit of the Red Guard formed, tore down the ancient city walls as atavistic reminders of feudalism, destroyed the decadent exhibitions of paintings, vandalized the park dedicated to the great poet Du Fu, and then closed the teahouses. The city's trademark smile became a rictus of paranoia as friend betrayed friend, son betrayed father, daughter betrayed mother, and the community betrayed itself. In the darker corners of the narrower streets the mutterings of secession started as the Red Guard splintered into competing factions. The city smoldered.

The fire exploded in 1967, when the rival groups of Red Guards waged pitched battles for possession of factories, post offices, and train stations. Machine-gun fire flashed across the Silk Brocade River, tanks rumbled down the boulevards, gasoline bombs tumbled from the carved balconies. The older people stayed inside and left the city to its youth, who fought each other in a frenzy of violence to determine who loved Chairman Mao the most. The city burned.

Even Mao had seen enough, and he ordered his young worshipers to cease fighting and respect authority. They had a hard time squaring this request with "permanent revolution" and decided that Mao was being coerced by treasonous bureaucrats, so they took the revolution up a couple of notches and attacked police stations and government buildings. Mao sent the army, and the People's Liberation Army rolled into Chengdu to put down the insurgency. The Red Guard resisted. Thousands were killed. Many of the survivors were sent to prison, or sentenced to labor camps, or packed off into the countryside to learn firsthand about the life of the masses. The city put on the ashes of mourning.

Years of sullen silence followed. Artists stopped painting, poets produced no verse, the great storytellers were either wise enough to tell no stories or told them to themselves inside their cells. The once-unbuttoned city buttoned itself up tightly and waited for this long afternoon rain to end.

*　　*　　*

Neal Carey heard a lot about Chengdu's history from Xiao Wu. Xiao Wu talked nonstop for three straight days as he took Neal around to every sight of any possible significance in the greater Chengdu area. It was marathon tourism, an endurance event. Neal wondered if Wu was just that proud of his hometown, or whether it was William Frazier that was on display and not the city. Maybe Wu was just drunk with the power of having a car, a driver, and the chance to practice his English.

Not that Neal minded all that much. Cooped up as he had been for three months, it felt great to be out in the warm sun, and if the sultry summer air wasn't exactly invigorating, it wasn't exactly painful either. And it felt wonderful to walk. At first his leg muscles sent him messages in the form of pins and needles, and he needed to rest a lot. But after the first morning he found that he and Xiao Wu were taking longer jaunts away from the government car, and that his legs seemed to be waking up from their long sleep.

And they did cover some ground, because Wu seemed unwilling for his guest to miss a single temple, shrine, park, panda, or rare bamboo plant in the city.

Some of it was great, like on that first wonderful morning. He had sprung out of bed like a kid at Christmas, bolted breakfast down, and was dressed and ready half an hour before Wu knocked on the door. Wu was excited also. This was his first important assignment, he explained, and he also confessed that it would be only the second time he had ever ridden in a private automobile. He hurried Neal through the hotel lobby and into the waiting car. The driver was a middle-aged man in a green Mao jacket, and he went to such great lengths not to appear to be listening that Neal made him for a fink right off the bat.

Wu launched into his soliloquy right away.

"You can now see the outside of the Jinjiang Guest House," he said before the driver started the engine.

"It's nice to see the outside of something," Neal said. Even the Jinjiang Guest House, which was a boring rectangular concrete box.

"The Russians designed it," Wu said, as if reading Neal's mind. He leaned over the seat and gave some directions to the driver, then looked at Neal with an expression that could only be described as "thrilled." It occurred to Neal that he thought of Xiao Wu as a kid, even though they were roughly the same age.

That first morning they drove west along the north bank of the Nan

River to Caotang Park, "home of the great Tang Dynasty poet Du Fu," Wu explained as they got out of the car in a small parking lot surrounded by tall bamboo trees. They walked for few minutes and came to a small shrine beside a narrow creek. Wu explained that the shrine had been built to honor Du Fu, and that the only reason it wasn't torn down by the Red Guard was that Mao had once written two lines of verse honoring the ancient poet.

"He was born in 712 and died in 770, but the shrine was not built until sometime around the year 1100."

Neal flipped through his mental reference cards. Du Fu was writing poetry around the time of Charlemagne, and this shrine had been built to honor him around the time William the Conqueror had fought the battle of Hastings. When my Irish ancestors were running around in skins, Wu's people were building a shrine to a poet because they had been reciting his work for four hundred years.

They lingered in the shrine for an hour, looking at a collection of landscape paintings that had been "lost" during the Cultural Revolution and had just recently been "found" and put on display. Neal thought briefly about Li Lan and wondered if she had ever stood here looking at these paintings. He shoved the thought out of his head and asked Wu to translate some of the other poems that were inscribed on wooden plaques. Wu did, and it turned out that old Du Fu was a dour fellow who wrote mostly about war, loss, and dislocation.

"He lived in a time of great chaos," Wu said.

They wandered around the park for the rest of the morning. Wu dutifully recited the name of every plant and bird, although Neal could tell it didn't interest him much. After a quick alfresco lunch of noodles, they got back into the car and drove to another park.

"Nanjiao Park," Wu said. "Site of the shrine to Zhu Geliang."

Neal knew his cue.

"Who was Zhu Geliang?"

"Come see."

They walked a path through a lush garden to a large, imperial red shrine where a large painted statue of a soldier sat complacently.

"Zhu Zeliang was a great military strategist during the Three Kingdoms era that followed the demise of the Han Dynasty. Chengdu was the capital city of one of the Three Kingdoms, the state of Shu Han."

"When was this?"

"Zhu lived from 181 to 234, but the shrine was not built until the Tang Dynasty."

"About the time Du Fu was writing."

"You have a good memory. Yes, that is correct. Chairman Mao had the shrine completely repaired in 1952. He was a great admirer of Zhu Geliang's military thought, and he would send young officers here to learn from Zhu's writings."

Sure enough, Neal thought as he looked around, there were a number of PLA officers scribbling earnestly in their notebooks from plaques on the wall. Neal found himself staring at them and getting sidelong glances in return. But there they were, he marveled, taking notes directly from writings that were almost two thousand years old.

Wu walked him around the park, again pointing out the various flora and fauna. They strolled the edges of ponds that had fallen into disrepair and were just now being revived. Then they stopped for tea at a newly reopened pavilion that needed some roof patching and a good cleaning. But the few customers who were there on this working day didn't seem to care. It was enough to get a cup of green tea and sit at the bamboo tables as a waitress came along with a kettle of hot water for refills.

Wu let the water steep in his lidded cup for a minute or so, and then poured the contents on the ground. The dark green tea leaves stuck to the bottom of the cup. The waitress refilled it, and Wu waited another minute before repeating the process. After the next refill, he let the cup sit for a few more minutes, removed the lid, and took a deep sip. Then he smiled with satisfaction.

"The first time, it's water," he said. "The second time, it's garbage. The third time, it's tea."

They drank a few cups, talked about *Huckleberry Finn* and *Innocents Abroad,* complained about the vicissitudes of college life. Turned out that Wu was a recent graduate of Sichuan University, where he had studied tourism. His father had been a professor of English, had been in jail for it, and was now a room service waiter in a Chengdu hotel. But the authorities, realizing that they would need English-speakers to service the tourist trade they now coveted, pulled Wu's file from a thousand others and admitted him to university. A job with CITS, the China International Travel Service, followed straight away. Wu's great ambition was to become a "National Guide," one of the elite cadre who escorted tourist groups for their entire stay in the country.

"Right now," he explained, "I am just a local guide, authorized for Sichuan only. But I would very much like to see the rest of China, especially Beijing and Xian."

"They put your father in jail for teaching English?" asked Neal, who knew a few English teachers who could profit from the experience.

"For *speaking* English."

"Why?"

Wu shrugged.

"Cultural Revolution," he said, as if the phrase explained everything.

"Do you think he'll ever get his teaching job back?"

"Perhaps."

I guess they don't have tenure in China, Neal thought. In the States, once a professor got tenure, you couldn't fire him if he buggered a goat on his desk during a lecture. You couldn't get him out of that professional chair with a tow chain and an ox. But here you had English professors getting the sack for . . . speaking English.

"So what do you think about Mao now?" Neal asked.

Mao now? How now, Mao?

Wu stared at the table. "He liberated the nation, but he made some mistakes, I think."

Wu was so clearly uncomfortable talking about it that Neal let it drop. It wasn't the time to push. At this pace, there'd be plenty of time for that later. Nobody seemed to be in any hurry, that was for sure. What were they waiting for, he wondered.

Wu must have figured the conversation had gone on long enough, because he brought them back to touring with a vengeance. They hit the Cultural Park and the tomb of Wang Jian, a Tang Dynasty mercenary and self-styled emperor. They dropped in on the Center of Traditional Chinese Medicine, which served to refresh Neal's memory of his bout with acupuncture. They wrapped the afternoon up with a visit to the People's Park, where seemingly thousands of would-be swimmers were jammed shoulder-to-shoulder in three Olympic-size pools.

"You sure have a lot of parks in this town."

"Chengdu people like to relax."

They were driving back to the hotel when Wu casually pointed out the Xinhua Bookstore.

"The what?" Neal asked. "Did you say 'bookstore'?"

"Xinhua Bookstore, yes."

"Stop the car."

Neal noticed that the driver hit the brake just a half-second before Wu gave the instruction.

"Let's walk," Neal said.

"You are not tired?"

"Suddenly I have all sorts of energy."

Wu told the driver to meet him in the hotel lot.

"Xiao Wu," Neal said as the driver pulled away, "do they sell English books here?"

Wu said, "They only sell textbooks at the university."

"No, I mean books in English. Novels, short stories, the dreaded nonfiction."

Wu shuffled his foot on the sidewalk. "Perhaps."

"Come on, Wu."

"I am not authorized to take you there."

"Were you ordered *not* to take me there?"

Wu brightened. "Noooo . . ."

"Wu . . . Wu, I haven't had anything to read in three months. Do you know what that's like?"

"Are you joking? Cultural Revolution?"

"So help me, Wu."

"I don't know."

"I'll tell you my best abusive words."

"Like what?"

"Cocksucker."

Neal watched anxiously as Wu put the compound together and a glimmer of understanding came to his eyes.

"Cocksucker," Wu intoned, his eyes widening. "Does that mean—"

"Yup."

Wu burst into a hysterical giggle. He repeated the word several times, each repetition sending him into a fresh paroxysm of laughter. He was bent over double on the sidewalk, oblivious to the stares of passersby, muttering "cocksucker" until he cried.

"And that is an abusive term?" he asked when he had caught his breath.

"Oh, you bet."

"In Chinese . . . *tsweh-tsuh.*"

"*Tsweh-tsuh.*"

That set him off again, and his fresh hysteria set Neal off, and they both stood on the sidewalk laughing until their stomachs hurt and they couldn't laugh anymore.

"Okay, cocksucker," Wu said. "Let's go to the bookstore."

Bookstore. *Bookstore.* Wu might as easily have said "Paradise" or "Heaven." Neal breathed it in as he went through the door. The smell of books, that clean paper smell, filled his nostrils and went straight to his brain. He looked around at the shelves filled with books—all in Chinese, all absolutely incomprehensible to him—and then went around touching them. He stroked their spines, and felt their covers, and examined them as if he understood their titles and could read their pages.

Wu went over to the checkout counter and had a quiet conversation with the clerk. Neal felt his heart sink when the clerk shook his head vigorously, but Wu kept talking patiently and quietly, and a few minutes later he had procured a key.

"Come on," he said. "There are some English books in the storeroom. Try not to look so . . . obvious."

Wu opened the door and Neal stepped into heaven. Hundreds of paperbacks filled some cheap metal shelves and were piled up on the floor.

"I love you, Wu."

"Cocksucker."

"I'll take them all."

"Just one. And hurry, please."

"Cocksucker."

They were mostly medical texts. Wu explained that there had been a medical college that had once been staffed by Americans and Canadians. But there were also some volumes of fiction. Melville's *Billy Budd,* Hawthorne's *The Scarlet Letter,* and Twain's *Huckleberry Finn* had found spots on the shelves amid the anatomy tests and emergency-aid manuals.

"Any Hemingway? Fitzgerald?"

"Decadent."

Then Neal spotted a pile of books in the corner. All Penguin Classics. Goddamn, he thought, could it be? Could I get so lucky? He attacked the pile like a rat in a garbage can. *Bleak House . . . Oliver Twist . . . Bleak House* again. *Jude the Obscure . . .* fucking *Beowulf . . .*

Then there it was. Unbelievably, in the middle of Chengdu, capital of Sichuan Province, southwestern China . . . Tobias Smollett . . . *Roderick Random.* There is a God and he loves me, Neal thought. He grabbed the book before it could disappear into an opium dream.

"This is it," he said.

"I never heard of it."

"You will."

"Good. Let's go."

"I want two books."

"Not safe. Too obvious."

"Please."

"Perhaps not."

"Have I told you about 'motherfucker'?"

"But two is all."

Neal took the copy of *Huckleberry Finn* off the shelf.

"Do you own it?" he asked.

Wu flushed. "No."

"Please. My gift."

"I am honored." Wu bowed deeply and quickly. "Now let's go."

Wu picked up two thin Chinese books in the main room and sandwiched the English volumes between them before he brought them to the counter. He took the appropriate amount of cash from Neal's wallet, paid the bill, and walked quickly out into the sunshine.

"Thank you so very much for the book," he said.

"Thank you so very much for bringing me here. Is it a problem? And is the book safe for you to have?"

"I think so, now."

Wu escorted Neal back to his room and said he would pick him up again at nine the next morning. Lest Neal have any illusions about his role, he heard the lock click with the shutting door.

The human mind is a funny thing, Neal thought. When he was lying in shackles in the Walled City, all he wanted was to get out of there. He would have given anything he had—his heart, mind, and soul—for salvation from that hellhole. When Li Lan had come, he had wept with relief and gratitude. In the long, sleepy days of his confinement he had simply given in to the care and comfort until first his body and then his mind came back.

But now his mind *was* back, and the funny thing was that it wasn't happy. He had all the necessities, all the creature comforts he had longed for in Hong Kong. He was well treated, out of danger—he even had books to read—but his mind started to think about other things.

First there was Joe Graham. When Neal had left him on the San Francisco street, he had thought it would be a matter of days or weeks, not months, before he would contact his mentor. Graham must be going crazy with worry, Neal thought. If he knew Graham—and he knew Graham—the leprechaun would have dogged him to Hong Kong, maybe even tracked him as far as the Walled City, maybe even now would be making deals to try to find him and get him out. But even Graham couldn't make this jump, couldn't have any way of finding out that he was sitting in Chengdu with a different identity, a prop in some sort of show-and-tell game run by his jailer-hosts.

Second, what was the game? He didn't buy this identity-wash bit for a second. They had him here for a reason, and Neal was beginning to think they were stalling before deciding just what that reason was. Maybe they were waiting for further developments, waiting for another move in the game to see which way they'd move him.

Which was the third thing that was troubling him. He had become a game piece, a passive pawn that other people moved around at their whim or will. Shit, he hadn't done anything active since his rooftop bomber routine on Waterloo Road. They had beat him, knocked the confidence out of him, and he was just starting to recover from it. It was time to get back in the game. Time to do something to get his own life back.

With his copy of *Roderick Random* and a pen, he got to work. He was still working when the waiter came with his dinner tray. Having devoured the meal, he took the book with him to read while he soaked in an almost scalding bath, and then went back to work at his table. He took the book with him to bed, and woke up with it on his chest when the waiter rattled the breakfast tray.

"Are you taking him out again today?" Xao asked. He lit his second cigarette of the early morning.

"Yes, Comrade Secretary," Peng answered.

"And no surveillance appeared yesterday?"

"Only our own."

"You are quite sure?"

"Yes, Comrade Secretary."

Oh, yes, Comrade Secretary, I am quite sure. None appeared because I ordered none.

Xao inhaled the smoke and worried. On the face of it, it was good that no government surveillance had picked up their "Mr. Frazier," but faces often lied. And young Frazier's American friends were raising quite a fuss in Hong Kong. Why had it not reached Beijing? If it had, they would arrest Frazier as soon as he appeared above ground. We certainly trotted him around enough yesterday. Better to be safe and put Mr. Frazier on display a bit more. If the security police picked him up, there would still be time to dig Li Lan and Pendleton in deeper. If the police were truly unaware of Frazier's true identity, then the rest of the operation could be activated.

"Show him around the city again today," Xao ordered. "If all stays quiet, take him to the countryside tomorrow."

"Yes, Comrade Secretary."

"Good morning."

Peng turned on his heel with the curt dismissal. Perhaps Comrade Secretary Xao will learn more courtesy when I have the opportunity to interrogate him. Perhaps I shall ask him to light my cigarettes and watch me smoke them.

But first to put them all together—the woman, the scientist, and the persistent young American. Yes, gather them at the scene of Xao's intended treason, these three strands of the rope with which Xao will hang himself.

Patience, he cautioned himself. Move slowly. Let Xao think it is safe.

Xao waited until Peng had left and then called in his driver.

"How is it?" Xao asked.

"Wu and the American get on well. They are becoming friends."

"Good. Good. You will be their driver again today."

The driver nodded deferentially. Xao handed him the pack of cigarettes and motioned him out the door.

I would have more men like him, Xao thought, instead of that snake Peng. He is not clever enough to win, just clever enough to cost me resources and trouble. But he has his uses.

"Good morning, cocksucker," Wu said.

"Good morning, motherfucker."

214

Wu giggled with delight and opened the car door for Neal.

"Today we see the east side of the city," Wu announced.

They started with the zoo.

Neal Carey liked a zoo as much as the next guy, provided the next guy thought that they were among the most depressing places on earth. He understood that they were necessary, probably even beneficial, in that they were used to breed species that mankind had succeeded in almost wiping out. He also knew that the animals in zoos spent their days pretty much the way their cousins did in the wild, sleeping and eating. There was just something about looking into cages—or even over the hedges and moats that the enlightened Chengdu Zoo featured—at the individuals of another species, that downright demoralized him.

Nevertheless, he feigned polite interest at the golden monkeys, the speckled deer, and the gibbon apes that led up to the featured attraction, Sichuan's own giant pandas. The two pandas had their own entire section, an "environment" of rocks and bamboo separated from the admiring public by a high railing and a moat. The pandas didn't actually do much, just sat there eating bamboo and looking back at the gawkers.

Wu was quite enthusiastic and gave Neal a thorough rundown on the history, physiology, and behavior of the giant panda, as well as on the government's efforts to save it from extinction. This was followed by a complete history of the Chengdu Zoological Association and its tribulations during the Cultural Revolution. Even the pandas had not been immune from political analysis, and might well have been liquidated as a symbol of bourgeois preoccupation with pets had not it shared a name with the Chairman—the Chinese name for panda being "bear cat," *Shr Mao*—and hence been immune from criticism. It was true that certain radical Red Guards had seen the zookeepers' confinement of the panda as symbolic of the bureaucracy's hemming in of Mao Tse-Tung, and demanded that the pandas be set free, but the zookeepers trumped them with an offer to release the pandas along with all the other *mao,* such as lions, leopards, and tigers, on the condition that the Red Guard open these cages themselves. The Guard declined.

"Too bad," Wu muttered. "I would like to have seen those bastards try to put a dunce cap on a tiger."

"Did they do that to your father?" Neal asked.

"Yes."

215

"I'm sorry."

"It doesn't matter."

Neal didn't answer, but from the hard, angry look on Wu's face he knew that it mattered. Big time.

They strolled through the zoo for a while longer, eating peanuts in place of lunch as Wu described the natural history, habitat, and folklore of every animal in the zoo.

"I never knew my father," Neal said as they neared the parking lot.

"You are a . . . bastard?" Wu asked. He was shocked, not only by the fact, but that Neal would choose to reveal it.

"Yeah."

"I am sorry."

"It doesn't matter."

Wu shook his head. "In China, family is everything. We are not so much individuals as we are family. A person will happily sacrifice his life to ensure that the family survives. Do you have no family?"

"No family," answered Neal. Unless, he thought, you counted Joe Graham and Ed Levine, Ethan Kittredge, and Friends of the Family.

"No brothers or sisters?"

"Not that I know about."

"That is very sad."

"Not if you don't know any different."

I guess.

"Perhaps not."

Wu was quiet as they drove away from the zoo, and he provided only cursory narration for the scenery of apartment blocks and factories that made up the northeastern part of the city. He brightened a little as they came to Sichuan University.

"What university did you attend?" he asked.

"Columbia, in New York City."

"Ah," said Wu politely, although he had clearly never heard of it. "What did you study?"

"Eighteenth-century English literature."

"Qing Dynasty."

"If you say so."

"I have read some Shakespeare."

"Oh, yeah? Which?"

"*Julius Caesar*. It concerns the oppression of the masses by first a militarist dictator and then a capitalist oligarchy."

"Are you kidding?"

"No."

"Do you believe all that?"

"Of course."

"So what is *Huckleberry Finn* about?"

"Slavery and the rejection of bourgeois values. What do you think it is about?"

"A boy on a river."

"Whose thinking is correct?"

"You have your interpretation and I have mine. One isn't any better or worse than the other. We're both right."

Wu chuckled and shook his head. "What you say is impossible. Thought is either correct or incorrect. Two different interpretations cannot be right. One must be right and the other wrong."

"They'd love you at Columbia."

"Yes?"

"Fuck yes."

Wu laughed but then looked serious and said, "You are joking with me, but I think this is the difference between our two cultures. I believe that wrong thought leads to wrong action. Therefore, it is very important that people be taught correct thought. Otherwise, how will they know how to act correctly? I think in your society, you believe that it is bad to insist on correct thought, but then, because your people do not have correct thoughts, they perform bad actions. This is why you have so much crime and we do not."

Neal almost answered that it is also why China could have a Cultural Revolution and the States couldn't, but he stopped. He didn't want to hurt Wu's feelings.

"We just don't believe that there is only one way to think."

"Exactly."

"I have a correct thought," Neal said.

"What is it?"

"Let's go out for dinner tonight. Can you arrange it?"

"I do not have money," Wu said unabashedly.

"I do," Neal said. Mr. Frazier had come to China loaded.

217

"I think that your thought is a correct one, then," Wu answered. "Would you like to eat at the Hibiscus?"

"Wherever you say."

"It is the best."

"The Hibiscus it is."

But before the Hibiscus, there was more touring. They hit the Cultural Palace, the People's Market, and the River View Pavilion, where an enormous terrace overlooked the Min River. It seemed to Neal that they were covering the entire city, putting shoe leather to every public place; the whole scene reminded him of a fisherman who casts his lure all over the pond, hoping for the big fish to strike.

But that's okay, he thought, because I'm going to be the first bait in history that catches both the fish and the fisherman.

"Chengdu is the best place to eat in China," Wu said. He had tossed back more than one *maotai*. "And the Hibiscus is the best place to eat in Chengdu."

Neal wouldn't argue with that. The decor wasn't much; in fact, it looked like any Chinese restaurant you might wander into in Providence, Rhode Island, if you were more interested in getting laid than in getting moo goo gai pan. You walked in a narrow doorway off the street into a minuscule lobby. A door to the right led to a large dining room packed with round tables with plastic covers. Neal started through that door, but Wu explained that the room was only for Chinese citizens; foreign guests ate in private dining rooms upstairs.

"What's the difference?" Neal asked.

"Privacy."

Yeah, right. Privacy and the prices. Not that he really cared, the Chinese having given him the money to be Mr. Frazier in the first place.

So they climbed the stairs to a room about the size of a large den. There were three tables, but only one of them had been set. A white linen tablecloth set off the black dishes, and black enameled chopsticks with blue and gold cloisonné were set on the plates. Linen napkins were rolled in black rings, and small black china cups completed the setting. The walls had been whitewashed recently, and several charcoal sketches of bamboo leaves and hibiscus blossoms on framed rice paper had been hung. The plank floor had been painted in black enamel, and someone had gone to some trouble to carry out a "theme" with limited means.

218

Neal didn't think the rat that scurried across the shiny floor was part of the theme, but he pretended not to notice it and took his seat in the black wooden chair offered by the waiter. Anyway, he thought, nobody from New York had any right to be picky about rats in restaurants.

And rats always seem to know the best places, because the food was fantastic. The banquet started with a single cup of a tea that Neal had never tasted before, followed by a shot of *maotai*. Neal could see that Wu wasn't much a drinker, because his face turned scarlet and he had to work hard to suppress a coughing fit. Neal hadn't had a taste of booze in four months, and it felt good—like getting a letter from an old friend.

The drinks preceded a parade of hors d'oeuvres: pickled vegetables, small *mantou* with meat centers, dumplings filled with pork, and several other items that Neal didn't recognize and was afraid to ask about. Wu exercised the proper protocol by selecting the best tidbits and putting them on Neal's plate, a task that became more complicated as the shots of *maotai* went south. The last appetizers were the little pastries of red bean paste that Neal remembered from Li Lan's dinner.

Then came the main courses: sliced duck, chunks of twice-cooked pork, a whole fish in brown sauce, steamed vegetables, a bowl of cold noodles in sesame sauce . . . the courses interspersed with small bowls of thin broth that cooled the mouth and cleared the palate. Somewhere in there, two or three more *maotais* sacrificed their lives for the greater good, and then the waiter brought out a dish of chicken with red peppers and peanuts—another one of Li Lan's greatest hits. Neal was beginning to pray that the Hibiscus didn't have a hot tub when the waiters brought out a tureen of hot and sour soup and then a big bowl of rice.

Neal watched Wu scoop up globs of the sticky rice and rub them in the sauces of the previous dishes. He did the same and found it was a delightful recap of the whole meal, a gustatory album of a recent memory. Wu looked as happy as a politician with a blank check.

Wu polished off his rice, leaned across the table, and said, "I have a secret to tell you."

"You're really a woman?"

Wu giggled. He wasn't drunk, but he wasn't sober either. "That is the best meal I have ever eaten in my whole life."

"I won't tell your mother."

"That is not the secret."

"Oh."

"The secret is—I have never eaten here before."

"That's okay. Neither have I."

Wu broke up on that one, but when he stopped laughing he turned terribly earnest. "Why must a foreign guest come before a Chinese can eat like this?"

"I don't know, Xiao Wu."

"It is an important question."

"You could eat downstairs, right? Same food."

Wu shook his head angrily, then looked around to see if anyone was listening. "I cannot afford it. Only party cadres can afford it."

"Home cooking is better anyway, right?"

"Do you think we can afford to eat like this at home?" Wu asked indignantly. "We have no money for pork, for duck. Even good rice is very expensive. This food is for festivals only, sometimes for a birthday. . . ."

He trailed off into silence.

"Let's go get blasted, Xiao Wu."

Wu was still smoldering in resentment. "Blasted?"

"Blasted. Hammered. Spiflicated. Shit-faced."

"Shit-faced?!"

Wu was fighting a grin and losing.

"Shit-faced. Bombed. Intoxicated."

"*Shit-faced?!*"

He was off and giggling.

"Drunk."

"It is frowned upon."

"Who cares?"

"Responsible persons."

"No. Cocksuckers and motherfuckers."

That did it. Wu was doubled over in his chair, gasping for air and mumbling, "Shit-faced."

"Where can we go?" Neal asked.

Wu suddenly got serious. "We have to go back to the hotel."

"Is there a bar there?"

"On the roof. There is a noodle bar."

"I don't want any more noodles, I want us to get shit—"

"They serve beer."

Neal signaled the waiter. "Check, please!"

Dinner should be surprises, Neal recalled as he and Wu finished off the last cup of tea at the Hibiscus Restaurant.

The meal wasn't surprising. Li Lan had made several of the same dishes in the Kendalls' kitchen in Mill Valley, although not as well.

"Were all these dishes Sichuan specialties?" Neal asked Wu.

"Oh, yes. Very distinctive. In fact, Chengdu is the only place in the entire world where you can eat some of these dishes."

Not exactly, Wu, Neal thought. You can suck down this home cooking in Kendall's dining room in Mill Valley, provided your chef is Li Lan.

They walked the two blocks back to the hotel. A cop stopped them at the entrance. More accurately, he stopped Wu, and spoke to him brusquely.

"What's up?" Neal asked.

"He wants to see my papers."

"What for? I'm the foreigner."

"Exactly. It is natural you would be in the hotel. Not natural for Chinese."

The cop was starting to look impatient, annoyed. It was the same imperious look that Neal recognized from small-minded cops everywhere.

Neal asked, "But you've been here all week, right?"

"Through the back door."

Neal saw the look of painful embarrassment on Wu's face. He was being humiliated, and he knew it. He fumbled in his wallet for his identification card.

"He's my guest," Neal said to the cop.

The cop ignored him.

Neal got right in his face. "He's my guest."

"Please do not cause trouble," Wu said flatly as he handed the cop his card. The cop took his sweet time looking it over.

"It's no trouble," Neal said.

"It is for me."

Right, Neal thought. I'm going home. Maybe.

"You mean to tell me you can't walk into a hotel in your own country?"

"Please be quiet."

"Does he understand English?"

"Do you?"

The cop shoved the card at Wu and nodded him in. No apology, no smile of recognition, just a curt nod of the imperial head. Wu's own head was down as he walked through the lobby. Neal knew that he had just seen his friend lose face, and it made him furious and sad.

"I'm sorry about that," Neal said as they got into the elevator.

"It doesn't matter."

"Yes it does! It matters a—"

"Let's just get shit-faced."

The noodle bar surprised Neal. It had an almost Western feel of the dreaded decadence. The lights were low, the small tables had red paper covers and lanterns, and the entire south wall was composed of windows and sliding glass doors to give a spectacular view of the Nan River and the city beyond. A wide-open terrace had tables and scattered lounge chairs, and you could lean over the balcony railing to see the street fourteen floors below. The bar itself ran at least half the length of the large room, and it looked like a real bar. Glasses hung upside down from ceiling racks, bottles of beer cooled in tanks of ice, liquor bottles glistened on the back wall, and wooden stools provided plenty of spots to belly up. Off to the side, a cook fried noodles on a small grill, but the whole noodle bit was clearly just a gimmick to get past the bureaucracy. The operative word in "noodle bar" was *Bar*.

There weren't many customers. A few cadre types were smoking cigarettes, drinking beer, and having a quiet conversation at one table, while a few Japanese businessmen sat silently at the bar. The tone was subdued but not sullen. It had the feel of any late weeknight in any bar in any city in the world, and Neal had to remind himself that it was only ten o'clock. The place closed at ten-thirty.

Neal dragged Wu to the bar, lifted a finger to the bartender, and said, "Two cold ones."

The bartender looked to Wu.

"*Ar pijiu.*"

The bartender popped open two bottles and set them on the bar. Neal tossed some Chinese bills down. Wu retrieved a couple and handed them back to Neal.

"Plenty," he said.

"Let's go out on the terrace."

"Okay."

They stood against the balcony wall and looked out at Chengdu. Lack of electric power made the city lights relatively dim, but their low glow made the night soft and somehow poignant. A few old-style lanterns shone in the windows of the stucco houses of the old neighborhood, while behind them the low electric lights in the new prosaic high-rise apartments made geometric patterns in the night sky. Just across Hongxing Road the Nan River made a lazy S-curve, and the lamps of a few houseboats reflected in the water.

The soft night took the edge off Neal, and the urge to get drunk left him as suddenly as it had come. He felt a little ashamed, too, about leading Wu into trouble. Better just to have a couple of beers, talk a little Mark Twain, and leave it at that.

Anyway, he thought, the kid isn't used to alcohol, and you're not in drinking shape anyway. Maybe they'll let you take a scotch back to your room.

He knocked back a long slug of the domestic Chinese beer and found that it wasn't bad. Wu didn't seem to mind it, either, sipping at it steadily as he drank in the view.

"Can we see your house from here?" Neal asked him.

"Other direction." He was still smarting from the scene at the door, nursing a grudge along with the beer.

Maybe that isn't all that bad, Neal thought. If I were him, I'd have a hell of a grudge, too, and it might be better to nurse it than to forget it. Come to think of it, I *do* have a hell of a grudge, and I'm not going to forget it either.

"Beautiful city," Neal said.

"Fuck yes."

"You want another beer?"

"I'm not finished this one yet."

"You will be by the time I get back."

Neal held up his empty bottle in one hand and two fingers in the other. The bartender responded with the requisite two brews and even made change for Neal. The cadres at the one table stopped their conversation to stare at Neal as he walked past.

"Hi, guys," he said.

They didn't answer.

Neal handed Wu his fresh bottle. "Here's to Mark Twain."

223

"Mark Twain."

"And Du Fu."

"Du Fu."

"And here's to Mr. Peng, who's coming through the door."

Peng nodded a hello to the boys at the table and came out on the terrace. He looked pissed off, and the sight of Wu with a beer bottle in his hand didn't do anything to improve his mood. He spoke rapidly to Wu and then stood looking at Neal.

"He is happy you are enjoying your evening."

Meaning exactly the opposite, Neal thought.

"If he's happy, I'm thrilled," Neal answered.

"He says to pack your bags tonight."

Neal felt his heart racing. Maybe they were going to put him on a plane.

"You will be gone for three days," Wu continued.

"Where?"

"Dwaizhou Production Brigade."

"What's that? A factory?"

"No. It is in the countryside, perhaps one hundred miles south of Chengdu. You would call it a commune."

"A collectivized farm."

"As you say."

"It's a tourist thing?"

Peng spoke quickly.

"Foreign guests love to see production brigades," Wu translated. "This is one of Sichuan's best. Highly productive."

Swell. They're finished displaying me in the city, so we're taking a weekend in the country. What for? More Mr. Frazier bullshit?

"How are you going to keep me down on the farm, after I've seen Chengdu?"

"What?"

"Nothing. Do me a favor, Xiao Wu? Last call is coming. Go to the bar and get us three beers?"

"I don't think—"

Peng told him to go. He and Neal stood staring at each other for a few seconds.

"Let's cut the translation crap, okay?" Neal said.

Peng smiled narrowly. "As you wish."

224

"What's the game here?"

"I have gone to great lengths to explain that."

"You have gone to great lengths to avoid explaining that."

"Things are not always what they appear."

"Grasshopper."

"Pardon me?"

"Nothing. Come on, Peng, what's the deal? Why are we going to the country?"

"You do not wish to go?"

"What are we talking about here?"

"Your returning home. The sooner you go on this trip, the sooner you can go home. Of course, if you wish to delay . . ."

"I'll be packed and ready."

Wu returned with the beers and stood on the edge of their conversation. He edged forward when he saw that they had stopped speaking, and offered the beers.

"I do not drink beer," Peng said. It wasn't a comment, it was an order.

"Yes," said Wu, setting the beers on a table, "it is late and we must start early in the morning."

Neal scooped up the beers. "I'll just take them to my room, then."

"That is against the law," said Peng.

"Arrest me," answered Neal. He popped Wu on the shoulder and walked out the bar. He could feel Peng's glare on his back, and it felt great.

Peng was furious. Until his conversation with the arrogant, rude young American, his evening had been going quite well. Persuading Comrade Secretary Xao to send Carey into the countryside had been ludicrously easy.

"I think we had better bring him closer to the asset," he'd told the secretary.

"Yes? Why? It seems he has attracted no attention at all."

Peng had furrowed his brow and stared at the floor.

"That is just what concerns me," Peng had said. "Perhaps they are waiting to be sure. Perhaps the young fool is even working for the opposition. He is, after all, the only one who could actually identify China Doll."

And that was the problem. Peng would have liked to put a bullet in the back of Carey's skull right away, or, better yet, seen how he enjoyed a decade or two in the salt mines of Xinxiang, but the rude young round-eye was the only one left who could point a finger at Xao's precious China Doll. Or bring her out of hiding, her and her American lover.

And the beauty of his own plan, to put that fear into Xao's head. Manipulate him into sending Carey out as a test, and find that the test would turn into the real thing. And Xao had fallen—no, not fallen, *leaped* into the trap.

"Yes," Xao said. "Send Carey down to Dwaizhou—"

"Is China Doll there?" Peng tried to keep the eagerness from his tone, and prayed that Xao hadn't noticed the trembling in his voice.

"Yes."

"Is Pendleton with her?"

Xao took a long time to light his damned cigarette.

"No," he finally said. "Do you think I would put them in the same place until we know that it is safe?"

Peng bowed his head. "You are always the wiser."

"So take Carey to Dwaizhou. If he sees her, observe how he reacts. If the police swoop in, we have lost China Doll and we shall have to keep the Pendleton hidden longer than we had hoped."

"Surely China Doll would talk."

"She would never talk."

In *my* hands, Peng thought, she will talk.

"And Carey?"

"I would then rely on you to see he does not get the opportunity to tell what he knows."

"And what if he sees her and keeps quiet?"

"Then we will know it is safe. You then take him on more touring to confuse the issue and send him home. End the howling of his American friends."

"And if he doesn't see her?"

"Then it doesn't matter."

So the conversation had gone precisely as Peng had wished, and he had been in such a fine mood until he found Carey and Wu, innebriated and still drinking on the hotel terrace. The rudeness of the American bastard, the foolishness of Wu, to be running around outside the pre-

226

scribed schedule! What if Carey had spotted the other American? What then?

Xao wasn't furious, but he was sad. The plan would work, of course, his plans always worked, but now he would have to put in effect the operation he had so hoped wouldn't be necessary. He had hoped to do this all without more loss of life, and now there would have to be a sacrifice.

Because of poor, stupid, disloyal Peng. It would be different if Peng had betrayed him out of political conviction, but that was not the case. Peng was merely treacherous and ambitious, with the poisonous jealousy of small minds. He had set his paltry trap, just as Xao wanted, but the trap would need bait, and Xao saw no way for the bait to survive the springing of the trap.

Neal drank two of the beers in the bathtub and sipped on the last one while he packed Mr. Frazier's country clothes. His big night out on the town was over, and in the morning they were going to haul him down to some bucolic commune and show him around. Or show him off. So what was on the farm? What's on any farm? Farmers, of course, pigs, cows, chickens, manure . . . crops . . . fertilizer . . .

Fertilizer? Super chickenshit? Pendleton? Li Lan?

He worked on the beer and *Roderick Random* for another hour before falling asleep.

16

His breakfast arrived shortly before dawn, so whatever they were going to do with him, they were in a hurry to get started.

The coffee went right to his head, grabbed his hangover, and slapped it around a little. The throbbing stopped, and there was enough Catholic in him to feel better for having endured this act of penance. It's hard to tell which an Irishman enjoys more, he mused, the high or the hangover.

Wu looked green around the edges when he came through the door, and his smile was somewhat constrained. He was decked out for the country in a white short-sleeved shirt and brown cotton trousers, although he was still wearing the stiff black leather business shoes. He carried a blue nylon windbreaker and a bright yellow nylon tube bag.

"Good morning," he said.

"Some night."

"Oh, yes."

"You want some eggs?"

Wu made a face of horrified disgust.

"Coffee?"

"I'll try some. But we must hurry."

They hurried, and were down in the car in ten minutes. Neal was surprised to see Peng in the backseat. Wu got in front with the driver.

"Do you own a car?" Peng asked Neal, apparently as a form of greeting.

"No."

"I thought all Americans owned their own cars."

"And I thought all Chinese played Ping-Pong. Do you play Ping-Pong?"

"I am quite good at it."

"Well, I am quite bad at driving."

"You joke."

"Okay, let me take the wheel."

The driver put it in gear and pulled out of the parking lot before Peng could take Neal up on it. He eased onto South Renmin Road and headed south. The route took them through some industrial suburbs, past the airport, and quickly into the countryside.

"How long a drive do we have?" Neal asked.

"Perhaps three hours," Wu answered automatically before looking deferentially at Peng.

"Three hours," Peng said.

"Three hours it is," Neal said. "Who brought the cards?"

"Perhaps," said Peng, "you would do better to learn from the peasants than waste your time in decadent bourgeois pastimes."

Man, you have some vocabulary for a guy who didn't speak English just a day ago. And don't call *me* bourgeois. Where I grew up, the bourgeoisie was anybody less than two months behind on the rent.

"Sure. What would you like me to learn?"

"What it means to labor for your food."

You never worked for Joe Graham, pal.

"Do *you* know, Mr. Peng, what it means to labor for your food?"

"Both my parents were peasants. And yours?"

Wu jumped in. "Have you noticed the mulberry trees, Mr. Frazier? The silkworms feed—"

"I suppose your parents were intellectuals," Peng said, pronouncing *intellectuals* as if the word had a bad smell.

"Sure. My mother graduated Summa Cum Stoned from Needle U., and my old man was an overnight success."

"You are very rude, Mr. Carey."

"Frazier. The name is Frazier."

Peng hit him with one of those laser looks, the kind meant to burn

229

right through you. Neal was discovering that people in China were either very calm or very angry, without a lot of middle range. He intended to push Mr. Peng into the very-angry zone. Very angry people make very stupid mistakes.

"Thank you for correcting me," Peng said, "Mr. Frazier."

"Don't mention it. I just don't want to get fucked up again by someone being careless."

Wu started to do little hops in the front seat. He was trying to think of something to say to change the subject, but nothing very clever was coming to him.

"Pretty country," Neal said as he turned his back on Peng and looked out the window.

The terrain was flat for a mile or so on each side of the narrow road. Low dikes, with tall, spindly mulberry trees, divided rice paddies into neat geometric patterns. In the background a range of hills rose from the plain. Their neat rows of terraces made them look almost like Central American pyramids overgrown with vegetation.

"Tea," Wu explained. "Some of the very best tea in the world comes from the hills. Have you heard of Oolong tea?"

"I think so."

"It is grown there."

"Is that some of the stuff we used to trade you dope for?"

Neal watched Peng squirm a little.

" 'Dope'?" Wu asked.

"Opium."

"Ah, yes."

"You guys had quite a little jones—addiction—going there, didn't you?"

Peng stared straight ahead as he said, "The problem of opium addiction—created by foreign imperialists—has been eradicated in the People's Republic of China."

"Yeah, well, if you just shoot them instead of shooting them *up* . . ."

"We treated them in much the same manner as we treated you after you had acquired the disease of addiction in the capitalist enclave of Hong Kong."

"I didn't think you had that many hotel rooms."

"Oolong tea is exported all over the world," Wu said.

The landscape was dotted with oval ponds about the size of large swimming pools.

"Fishponds," Wu said. "An excellent source of protein."

"No space can be wasted," Peng elaborated.

This is certainly true, thought Neal. As far as he could see, every bit of ground was being used in some way. Most of the flat land was flooded for rice cultivation, and the hills were terraced to the very tops. Every hollow seemed to hold a fishpond, and vegetable patches clung to the ground in between.

"China has four times the population of the United States, but only one-third the arable land," Wu said. "Much of China is desert or mountain. So we must make the best use of all the arable land. Sichuan Province is often called the Rice Bowl of China, because it is a fertile plain surrounded by high mountains. You are now in the middle of the Rice Bowl."

"It's beautiful," Neal said, addressing himself specifically to Wu.

"Yes, it is," Wu answered happily.

It was so beautiful that Neal forgot his skirmishing with Peng for a while and just took in the scenery. He hadn't seen such open spaces since his days on the Yorkshire moor, days that seemed like a distant memory now. And while the moor was vast and lonely, the Sichuan Plain was vast and peopled. It wasn't crowded, but it was definitely occupied. Lines of people moved slowly across rice paddies, children led buffalo along dikes, men in wide straw hats pushed wheelbarrows on narrow dirt roads. Old women, their heads wrapped in black turbans, sat beside the vegetable patches and smoked long-stemmed pipes as they scolded birds away. Younger women, often with babies slung on their backs, stacked piles of rice husks along the roadside. Just as every bit of land was used, thought Neal, every person on it was useful.

And where the moor was brown, southwest China was green. The paddies were green, the vegetable gardens were green, the hills of tea on the horizon were green. Here and there a metal rooftop shone silver, or a pond sparkled in blue, but they were like buttons on a gigantic emerald cloak.

"The rice in this area," Wu said, "produces two crops a year, so the peasants are always busy planting, harvesting, or tending their fields. Two crops a year is wonderful! If we could ever find a way to grow three, there would be no growling stomachs in China ever!"

231

He laughed at what seemed to be an old joke.

"Three crops," Peng muttered. "A typical Sichuanese dream. We do not need more harvests, we need more factories."

After a couple of hours they came to a sharp bend in the road where a small teahouse and a few shacks were clustered.

"Do you need to use the toilet?" Wu asked Neal.

"Wouldn't mind."

Wu led him around the back of the teahouse. A bamboo fence screened the lavatory from view. The toilet was an open trench about three feet deep, graded so that the urine ran down a slope but the feces remained. Neal discovered the physics of the operation as he relieved himself of the morning's coffee and Wu squatted down to do something more serious.

"What do they do?" Neal asked. "Burn it off every day?"

"Oh, no. The shit is valuable fertilizer. The night-soil removers come with buckets and carry it into the fields."

"Is there a lot of competition for that job?"

"It is assigned by class." Wu's voice dropped to a whisper. "Very often, intellectuals or their families who were exiled from the city perform this job. My father was a night-soil remover after he was freed from prison."

"Is it a punishment?"

"Not really. It is just that city people do not know the skills of farming, and this is something simple they can do. It is very hard work, though."

So, after a few thousand years of taking shit from the gentry, Neal thought, the peasants are giving it back, literally.

"We cannot waste anything in China," Wu said. "What do you do with shit in America?"

"Send it to Washington."

"That is a joke."

"You're telling me."

Wu stood up pulled his trousers up. "Yet you purged President Nixon and sent him to the countryside."

"I don't think he's lugging around buckets of night soil, although it's an appealing image."

"President Nixon is a very great man. You should rehabilitate him."

The stuff you hear in men's rooms.

"Perhaps if he corrects his thinking," Neal answered. "Does Peng ever have to piss, or is he really a robot?"

"You should not fight with Mr. Peng. He is an important man."

"That's why I'm fighting with him, Xiao Wu."

"I do not understand."

Neither do I, Wu, but I'm beginning to.

"Dwaizhou Production Brigade Central Committee Headquarters," Wu translated from the signpost at the road junction.

Neal didn't see anything that looked remotely like a Production Brigade Central Committee Headquarters, just a long, straight dirt road that stretched through rice paddies and wheatfields and disappeared into some low hills on the horizon.

They drove down the road for about three miles before coming to an S-curve among a copse of trees. On the other side, the road dropped into a valley in which Neal could see several villages, a dozen concrete grain silos, and a group of larger buildings that resembled a town center: the Production Brigade Central Committee Headquarters.

The car pulled into a parking lot in front of the largest building. A greeting committee of sorts had formed, and met Neal with broad smiles and an array of bows as he stepped out of the car.

"Mr. Frazier, please meet Mr. Zhu," Wu said.

"Welcome, welcome," said Zhu.

"Thank you very much," Neal answered. *"Xie xie ni."*

Zhu smiled at Neal's attempted Chinese, took him lightly by the wrist, and repeated, "Welcome, welcome."

Let the games begin, Neal thought as he looked around at his new surroundings. The building in front of him was a concrete and brick structure, three stories tall, with a broad set of concrete steps and a front landing. To the left, about a hundred feet away, was a single-story brick building that looked like a dining hall. To his left, surrounded by a cement patio with several wrought-iron, umbrella-shaded tables, was a swimming pool.

"Does Mr. Zhu speak English?" Neal asked Wu.

"Only 'welcome, welcome.'"

"Why is he holding my wrist?"

"He likes you. It is a traditional greeting in this part of the country."

"Who is he?"

"The Production Brigade leader."

"He looks too young."

"Everyone calls him 'Old Zhu.' "

Old Zhu led Neal over to the patio, reached into a barrel, and came out with a bamboo fishing pole, which he handed to Neal. He pointed to the swimming pool, which Neal then saw wasn't a swimming pool at all, but a fishpond. A closer look revealed that it was crammed with carp; the whole bottom of the pond looked like it was moving.

Zhu took a pole of his own, fixed a large breadcrumb on the hook, and cast it into the middle of the pond. A carp hit it right away. Zhu dragged in the fish, unhooked it, and handed it to a young man who was standing by for just that purpose. The boy ran to the dining hall with the fish. Zhu gestured for Neal to do the same, and by the time Neal had baited his hook, Wu and Peng already had their lines in the water and were waiting intently for the carp to strike. Neal thought of asking for a rifle, so that it would be *exactly* like shooting fish in a barrel, but didn't want to hurt Zhu's feelings. So he dropped his hook in and watched it land on a carp's head. The fish tapped at the bait with no great enthusiasm, and Neal watched Wu, whooping with delight, haul in his catch. Peng caught one too, and broke his wooden demeanor with a triumphant yell as the boy came running back from the dining hall to collect the catch of the day.

Just my luck to get a racist carp, Neal thought.

"Fresh fish for lunch!" Wu called to him.

"Wonderful!" Neal answered, fervently hoping they weren't going to hunt their own fresh pork for dinner.

They repaired to the dining hall, a utilitarian rectangle with a lino-leum floor and wooden tables. The fish was prepared quickly, and they ate it with some greens Neal didn't recognize, along with bowls of sticky white rice. Some bottles of beer made a quick appearance and departed just as quickly in the midafternoon heat. Peng, who had announced only the night before that he did not drink beer, drained one with little difficulty. After lunch, the group went to a second-floor meeting room in the headquarters building so that Zhu could answer Mr. Frazier's questions about the Dwaizhou Production Brigade.

Neal didn't ask the only question he was really interested in: What am I doing here at the Dwaizhou Production Brigade? Instead he launched a battery of interrogatives and nodded sagely as if he understood or even cared about the answers that Wu worked so hard to translate. What is the annual rice yield? How many people work on the brigade? How many families are there? How is it organized? What crops besides rice do you grow? How many hogs? How many chickens? How is silk produced?

Zhu seemed particularly proud of his new fish-farming project, explaining that the pool out front was just for the recreation of party cadres; the real ponds were harvested with nets, and were an enormous success. Neal said that he would like to see them, and was rewarded with a huge smile and a promise that they would do so that very afternoon.

Even Peng was pleased with Neal's performance, nodding and even smiling at Neal's questions, then nodding vigorously at Zhu's answers and listening intently to Wu's translation. He apparently thought the whole dog-and-pony show was so wonderful that he passed cigarettes out to everybody. The three Chinese men smoked solemnly while Neal sucked on some hard candy.

Neal also thought that the show was pretty good, especially Mr. Zhu's eloquent soliloquies on agriculture. The guy seemed to care passionately about farming in general and this farm in particular. His eyes shone with pleasure when he discussed gains in food production, and went dull and sad when he spoke about the lack of modern equipment and fertilizers. Neal figured that Zhu was either a terrific actor—sort of an Oriental Mr. Greenjeans—or that he wasn't in on the whole "Mr. Frazier" scam.

Why should he be? Neal wondered. I'm not in on the whole "Mr. Frazier" scam, and I'm "Mr. Frazier."

"I really want to see those fishponds!" Neal said before the boys could light up another round.

He saw the fishponds, which were actually huge, square, sunken concrete tanks with plank catwalks. He saw the rice paddies and learned how rice was planted, harvested, chaffed, packaged, and transported. He saw fields of wheat, sorghum, and sunflowers, and received instruction in the fine art of chewing sunflower seeds and spitting out the hulls. He saw chicken coops, duck ponds, and hog pens, and learned that pork was a major part of the Chinese diet. He saw water buffalo, petted water buffalo, and reluctantly rode on a buffalo while its little girl owner sobbed in anxiety for her pet. He saw a twenty-acre square of uncultivated land—woods and brush—and learned that it was set aside to

235

encourage the rabbits that were a major game crop. He saw a party of hunters, armed with ancient, muzzle-loading, curve-stocked rifles, go into the wood and emerge with several rabbits. He saw the complicated, integrated, and enormous effort it took for the people of this area to feed themselves and try to get ahead a little bit at the end of the year. He saw the tranquil beauty of the countryside.

He saw a maintenance shop where mechanics cannibalized the older trucks and tractors for the benefit of the newer trucks and tractors. He saw a clinic where a "barefoot doctor"—a woman paraprofessional—dispensed a combination of acupuncture, traditional herbs, and rare Western pharmaceuticals. He saw a school where male and female teachers handled enormous groups of uniformed children without apparent strain. He saw the presentation that the elementary kids had cooked up for him, a charming montage of song, dance, and parade that left him laughing and touched at the same time.

He saw Li Lan.

She was in a classroom, bent over a little girl, guiding the girl's hand and paintbrush over a sheet of white paper. She wore a plain, loose-fitting white blouse over blue "Mao" pants and rubber sandals. She wore no makeup, and her hair was tied into two braids with red ribbons. She looked up, saw Neal, and shook her head almost imperceptibly.

Neal moved on to the next classroom.

Because then he understood it. Not all of it, but enough. He sleep-walked his way through the rest of the tour, putting the whole thing together in his head. He didn't know where everybody fit in, but at least he knew now what he had to do.

Nothing.

Nothing, he told himself. Do nothing and just shut up.

Which was something he had never done before.

Neal finally figured out how to work the kerosene lantern and then fell into bed. What did they call it? A *kang*. A straw mattress on a low platform covered with a cotton quilt and remarkably comfortable. Zhu had offered to put him up in the little recreational club the cadres used, but Neal opted to stay in a typical peasant house. So the boys drove him into the middle of the commune somewhere and left him with a nice family, whose house had an interior courtyard full of chickens and pigs, a big charcoal-burning stove, and about a dozen kids who played with him until the simple dinner was served and they went to bed. He had walked about a million miles over the commune, and his body wanted to drop right into the arms of Morpheus, but his mind still wanted to pace around.

So Li Lan had made it home, he thought. Home was in Sichuan, where she had learned to cook, not surprisingly, Sichuanese food. Home was on a farm, and that was why she'd taken Pendleton. Doctor Bob didn't make herbicides, idiot. Simms's story was a cover, which Pendleton mimicked perfectly. Neal thought back to his drunken evening at the Kendalls', to Olivia's request for Pendleton to kill the weeds. That's not my line, he'd said. *I only know how to make stuff grow.* Like rice, maybe? Like three crops a year, maybe? *No more growling stomachs in China. The same old Sichuan dream.*

But why have they brought me here? Why go to all that trouble and then bring me here where I can see her? And where is Doctor Bob? Why did Li Lan shake me off this afternoon? Was I supposed to see her and *not* see her? How do I resolve *that* contradiction? What the hell do they want?

Make up your mind, guys, he thought.

No, not "mind" . . . *minds.*

Yeah.

He picked up *Random* and worked on it for an hour before crashing into sleep.

Peng squeezed the trigger. The pellet smacked into the paper target with a satisfying *thwack.* Along with the fishing pool, the BB gun range was his favorite part of visiting Dwaizhou. He had gotten the key from Zhu, opened up the big room, and liberated some beer and cigarettes from the locker. There were, after all, privileges that came with his high position and heavy responsibilities. He shot again, and the pellet hit the silhouette target right in the forehead.

"Good shot," the American said.

"If only you had shot as well," Peng observed.

The American shrugged.

Peng couldn't help rubbing it in. He didn't like the American, and the American had been drinking heavily.

"You missed," Peng said. "You shot at the wrong man, and then you missed."

"It could happen to anybody."

"But it didn't. It happened to you."

The American took a long pull on the bottle of beer.

"It won't happen again," he said. He raised the pellet gun to his hip and casually pulled the trigger. The pellet hit the target between the eyes. So did the next four shots.

"Let us hope you get the opportunity," Peng said.

"That's your job."

And a good thing, Peng thought. The plan was working beautifully. Carey had spotted China Doll and had not so much as blinked. The same could not be said for her; her eyes had widened and her breath had caught. She could not have been more obvious, and Peng would have arrested her on the spot if he hadn't had bigger plans.

She will run, now that she has seen Carey. Run like a rabbit, right to the burrow, to hide from the Carey dog. Well, you may have seen the dog, but you missed the fox. And you will lead me right to your lover, the great scientist, the great expert.

Xao will go, too, of course. The great romantic will not be able to resist. Then I will bag you all. Rightists, capitalists . . . traitors.

He squeezed off another shot.

Xao Xiyang put out his cigarette in the overflowing ashtray and answered the phone.

"Yes?" he said.

It was his driver.

"Your foreign guest had a good day."

"Did he have any complaints?"

"If he did, he didn't say a word."

"Perhaps you can take him to see the Buddha tomorrow."

There was a silence, a hesitation. Xao lit another cigarette.

"So you do not wish to change Mr. Frazier's itinerary?"

"Not at all."

"As you wish, sir."

The driver hung up.

It is not as I wish, Xao thought. It is what I must do.

The smoke tasted bitter in his mouth.

17

品

Neal Carey looked up at Buddha.

Buddha didn't look back. Buddha just sat there and gazed serenely across the water and ignored Neal entirely. Buddha was 231 feet tall and made of stone. Buddha was carved from a red rock cliff that rose straight up from the broad Min River.

Neal was standing on Buddha's big toe. So were Wu, Peng, and a couple of PLA soldiers. There was plenty of room.

"Pretty big Buddha," Neal said stupidly.

"It is the biggest sitting Buddha in the world," Wu said.

"A relic of the superstitious past," Peng said.

"Where's Mao's statue?" Neal asked. "Upriver? Next to the Gang of Four montage?"

Neal was back on his Piss Off Peng Program. Peng had whipped him out of Dwaizhou like they were trying to stiff the bill. They had driven about an hour before coming to the industrial town of Leshan, a squat gray battlement on the green floodplain, and boarded a ferryboat across the river. The ferry had dropped them off at Buddha's right foot.

"There are no statues to the Gang of Four," Peng said. "They betrayed Chairman Mao."

"Yeah, by carrying out his orders."

Neal turned around to look at the river, which was dotted with fishing boats. Fishermen, balanced precariously on the back ends of their small boats, maneuvered in the swirling currents with large poles that were both oar and rudder. Larger boats had crews of oarsmen to struggle with the fast-moving water. The Min River was deceptive. From a distance it had looked lazy and muddy. Up close it looked dangerous, almost evil, and it was small wonder that the local people had built a large Buddha to watch over them on a large river.

"Would you like to see Buddha's head?" Wu asked.

They climbed up a white wooden staircase beside Buddha's right arm. A wide railed landing wrapped around Buddha's head, and Neal stood about twenty feet away from Buddha's left eye, which was about the size of a small boat, and contemplated Buddha's face. It was certainly serene, he had to admit. Of course, anything that big, made of rock, and almost one thousand years old had pretty good reasons for being serene. And Buddha had a nice view. The wide river and its valley stretched out directly below, and if Buddha shifted his eyes to the right or left, he'd be treated to the sight of dramatic red cliffs topped with lush green vegetation.

The scenery hadn't changed much for Buddha over the millennium, except for the big smokestacks that poked up from Leshan's gray walls and the smaller smokestacks on the few power boats that plied the river.

Buddha had seen a lot change in China in a thousand years, but he'd seen a lot stay the same, too.

"It's beautiful!" Wu said.

"Haven't you been here before?" Neal asked.

Wu whispered, "I'd never been out of Chengdu until yesterday."

It was funny, Neal thought, standing around a gigantic head, gazing at the huge, unblinking eyes. Sort of ludicrous and awesome at the same time. He wondered about the depth of faith it would take to carve something this large on a dangerous cliff above a dangerous river.

"How did this Buddha make out during the Cultural Revolution?" Neal asked. He saw Peng's jaw get tight.

"The Buddha itself was not damaged. But the temple and the monastery behind us," Peng said, pointing into a manicured forest, "suffered significant damage, which is still being repaired."

"Why didn't the Red Guard vandalize the Buddha?"

"Afraid to," Wu said.

240

I'd sure as hell be afraid to, Neal thought. One look from those stone eyes would stop me in my tracks. Not to mention the thought of hurtling two hundred feet down into those currents. Old Buddha didn't last here a thousand years by being an easy mark.

"So they didn't have the balls to put a dunce cap on old Buddha here, huh?"

Peng's glare cut short Wu's nervous laughter.

"We should get you settled in your room," Peng said. "The driver took the car there directly."

"I'm staying in a garage?"

"You are staying in the monastery's guesthouse. It is back behind the temple, through those trees."

"Where are you boys staying?"

"The guesthouse is for foreign guests, but Mr. Wu will stay there to serve as your translator. I will stay at a Party facility nearby."

"I'll miss you."

Peng smiled. "It is only for the night. This afternoon we will escort you on a walk, and take you to dinner."

Swell.

"Then tomorrow you may start your journey home."

Well, you slipped that little tidbit in, didn't you? Well, well, well . . . you've found out whatever it was you wanted to find out. Now what could that be? I saw Li Lan, and I kept my mouth shut, and I didn't start screaming about her or Dr. Robert Pendleton . . . and that's what you needed to know. That I'm beat . . . that I don't want any more trouble . . . that I'm going to be a good boy . . . that you could snatch Pendleton and get away with it and that Tar Baby here ain't saying nothing.

And that's why Lan warned me off. She knew that if I opened my mouth I'd be here forever. Well, thank you, Li Lan.

Thank you Li Lan?! What the fuck are you talking about?! She's the one who dumped you in the shit in the first place, and now you're eaten up with gratitude because she's rescued you?! And what's *her* story? What had Olivia Kendall said about Lan's paintings? Some artsy-fartsy babble about "the duality of the mirror images reflecting both conflict and harmony"? No shit. The woman is a schiz, that's all. No wonder Pendleton is so pussy-whipped—he has himself a one-woman harem.

Well, he can have her. I'm getting out of here.

But first, the monastery.

He followed his guide-guards around the back of Buddha's head, where the cliff flattened out to a wooded plateau. An enormous temple, made entirely of dark wood, blended into the forest like a shadow. On the other side of the temple was a large garden with twisting paths, and Neal could only orient himself by looking over his shoulder at the back of Buddha's head. Bamboo, ferns, and creeping vines competed for space under a canopy of fir trees, and the garden was dark even at midday. The path eventually led past two smaller temples and another wooden building that looked like a barracks. There were a bunch of brown-robed monks doing chores around these buildings, so Neal quickly put it together that this was the monastery. The path ended at a circular gateway.

Neal expected something grim, but the monastery's guesthouse was actually cheerful. He stood in a square, open courtyard defined by four three-story wooden buildings. Every floor had a balcony running the length of the building and was sheltered beneath a sharply pitched black tile roof. There were about eight rooms on each floor.

A pond dominated the center of the courtyard. Stepping-stones and arched bridges wended through tall ferns and stone statues of frogs and dragons. Golden carp hid under the bridges or swirled lazily underneath huge lily pads.

Small pavilions, resembling neat caves, interspersed the ground-floor rooms. Tall covered jars served as stools around circular tables, and Neal figured that these shelters were built for alfresco tea parties during what had to be frequent rains.

The whole effect was lush, hospitable, mystical, and decadent.

Neal's room was on the top floor. It was small, but clean and comfortable. A mosquito net covered the *kang*. For washing, there was a basin, with pitchers of hot and cold water. A thermos of hot water, a lidded teacup, and a jar of green tea had been set on a side table. There was a single chair and a small desk. One window looked out on the courtyard. Another, on the other side of the room, gave a view of the forest and the roofs of the temple. The room had no bathroom, but a lavatory was four doors down. It had a room of toilets and another room with large cedar tubs.

Neal washed up and then joined Wu and Peng for a quick lunch of fish, rice, and vegetables. After lunch they worked their way back through the garden maze to Buddha's head, and then followed a cliffside path along the river. They were headed for another large monastary, about three miles up the river. Neal could see its tiled roof, shining golden in the sun, peeping through trees on a knoll ahead.

I wonder what they want me to see up there, Neal asked himself. Maybe Mao is alive and living as a monk, and they want to see if I'll keep my mouth shut again.

Mao wasn't there. Or if he was, Neal didn't see him. Neal did get a tremendous view of the Min River Valley from a pavilion on top of the knoll, and the temple housed the usual array of Buddhist saints, but none of them was Mao, and Neal was impatient to get going.

He posed for the cliché tourist photos: at the pavilion, at the temple, on the trail back to the Buddha, standing on Buddha's toenail, standing by Buddha's head. He perfected the wooden tourist smile, the self-conscious "Here I Am at ———" stance, and the classic Staring Off into the Distant Horizon profile. It felt strange to him. After all, he had spent a lifetime trying to stay out of photographs, and here he was posing for them. But he knew they would need them for his Frazier cover, so he stood, smiled, and stared.

Finally the sun dropped behind Buddha's head, putting a halt to the photo opportunities, and after an austere dinner at the monastery Peng took his camera and left. Neal and Wu repaired to one of the courtyard pavilions and shared a cup of tea and a little Twain chatter, and then Neal pleaded fatigue and said good night.

He lit the kerosene lamps in his room, poured himself a cup of tea, and settled into *Random* for an hour or so. He had a hard time concentrating. Is this thing really over? he wondered. Do I really start the trip home tomorrow? And what then? What will Friends say? I've fucked up the gig completely, and it's unlikely they'll reward me with a ticket to grad school. No, that's out. Well, I still have some money in the bank, maybe I can go somewhere else. Yeah, right, with a whole file of "incompletes."

And what will Graham say? He's probably been worrying himself sick, rubbing a hollow into his real hand with his artificial one. He'll be glad to see me, but royally pissed off. Maybe I can make it up to him.

So I'll get out of here, fly to Vancouver, call Dad, and see what's what. Probably the best thing is to keep going, go back to the cottage in the moors for a few weeks and try to sort things out.

Like Li Lan.

Yeah, face it. Almost everything that's happened in this whole sad gig has happened because you were obsessed with Li Lan. You got shit-faced and gaga at the Kendalls', you went off half-cocked, so to speak, to Hong Kong, where you walked into not one but two traps, and then you had to be spirited into mainland China, all because you were thinking about her and not the job. Now Pendleton gets to spend his life working for the Chinese, your so-called career is dusted, and why? Because you're in love with Li Lan.

And that's the saddest thing, he thought. I still am in love with Li Lan.

He got up from his chair. He was too restless to work, too wired to sleep, and there was no booze. Time to go see Buddha.

A thick mist had settled in the night air, and torches barely lit the courtyard. He found the gate and made his way through the garden. The monks had set torches in large stone holders around the Buddha, and Neal could just discern the shape of Buddha's head as he approached it.

So it took him a minute when he saw the woman to decide that it really was Li Lan.

She stood in the gray mist with the giant Buddha at her back. She was wearing a black silk jacket and black pants. Her hair was long and straight, with a single red comb on the left side. Her eyes were delicately lined, and she wore red lipstick. Her hands were clasped in front of her thighs.

She saw him first and stood still until he recognized her.

"I came to find you," she said.

A solid ache gripped his chest.

"Why?"

"I wish to explain."

"I'd sure like to hear that."

"Can we walk?"

"Wait a second. You want me to follow you down another dark path? What do you have waiting out there this time? Guys with knives? A bamboo cage? Or a nice deep drop into the river?"

She dropped her head. Neal could just see the tears well in her eyes and then spill over. She's good, he thought. She's very good.

"You have no reason to trust me," she said.

"You got that right."

She looked up at him. "You may choose the path," she suggested.

"Turn around. Put your arms over your head."

He patted her down. No knives, no guns. But she hadn't had a knife or a gun when she'd punted Ben Chin's head into the wall, either. His hands got sweaty as he touched her. He was shook up, and he didn't like it.

"What are you doing?" she asked.

"They say I'm going home tomorrow. I'm trying to make sure it's not home to Jesus."

"I am not carrying any weapons."

"You *are* a weapon."

"I only want to talk."

He turned her around, which was a mistake because then he could see her eyes. They took a lot of the tough out of him.

"So talk," he said.

"Not here."

"Why not here?"

"It is dangerous."

Well, we wouldn't want to do anything dangerous all of a sudden, would we?

"Where, then?" It was a rhetorical question, because Neal Carey wasn't following her anywhere.

"Perhaps your room?"

Except maybe there.

18

꘎

She sat on the bed. He closed the bamboo shades and turned the lamp down low. There was no lock on the door, so he set the chair against it and sat down. She closed her hands in front of her and looked at the floor.

He wanted to get up and hold her, but he couldn't seem to move. He felt like he was living inside a marble statue.

"So talk," he said.

"You are angry."

"Goddamn right I'm angry," he hissed. "Do you know what it was like in that shithole in the Walled City?!"

"Yes," she said quietly. "You are well now?"

"Terrific."

"Good."

Yeah, good. Except I don't know if I want to kill you or love you. Get out of here or stay here with you.

"So what's your story?" he asked.

Li Lan

My mother's family were rich landowners in Hunan Province, very important members of the Nationalist Party, the Kuomintang.

246

Mother grew up in privileged household, cultured . . . genteel. Her parents were very progressive. They believed that boys and girls should be equal. And they thought that China must become modernized. So they sent their oldest son to England, the youngest son to France, and the middle daughter to America. Middle Daughter was my mother. So as a young girl, just seventeen, she traveled to America, to Smith College.

But she did not stay very long. The Japanese invaded and killed very many Chinese. Mother came home. Her father was very angry with her, very worried. But Mother was patriotic. She ran away to join the fight.

She became a legend. She ran far away from Hunan, north to the area controlled by communist guerrillas. She trained hard in the mountains. She learned to shoot a rifle, to plant a mine, to make a deadly spear from a bamboo stick. Her officers also gave her political indoctrination, and she became a devoted communist. She learned how her own family's huge landholdings oppressed the masses, and she longed to purge the burning shame of her class background. She became at first a courier, and then a spy. It was a role in which her family background and her education was useful. She spoke beautiful Chinese, and she could understand Japanese and English. Mother could walk among any kind of people and keep her ears open.

Her work was dangerous and she loved it. Every dangerous act was a redemption, every contribution to the war helped to build a new woman in a new China. And she fell in love.

He was a soldier, of course. A guerrilla leader and a brilliant political officer. She met Xao in the mountains when she smuggled a message from an enemy held in a town nearby. He admired first her courage, then her beauty, and then her mind. They went to bed that night. It was her first time, and it was all somehow the same thing: the war, the communist struggle, and Xao Xiyang. She knew their futures would always be together, hers, Xao's and China's. The war was long, so long, and after they defeated the Japanese, they began to struggle against the fascist Kuomintang and its leader, Chiang Kai-shek.

In the battle to liberate the country from the Kuomintang, my mother's background became even more useful. She pretended to become obedient to her father. She went home, she attended parties, she "dated" American officers and spies. All this time she passed information to the Party, many times through her husband, Xao. When the communist forces appeared to be victorious, her family fled to Taiwan, but Mother hid, and stayed behind. She traveled to Beijing and found Father there! They were together on the birthday of the new China. Many times Mother told us the story of how she and Father stood in Tiananmen Square, with thousands of red flags waving in the wind and thousands of people in the square, how they stood there cheering Chairman Mao and weeping with joy as the Chairman declared the People's Republic of China. Father stayed with the Party and was assigned a government post in Chengdu. Mother became a propaganda officer. I was born two years later, in 1951.

Poor father . . . he was destined to have only girls. But he did not mind. He loved us very much, and would buy us dresses and pretty things, and tie ribbons in our hair. Blue for me, red for my sister. So we became called Lan Blue and Hong Red. Xao Lan and Xao Hong.

At first, everything was well. We were so happy! Although we were sisters, Hong and I were so different. I was shy, she was very forward. I studied painting and music. Hong studied acrobatics and theater. I liked to walk in countryside, Hong liked to make fight. Mother and Father would joke that perhaps they had daughter and son also. There was much laughter in our house, much laughter and music and art. Great happiness.

Then the bad times came. When Chairman Mao said, "Let a hundred flowers bloom." That was 1957, when the Chairman invited all people, most especially intellectuals, to criticize the Party.

Mother did so. With enthusiasm. She loved the Party, but she also loved freedom, and she thought that the Party had become too . . . authoritarian, too "one way." Mother did not believe in "one way." She said the world was too large for that. So she taught us everything. Chinese, but English also. Communist thought, but also Jefferson thought, Lincoln thought. Chinese music, but also Mozart. Chinese painting, but also Western painting, Cézanne, Mondrian. So Mother criticized the Party, thinking that was her duty. She wrote letters to newspapers, she joined the students at Sichuan University who were putting up posters. She even criticized Father for not listening enough! This was also a joke in our house, because after that Father would cook and ask Mother to criticize his soup!

But Hundred Flowers Movement was a trap. It lasted one month only, May to June, one breath of fresh spring air before the doors slammed shut. Those who made criticisms were called traitors, called Rightists, and a new campaign replaced Hundred Flowers Campaign. They called it "Anti-Rightist Campaign."

The Chairman did not really want free speech. Police suppressed newspapers, silenced speakers, and tore down the posters. Students in Chengdu rioted.

Mother came home in tears. She had seen the police use batons on the students and beat them bloody. Father argued that order had to be restored, and she became very angry with him. That night the police came for her.

We were little and didn't understand, but we were very frightened. Mother did not return for two days, and when she did, she looked older and sad. We discovered later that the police asked her about her family, accused her of being a Kuomintang spy, waved the letters she had written at her, and ordered her to write out a "confession" of her mistakes. She refused. A week later the police came back and arrested her. Father explained that she had gone back to school to learn more about Mao's thought. I remember that I asked if I could go to school with her, but Father said that I was too young. Hong wanted to fight the police, of course, but Father said that they had just made a mistake and would correct it soon. Why, Mother was a war hero and a patriot!

Mother was in jail for over a year. We visited her twice, which was all we were allowed. Father helped us get into our prettiest dresses and our ribbons, and get together a bundle of flowers. We went to a big building on the edge of the city. Mother came to a table behind a wire fence, and we took the petals off the flowers and pushed them through the wire to her. I tried not to cry, but I cried. Mother tried not to cry, but she cried. Hong did not cry and Father did not, but he looked sad and angry. I asked Mother what she had done wrong, and she said that she was a Rightist, because her parents were Rightists. I did not know what a Rightist was, but I remember I said that if she was one because her parents were, then I must be a Rightist, too. I remember that Father laughed a harsh laugh, but Mother looked serious and told me that I must never say that, that we children must be good communists and study the thought of Chairman Mao. She said that she was studying hard and had written many confessions, and when she had learned to overcome her own

Rightist thought, she could come home and we would be together again.

We were together again, but not at home. Father was sent to the countryside "to help reorganize the peasants," but really because he refused to divorce Mother, or even denounce her. This was the beginning of the Great Leap Forward, when the land was divided into production brigades, and Father was to educate the peasants about the great changes. We left our apartment in Chengdu and moved to a small village—Dwaizhou. It was very strange to us, very new, and we were frightened. The peasants did not want us there at first, because we were more mouths to feed and we knew nothing about farming. Father worked very hard, though, and learned much, and helped the peasants explain their problems to the Party cadres. The peasants began to respect him, and then love him, because he fought for them and got them equipment, and fertilizer, and medical supplies. He taught classes at night also and conducted political struggle sessions to explain to the people the great goals of the revolution. Mother joined us after a year, and we were so happy! We wore peasant clothes now, and had no pretty dresses, but we were happy to have our mother back. And we could see that Father and Mother were so happy to be together.

We came to love Dwaizhou. I helped in the fields and the kitchens, and wandered all over with a stick of charcoal and rice paper, making little childish drawings. Hong played that she was a brave PLA soldier, and she acted out stories of revolutionary heroes for the peasants. And she was so proud of her nickname—because red was the color of the Party, and she was Red!

But then food became scarce. The Great Leap Forward had failed, and even Sichuan began to feel hunger.

Father tried to stop the foolish edicts. He fought the cadres when they ordered the peasants to slaughter all their livestock because livestock was property and ownership of property was Rightist. But the cadres overruled him, and the peasants had to kill their pigs and chickens and ducks, and send the food to workers in the city. But then, of course, there were no animals left to breed. I remember Father standing with the peasants as they killed their cherished breeding stock, remember him standing in puddles of blood, weeping along with the farmers. I remember the trips through the countryside, where I saw farmers standing in once fertile rice paddies and begging for food. I remember families who were once good friends fighting each other over a few fish or vegetables. I remember hunger.

My family did not starve, because Father was still an official, and had *yuan* to buy food. But there was often not a lot of food to buy, and many meals were made up of some cabbage and perhaps some peanuts. Sister and I missed the bowls of white rice and the steamed rolls and the "mooncakes." But we did not complain, because so many people around us were worse off, and it was the price we all had to pay for the revolution.

But I never forgot. Hong and I would eavesdrop on Father when he would tell Mother about his latest inspection tour. He would whisper to Mother about the sights he had witnessed: dead bodies on the roadside, men chopped to pieces by villagers for stealing grain, children with open sores from malnutrition. He would sit, smoking one cigarette after another, saying that they must put a stop to it, and never let it happen again. And Mother would ask, "What is wrong with the Chairman? Has he gone mad?" Father would just shake his head.

Then suddenly it seemed that Father became very important. We learned later that he had joined with a group of reformers led by Deng Xiaoping. It was in 1960, I think, that investigations were started, and then reforms, and Father was a leader of the reforms in Sichuan and the cadres hated him. But the hunger ended, and Deng Xiaoping supported my father, and after two more years we moved back to Chengdu because Father had been made Party Secretary, a very important position.

We didn't know then, of course, that Chairman Mao was just biding his time. We were once again very happy. We had our family and we had our dreams. I was to become a great painter and Hong was to be a great actress. We studied our arts and worked hard in school, and our evenings at home were wonderful. Mother was always curious about our work, and we always had to tell her about our day at school. I would show her my painting and Hong would perform. Father would come home late and then we would have to do it all over again, but that was wonderful, too.

And mother had been "rehabilitated." She even began to write for the newspaper. We all went together for walks in the parks or strolls through the city streets or drives in the countryside. We often went to visit Dwaizhou, because the people there were our family now. It was a happy time and we were still children.

But our childhoods ended in 1966. Then the Great Proletarian Cultural Revolution turned all the children into Red Guards.

I was fifteen and it was springtime. Why do all the campaigns start in springtime? I was old enough then to have some small understanding of politics, so when the attacks began on Peng Zhen, the mayor of Beijing, I understood that it was really his sponsor, Deng Xiaoping, who was under attack. That was the method, you see—attack the subordinate to erode the ground beneath the superior. I was afraid, because Father worked for Deng. Then Chairman Mao himself attacked the Party professionals—such as Father—accusing them of taking the capitalist road, and we became very worried.

But also excited, because all the students at school were buzzing with Mao Thought and Making Revolution. We painted big posters supporting Chairman Mao and urging revolution. I felt badly, thinking that I was perhaps being disloyal to Father, but Hong explained that our duty to Chairman Mao and to the revolution came first, and that Father would be proud of us for our honest criticisms. She criticized our teachers for lack of revolutionary ardor and purity. She even criticized me for making "useless" paintings of hills and trees instead of "useful" paintings with revolutionary themes. I tried at first, but the pictures just would not come. Soon I did not make paintings at all.

Then the Red Guards began to appear, first in Beijing, then in Shanghai, soon after in Chengdu. Hong was one of the first to join, of course. She was so proud in her green uniform and red armband. I remember when she first walked into the house in her uniform. Mother turned pale and said nothing, and Father only observed that revolution was a complicated and sometimes painful thing. Hong was angry and said that they should support her in making revolution, in wiping out "The Four Olds": Old Customs, Old Habits, Old Culture, Old Thinking. Father asked her if she wanted to wipe out Old China entirely, and she answered that the Red Guard was supporting Chairman Mao.

That August, Mao stood on Tiananmen Gate and reviewed a big parade of the Red Guard. That loosed the flood. Students all over China went crazy with power. Red Guard groups started everywhere, sometimes three or four groups in a single school! Mao officially announced the start of the Cultural Revolution. Students denounced teachers, professors, and party officials. They stopped going to classes. Schools shut down. All we did was make revolution.

I did as little as possible, but Hong was involved in everything. She marched with the Red Guard, she organized a theatrical troupe to act out revolutionary plays in the streets, she sometimes spent days away from home, staying at our school that the Red Guard had turned into a barracks.

Father was denounced that autumn. I was surprised and hurt that Deng joined the attack on Father to try to save himself. It didn't work, of course, and Deng was toppled shortly after. The Red Guard went to Father's office, tied his hands behind his back, and dragged him into the street. I was at home on the second floor of the house and heard the noise in the street. Mother went to the window first, then quickly closed the curtains. I pushed them aside and stood there watching as they put a dunce cap on Father's head . . . and a rope around his chest . . . and paraded him down Renmin Road. I saw some of my schoolmates throw garbage at him . . . and spit in his face . . . as the Red Guard chanted "Capitalist Roader" and "Western Stooge." Father just looked straight ahead. His face was calm and composed, and two feelings fought in my heart: hatred and pride. Hatred for the Red Guard and pride for Father. How could such opposite feelings live in the same heart?

Hong came home that afternoon. She was sobbing. I thought she was weeping for Father, but that was not the reason. She had been thrown out of the Red Guard because of Father. Her armband had been ripped off and her uniform was torn. She had bruises on her face. Mother tried to talk to her. I tried to comfort her, saying that Father had suffered a great injustice, but that it would be corrected soon, and she would have her revenge on the Red Guard. But she wasn't angry at the Red Guard, she was angry at Father! Father had caused her downfall! We did not speak after that.

Father did not come home. We heard that he was in jail. Later we heard that he had been sent to a work camp in Xinxiang. We stayed in the house after that. We knew that it was only a matter of time before we would be attacked. The Red Guard had come to the homes of other purged officials, searching for evidence of Western influences or decadent belongings or just to loot. It was a terrible time. I was worried about Father, Mother sat for hour after hour saying nothing, doing nothing, and Hong sank into silence and acted as if she could not stand the sight of us.

Finally in November it happened. It was cold for Chengdu, and I was huddled beneath my quilt, late at night, when the front door crashed open. We all ran downstairs to see what had happened. There were at least twenty Red Guards. The leader was a tall young man. His face was flushed with rage! He screamed at Mother, "American spy! You must confess now!" Mother glared back at him and answered, "I have nothing to confess. Perhaps it is you who has something to confess." He grabbed her by the neck and threw her to her knees. I rushed at him, but he easily threw me off, and two other Red Guards—one of them a girlfriend from school—held me down. The leader screamed again for Mother to confess, but she just shook her head. He hit her on the back of the neck and she fell flat on the floor. I screamed for him to stop and my old friend slapped me in the face. The leader kicked Mother and pulled her back up to her knees.

"You are a spy," he said, "and the wife of a traitor. We are here to express the outrage of the masses and give you revolutionary justice!"

"You know nothing about justice," Mother answered, "so how can you give it?"

He kicked her again and pulled her arms behind her back and handcuffed her. It was a very painful position, but Mother did not cry out. Then he ordered his helpers to search the house. All this time Hong stood in a corner and said nothing.

They tore our house apart. They ripped the beautiful paintings with knives, they smashed the record albums into pieces. When they found the writings of Jefferson and Paine, they let out shouts of triumph. The leader slammed these books down in front of Mother.

"English books!" he screamed. "Who are these American thinkers you admire?!" "

"They were true revolutionaries," she answered. "You should learn from them."

The leader spat on her and made a pile of the books in front of her face. Then he lit a match and tried to set them on fire, but he did not know what he was doing and could not get the fire to take flame. He became so angry that he picked up the books and threw them at Mother's head, giving her cuts and bruises. All this time, I was held down on my knees, and I cried and cried . . . and Hong stood silently in the corner.

The Red Guard stayed for hours. The sun was coming up as they were getting ready to leave.

"We will be back for you later," the leader warned. "So you can face the people and tell your lies!"

He took the handcuffs off Mother and stormed out of the house. I went to Mother and held her. She shook with pain and anger, but she got up and we walked through the house. Everything was destroyed. Even our beds were ripped up, so we put our quilts on the floor and tried to sleep. I could not sleep, because when I closed my eyes I saw them beating Mother.

They were back in a few hours. They handcuffed Mother again and ordered us to follow. They took us to the same government building where Father's office had been. There was a large room there, full of people. Posters denouncing Mother were all over the walls. "American Spy!" "Kuomintang Snake!" "Treacherous Class Enemy!" They sat us down in the front row and carried Mother up on the stage. They hung a poster around her neck. "Death to American Spies!" it read. The crowd chanted these slogans and hurled insults, but Mother refused to lower her head. She stared back at the people, some of whom had been friends of hers and Father's. At one point, the young man from the night before even pushed her head down to make her look ashamed, but she raised her head again.

"What do you have to say for yourself?" an older man asked her.

"I have nothing to say to a mob," she replied.

"Then you will speak to the Committee of Revolutionary Justice," the man answered.

Then several men grabbed Mother and walked her through the crowd. People hit her and spat at her as she passed through. After an endless hour, a young Red Guard came to Hong and me and took us upstairs to the fourth floor. We were left on a bench in the hallway by a door, but we could hear shouting from inside the room. They were screaming at Mother to confess to being an American spy.

"Your father was a Kuomintang official, a traitor! You are his spy! Didn't you fraternize with Americans during the War of Liberation?!"

"Yes, that is true! I was spying for the Party!"

"Liar! You were working for the Kuomintang. You are still working for the Kuomintang!"

"That is a lie."

"You hate China! You have American books and American music!"

"You are being ridiculous. Please spare yourself further embarrassment and stop being so foolish."

This went on for some time. I flinched with every shout, and sometimes I could hear them kicking and hitting her. They were desperate for a confession. I realize now that Father's powerful enemies were behind it, seeking to discredit him further, but Mother must have known it then, because she refused to give them anything. She knew that they had no real evidence against her, because she was innocent.

Finally, the young Red Guard who had destroyed our house came out. He was very red in the face, almost out of breath, and he ordered us to enter the room.

Mother was standing in the "airplane" position, her knees bent and her arms stretched behind her. She was in great pain, but she remained composed. Hong and I were pushed against a wall, opposite a draped window. It was dim and hot in the room.

"Denounce her!" the older man demanded.

I shook my head. Hong remained silent, and I was very proud of her.

"Tell us what you know," he repeated. "You will be helping her. If she confesses, she can be rehabilitated, but if she does not, she can be executed a a spy. Help her to confess!"

I stole a look in Mother's eyes. She shook her head so gently that only I could see it. I loved her so much and I started to cry, but I refused again to denounce her. So they tried another tactic.

"Then you are as guilty as she is! You are against the revolution! You hate Chairman Mao! Do you want to go to prison?! To a work camp?!"

I didn't care. No prison could have been worse than that little room. All of China had become a prison to me. I remained silent. Hong remained silent. I felt that we were sisters again.

"You must correct your bad thought!" the young Red Guard screamed. "Your mother has poisoned your mind with bourgeois thought! She is a criminal! Denounce her!"

I do not know where I found the courage to answer, but I said, *"You* are the criminal, and I denounce you." And I saw Mother smile. They gave up on me then, and talked only to Hong.

"Denounce her!"

Hong shook her head.

The older man spoke quietly to her. "Xao Hong, you were a Red Guard. Now you are in disgrace because of your parents. Do you want to be rehabilitated? Do you ever want to be a Red Guard again?"

Hong dropped her eyes to the floor. She shook her head, but very gently.

"Xao Hong, we know you love Chairman Mao. We know you love the revolution. Your mother wants to destroy Chairman Mao. She wants to destroy the revolution. She is your mother in body only. In spirit you are a daughter of the revolution."

He lifted her chin up and looked her in the eyes. "You are Chairman Mao's good daughter."

"Yes, I am."

"But you must prove that. You must prove yourself before you can become a Red Guard again. Help us to foil this woman's conspiracies. Denounce her."

I could not breathe. I could only watch Mother as she looked at Hong, looked at her with such gentleness, with such love, even as Hong suddenly shouted, "Yes, it is true! She is a spy! She hates Chinese things! She taught us to read American books, and to listen to American music!"

The older man smiled. "Yes, yes. But surely there is more!"

You see, he still didn't have anything on Mother that he didn't already know. These things were mistakes, but not crimes.

Hong was really yelling now. She was almost hysterical. "She encouraged my sister to make decadent paintings!"

"Comrade Xao, we need to know more."

My sister's eyes were wild. She shook her head furiously and almost seemed to be choking. I felt for a moment that we were both going to die. Then she pointed a finger at my mother and screamed, "She said Chairman Mao was insane! I heard her!"

At first I didn't know what she was talking about, but then I remembered when we were little girls in Dwaizhou and eavesdropped on our parents and Mother had wondered aloud if Chairman Mao was mad. It had happened nine years ago, and in her desperation Hong recalled it.

"I heard her say it!" she repeated. "I heard her say that Chairman Mao was mad!"

Then my mother dropped her head and began to cry, not because she was guilty of treason, but because her own daughter had betrayed her for a green jacket and a red armband.

I tried to go to Mother, but the Red Guard grabbed me and took me into the hallway. They were all congratulating my sister, and they locked my mother in that small room and took us downstairs. They yelled to the crowd of their great victory as we entered the auditorium, and the crowd started to chant, "Xao Hong! Xao Hong! Xao Hong loves the revolution!" Her former Red Guard comrades ran up to her and draped a jacket on her. Then they gave her an armband. The crowd was shouting and celebrating the victory over Mother, and the demonstration swept out of the building onto the street. Hong was pushed to the front of the parade as it marched around the building underneath the window of the room where Mother was held. Hong herself held up a placard denouncing her.

They were not finished humiliating Mother yet, you see, and I believe to this day that they meant to leave her unguarded. They knew that she was a proud woman whose spirit had been broken, and they wanted to make an example of her.

Mother kicked out the window first, so we were all looking up when the curtain fluttered open and she plunged through.

I started to shut my eyes, but then I opened them because I wanted to remember, always.

She shut her eyes tight, but the tears came anyway. Neal sat down beside her on the bed and put his arms around her shoulders. She put her face in the crook of his neck and started to sob. The tears ran down her cheeks onto his neck and he held her tighter. She cried in choking gasps, as pain that was ten years old flowed out of her, and she cried for a long time. Neal leaned back and brushed a tear off her cheek, then he kissed one off, then kissed a tear on her neck, and then she brought her mouth to his.

Her lips were soft and warm and her tongue was hard and probing and her jacket seemed to unbutton itself and the silk slid down her legs and then he was inside her. She lay back on the bed, her long black hair rippling under her as she moved beneath him. Her legs clasped him tightly as her hands fluttered up and down his back, or stroked his hair, his face. She kissed his forehead, then his eyes, then his mouth again, before she clasped her legs tighter and rolled them both over.

She rubbed his chest with her hair as she moved back and forth on him, and he reached between her legs and stroked her as she stretched up and kept him just inside her. She slammed back down on him and they moved together and he could see her beautiful face, touch her breasts and her stomach; she was shiny with sweat. She rose and fell and twisted on him and then collapsed on his chest and he held her tight and still and thrust to the center of her once, then twice, and then again until they smothered the sounds of their joy in each other's mouths.

They lay together under the quilt and she nestled her head in the crook of his arm as she went on with her story.

For weeks after Mother's death I just wandered the city. I didn't want to be at home among all the memories and where the Red Guard could find me. I took food from garbage piles and slept in the parks. I was not unusual; there were many "political orphans" and nobody seemed to care. The city was in chaos. The Red Guard splintered into several groups. They seized weapons from the armories and fought the police and each other. From time to time I caught a glimpse of Hong, always in the lead of something: a parade, a demonstration, a street battle. We never acknowledged one another. She was always in the center of the action; I existed on the margins.

In January the Beijing Red Guard tried to seize control of the government itself, and the army stepped in. Soon the Sichuan garrison did the same, and they fought bloody battles against the Red Guard all over the province, but especially in Chengdu. The fighting went on for weeks, and the last of the Red Guard seized a factory building in the northern part of the city. It took the army three days of hard fighting to get them out.

With the Red Guard shattered, there were so many young people wandering the streets! Schools were still closed, families disrupted. The police and the army rounded up thousands of the youth. The government made the decision to send the urban youth to the countryside, "to learn from the peasants." I was arrested and spent weeks in a detention center. When I was identified, I was sent away to the far southwestern part of the province, up into the mountains.

It was not really a village, just a group of huts on the lower slopes of a great mountain, and the people there were not even Chinese. They were from the Yi tribe, primitive people who grew a little tea and some vegetables and hunted in the mountains. Only the headman spoke any Chinese, and he assigned me to live in his cousin's hut. I was like a slave. They worked me very hard, and the cousin's wife hated me because she suspected that her husband . . . wanted me.

I was numb from hunger, hard work, and the cold, but perhaps this was good for me, because it also numbed my grief. And the mountains were beautiful. As I worked in the vegetable gardens I could see the snowy peak on the Silkworm's Eyebrow—Mount Emei—a mountain sacred to Daoists and Buddhists. It is part of my story, because I ran away from the hut and fled up the mountain.

The husband came to my *kang* one night. He was filthy and drunk and tried to press himself on me. I fought, and the wife heard the noise. She came in and beat me. Later that night I put my few things in a cloth and walked up the mountain. I was very afraid, because I had heard stories of the many wild animals there—tigers, snakes, big monkeys, even pandas.

I followed the path of the Buddhist pilgrims, stone steps up through the forest to the very top of the mountain. For a thousand years Buddhist . . . pilgrims . . . have climbed to the summit of the mountain to look into Buddha's Mirror.

At the very top of the mountain you can look over into an abyss, thousands of feet deep, filled with mist. But magical light hits this mist and makes reflection. So when you look over edge, you see Buddha's Mirror, and you see your true self. You see your soul.

That is called "enlightenment," which is the goal of all Buddhists. So the mountain is sacred, and many pilgrims make the climb to Buddha's Mirror to find enlightenment. The climb takes at least three days, so pilgrims sleep at monasteries along the trail.

There are many monasteries hidden deep in the forest, far away from the stone path, and I thought I would stay on the main path until daylight, then try to find a very remote monastery to hide in. As a good communist, I did not believe in God, but I hoped to find refuge among the monks and nuns.

But I became lost. It was dark and the path seemed to disappear beneath my feet. All around me was thick bamboo, and I heard the howling of wild animals. And it was so cold! Snowing now! I was freezing in my thin clothes. I sat down in a tiny clearing and hugged myself. I rocked back and forth and cried and cried. I did not know what to do. I just sat down to die. Then the miracle happened. A light appeared in the woods! A lantern! I walked toward it and then I saw that light was in a small cave, and in the cave was a man—a monk—and an ancient little statue of a beautiful woman—Kuan Yin, the goddess of mercy—one of the many faces of Buddha. The monk wrapped me in a blanket. He built a little fire and it was still cold, but not *dying* cold, and I fell asleep. When I woke up, it was morning, and the monk said it was time to go. I followed him up the mountain for many *li*. My feet hurt, and my legs ached, but I was happy. In Kuan Yin I had seen the beautiful face of my mother, guiding me to safety, and then I believed in God.

We climbed and climbed! I saw so many wonderful sights! Wild rivers, sheer cliffs, lovely pavilions from which you could see forever. The walk became harder and steeper, and the monk strapped spikes to my shoes so I could climb through the ice and snow. The first night we stayed at a monastery. I went into the temple and found Kuan Yin and sat with her for hours and my mind was at peace. I got up that morning ready for the climb. We walked along narrow paths across deep canyons. To fall would mean death, but I was not afraid.

At last we reached the top. There was a large beautiful temple there, and we slept there before making the final short walk to Buddha's Mirror, because the monk said it was best to go at dawn.

We were off before the sunrise, and sitting at the edge of the great cliff as the sun appeared on the eastern horizon. The world became red and then gold, and finally we stood up and looked over the edge and I saw . . . saw my sister, and I knew that I would never be at true peace while her soul was tortured. It was the vision Kuan Yin had given me. It was Mother telling me to purge my hatred and save my sister.

The monk took me to a monastery on the far western side of the mountain, far away from anything. He brought me before an old nun, who asked me to tell my story. I told her everything. When I had finished, she said I could stay. She gave me a little room and some plain clothing. I had a job in the kitchen, carrying water, gathering wood . . . later, cooking . . . cleaning bowls and cups. I sat with Kuan Yin every morning and every night. Later I studied all the Buddhist arts—t'ai chi, kung fu. I began to paint again. I was very happy.

I stayed there for almost four years.

Then Father returned from prison.

One day I came to the kitchen, and a monk I didn't recognize was there. He was from lower down the mountain. He said that there were soldiers going from monastery to monastery looking for Xao Lan, searching cells, breaking things. Was I, perhaps, this Xao Lan? I admitted that I was. I asked who was behind this, did he know? Yes, it was Xao Xiyang, the new county commissar from Dwaizhou, a powerful official. He wanted his daughter back.

You see, Deng had been rehabilitated and slowly, slowly he began to locate his allies and supporters, including Father. The idea was to eventually gather them in Sichuan, to build a power base there to continue the reforms that had been destroyed by the Cultural Revolution. Father was on the rise again! But he was turning the Silkworm's Eyebrow upside down to find me.

The old nun left it up to me. She said that they would do their best to hide me, if that was my wish. I was so torn! I loved my life on the mountain and I loved my father. I wanted to be away from the cares of the world, but I wanted to help Father's reforms. I prayed to Kuan Yin, but I knew the answer. Father would never stop, and I could not hurt the people who had rescued me, given me a shelter and a home. I went down the mountain with the monk and turned myself over to the soldiers. But it broke my heart to say good-bye to the mountain I loved so much.

I was overjoyed to see Father again, but there was great sadness between us. Mother's death, my sister's betrayal. I asked Father if he had found her. When he didn't answer, I became frightened. I asked again. Finally he said yes, he had found her—she was dead. She had been killed in the fighting at the Chengdu factory. Now I was the only daughter, he said, and I had to live for both.

Then Father surprised me. He said I must leave China. He had lost all his family to China, except me, and he couldn't stand the thought of losing me as well. He said I must go away until the country was safe to have a family. I argued, I cried, I begged, but

Father was firm. I asked if I could go back to the mountain, but Father said that no place within China was safe. I must go away.

We spent but a few days together. Then we said good-bye and I was taken secretly to Guangzhou and put aboard a junk. I was smuggled into Hong Kong much the way you were smuggled out. I was put onshore at the typhoon shelter at Yaumatei, and that neighborhood became my new home.

But how to live? Yaumatei was very dangerous for a single young woman without connections. But Father had seen to that. I was soon visited by a local 14K Triad member. I knew nothing about Triads then, but this man told me that 14K was closely allied with mainland China, that I did not have to worry about my safety. He gave me money to live on. I thought about what I wanted to do. All I knew to do was to paint, but I could not use my own name for fear of damaging Father. I took my mother's name, Li, a very common one in China. And I did begin to paint. The freedom of Hong Kong was wonderful, and my painting began to thrive. I saw new possibilities, new forms, new colors. And there was no one watching over me to tell me what I could do or not do. I was lonely, but I was happy.

Then I met Robert. Robert had come on a holiday . . . let me see . . . two years ago? We met at the opening of a new office building where I had done murals. Robert's company was doing business with a Hong Kong company, and—

Neal tightened his grip on her shoulder.

"Wait a second," he said. "You met in Hong Kong? Not In San Francisco?"

"Hong Kong."

"You told me San Francisco before."

"Yes."

"Are you lying now or were you lying before?"

She covered his hand with hers.

"I was not in bed with you before."

"Was it love at first sight?" Neal asked. "With Pendleton?"

She hesitated before answering, "For him."

Neal's chest hurt. "But not for you?"

It seemed to take her about a week to answer, "No, not for me."

He was surprised to find himself using interrogation techniques with

263

her, varying the pace of his questions, or using silences to hype her anxiety. Was it just habit, he wondered, or did he still consider her the adversary, this woman who was lying in his bed? He waited for her to go on.

"We were together perhaps one week," she said, "before Robert had to go home. He was very sad to say good-bye, and I promised I would write."

"Did you?"

"Yes, I promised! He wrote back, or sometimes telephoned. Then . . . I was contacted by a Triad leader. He had a message from Father. Father said that Robert's knowledge would be very valuable to China."

"I'll bet."

"He asked me to 'nurture' my relationship with Robert and persuade him to come to China."

A goofy symmetry occurred to Neal: Li Lan's father summoned her to talk Pendleton into going to China; Neal's "Dad" got him to persuade Pendleton to go home.

"At first I refused. I wanted nothing more to do with politics. My life was so happy. I sent a message back begging Father to release me from this request."

I did a little begging myself. Did you do any better at it than I did? And what card did your father play?

"Then Father sent back the message that persuaded me. My sister was alive."

The ace of hearts.

"Sister was alive, but in prison. Robert was to be the price of her release."

Family is fate.

"I could not then refuse. It was my duty, and the fulfillment of the vision Kuan Yin had shown me in the Buddha's Mirror. I could not realize my true self until I confronted the face of my sister. I could not be released until she was free.

"Through Chinese agents in Hong Kong, I received more training. Training was easy for me because of my Buddhist discipline. I continued to write Robert. Then he wrote saying that he was coming to California. Would I meet him there? I told Father this news. He urged me to go. 'Now is the time,' he said.

"I had met Olivia Kendall in Hong Kong some time before. She liked my painting and had invited me to have a showing at her gallery. I wrote to her and accepted. I met Robert at his conference."

"And everything was working out just fine until Mark Chin showed up."

"We went to Olivia's. And then you came."

"So now they have Pendleton, and you have your sister back, and you can both go back to being Daddy's good little girls."

"Hong will be released when Robert begins his work here. Robert is in hiding, and we will only bring him out when it is safe."

"When will that be?"

"When you leave."

Ouch.

He traced the bones in her fingers and was surprised when she did the same on his other hand. "Let's be grown-ups here for a minute," he said. "You and I and all your buddies know that—once I'm home—there's nothing to stop me from telling everything I know."

She gripped his hand. "They would kill me."

That would stop me.

"They're bluffing."

" 'Bluffing'?"

"Making an empty threat."

She squeezed tighter. "I am a hostage to your honor."

Boy, are you in trouble.

"Wouldn't it be safer just to have me killed?"

"Yes."

"Is that why you came to tell me your story? So I would understand? Sympathize?"

"Yes."

He swallowed hard before asking the next question. "So you made love to me to improve the odds, is that it?"

She whispered the answer in his ear. "No. I made love with you because I wanted to make love with you."

So there it was. The deal was pretty clear. Her life for his, his life for hers. Talk about symmetry. Talk about Buddha's Mirror.

"I have to ask you something," he said. "Is Pendleton a volunteer? Does he want to be here, or is he a prisoner?"

"Does this make a difference?"

"It makes all the difference. You have to understand that if Pendleton wants to go home, I have to help him. I can't stay silent. So if that's the case, let's find a way to get all three of us out of here."

"Robert is very happy. He has his work. He has me."

Then Robert is very happy.

"That brings up another ugly question. Just what *is* Robert's work?"

She looked at him oddly, an I-thought-you-knew-this-already look. "To make things grow."

"And he's worth all this? Just because he can make things grow?"

"You have not seen hunger."

This is true, Neal thought. I always thought I had it tough after midnight when the Burger Joint stopped delivering and I had to walk down there.

"But you must have plenty of agricultural experts here."

"No. So many were killed! And none with Robert's knowledge."

So Pendleton gets to spend the rest of his life growing rice and loving Li Lan. Okay. But what about Li Lan?

"What about you?" he asked.

"What about me?"

"Do you love him?"

"He is good. He is kind. He will do wonderful things for my country."

"Right. Do you love him?"

She rolled over on top of him, stroking his face as she spoke. "You and I, Neal Carey, we are from different worlds. Your 'love' is not our 'love.' "

"I love you."

"I know."

In a lifetime of questions it was the hardest one.

"Do you love me back?"

She looked him in the eyes, and it was heartbreak and grace at the same time. "Yes."

"You're breaking my heart."

"I know this, too."

"How can you send me away?"

"To save our lives."

"I'll risk it."

"To save our souls."

He saw himself in her eyes. Buddha's Mirror.

266

"It is still dark out," she said.

"Yeah."

"We have some time."

He shrugged.

She slid down and took him in her mouth. He tried to focus on his anger and hurt, but soon he turned her around and then he was drinking from her. Then he entered her and they laid side by side.

"Tell me," he said.

"I love you."

"Say it in Chinese."

"*Wo ai ni*, Neal."

"*Wo ai ni*, Lan."

Their world erupted into the clouds and the rain before they fell asleep. He woke up a while later and listened to her breathing.

Li Lan's life for my silence, he thought. The Book of Joe Graham, Chapter Eight, Verse Five: Every undercover operation ends in a betrayal. I wonder if Graham expected this one to end in me betraying him and Friends.

It was still dark when he woke her up.

"It's no good," he said.

"What is no good?" she mumbled sleepily.

"I have to hear it from him."

"You are having a dream. Go back to sleep."

I wish I could, Li. I wish I could put my conscience to sleep, make love with you once more before dawn, and then sleepwalk my way through the rest of this deal. But it is no good. I have to hear from Pendleton that he wants to stay. I was sent to save him from his infatuation, and that's what I still have to do.

"I have to talk with Pendleton myself."

"Not possible."

"He has to tell me himself that he wants to give the rest of his life to this little 4-H project you have cooked up for him."

She reached between his legs and stroked him. "Do not be so silly."

He grabbed her wrist and held it still. "Take me to him. Let me talk to him alone for five minutes. If he still wants to stay, okay. I'll go home and keep my mouth shut. Word of honor."

He could feel the muscles in her wrist tighten against his hand.

"What if he says he wants to leave?" she asked.

"Will he?"

"No."

"Then why bring it up?"

She snatched her wrist away and sat up. "What if?"

He looked at the sudden anger in her eyes. It looked odd against her sleepy face and tousled hair.

"Then I have to try to take him home," Neal answered.

"You do not trust me," she said.

"Don't take it personally. I don't trust anyone."

He watched as her angry glare turned thoughtful. Then the look became seductive. She was an actress changing emotions for the camera.

"Go home tomorrow," she said. "I will visit you once a year. For a week in San Francisco. Every year until you are tired of me."

We're right back in the hot tub, he thought. Nothing's changed, including the sorry fact that I want to say yes.

"That's sick and desperate," he said.

She jumped out of the bed and grabbed her clothes, throwing them on as she spoke.

"You are the person who is sick and desperate," she said. "You chase, chase, chase—then, when you are given what you chase, you do not accept. Answers . . . truth . . . me. I make this offer to make you happy . . . to make *me* happy. Never mind. You have no choice. You do not know where Robert is, where I go. You cannot chase anymore."

"Lan, I—"

"Go home! That is all! If you say what you know, I will die! Do what you want!"

She stormed out the door.

It took him a few seconds to get his shirt and pants on and follow her. It was still dark and foggy and he could just see her as she passed through the gate into the garden. He ran down the stairs and across the little bridge. When he got through the gate she was gone.

All he could see was fog and the eerie shapes of the garden statues: dragons, birds, and giant frogs. He could hear footsteps ahead of him and he followed the sound. The garden was a maze.

When in doubt, Neal thought, go to Buddha. The gigantic head was about the only thing he could make out in the fog. It glowed palely at the edge of the cliff. He ran for it.

Her black-clad form appeared in stark silhouette against the whiteness of the Buddha's head, about twenty feet away. She was inching her way along, trying to feel for the railing that led down the stairs.

Neal realized that she was heading down to the river. She had a boat waiting. He couldn't let her meet it. He broke into a sprint.

The bullet hit Buddha square in the ear. Li Lan dropped to the ground.

"Shit."

Neal heard the voice. It was about fifty feet away, in a copse of trees to his right. He peered through the fog but couldn't see anyone. He lay on his stomach, wishing his breathing didn't make so much goddamn noise. Li Lan hadn't gotten up, so she was either hurt or just being smart. Staying flat on his stomach, he crawled to where he had seen her fall.

His hand touched her elbow and she flinched. He grabbed her arm and pulled himself against her.

He heard cautious footsteps. The shooter was maneuvering for a better angle. If he was smart, he'd work his way back onto the path and come straight onto the landing. She heard it, too.

"Are you hurt?" he asked her. It was just the slightest whisper, but it sounded like a PA announcement to him.

She shook her head.

The footsteps stopped.

"You have a boat down there," he said.

She nodded.

"You can back down the stairs without being seen."

"There is not the time. He will shoot me on the stairs."

"I'll take care of it."

The footsteps started again, slow and patient.

"Get going," he said.

"Why would you do this?"

Good fucking question.

"Because you're going to take me to Pendleton."

If I live that long.

And you might as well tell the truth as long as you're probably going to get killed anyway.

"And because I love you. Now crawl backwards onto the stairs. When you're down to the next landing, get up and make all the noise you can going down. Got that?"

"Yes."

269

"Where can I meet you?"

She didn't answer. The footsteps had stopped. The bastard was in position and just waiting for the right moment. As soon as his quarry flinched, he'd move in for the kill.

"Look," Neal whispered. "I know where your mountain is. I know it from your paintings. I can track you down, and I won't give up. It will never stop until you let me speak with Pendleton. Never. Now tell me where I can meet you, and get your ass in gear before we both get killed."

She squeezed his hand. "At the elephant."

"Where?"

"You can find it. I will be there."

"Get going."

"I am very frightened."

"I'm scared to fucking death. Now go."

She squeezed his hand again and started to crawl backward, feeling for the edge of the stairs with her feet.

Neal could just hear her make contact with the wooden steps. Now what? he thought. The opposition has a gun, and you're armed only with your fine sense of irony. Of course, he's missed once already. Maybe he's a lousy shot.

Then he heard the sound of footsteps running down the stairs to the river. She was making a real show of it, and that was just what he needed, because then he heard the shooter running along the path straight toward him.

The fucker doesn't know anyone's here, Neal realized with relief. He's running straight, hard, and fast toward the stairs, where he'll have her pinned against the river. He'll have all the shots he wants.

Neal gathered his knees underneath him.

Simms burst out of the fog, holding the pistol, barrel up, in his right hand, running hard. He was almost on top of Neal.

Neal lowered his head and sprang. The top of his head smacked Simms on the bottom of the chin.

Neal figured it worked better when you had a football helmet on, and his head spun with pain as he fell. But Simms was out, and this gave Neal a few seconds to recover. He found the pistol just a few feet from Simms's hand and picked it up.

Do it, Neal thought. You can pop him right now and toss him into

270

the river. The currents will take care of the rest. Do it. He raised the pistol and lined the sights up on Simms's forehead. Then he waited for Simms to come to. It didn't take long. Simms sat up groggily and put his hand to his chin. He looked at the blood on his palm and shook his head.

"That's twice you've missed an easy shot," Neal said.

"Carey! It took you long enough to fuck her."

"It's not too late for me to shoot you."

"You won't. You're not the type. If you were going to use it, you'd have done it when I had my eyes closed. In fact, give me back the gun before you hurt yourself. I think I need some stitches."

"Put your hands up where I can see them."

Simms didn't move. "Did you hear that line on television? It won't do you any good, Carey. As soon as the cobwebs clear, I can take you, pistol and all."

"So maybe I should shoot you right now."

"You won't. You're a pussy-whipped, sniveling little traitor, but you don't have the balls to squeeze the trigger."

Which pretty much sums it up.

"Get up," Neal said.

"Okey-dokey."

Simms wobbled to his feet. Blood dripped from his chin.

"Walk over to the edge of the cliff."

"Oh, come on."

Neal's shot whizzed well clear of Simms's head, but made its point anyway.

"Well, well," Simms said. He started walking. "That was a pretty nifty block you threw on me. Did you play football in school?"

"No, I saw it on television. How about you?"

"I'm from basketball country. Used to be a white man's game."

"Sit on the railing, facing me."

Simms looked at the spindly wooden railing that served as a shaky barrier between him and a three-hundred-foot sheer drop.

"Uhhh, Carey . . . this doesn't look like it was built by the Army Corps of Engineers."

"Gee, you might fall. Hippety-hop."

Simms eased himself onto the railing, gripping it tightly with both hands. Neal sat down on the ground and steadied the pistol on his knees. "Let's talk."

"Can I smoke?"

"No."

"You are a vindictive little bastard, Carey. You have got to stop taking these things so damn personally."

"Pendleton doesn't make herbicides, never did."

"You just figured that out?"

"Yeah."

"You're a minor-leaguer, Carey. A good minor-leaguer, but you don't have what it takes to make it in the bigs."

"So what's the big deal? Why is he so important? Why not let him come over here and grow a little food?"

Simms gave him that arrogant sneer that made Neal want to pull the trigger.

"A little food?" Simms echoed. "A little food, Carey? Grow up."

"Age me."

"It's all about food, boy. All about food. China has one quarter of the world's population. One out of every four people filling his mouth on God's good earth is a citizen of the People's Republic of China. And that's not to mention the countless Chinese in Hong Kong, Taiwan, Singapore, Vietnam, Malaysia, Indonesia—"

"I think I get it."

"No, you don't. Indonesia, Europe, and yes, America. Let's talk about America for a second, Carey, as if you cared. How many Chinese did you ever see on welfare? Cashing in food stamps, in prison?"

"What the hell are you talking about?"

"These people work their asses off, Carey. They save their money, they study like hell, they break their balls to make it. And they do. You let them out of this enormous open-air prison here, and they make it. In fact, they kick our butts. Now, what do you think would happen if mainland China stopped being a prison? What would happen if the Chinese here could do what their expatriate relatives have done?"

"Gee, I don't know. What?"

"We'd be finished, Carey. The good old U.S.A. couldn't hack the competition. Not with our standard of living, our unions, our big cars, our little savings accounts . . . our small population, our lack of disipline. The Chinese are organized, Carey, or haven't you noticed? Have you seen a dirty street here? Litter on the roadside? They organize brigades to sweep and clean. In three years, during the Great Leap Forward, they reorganized their entire population into teams and brigades. Why, you let these people finally get their act together, and we couldn't sell so much as a dress shirt on the world market. It would start with textiles, then it would be electronics, then steel and iron, automobiles, airplanes . . . then banking and real estate, and you can kiss us good-bye. One quarter of the world's population, Carey? Unchained? Shit, look at what the Japs have done to us in thirty stinking years. China has ten times the population, and one hundred times the resources."

Neal's head hurt like crazy. He glanced sideways at Buddha's head, and wondered about the organization and discipline it had taken to build the gigantic statue. One thousand years ago.

"Thanks for the geography lesson," he said, "but what does this have to do with Pendleton?"

Simms started to raise his hand for emphasis, but grabbed the railing again when it shook.

"Food," he said. "There are two things that are holding the Chinese back. The first is food, and the second is Mao."

"Mao's dead. It was in all the papers."

"Exactly. Mao's dead and Maoism is on the rocks. There's a battle going on here between the democratic reformers and the hardline Maoists, and the major weapon is food. It's China's age-old issue: What system will provide the most food? Some boys down here in Sichuan have figured out that privately owned land is more productive than state-owned land. You get it? You take an acre and give it to a family. You take the next acre and have the government run it, and guess what? The family acre kicks significant butt. No contest."

"How's your backflip, Simms? Pretty good?"

"Don't get itchy, I'm getting to Doctor Bob, I am."

"Hurry up."

"The boys down here are quietly converting the whole province to privately owned land. The only way they can get away with it is by being so successful that no one will dare to purge them. Old Deng Xiaoping knows that his road to Beijing runs right through the farmland of Sichuan, and he's started his own little Sichuan Mafia down here. It's going to surface if and when the agricultural experiment becomes an undeniable success. Then he'll use that success to rout the Maoists and launch democratic capitalist reforms over the whole country."

Neal's head was whirling.

He asked, "Wouldn't we want to get behind that? The democratization of the largest country in the world?"

"On the surface, sure. But think about it, Carey. Even you can think this through. Think about a China that looks like Japan. All those people, all those international connections, all that organization and discipline. You modernize that, you shrug off the Maoist yoke—I'm telling you Carey, when these people can feed themselves, it's all over for the white man in the good old U.S. of A."

Neal's wrist started to ache. The pistol was heavier than it looked, a lot heavier than it looked on TV.

"Are you telling me," Neal asked, "that we're supporting the Maoists in this battle?"

"We're supporting the legitimate government of the People's Republic of China. Yes, it happens to be hard-line Maoist at this time."

"And we want it to stay that way."

"I believe I've explained the doleful alternatives."

"It's a long fall and I'm getting impatient."

Simms smirked. "That's just like you, Carey. I'm talking about the lives of a few hundred million people, and you're bitching about your delicate emotional condition. My head's getting clear, Carey. I can take you with one rush before you squeeze off a shot."

"Come on."

"When I'm ready."

"I'm ready to hear about Pendleton."

"You just don't get it, do you? Pendleton was on the verge of developing Supershit, Mighty Manure. It maximizes the nitrogen content of the soil, accelerates the growing process."

"So?"

"So it would give these agrarian reformers down here a third crop. Get it, Carey? They get two harvests of rice a year now. With Doc Pendleton's Homegrown Formula they could get three. That's a thirty-three percent gain. You add thirty-three percent to what they're already doing, and . . . well, it's a lot of rice. More than enough rice to make Deng the top chink, more than enough rice to turn this fucked-up shithole into a modern country. We can't let that happen, Carey."

274

"Maybe *you* can't."

Neal watched Simms's eyes. They were getting clearer and his breathing was slowing down. If Simms was going to make a rush, it could come anytime. Neal tightened his finger on the trigger.

"Well, it ain't just me, Carey boy. It's the Chinese government. They don't want Pendleton here, either."

"Why don't they throw him out, then?"

"Boy, you are just dumber than mud, aren't you? That slant must have balled your brains out! The Beijing boys didn't bring Pendleton in. They don't know where he is, and they can't even prove he's here. They have their suspicions, but suspicions aren't enough anymore. Things are a bit delicate around here lately. Do you know how hard it is to hit somebody with a pistol shot, even from this range? Have you ever shot anybody?"

"Want to find out?"

"It was a rhetorical question, Carey. Anyway, it's a renegade group running this Pendleton operation. Hard to say how high up it goes. Hard to say if Deng even knows about it. But I'll tell you this, the Beijing boys and I are of one mind about this. I have free rein to find your friends and dispose of them as I see fit."

"How did you find us?"

Neal saw Simms's hands loosen their grip. He had found his balance and was getting set.

"You helped, in your debriefing. You told me all about the scrumptious dinner old Li Lan made for you. She could only come from around here, boy. Then I got hold of one of her brochures. She cooks Sichuan, she paints Sichuan . . . hell, I figured she's from Sichuan."

Bullshit. Good bullshit, but bullshit. Recipes and paintings couldn't tell you my exact schedule and location, but what could? The Sichuan Mafia has a mole, a double, an informer. I wonder who?

"So how do you and Peng get along?" Neal asked. "Okay?"

The reaction was infinitesimal, but it was there. You're good, Neal thought, very good, but I'm better. I've been watching people blink all my life, and that was a blink.

"Who's Peng?" Simms asked.

"Yeah, okay."

"You picked a hell of time to stop being stupid," Simms said. "I was going to let you walk."

275

"Where did you go to school?"

"North Carolina."

"They have a diving team? Were you on it? How did you do in the three-hundred-foot freestyle?"

"You're just not a killer, boy. You're a disaster. The big mistake the girl made was coming to see you. We didn't have a line on her until now. And now it's just a matter of time. You fucked her good, all right."

Time, Neal thought. Time is the issue right now. Simms had missed with his shot intentionally. He didn't want to kill Lan, he wanted to make her run. Just as he'd done every step of the way. What we need here is a little time, a little lead.

He stood up and raised the pistol.

"Let's go," he said.

"Where?"

"Down the stairs."

"You're kidding."

"I'm a funny boy. Come on."

Simms eased himself off the railing and stepped onto the landing beside Buddha's head. Neal gave him plenty of room and left four steps between them as he followed Simms down the steps. They walked down past Buddha's chin, then his chest, paused at a landing by his belly, and finally made it down to his big toe. The brown river swirled just beneath them.

"Sit down," Neal said.

Simms hesitated. He was thinking about taking his chance, but Neal stayed on the steps, out of reach but within pistol range. Simms sat down.

"Take off your shoes," Neal said.

Simms untied his leather saddle shoes.

"Wallet and watch," Neal said.

"What is this, a mugging?"

"You might want to take off your jacket."

Simms got it just then.

"Carey, you don't think I'm going to jump in the river, do you?"

"Now jump in the river."

"I can't swim."

"Float."

"Shoot me."

Neal raised the pistol.

It was no good. He wasn't going to shoot. He knew it and Simms knew it. Even Buddha knew it.

Neal stepped off the landing onto Buddha's foot. Simms smiled and started to circle. He did a good job, maneuvering Neal between himself and the river. Neal kept the gun pointed at Simms's chest, an easier target than his head.

"I can't miss from here," he said.

"Then shoot."

Neal tightened his finger on the trigger. It was just enough to make Simms move. He jolted forward like he was on springs. He came in low, fast and hard, with his head down and his arms forward, straight at Neal's chest.

Neal's chest wasn't there. Neal had dropped to the ground a half-second after bluffing with the trigger. All Simms hit was air, and then the water.

Neal watched the current carry Simms away.

Neal scurried back up the stairs, through the garden, and into the monastery. He went to his room and packed a few things into his bag. Then he went to Wu's room and tapped on the door.

A groggy Wu came to the door, and Neal pushed him back inside the room.

"Are you drunk?" Wu asked.

"Where's the Silkworm's Eyebrow?"

"What?"

"Where's the Silkworm's Eyebrow?"

"On the silkworm?"

"No, it's a mountain. In Chinese, what's the Silkworm's Eyebrow?"

Wu came awake. "Oh! Mount Emei. 'Emei' means Silkwo—"

"How far is it?"

"Not far. Perhaps ten or twenty *li.*"

"I want to go there, right now."

"Not possible at any time. Absolutely not."

"I have to go there."

"I cannot take you. I would get in big trouble."

"Tell them I forced you."

Wu chuckled. "How are you going to force me?"

277

Neal pulled the gun from his jacket and pointed it at Wu's nose. Wu doesn't know what a wimp I am with guns, he thought.

"You are crazy," said Wu.

"This is a good thing for you to keep in mind. Now let's go wake up the driver and go to Mount Emei."

Wu flapped his hands in frustration. "Why do you want to do this?"

"Because I'm crazy. You have one minute to get dressed. Go."

Wu got dressed and led Neal to the driver's room. Neal greeted the driver with the pistol and held it on him while Wu explained the situation. The driver smiled calmly at Neal and shrugged.

"Emei?" he asked.

"Emei."

The driver pulled his shoes on. Five minutes later they were in the car. Neal sat in the backseat and kept the pistol pressed to Wu's head.

They were at the base of Mount Emei just as the sun came up.

19

品

The car climbed dirt switchbacks up the foothills of the mountain until
the road ended on a broad knoll. A few thatch-roofed huts huddled on
the edge of the treeless hill. The Sichuan basin stretched out below to
the north. To the south and west, the heavily forested slopes of Mount
Emei dominated the skyline, and to the far west the snow-capped peaks
of the Himalayan foothills loomed like a promise and a threat.

The village had the tattered, dirty look of rural poverty. Acrid smoke
poured from holes in the roofs of shacks. A scraggly garden plot fought
for survival in a sea of wild grass. A few skinny sheep and goats bleated
indignant protests at the arrival of the strange motorcar.

"This is as far as he can go," Wu said as the driver pulled to a stop.

Neal could sense rather than see the eyes of the villagers observing
the government car. No one came out to greet them. He pointed to a
trodden dirt path that scarred the grass.

"Is that the only way up the mountain?"

Wu spoke to the driver.

"It's the only way up," Wu translated. "You go down on the other
side."

"What about airstrips? Helicopter pads?"

Another exchange.

"The only thing you can fly to that mountain is a dragon."

"Good."

Neal started to gather his bag together.

"The police will be right behind you, you know. You cannot escape."

"I don't need to escape. I just need a little time. If they have to walk, they won't get there ahead of me."

"I will come with you."

Neal smiled at him. "I'm honored. But no thanks."

"Why are you doing this?"

"Because your father went to jail for speaking English."

"Do not joke."

"I'm not."

Neal got out of the car. The driver looked straight ahead, still smiling calmly. Wu looked as if he were about to cry.

"Good-bye, Xiao Wu," Neal said.

"Good-bye, Neal Carey."

"We will see each other again."

"Fuck yes."

"Fuck yes."

Neal took the pistol from his jacket, pointed, and pulled the trigger. The right front tire hissed its death throes before expiring. Neal was pleased—he had never shot anything before. He executed the left rear tire in the same fashion.

"Sorry," he said to the driver. "It'll give me a little more of a start."

The driver shrugged. He seemed to understand.

Neal walked backward along the trail and kept his eye on the car, just in case Xiao Wu and the driver were thinking about trying to catch him and wrestle him to the ground. The path took a dip out of sight about fifty yards away, so he turned around and headed for the mountain.

He felt exhilarated, almost carefree. It was strange, because he had nothing but cares. He had to catch Li Lan before Simms and Peng did—warn her that her organization had a mole and that she and Pendleton would never be safe. And he was now the proverbial man without a country—not America, not China. If he survived the next few days, which was a poor bet at best, he had nowhere to go, nowhere to hide.

But he felt the energizing simplicity of desperation. It felt great to be done with the myriad complexities of intrigue, with the subtle maneuvers, with the twisted emotions, with the damn *thinking*. The whole mess had come to a race up a mountain, and the fresh air and open spaces sang to him as he settled into a pace.

He realized he hadn't been alone in three months, not for a single hour, and he certainly hadn't been free. Now he looked up at the magnificent panorama of mountains and valleys, and he felt . . . clean. He hadn't felt clean in a long, long time.

The climb began abruptly as the grassy plateau gave way to a narrow saddle and the dirt trail yielded to a more formal stone path. The saddle emptied into a thick grove of bamboo, beyond which was a stone bridge over a fast, narrow stream. On the other side of the bridge, Neal passed under a large open gate to the bottom of a steep knoll. The stone steps flanked the edge of a wall, behind which was an enormous temple. Neal paused at the first landing and felt the pins and needles in his legs. The trail ahead of him went straight uphill for as far as he could see. It was going to be a long day.

And he had to find an elephant.

No, not an elephant. *The* elephant. On a Chinese mountain.

Speaking of elephants on Chinese mountains, he thought . . . I'm probably pretty conspicuous now that daylight's here.

He walked up the stairs until he came to an open arched gate, then stepped inside. He was standing at the edge of a large courtyard where a small battalion of monks were doing t'ai chi. Other monks, who looked like young novices, scurried about with wooden buckets of water and bundles of firewood. Neal surmised that they were getting ready for the old after–t'ai chi breakfast. Neal sidled along the edge of the courtyard beneath a tiled portico, then slipped through the first open door.

The sanctuary was full of statues, sticks of incense smoldering in their stone hands. Neal hit the staircase just inside the door and found himself in a hallway in front of a row of rooms. In the trusting, cloistered atmosphere of the monastery, the rooms were unlocked.

So much for trust, Neal thought, as he went inside the first room. A heavy shirt and a pair of peasant trousers hung on a wooden peg. Working clothes, Neal thought, as he held the shirt up against his chest. It was much too large, so he tried the next room. Still too large.

He hit the jackpot at the end of the hallway, where a larger room had eight *kangs* and eight sets of work clothes. Must be the novices' dorm, he thought. He found a set of clothes that fit loosely, then stripped off his own Western clothes and changed into the Chinese workaday outfit. He kept his tennis shoes, though, figuring that a change of footwear didn't make sense for a long climb up a mountain. Besides, if anyone got close enough to notice his shoes, they would also notice his round eyes.

A few more minutes of scavenging got him a wide straw hat, which he slanted down over his forehead.

There was still the problem of his modern Western bag. He gave a resigned sigh, then removed his copy of *Random* and Li Lan's brochure from the bag and put them in the shirt's wide hip pocket. He took out his toothbrush, toothpaste, and razor and put them in the other pocket, and shoved Simms's pistol into the back of his pants at the waist. Then he rolled the bag up tightly and put it under his arm until he could find a safe place to dump it.

He paused at the top of the stairs and listened. The t'ai chi was still going on, and he could hear the clatter of kettles and plates from the kitchen. He hustled down the stairs and went to find a back exit, then passed through the row of statues and under another arch into a broad courtyard.

To his left, a small pagoda supported a bronze bell about nine feet high and eight feet around. A monk sat by the ladder leading up to the bell, but he didn't seem to notice Neal. To Neal's right, a twenty-foot tower rose over the monastery walls. It had fourteen levels, with large characters inscribed on each level. Neal walked through the courtyard and up some steps into a large temple.

The usual saints were there, and a large Buddha, but the central figure was a sixteen-foot-tall bronze statue of a man sitting astride an elephant.

Okay, Neal thought, now we'll see if Li Lan's word is any good after all.

"Did you steal those clothes?" he heard her ask.

"Yup."

She came out from behind one of the statues. She was wearing cotton peasant pants and an old Mao jacket and cap. Her eyes brimmed with tears and she threw her arms around him.

"You are alive," she whispered.

He hugged her back. It felt great.

"We don't have a lot of time," he said. "They'll be coming after us. There's a traitor in your old man's operation."

He felt her body tense.

"You led them here?" she asked.

"They know anyway. Listen to me. One of your father's people, Peng, is a mole, a traitor. He's working for the other side. You didn't tell me your father was working against the government."

"He is working to become the government."

"Is he part of this 'Sichuan Mafia'?"

"I have heard it called that, yes."

"Pendleton's on the mountain?"

She hesitated. "Yes."

"Is there any other way off the mountain? An escape route?"

"It is very dangerous. Over the top and down the western side. Then by foot road to Tibet. It is very long and very dangerous. But the Yi people hate the government. They would lead us. And hide us."

"Okay," he said, "here's the deal. You take me to Pendleton. If he wants to stay, fine. He stays and takes his chances. If he wants to leave, your people give us a guide and supplies and we hit the road to Tibet. Deal?"

"Deal."

Well, half a deal anyway. Peng wasn't sitting at the table.

"Tell me the truth," he said. "If Pendleton decides to stay, is he committing suicide? Is there a chance you can make it while Peng knows what's going on?"

She nodded. "Father is very powerful. Peng will be afraid to move against him without proof. He will need possession of Robert and me, and to connect us with Father."

"Can he do that?"

She nodded again. "Father is on mountain."

"Jesus Christ! Why?"

She smiled wanly. "To see Robert, to see me, to see my sister. It was to have been a happy family reunion."

Maybe it still can be, Neal thought. If two can walk to Tibet, so can five. But none of that can happen unless we can get to the top before we get caught.

"Let's get going," he said.

The path led out the back of the monastery on a narrow raised road flanked by fields where a few farmers were at work. Neal and Li came

283

to a bridge over a rapid creek, and Neal tossed his bag into the water.

The path was level and the walking easy as the path ran beside another creek, past ancient, gigantic banyan trees. The countryside was still fairly open, and they could see the rocky crags of Emei's lower slopes. They came to a village of about a hundred pleasant, thatch-roofed wooden houses amid a grove of tall bamboo. Neal sat at the edge of the path as Lan stopped at one house and came out a minute later with two *mantou* and two bamboo cups of tea. They sat under the bamboo and ate quickly, then started back up the path, which went across another bridge and then up a steep incline through a thick forest of fir trees.

It emerged into open country between the creek and a high, rocky knoll on which was perched a large monastery. It was midmorning, the sun was out, and Neal felt sweat beginning to break out on his back and then trickle down his spine. Li Lan was setting a healthy pace, and the increasing pitch didn't seem to bother her. Neal had thought that walking up the stone steps would be easier than struggling up an incline, but the backs of his thighs were already starting to ache and the soles of his feet felt the pounding.

Another half hour of climbing took them under a wooden arch where four wooden poles supported three tiled, curved roofs, and then up along the edge of a knoll to an ornate monastery. A broad terrace looked out over a deep, forested chasm.

"We will rest here," Li said.

"If you really want to," Neal said between gasps.

"This is an historic place," Li said, "where Emperor Kang-hsi visited and gave the abbot a jade seal."

"When was this?" Neal asked, eager to keep up the conversation—and the breather.

"Qing Dynasty. In your time, the late sixteenth century."

Around the time of Shakespeare, Neal thought.

"Emperor Kang-hsi gave this place the name 'Dragon's Abode.' "

"Did dragons live here?"

Li laughed. "No, but wolves and tigers did, down the hill, until the abbot built a watchtower with fire to scare them off. The fire at night looked like a dragon's mouth. So the name is a funny joke."

"Pretty droll emperor."

"The resting time is finished."

Which will teach me to mouth off about the emperor.

To Neal's surprise and relief, the path went downhill in a switchback around another steep knoll. It crossed and recrossed the curving river on stone bridges, finally working its way down to a waterfall about twelve feet high.

They crossed the river just downstream of the waterfall, and Neal enjoyed the spray of the cool water as he passed by. He looked over the bridge into a pool, where smooth stones sparkled like jade. Then he followed Li around what looked to be an enormous monastery. Li went in a side gate and emerged a few minutes later with two wooden bowls of rice and some pickled vegetables. Neal shoveled the food down gratefully while sitting on the path, and then they started off again.

The path led to a ferociously steep, zigzag incline surrounded by a thick bamboo forest. Each switchback led to just another switchback, higher than the last, on the very edge of the mountain. The view was stunning, overlooking the valleys and plains to the east and the path they had just ascended, but after three or four switchbacks, Neal stopped looking. He just put his head down and concentrated on putting one foot in front of the other. His shirt was soaked with sweat, and his eyes stung from perspiration and fatigue.

He almost missed the tree with the "wanted" poster on it.

"What's this?" he asked Li.

A sketch of a monkey's face had been nailed to a tree.

"Bandit monkey," she said matter-of-factly.

"Bandit monkey?"

"Yes, it offers a reward for this monkey . . . named One Fang . . . because it has been robbing pilgrims. There are many bandit monkeys on Emei. Only the very worst get a poster."

She started back up the hill.

Bandit monkeys, Neal thought. He pictured Central Park with gangs of simian muggers running around, dropping on people out of trees . . . taking their peanuts . . . then gave up the fantasy. Central Park was bad enough.

"What do the monkeys steal?" he called ahead.

"You will see!"

Say what?

"What do you mean?!"

"Monkeys any time now!"

Monkeys any time now. Neal stopped for a second to break a dead branch of bamboo and strip it down into a walking stick. Then he remembered that he had a gun and felt a little foolish. I wonder if the monkeys understand what a gun is? he wondered.

They didn't.

It was three switchbacks later when about half a dozen monkeys came scrambling down through the bamboo and blocked the path in front of them. They were about the size of cocker spaniels and had a good sense of terrain, because they plopped themselves just where the path took a wicked outside curve over a deep canyon. Two of the monkeys stayed in the bamboo on the uphill side to block that escape. The monkeys looked for all the world like a hairy street gang extorting passersby on their turf. The head monkey wasn't One Fang, because he had two very large, healthy incisors that he displayed in a a growl of anger and arrogance.

He got angrier when Li Lan whacked him in the legs with her walking stick. He leaped in the air, snarling and snapping, and rushed toward her legs. She stepped back and swung at him again, missing him by an inch as he somersaulted backward. Another monkey rushed at her from the side. Neal couldn't swing at it with his stick without hitting Li, so he kicked at the monkey, which retreated up the path and hunched into a threatening crouch. The rest of the monkeys contributed screams and howls of intimidation and hilarity and waited for the next round.

Neal pulled the pistol from his waistband. He leveled it at the lead monkey, who sat staring at it curiously and issued a low growl. He might not have recognized a gun, but he knew a threat when he saw one. He started to back away, still growling. His gang followed him as he scrambled back up the hill into the bamboo.

Neal pulled the pistol up and blew into the barrel before sticking it back in his pants.

Li didn't get it.

"You'll be okay now, ma'am," Neal said, "as long as I've got this here Winchester."

Then a small stone hit him in the side of the head. This was followed by a barrage of rocks, sticks, nuts, and fruit that followed Neal and Li as they retreated about fifty feet down the path.

Son of a bitch, Neal thought. The bastards understand firepower.

Sure enough, four monkeys were still launching missiles while their comrades hustled around the hillside collecting ammunition. Neal picked up a handful of small, sharp stones and flung them toward the monkey battery on the hillsides. He found the resulting cries of indignation extremely satisfactory, especially when his adversaries retreated up the hill.

Joe Graham is wrong, Neal thought. I *can* outsmart an ape.

He found this wasn't exactly true, however, when it became apparent that all the monkeys had done was set their blockade up on the next switchback. Two of the largest were sitting in the middle of the path, grinning with immense glee while their supporting troops crouched in the bamboo, ammunition already at hand—or paw.

"Uh, how many switchbacks are there?" Neal asked, aware that this could go on all day.

"Many."

"What do the monkeys want?" Maybe it would be easier to pay the toll and get on with it.

"Food."

"Do we have any?"

"No."

"Right. I'm going to shoot one."

"No!"

"We could collect the reward."

"For a live monkey only."

"We don't have time to fuck around here, Li."

She looked at him curiously and with a trace of indignation until he realized that she hadn't understood the idiom.

"I mean we have to get going."

The monkeys, fully aware of the humans' hesitation, sensed victory and inched closer. Great grimaces of dominance spread across their faces and they scratched vigorously.

"You may not shoot them," Li said firmly.

Besides, Neal thought, I probably couldn't hit one anyway. And they are kind of cute, in a repulsive sort of way. He drew the gun anyway and pointed it at the leader. The leader didn't show any signs of intimidation this time, unless rubbing one's genitals could be interpreted as a sign of terror. Then he shot back, so to speak, with a stream of urine.

"That does it," Neal said. "Can you stand them off for a few minutes?"

"I think so."

Neal retreated down to the edge of the last curve and then headed up the hill through the bamboo. He scratched his way up to the next level of the path until he was looking down at the monkeys. He gathered up rocks, sticks, and fruits and then headed down toward the spot where the monkey gang was in its standoff with Li Lan. He snuck from tree to tree, being as quiet as a city-bred klutz can be in a bamboo jungle, until he stood about twenty feet above the gang.

He took a Ron Guidry windup and launched a rock at the leader, scoring a strike on its haunches. The monkey yelped more with surprise than with pain and turned to see where the rock had come from. Neal then threw as many of his missiles as he could get off, and screamed obscenities.

The startled monkeys froze on the path and glared up at him. For one ugly moment, Neal thought they were going to charge him, but his last pitch was a wicked curve with a bamboo stick that hit the leader in the left shoulder.

The leader turned tail and the monkeys ran, downhill this time, and Li Lan scurried up the path to Neal.

Neal waited for her praise and gratitude.

"I perhaps should have told you about the snakes."

"Snakes?"

"Poisonous snakes, yes."

"Yes, you perhaps should have told me about them."

She nodded solemnly. "There are many poisonous snakes in the bamboo forests here."

"Thank you."

"You are welcome. Shall we continue?"

She started up the switchback. Neal picked up some stones and put them in his pockets in case the monkeys tried to gain the upper hand on them again.

He shouldn't have worried. No monkey on earth was ambitious enough to tackle the next few switchbacks, which were made up of narrow stone steps that rose at an impossible grade up to the very edge of the mountain. It seemed like some endless torture of running up stadium steps, prescribed by some goofy, sadistic Chinese football coach.

Neal knew that the top of each stairway had to be—*had* to be—the last, but each time he reached a landing it was only a prelude to the next zigzagging staircase. His thighs and calves strained and ached, and his lungs started to struggle for air.

In addition to the exertion, there was the bonus of fear. They were walking along the edge of the mountain, on the rim of steep cliffs and deep chasms, on steps that were a thousand years old. The steps were gullied and chipped, and where water ran down from uphill, they were slippery as well. Most of the trail wasn't that dangerous, and a fall would have been broken quickly by the thick bamboo, but other spots offered the prospect of a dramatic free fall into jagged rocks, rushing streams, and waterfalls. It was a painter's dream, no question, but a nightmare for Neal Carey, who was afraid of heights.

So he was exhausted, hungry, aching, and nauseated with fear when the trail finally leveled out before narrowing into an arched stone bridge.

"The Bridge of Deliverance!" Li announced over the roar of a huge waterfall above them.

"Why is it called that?!" Neal shouted, praying that the answer didn't involve an albino boy and a banjo.

"Here, all fatigue disappears, because the sound of the rushing water is so beautiful! Sit and listen!"

She crossed the bridge to a small level spot and scooped some stones from a pool in the river. She came back and handed the stones to Neal.

"These are stones from the Great Lake above, and they have great medicinal qualities! You boil them in water and drink the water and you will never have a heart attack!"

"You'd better keep them on hand."

"Are you rested?"

"Why did you have to hide Pendleton on the *top* of the mountain?!"

"Because it is hard to get there!"

"One more minute."

He stood up and leaned gingerly on the bridge wall. He had to admit that the sound of the water was lovely, and the panorama was sensational. He could see the peak of the mountain, their goal, shining in the sunlight above him. The waterfall cascaded right beside him, casting a small rainbow where it smashed into the rocks. The bamboo forest was a sea of emerald. And there was always Li to look at. He was sadistically pleased to see sweat on her face.

She frowned. "Now I am afraid perhaps the trail becomes difficult."

"Oh, *now* it does?"

"I am afraid perhaps yes."

Neal had come to understand that the more modifiers a polite Chinese person threw into a sentence, the worse the situation was.

"More steps?" he asked.

"Yes." Then her face brightened. "But they are not stone!"

"Nails?"

"Wood!"

Wood. Hmmm . . .

"For how far?"

"Perhaps maybe one thousand feet."

"Pendleton walked up here?"

"Oh, yes!"

"Let's do it."

Yeah, right, let's do it, he thought about a half hour later as his heart slammed and his chest pounded back. The beauty would have been breathtaking if the climb hadn't already done the job. But fear is a wonderful motivator. Neal was tired from the climb, but his mind reminded his body that there were angry people chasing them up that slope, and mind and body got together to make a batch of adrenaline to help him finish the climb.

The path finally flattened out on a level shelf that skirted yet another promontory. A sharp cliff dropped off on Neal's right. To his left, a dramatic complex of balconies and terraces had been built into the steep hillside. Under different circumstances he would have wanted to stop and explore the buildings, but the sun was dropping along with his energy and morale, and the morning's adventure had become the afternoon's grim march.

The path dropped steeply downhill, which Neal found almost as wearing as the uphill struggles, through a stretch of sparse scrub pine, across another narrow stream, and then uphill again. He and Li passed a few monks here and there, but otherwise the mountain seemed empty. Where, Neal wondered, were all these pilgrims trying to find enlightenment? He hadn't seen one stinking pilgrim. He made a mental note to ask Li, when they stopped. *If* they stopped.

They would have to stop soon, he thought as he forced his legs up another steep stretch of stone stairs. It would be impossible to hike this trail at night, even with lanterns. He was nervous walking along it even in daylight, afraid a tired misstep would send him hurtling to his own enlightenment in the canyons below.

And they would have to sleep. He was exhausted and numb. She must be tired, also. And whoever was chasing them had to be beat, as well. He figured he and Li had at least a four-hour jump on them, and their pursuers wouldn't be able to move at night either.

He was about to share this analysis with Li Lan, when he heard her chanting.

"*Yi, ar, yi, ar, yi, ar, yi* . . ."

"What are you doing?"

"Counting. One, two, one, two, one, two . . ."

"Why?"

"It takes mind away from the pain in your legs. Try it."

"What I had more in mind was a hot bath, a bed, and a bottle of scotch."

"Try it."

He tried it. He chanted along with her, matching his steps to the beat. He felt stupid at first, but then it began to work. It was so silly and so childish that he began to laugh. Then they laughed together, taking turns at counting off the cadence, and the game took them across more stone bridges, through more thick bamboo forests, up an incredibly vicious series of switchbacks, past three more monasteries and temples, and along the edge of a terrifying cliff.

"*Yi, ar, yi, ar, yi, ar, yi* . . ."

"*Yi, ar, yi, ar, yi, ar, yi* . . ."

They were heading up some stairs when he fell.

It was stupid, really. He simply missed the switch in the switchback and walked straight off the edge of the trail. One second he was mindlessly chanting, the next second he was in midair.

A fir tree broke his fall and cracked at least one of his ribs.

His shriek echoed through the canyon, so he had the rare opportunity of listening several times to the sound of his own pain. The jolt of agony sped like an express train from his chest to his brain. His brain told him to shut the fuck up, so he clamped his jaws together and whimpered. He wanted to roll around on the ground, but he was afraid to move because his position—feet jammed against a tree on the side of a cliff—was somewhat precarious. When he looked up he saw that he had fallen about fifteen feet. When he looked down he was quite content with his broken ribs; he had another thousand or so feet to fall if he wanted to throw back this card and draw another one.

He rolled over gently on his stomach so that he was facing uphill, and began to claw his way back up to the path. Li stretched her walking stick out. He grabbed it and she pulled him up. Back on the relative safety of the path, he rolled around on the ground in agony.

"Is anything broken?" she asked.

"I think a rib or two."

"That is too bad."

She was a bit too cool for his taste. He would have liked her to be a little more upset. A few tears would have been okay.

"Does it hurt much?"

"No. I'm just cleaning the steps with the back of my shirt."

"Yes. It would be better if you would be still."

"It would also be better if you'd shut the fuck up."

"Better also to be calm."

Calm. Right. My stomach feels like it's been napalmed. We're halfway up a mountain, it's getting dark, I can't breathe or walk, and some very heavy types who are chasing us just got a major boost. So let me indulge in a little panic for a minute.

Not to mention self-pity.

"Do not worry," she said. "I can carry you."

"Lan, don't be offended, but you don't resemble—in any way, shape, or form—a mule."

"I can carry you."

"I have at least forty pounds on you."

"We must take off shirt and take care of ribs."

"You touch that shirt, you go off the edge."

"Tough man."

"That's 'tough guy.' Aahhhh!!!"

She opened his shirt. His rib cage was turning purple. His head whirled and he almost fainted, but a silly sense of male pride kept him conscious.

"I will do some pressing," she said.

"I'll shoot you."

She apparently didn't believe him, because she dug a finger into the muscles above the ribs. The pain didn't stop, but the piercing stabs settled into a dull, sick ache.

"How did you do that?"

"Be still."

She did more pressing. Then she manipulated the broken rib. This time Neal fainted.

He awoke to the sound of her *yi-ar* chant. She was climbing a hill, carrying him piggyback, her knees bent to adjust to the extra load. The sky was slate gray.

His ribs throbbed to the rhythm of her gait.

"Put me down."

"No."

"You can't carry me up this mountain!"

"What am I doing now?"

Carrying me up this mountain.

"It is an old tradition. Buddhist grooms used to carry their brides up the mountain."

"I've been meaning to ask you, why haven't we seen all these devout pilgrims climbing to Buddha's Mirror?"

"Cultural Revolution."

Cultural Revolution, Cultural Revolution. It seemed like the answer to every question. Why did the chicken cross the road? Cultural Revolution.

"It was very dangerous to be religious," she continued, "so people could not travel to Emei to make climb. Even some monasteries on the bottom of the mountain were destroyed by the Red Guard. Very sad."

"I'll slow you down."

She stopped. "You are slowing me down by making me talk. Interrupting my chanting. With the chanting, you are light. Without it, you are heavy. We have far to go and darkness comes soon. So be quiet. Please."

He sank back down on her back. Before long the sky around them turned golden, then orange, then red, setting the mountain off in an almost surreal glow. The miles passed with the litany of *yi, ar,* throb, throb.

Just as the sky turned black, Li carried Neal through the gates of a monastery. Neal recognized the statue of Kuan Yin, Goddess of Mercy, before Li collapsed in exhaustion.

*   *   *

Neal lay on his *kang* later that night. The monks had wrapped his rib cage in a cloth boiled in an herbal mixture. They had forced some noxious, hot liquid down his throat that eased the pain. Then they had stretched a course net over the top of the bed and left him to get some rest.

What's the net for? Neal wondered. We have to be at least nine thousand feet up here, well above the mosquitoes. Besides, the net was too coarse to keep out anything but a mutant giant mosquito. What was it for? He had his answer a few seconds later, when he heard the scurrying of paws across the floor. He looked down to see at least eight pairs of red eyes studying him.

Rats.

They were all over the place, scratching at his discarded shoes, sniffing at the edge of the *kang*, scavenging for food. Neal huddled up in his clothing, trying to cover up every bit of his person he possibly could. He closed his eyes and tried to sleep, but the thought of a rat nibbling at his foot kept him awake. Just then a rat ran straight across the top of the net over Neal's chest. Neal heaved himself up and screamed. His chest responded with a stab of fire that put Neal back in a prone position. It was probably just his imagination, but he thought he saw the rat grin at him. The rat chattered busily. Neal figured that the rodent was telling his buddies they had a helpless victim here.

Bandit monkeys, marauding rats ... It's a good thing there aren't any wolves or tigers left on this damn mountain—or are there? He entertained himself with visions of tigers and wolves creeping stealthily up the stairway. Well, at least they'd scare off the rats. He finally dozed off to that pleasant fantasy.

He screamed as he felt the tiny claws scrape his chest.

"It is just me," Li Lan said as she climbed into bed.

"Don't let the rats in."

She snuggled against him carefully.

After a few moments she said, "The climb tomorrow is difficult and treacherous. You cannot go on, I think."

"I have to see Pendleton."

She thought for a moment.

"I can bring him down here in two days."

"We don't have two days, Lan. I'll be caught by tomorrow morning."

As soon as Li settled in, the rats became active again. Neal listened to the scraping sounds of their claws on the wooden floor.

"Don't the rats bother you?"

"This is why we use the nets."

"Why not traps?"

"Killing is wrong."

Killing is wrong. Neal tried to tally the number of people who had been killed to bring Pendleton to the top of this mountain. Jesus, had it only been two? The Doorman and Leather Boy One? Only two? What am I thinking about? Two are enough. More than enough. And we ain't home yet.

"We must leave as soon as it is light," Li said.

Good, Neal thought. She's accepted that I'm going with her.

"Sure," he said.

"Sleep now."

"Okay."

She stroked his chest. "I would like to do more than sleep, but you are wounded."

"Well, maybe if you were real gentle with me . . ."

"Oh, I can be very gentle."

She was, Neal thought later, remarkably gentle.

"Li Lan," he said, "when I go down the mountain . . . on the other side . . . will you go with me?"

She took a long time to answer.

"Tomorrow," she said, her voice edged with excitement, "we will look into Buddha's Mirror, see our true selves. Then we will know everything."

He wanted to talk about it more, but she made a show of being sleepy. Her breathing deepened and steadied, and soon she was sleeping.

Neal listened to the clawing of the rats before finally willing himself to sleep. Dawn would come all too soon.

20

꤫

Xao Xiyang stepped out from the modest pavilion at the top of the promontory and waited for the sun to rise. The air was so clear, so lovely, so peaceful that he almost did not wish to light the cigarette in his hand. The long climb and the pure mountain air had cleared his lungs, and the serene panorama almost inspired him to begin a more healthy regimen. The Yi guide had put him to shame, but of course he was much younger, and a native. Xao accepted the rationalization and lit the cigarette.

So . . . soon he would see his true nature. A dangerous undertaking, considering what he was about to do. He was by no means certain he wanted even a glimpse at his own soul. He leaned over the low railing and sneaked a peek at the mists below. He saw no mirror; it looked like a bowl full of clouds, that was all. But hadn't the Yi guide assured him that the Buddha's Mirror appeared every day at dawn and dusk? Superstitions, he thought. They will hold us back.

He felt the quiet presence of his driver behind him. If I am tired, he thought, this good soldier must be exhausted, having raced all the way around to the west side of the mountain and then climbed the treacherous western trail. A true soldier, a good man who should not fear seeing his own soul.

"Is the American with you?" he asked.

"Yes, Comrade Secretary."

"Good. He is well?"

"He is breathing somewhat heavily."

"We do not all enjoy your sturdy constitution."

He offered the driver a cigarette, which the man accepted.

"I take it, then," Xao said, "that young Mr. Carey took the bait."

"You have seen the fish in the pool at Dwaizhou?"

"Yes."

"Like that."

"Ah."

Xao considered his contradictory emotions: satisfaction that the plan was working, sadness that the plan had to work to its unrelenting end. The duality of nature—that a great good was always coupled with a great evil, a wonderful gift with a tragic sacrifice. Perhaps the Buddha's Mirror will show me two faces.

"When do you think they will arrive?" Xao asked.

"For the sunset."

So it will be sad *and* beautiful, Xao thought. Appropriate.

"Have him ready," Xao ordered.

He could sense the driver's unease.

"Yes?" Xao asked. "Speak up, we are all socialist comrades."

"Are you certain, Comrade Secretary, that you want to . . . complete the operation? There are alternatives."

"You have become fond of him."

There was no answer.

Xao said, "There are alternatives, but they are risky. Risks are unacceptable when so much is at stake. Our personal feelings cannot matter."

"Yes, Comrade Secretary."

"You must be hungry."

"I am fine."

"Go eat."

"Yes, Comrade Secretary."

The driver stepped away. Xao watched the sun rise over the Sichuan basin. He knew what the driver had been hinting at—there was no operational reason for Xao to be here at all.

True, he thought, but there is a personal one. A moral reason. When

297

one orders the death of an innocent, one must have the character to watch it.

Xao peered into the mists below him to search for his soul.

Simms was just goddamn miserable. He had spent the night in a damp, dirty, rat-infested Buddhist Disneyland, had to squat over an open trench to take a dump, and now he was standing in the cold fog, trying to choke down a bowl of rice gruel, waiting for the sun to rise so he could climb a few thousand more steps.

He yearned for the comforts of the Peak: a decent meal, a good bottle of bourbon, a young lady wrapped in silk. The thought of spending the rest of his life in the PRC made his stomach turn more than the rice gruel did. It was so dull here, so frigging monotonous, so spartan.

The thought galvanized him, made him urge the sun to hurry up. If he didn't do what he had to do—grease Neal Carey—he might very well have to spend his remaining days here in this communist paradise. If Carey made it back to the States and slobbered about what the mean Mr. Simms did to him, the folks at the Company might notice the conflict with his job description. They might start asking some unfortunate questions. Then even those shit-for-brains might figure out that he was taking a regular paycheck from the Chinese. And that could get ugly. Probably even that stupid geek Pendleton had put it together.

He unzipped the long case and pulled out the rifle. The Chinese 7.62 Type 53 was by no means his favorite, but it would do. He favored bolt action, and the telescopic sight adjusted nicely. He sat down behind a large rock and screwed the sight onto the barrel. Then he hoisted the rifle to his shoulder, braced it against his cheek, and checked the sight out in the gathering light.

He spotted a band of monkeys in some bamboo about two hundred yards down the slope. He thought about his confrontation the day before with the fucking little bastards. I'll show them an ambush. He centered the cross hairs on the chest of the largest monkey in the group, and squeezed the trigger. The shot threw high and to the left. He adjusted the sights accordingly, and aimed again. The monkey continued to gnaw on some exotic piece of fruit. The bullet slammed squarely into his chest and sent him tumbling down the hill.

Okey-dokey, Simms thought as he slung the rifle over his shoulder. He tried to force the excitement of imminent revenge out of his system, but every time he thought about struggling out of that fucking river, he got angry. He had damned near drowned, and he had sure as hell scraped the shit out of his legs crawling onto those rocks and pulling himself out. So, while revenge might be unprofessional . . .

He walked back to the old dining hall to find Peng and that other little slant. He'd probably need a crowbar to pry them from their rice bowls. He'd just about needed a gun to force them to walk in the dark last night, the little chickenshits. What did they think flashlights were for, the movies? Well, anyway, they'd picked up a couple of hours before packing it in for the night. Now it was time to get moving again.

Neal struggled out of the *kang*. Just turning to put his feet on the floor hurt, and bending over to put on his shoes was an exercise in advanced masochism. Lan wanted to do it for him, but Neal figured that if he couldn't put his own shoes on, he damned well couldn't climb the rest of the mountain.

Lan diplomatically withdrew as Neal winced with pain, and reappeared a few minutes later with two steaming bowls of porridge.

"What's that?" Neal asked.

"Congee," she replied. "Rice gruel."

Neal ate the Chinese version of oatmeal gratefully—the thin cereal warmed his stomach in the early morning cold. He ate standing up; he didn't want to put himself throught the small torture of having to sit down and get up again. They finished their breakfast quietly, the tension between them palpable. The mountain's summit would be the deciding point in their relationship, and they both felt it but didn't want to talk about it. First they must get to the top of the mountain.

The trail started gently and led through a thick cedar forest. It was cold and dark, and Neal shivered. The altitude was starting to get to him, and he noticed that he was starting to breath heavily. He couldn't help but notice; each breath stabbed his rib cage.

They walked for about twenty minutes to the far edge of the woods. Neal looked ahead on the trail and wished that he hadn't; the steps ahead seemed to go straight up.

"Three Look Stairway," Li said. "Pilgrims look at it three times before they want to climb it."

"I've looked at it three times," Neal answered, "and I still don't want to climb it."

The grade was so steep that his knees practically touched his chest with every step. He consciously pushed off the balls of his feet, trying to concentrate on his legs as his ribs burned and stabbed him. He had to stop after the first twenty steps.

Li turned around. "Please go back to the monastery. I will bring Robert down."

"Right."

"I promise."

"I started out to climb the fucking mountain. I am going to climb the fucking mountain."

"You are a fool."

"I'm not arguing."

She turned and started back up. He caught his breath and went after her. *Yi, ar, yi, ar, yi, aaarrgh!* His ribs threatened him. He felt the sun begin to beat on his hunched-over back. *Yi, ar, yi, ar . . . yi . . . ar . . . . . yi . . . . . ar . . . . . . yi . . . . ar . . . . yi.* He stopped to rest again. He wanted to collapse on the stairs, to lie down and rest, but he knew he probably couldn't get up again, so he forced himself to take another step. Wrapping one arm around his ribs, he took another step. The pain nauseated him. Another step. More pain. Another. *Yi, ar, yi, ar.* Another rest.

He started out again. The trail curved sharply and then opened out onto the edge of a cliff. To Neal's right a sheet or rock rose as high as he could see. To his left—much to closely to his left—was a drop of at least a thousand feet.

Don't look down, Neal warned himself. Isn't that what they say in all the movies?

He peeked again. His stomach lurched and his head spun. That's probably why they say not to look down, he thought. He felt as if he were hanging on to the edge of the world as he began his trudge up the mountain again. *Yi, ar, yi, ar, yi . . .*

Just focus on counting, he thought. Don't think about the pain, don't think about the fear, don't think about Pendleton, or about her, and for God's sake, whatever you do, don't think about the fact that they're gaining on you. At this pace, they have to be gaining on you. Gaining fast. But don't think about that. Think about *yi, ar, yi, ar . . . yi . . . ar . . . yi . . . ar . . .* for two solid hours straight up the hill.

Li was waiting for him on a broad landing.

She pointed up ahead of her. He could see a huge peak, shaped like a big nose, rising above the rest of the rocks.

"The summit," she said.

"How far?"

"Four hours. Perhaps for you six."

Perhaps for me death.

"Is it all this steep?"

"Most. One place is gentle, almost level. But, I am afraid, it is also very frightening."

Swell.

"Why frightening?"

"The path is very narrow."

"Over a very long fall?"

She nodded and frowned. Then she smiled and added, "But after that, it is a short climb to summit."

Neal looked at the summit again. Fuck you, Silkworm's Eyebrow! I'm coming and you can't stop me! You took your best shot and I'm still on my feet, still climbing!

"Let's get going," he said.

Xiao Wu crossed the Bridge of Deliverance. The spray from the waterfall felt good. The day was very hot, even up here on the mountain, and his feet hurt. All he had to wear were his leather city shoes, and the blisters had already started to form the day before. Today they were raw, and he wished he could stop and dip his feet into the pool below the bridge.

But the American was setting an unrelenting pace. Even fat Peng was keeping up with it, so Wu thought that he had to do it as well. Besides, they were still angry with him for letting Frazier get away, and they only brought him along so he could point out exactly where the fugitive had started up the mountain.

Perhaps, Wu thought, I should have misled them. That would have been treason, of course, but why is the American carrying the rifle? Why is the American here at all? It doesn't seem right.

They were going to kill Frazier, he knew that, and that didn't seem right, either.

He forced the thought from his mind and picked up his pace.

* * *

Neal collapsed at the top of Three Look Stairway. He turned over on his back and gasped with pain and fatigue. He didn't even try to stop the tears from rolling down his cheeks. His chest heaved and his ribs hurt like they were breaking all over again. He could barely hear Li walking back down the path toward him.

In fact, he could barely hear at all. An incredible roar of rushing water echoed in the canyon and reverberated inside his head. The path was enclosed in a heavy mist.

Maybe the nuns were right about Purgatory, Neal thought.

"Thundering Terrace!" Li yelled. "The dragon and the thunder live below!"

Neal nodded.

"You are in pain?"

Neal rolled his eyes and nodded.

"There are caves just up the path! We will rest!"

She helped Neal to his feet. He staggered behind her, out of the mist and onto a broader terrace, behind which a cave burrowed into the cliff. She helped him to sit down. Even seated, they could now see the path below them. They could see the roofs of several monasteries, the trail below, the torturous stairs. They could see three figures climbing the trail near where Neal had fallen the day before.

"They have followed you," Li said. She sounded devastated.

"I'm afraid so."

"You should have let me go at Leshan."

"You'd be dead if I had."

"It would still be better."

They sat quietly for a moment.

"Two Chinese and one American."

"How can you tell?"

"By the way they walk."

She stood up. "The resting is finished."

He struggled to his feet. "We can still make it, can't we? Get to Pendleton in time to hide? To keep running?"

She stood for a moment, calculating. "Perhaps. Perhaps. There is left the Eighty-four Switchbacks, the Elephants's Saddle, and the Buddha's Ladder. Perhaps three hours."

"We can make it."

"We can at least warn Father."

It doesn't sound good, Neal thought. The Saddle sounded easy, but the Eighty-four Switchbacks? A ladder? Their pursuers were maybe three hours behind. Maybe. But they were gaining.

"You'd better go ahead," he said.

"They will kill you."

"Nah, they'll just criticize me severely. I can take it."

"They will kill you. Come."

She started out, and he fell in behind her. Five minutes' walk along the shelf took them to the first switchback. He looked up and saw what looked like an endless series of stone fire escapes zigzagging up the precipice. The first few switchbacks were fairly easy, but grew steeper as they worked higher up the mountain. About ten switchbacks in, the grade became almost as tough as Three Look Staircase, and Neal found his knees brushing his chest as he ascended the steps.

The sight of their hunters gave him a good shot of adrenaline, which lasted for a good forty switchbacks. After it had worn off, Neal had to search for a motivator. Fear didn't do it, neither did anger. Duty gave him five switchbacks, loyalty another seven, love another twelve. Contempt only got him one, pride less than one-half, a reprise of loyalty got him over the next difficult two, guilt took him for three, and then he dropped.

"Fourteen more and then level!" Li Lan shouted down from the switchback above.

Neal lay in a fetal position on the steps. Fourteen? I don't *have* fourteen more steps. I have nothing left.

"Go ahead!"

From the corner of his eye he saw her stand for a moment, and then begin a slow trudge away. She's beat too, he thought. Christ, I've lost everything.

And when you've lost everything, you have nothing left to lose. Clever boy. He pushed himself up with his hands and stood on unsteady feet. I've lost everything, so what the hell? When you've lost everything, there's nothing left to do but keep going.

Come on, one foot in front of the other. Just one, and then just one more. Just one and then one more. Just one. *Yi. Yi. Yi. Yi.* Fuck the mountain. Fuck Mr. Peng. Fuck Simms. Fuck Friends of the Fucking Family. Step. Step. Fuck my whole stupid, useless life. Step. Step. *Yi. Yi. Yi. Yi.* Look behind you. The bastards are gaining. Really stepping out.

Well, boys, wait until you hit old Three Look Staircase. Wait till you come up the greatly beloved Eighty-four Switchbacks. We'll see how chipper you are when you step over my dead body.

This huge guy comes into a bar, see, and asks, "Which one of you bastards is O'Reilly?" Step. Step. And this skinny guy sitting at the bar raises his hand and says, "I'm O'Reilly." Step. And the big guy grabs him by the neck, turns him around, punches him three times in the face, step, slams him to the floor, step, kicks him in the groin, picks him up, step, step, hits him in the stomach, throws him down again, step, step, step, kicks him in the balls, stomps on his face, step, step, step . . . step, step . . . and storms out of the bar. Step. Step. Step. Then the skinny guys sits up, step, starts to laugh, step, step, step, and says, step, "Boy, did I put one over on him!" Step, step, step.

"I'm not O'Reilly!"

Step, step, step.

Boy, am I putting one over on them.

Step.

Simms spotted them first, but then again he was looking the hardest, and they were outlined pretty clearly against the cliff face. One of them looks hurt, Simms thought. The other is dog-tired.

He nudged Peng and pointed. "There are your puppies!"

Peng was bathed in sweat. Three Look Staircase was worth more than three looks.

"Will we catch up with them?"

"If you can shake your ass!"

"Remember, I want her and Pendleton alive!"

Maybe you do, Simms thought. But I don't want to take the chance of one of them being part of a spy swap some day and telling all kinds of stories in the debrief.

"Remember," Peng said. "They are evidence!"

Corpses are evidence, too, Simms thought.

"Let's worry about that when we catch them, all right?"

Simms saw that this fired up Old Peng and made him waddle a little faster. The kid behind them was fading.

It doesn't matter, Simms thought. As long as I don't fade. And I don't have to catch them, I just have to get in range. The bullets will catch them.

Neal lay down at the top of the eighty-fourth switchback. The path in front of him was fairly level, just a mild grade across a bottomless chasm. Li was laying down also—on her back, rhythmically slowing her breathing, getting ready for the next phase.

"I've lost sight of them," Neal gasped.

"That is bad. It means they are closer. We cannot see them because of the angle."

"I'll bet the resting is finished."

She stood up. "We are on the Elephant's Saddle. If we cross quickly, we can reach the summit ahead of them. I think, perhaps, in time."

Neal knew a cue when he heard one, and forced himself up. He indulged in a look over the edge of the trail. It was a mistake. You wouldn't want to go off either side without a parachute. You wouldn't want to go off either side *with* a parachute.

"Is this the time to tell you that I'm afraid of heights?" Neal asked.

"No," she said as she stepped out.

No sense of humor, Neal thought. Maybe I should try the O'Reilly joke on her. He picked his way carefully along the dirt trail. Bits of shale slid out from under his foot and rattled off the edge. Neal resisted the temptation to watch them fall into eternity. His rib cage felt as if Reggie Jackson had used it for batting practice. His legs quivered and his ankles shook. He didn't even want to check in with his feet. He heard noise and looked up to see Li Lan break into a trot ahead of him.

He limped along the path.

Xao's driver handed his field glasses to his boss.

"They are on the Saddle," he said.

Xao looked through the glasses. He could make out the figure of Li Lan, strong but tired, jogging up the slope. Carey seemed to be limping far behind her.

"He is injured, I think," Xao observed.

"Or merely unfit," the driver answered.

Xao handed back the glasses.

"What about Peng? Can you see him?"

"I lost them when they entered the Thundering Terrace. They must be well up the switchbacks now."

"You said there were three."

"Yes, and I could swear one is a Westerner. The one with the rifle."

"Impossible. Probably a Yi tribesman, a hunter."

The driver shrugged.

"How long?" Xao asked.

"An hour at the most. Longer for him."

"Go and get things ready."

"Yes, Comrade Secretary."

An hour, Xao thought. After all these years, one hour to the family reunion.

She reached the Buddha's Ladder well before he did, of course. It wasn't a ladder at all, but a severe rise up the side of the summit to the edge of a precipice. On the other side was the Buddha's Mirror. There were few actual steps here, mostly just a treacherous, slippery dirt path.

She stopped and waited. The view from here was lovely, she thought. Rock peaks seemed to rise straight up from verdant bamboo jungles. Swirling rivers and waterfalls like sapphire brocade on green silk. The entire Sichuan Valley stretched out in front of her. Behind her, Emei's final peak, gray and austere, waited for her. The sight of her own soul waited for her, and she had waited a long time for it.

The sunset would be scarlet. She could tell that already. How appropriate, she thought, that she would meet herself under a red sky.

"Hurry up!" she shouted to him.

There was much to love about him, she thought as he broke into a jog. It was more like a shuffle, but she admired him for it. What pain it must be costing him! What a stubborn man! And what a price his stubbornness had cost!

"Can you go on?" she asked when he reached her side. He was bathed in sweat. His face was green with pain.

"Yeah. How far behind do you think they are?"

She shook her head. "I think we can make it, but we have no time to waste. Please do not fall behind."

She squeezed his hand, then turned and started up the last climb. She had tried to encourage him, and perhaps herself, but in her heart she knew it was too late.

* * *

306

Simms watched her. If he'd had a better weapon he might have tried it right there, but that would still have left Carey and Pendleton to deal with. No, better to wait until they were all nice and cozy at the top.

He looked down to where Peng was huffing up the last couple of switchbacks.

"Jesus H. Christ, put it in gear!" Simms yelled.

Nothing more useless than a fat chink, he thought. And the young one is completely useless.

Well, shit, I can't afford to wait for them.

Come on, he told himself. Let's get it done.

He pushed out onto the saddle.

Neal worked his way up the slope on his hands and feet. The grade was so severe he couldn't stand up and walk, so he used his hands to balance. Li Lan was using the same method just above him, only she was making much faster progress. Every few paces Neal's ribs scraped against the slope, and the fiery pain would stop him for a few precious seconds.

He heard her yell, "There is a flat spot just up here! You can make it!"

He pulled himself along, digging into the dirt with his fingers, literally clawing his way up. It seemed like hours before he made it to where she was sitting behind a large rock on the uphill side of the path. She pulled him behind it with her.

He could see the summit clearly now. What looked like a rough wooden pavilion was perched on the edge of the far side. Two men—no, three—stood on the pavilion and looked down toward the path. Two were of medium build and stocky, one was tall and thin. Pendleton? Neal couldn't be sure at the distance and angle.

Then he heard voices echo below. Li Lan stood up and peeked over the rock. Then she slammed her fist on the rock in rage and frustration. She turned back to Neal.

Tears of anger streamed down her face.

"It is too late!"

Neal leaned out over the rock. His ribs exploded in a burst of pain. He saw Simms pacing steadily across the saddle, almost to the base of the ladder. Peng waddled about a hundred yards behind him, followed closely by Wu, who was shuffling along in his distinctive pigeon-toed gait.

He turned back to Li.

"We can run. We can make it. We can warn them."

She looked steadily in his eyes. "Fate is fate. You cannot change it. You Americans always think you can change it. You must learn to face your fate, learn to face the truth. Face what your stubbornness, and selfishness, and lust have done."

"Love."

"No, lust. I begged you to stop, but you wouldn't stop. Now see what you have done. See what *we* have done. Accept it."

Neal slipped the pistol from the small of his back.

"Go. I'll buy you the time."

"Neal Carey, listen for one time. I do not love you. That is the truth. I love Robert. *That* is the truth. I was never going to go with you. That is the truth. I made love with you to deceive you, to buy your silence. But now your silence is worthless."

She pointed down the hill.

She's right, he thought. Everything she says is true. Everything I've done, I've done because of her. Because I wanted her and couldn't have her.

"Run," he said. "If you run you can make it."

"Do not make this sacrifice for me. I do not lo—"

"I know. You don't love me. But neither do I."

But I do love you, he thought.

She turned and ran.

Now think, he told himself. For the first time on this whole fucking job, think. Simms can pick you off from here, and that's no good. You need to shorten the range so that your pistol is as good as his rifle.

He looked uphill to where Li Lan was scrambling up the slope. There was a slight curve in the path, and some rocks off to the uphill side.

If I can make it there, that might do.

He rolled onto the path and started on all fours. His ribs slammed at him, but he didn't stop. He didn't look up, either, but he could hear Li Lan running, as bits of rock and shale slid down behind her.

Go, go, go, he thought.

Now he could hear Simms on the path behind him. Also running.

Shit. Have to make it to that curve. Have to make it there with a few seconds' lead.

Neal stood up straight and burst up the hill. He screamed as his ribs exploded and screamed again as he reached the curve and threw himself behind the rocks. He could see a bit of the path below him and all the path in front of him. He saw Li Lan on all fours, and then he watched as she stood straight up, waving her arms and shouting, trying to warn the three men to get off the edge of the summit.

"She is waving!" Xao said. "But where is Carey?"

"He must be resting."

"Can he see from there?"

"I am sure."

I hope so, Xao thought. I hope so. Come on, Mr. Carey. Where are you?

Where are you, you little bastard? Simms wondered. The Chinese babe was flattened against the hill like a bug, but Carey had disappeared. Planning another little ambush, are you?

Simms saw the path curve about forty yards above him.

Okay, he thought.

He left the path, working himself down the slope on the seat of his pants. There was a nice rock down there to steady the rifle on, and it would give him a beautiful fire angle at the summit. They would be silhouetted, backlit by the setting sun.

Then he could deal with Carey at leisure. Leisure . . . what a nice concept. He sure could use a little leisure.

Simms slid down behind the rock.

What the hell is he doing? Neal wondered as he watched Simms's maneuver. Then he saw Simms drop into a shooter's crouch, wrap the rifle sling around his wrist, and lay the barrel against the rock. He watched as Simms put his eye to the scope and began to scan the summit.

Li Lan reached the top. She stopped again and waved her arms. They were about a hundred yards away, heading toward her, arms spread out in welcome—the largest possible targets they could be.

* * *

Neal saw it too. Pendleton was wrapped in a native black serape, and he looked like some sort of giant bat as he strode toward Li Lan. The Chinese man was older, shorter, but he also walked purposefully toward her as she ran toward them.

He looked down and saw the rifle barrel wave gently as Simms picked a target.

Now this, Simms thought, is what I call a target-rich environment. Now let me see. . . . Well, first things first.

He tightened his grip and centered the cross hairs.

Neal knew he couldn't hit Simms from that distance with the pistol in a thousand years, but he gave it a try. The pistol bucked in his hand as he pulled the trigger.

The shot didn't even distract Simms. He chuckled to himself as he followed his target, waiting for the two of them to get closer together so he could make an easy adjustment for the second kill. Or should I try for a double kill with one shot?

No, that would be vulgar.

He practiced his lead once and waited for the ideal shot.

Neal put both feet to the rock and pushed. His ribs strained and screamed as he as he pushed, wedging his back against the slope. Then the shale began to give way underneath. The rock began to slip.

Time to stop fucking around, Simms said to himself. He began to put just the right amount of pressure on the trigger.

The boulder gave way and started to roll. Neal watched it bounce over the path and pick up speed as it tumbled toward Simms. Please, God . . . please, please, please.

He heard the shot go off a half-second before the boulder hit.

He looked up and saw Pendleton drop.

Like he'd been shot.

Then he heard Li Lan scream.

He sprang to his feet and ran toward her.

*　*　*

Simms was about to grease the babe when he felt a jolt through his hands as a big fucking rock hit the gun barrel and tore the rifle from him.

Son of a bitch, he thought. They just don't want to make this easy. Well, he'd just have to do her with the knife. He wished she'd quit screaming, though.

Neal heard her wailing as he made it to the summit.

She stood with her back to him, Pendleton in her arms. There was a big hole in his back. The other two men stood as still as statues on the edge of the pavilion.

She was dragging Pendleton to the edge of the cliff, to the Buddha's Mirror.

"No!" Neal screamed as he ran toward her. "Noooo!!!"

She turned toward Neal as she reached the edge.

The two Chinese men started to run toward her.

Neal was close enough to see her eyes, close enough to see her smile, close enough to reach her with one lunge as she turned, looked into the Buddha's Mirror, cradled Pendleton in her arms, and jumped.

Neal sprawled on the edge. He peered into the mists below, into the Buddha's Mirror, but he couldn't see them. All he could see was the mist, and golden circles of light, and in one golden circle his own face. His own soul.

He closed his eyes and sobbed.

"We thank you for your assistance," Xao said. He raised his teacup in the form of a toast.

"You are very welcome," Simms answered.

They were sitting at a pavilion on the summit.

"I must confess," Xao continued, "that when we started to lure the traitors here, we did not know we would have the assistance of the Central Intelligence Agency. Mr. Peng has been most thorough."

Peng blushed. He was burning with rage, but could not let it show. Xao's plot had been foiled, but Xao would come out of it as a hero. Without the bodies, Peng could prove nothing. It would be his word against Xao's, and he knew he would come out the loser.

"The woman was obviously unstable," Xao continued.

"Apparently," agreed Simms.

"Perhaps she loved him."

"Emotional involvements are dangerous in our type of endeavor."

"Just so."

Xao turned to Peng. "You have been very loyal, Xiao Peng, almost to the point to cause concern. For a while it seemed that you thought that I was a traitor, and yet you were willing to conspire with me."

Xao's eyes burned into him.

Peng said, "Comrade Secretary, it is not for me to question your instructions, but merely to carry them out."

Xao's smile had the warmth of a dagger.

"Even so, accept my gratitude."

"Humbly, Comrade Secretary."

Xao turned to Simms. "You will inform your superiors that the problem of Mr. Pendleton is resolved?"

"They will be most grateful."

Jesus, thought Simms, can we cut the Oriental bullshit and get out of here?

"What about Carey?" Simms asked. "It would be awkward to bring him back to the States."

"A reckless young man," Xao answered. "Prone to the sort of rash behavior that leads to accidents. This is a dangerous mountain, particularly on the stretch known as the Elephant's Saddle. Careless hikers have been known to slip and fall, especially if they were foolish enough to attempt to traverse it at night."

"But I am afraid I have little choice, Secretary Xao. I wonder if I could borrow a flashlight?"

"Of course. Xiao Wu and my driver will escort you. Mr. Peng will stay here for the night. We have much to discuss."

Xao smiled pleasantly at Peng. So pleasantly that Peng wasn't looking forward to the conversation. Xao stood up and offered his hand to Simms.

"Thank you for all your help," he said.

"Don't mention it."

They both laughed at his joke.

Wu sat with Neal at the pavilion near the summit. Neal's hands were tied behind him. In the three hours since Pendleton's murder and Li's suicide he hadn't uttered a sound, just stared into the distance.

312

Simms came up, stood in front of Neal, and then kicked him in the ribs. Neal toppled over on his face.

"That's for the swim in the river," Simms said.

The driver picked Neal up gently and lifted him to his feet.

"You like to walk, Neal," said Simms. "We're going for a walk."

Simms held a large flashlight in one hand. So did the driver.

The soldier led the way. Simms pushed Neal in behind the soldier, and Wu brought up the rear. They trudged slowly down the Buddha's Ladder as the driver carefully pointed out the trail with his flashlight. They reached the bottom and started along the Elephant's Saddle.

"You want to be real careful, Neal, so you don't slip and fall."

Neal heard the words with intense relief. They were going to kill him after all.

They'd walked for a couple more minutes when he heard Simms say, "I guess this will do."

Neal waited for the push. Neal wanted the push.

"Cocksucker."

Neal turned and saw Wu kick Simms's feet out from under him. Simms tottered on the edge for a long moment, flailing his arms as he tried to regain his balance. Then he tumbled into the darkness. His scream echoed in the night.

Then the driver lifted Neal into his arms.

21

嚞

Robert Pendleton squatted in the muck of the rice paddy for a moment and came up with a beaker full of mud. He held it up to the light, swished it around, and looked at it carefully.

"It's the nitrogen content that's crucial, as you know."

Zhu smiled and nodded.

"We'll take this back to the lab and see what's what," Pendleton said. He waded up to the dike, shook the mud off his shoes, and looked around him. Dwaizhou's broad paddies and fields shone green and fertile in the morning sun. He inhaled the fecund scent of the rice crop, so different from the sterile smell of the corporate labratory, so much richer.

AgriTech, he remembered, had always bragged that it was "where the action is." No, he thought, *this* is where the action is.

And what would the boys in the office say if they could see me now? In my green Mao suit, little Mao cap, and rubber sandals? They probably wouldn't give me a tee time on the company course.

Gee.

He decided to stop off at home for lunch, handed Old Zhu the beaker, and said he'd meet him at their makeshift lab later. The lab was actually pretty good. Nothing like AgriTech, but still pretty decent, all things considered, and he'd given Xao a shopping list to fill as time, money, and secrecy allowed.

Pendleton walked along the dike, then along the road past the rabbit wood to his plain, tin-roofed, cinder-block dwelling on the brigade's far edge. He found a bowl of cold rice with some fish in it, and a warm bottle of beer, and sat down at the plain wooden table.

The food was good, the beer better, but he would be happy when Li Lan came home. Everything was better when she was there. Well, she should be home from the mountain any day now, any day.

He shoveled down some rice and speculated about the nitrogen content in the Dwaizhou soil.

Neal Carey steadfastly refused to eat. He sat on the *kang* in his dark monk's cell not even looking at the bowl of rice that the monk brought in every day. He had a vague awareness of hunger somewhere in his body, but the pain and guilt more than drowned it. Li Lan was dead because of him. Pendleton was dead because of him. He wished the driver had thrown him off the cliff instead of carrying him to the remote monastery on the west slope of the mountain. He wished that Xiao Wu had killed him instead of Simms. He wished he were dead. He wouldn't eat to keep himself alive.

The monk opened the shutter of the window to let the noonday light in. How many days had it been, Neal wondered. Seven? Eight? How many days did it take to starve?

"You must eat," he heard a woman's voice say.

The English startled him and he looked up. Who spoke English on this damn mountain?

Li Lan stood in the doorway. She was dressed in a white jacket and white pants. White ribbons held her hair in two braids. White, he recalled, was the Chinese color of mourning. Behind her stood an older man. The resemblance was startling, even though he wore a green Mao suit with a plain white armband.

Neal blinked twice to try to clear the hallucination from his head. He understood that his subconscious was desperate to relieve the feeling of guilt, so it had produced Li Lan alive for him. But the vision didn't go away. It stood framed in the doorway, backlit by the sunshine.

Then he understood. It was not Li Lan, it was her sister. They were twins.

"You must eat," she repeated.

He shook his head.

"You used to like my cooking."

He looked up again.

"I am alive," she said. "So is Robert."

"I saw—"

"My sister, Hong. My twin sister. When we were babies, Father and Mother tied blue ribbons in my hair and red ribbons in her hair to tell us apart."

Twins.

"It was my sister who took you from The Walled City, my sister who came to you at Leshan and asked you to go home, my sister who made love with you."

Sister Hong. The actress.

"She told me a story, about her sister killing her mother."

"She was talking about herself. She could never overcome her guilt. She found herself in the Buddha's Mirror."

Neal felt the room spinning. "Why? Why did you do all this?"

The older man stepped forward. "Mr. Carey, I am Xao Xiyang, Party Secretary for Sichuan Province. Lan's father. Hong's father. I am the responsible person in this matter."

Neal could only stare at him.

Xao continued, "You must understand how desperately we need the expertise that Dr. Pendleton can offer us. You have never seen hunger, Mr. Carey. You have never seen starvation. I have seen both. I never want to see them again, no matter what the price.

"When Lan began her relationship with Dr. Pendleton, I was overjoyed. I saw a wonderful opportunity, one that might never come again. As you know, I asked Lan to bring Dr. Pendleton into China. But such an operation was fraught with danger. Your own CIA, the Taiwanese, even our own government—especially our own government—would seek to prevent his defection at all costs.

"You see, Mr. Carey, we are engaged in a desperate struggle for control in China, a struggle between the hard-line Maoists, who seek to reimpose tyrannical madness and backwardness on us, against progressive, democratic reformers. I need not tell you that I am numbered among the latter. I need not tell you it is imperative that we prevail in

316

this struggle. The agricultural advances that Dr. Pendleton could provide may be a critical weapon in that struggle.

"He who feeds China, Mr. Carey, controls China."

Xao paused for comment or agreement, but Neal remained silent.

"We exercised every caution in our seduction of Dr. Pendleton. There were two factors that we did not predict: Lan actually falling in love with the man, and you. Lan shook you off easily in California, but we did not expect you to follow her to Hong Kong, which was the midpoint of the operation. We had to keep Pendleton in Hong Kong until our internal arrangements were complete. You were never supposed to leave San Francisco. The fact that you did was the fault of Lan's local case officer, a certain Mr. Crowe. He failed to delay you, failed to deflect your search."

It's all about making money now, Neal. Is that what Crowe said? Is that why he came so quickly to Mill Valley to pick me up?

"Was it Crowe who tried to shoot me that night?"

"No. To the best of our understanding, that would have been Mr. Simms. It appears now that Mr. Simms was working for our government, and he wanted Lan and Pendleton to make it into China, where I could be implicated along with them. He apparently mistook you for Pendleton, but the shot was intended to miss.

"When you made such a bother of yourself in Hong Kong, Lan argued that she had to meet you, to persuade you to give up your obsession. Frankly, I would have preferred to have you killed."

"You tried," said Neal, remembering the gang with the choppers and the Doorman's bloody death.

"And Simms intervened and saved your life. He had further use for you. You confirmed his good judgment when you tracked down Lan that night and 'persuaded' her to defect. After you saved her life that night from the Taiwanese thug, Chin, Lan would no longer countenance your being eliminated."

Neal turned his gaze to Lan. "So you lured me into the Walled City and dumped me there."

"May I remind you," said Xao, "that she also rescued you?"

"Why?"

"Again, this arose from a miscalculation. Your friends and employers were creating a stir. Lan would not let you simply perish in the Walled City, and we could not let you return to your employers and tell what

317

you knew. The only solution was to bring you here and either buy your silence or give you convincing disinformation to take home with you."

Neal's head was starting to clear. They had run him past Li Lan at the commune to see if he'd keep his mouth shut. Encouraged when he did, they'd sent Li Hong, pretending to be her sister, to sleep with him to ensure his silence when he went home. But he had screwed that up when he demanded to see Pendleton personally. Queered the deal and also sentenced Hong to death.

"You knew that Peng was working for the other side," Neal said.

"Of course. We knew that you would lead him to the rendezvous on the mountain. Your obsession with Lan would not let you turn back. So we wanted both you and Peng to see Lan and Pendleton commit suicide. That was the word we wanted you to take to Washington and Peng to take to Beijing."

Neal looked at Lan. "Your sister was willing to do this?"

Lan nodded. "She was eager. Life had become a torture for her after Mother's suicide. I had hoped her sacrifice would not be necessary, but your obsession with me demanded it."

"Let us be honest, Mr. Carey. Hong never forgave herself, but neither did I. After my wife's death, Hong took part in the worst of the Red Guard infighting. She trained as an agent, a killer. She was consumed with self-hatred. After the chaos, when I came back to power and influence, I had her found. And I imprisoned her myself. We were chained together by our guilt and sorrow. I asked her to perform this mission."

"Your own daughter?"

"I do not expect you to understand."

"And it was Hong I was with on the mountain."

"Everything went according to our plan, except for the presence of Mr. Simms. That was something we didn't expect. We didn't realize he was working with Peng until he fired his rifle."

At the tall man in the black cloak. A. Brian Crowe.

"How did Crowe happen to catch that bullet?"

"He was my handler," Lan said. "He introduced me to the artistic community in California. He arranged for me to go to the correct parties and meet the correct people."

"Why?"

God, Neal thought. I'm still jealous.

318

"Money," Xao answered. "We paid him a great deal of money. But with Lan returning to China, Mr. Crowe saw that income about to disappear. He sought out the Taiwanese and tried to sell his special knowledge. They laughed at him and threatened to turn him in to the FBI. He panicked and ran. We arranged his defection to protect ourselves. It was fortunate timing."

"Not for Crowe."

"He was a mercenary. Mercenaries get killed."

Neal turned back to Xao. "So it all worked out for you. Peng and I saw your two stand-ins go off the edge. So why am I here? Why aren't I back in the States, spreading your 'disinformation'?"

"Simms. Mr. Simms was going to kill you. For reasons I have explained, we could not let that happen. So we had to kill Mr. Simms to save you."

"You trusted that job to Xiao Wu, a lit student, a tour guide?"

"You are somewhat naive, Mr. Carey. Xiao Wu was graduated in literature, but his tour guide status is what you would call a cover. He works for us in a different capacity."

"That still doesn't tell me why you're holding me."

"Several reasons. First, we are afraid you will talk about Simms's death. Killing a CIA agent . . . even a renegade one . . . is a serious matter we would just as soon avoid. So the word had been put out that Mr. Simms has defected. It is Mr. Frazier that fell off the mountain."

"But I'm Mr. Frazier."

"Just so. Your employers will be informed that you used this alias to enter the People's Republic, where you met your untimely death. Second, Mr. Peng had been quite conscientious in telling all parties concerned about the suicides of Dr. Robert Pendleton and the treacherous Li Lan."

"So the CIA will stop looking for them, and my people will stop looking for me."

"Third, I am afraid you know too much."

"Why did you tell me?"

Li Lan walked over to him and took his hand. "You were dying from your guilt. If we had sent you home, you would have died there."

Neal shook her hand off.

"Can I ever leave?"

"Perhaps someday, when we are secure in power and it will no longer matter," Xao said. "When it is safe."

Neal thought about Graham, about Graham becoming another victim of this damn mess.

"You will stay here at the monastery," Xao explained. "As your injury heals, you may move about. You need not become a Buddhist, of course, but you will be expected to share in the work. If you attempt to escape, you will be executed. Do you understand?"

Neal nodded.

"I am sorry for your situation, Mr. Carey. But you are—as are we all—responsible for your own fate."

Xao walked out into the sun.

"I am sorry," Li Lan said.

Neal shook his head.

"I mourn her deeply," she said. "I mourn for all of us."

She knelt in front of him, forcing him to look at her face.

"When you looked into the Buddha's Mirror," she asked, "what did you see?"

He stared into her eyes before he answered.

"Nothing."

She squeezed his hands and then left him alone.

Joe Graham stepped out of the chauffeured limousine and walked the last hundred yards to the border checkpoint. The August heat was brutal, and he sweated even in his light khaki suit. A hot wind blew in his face as he scanned the checkpoint, where a chain-link gate topped by concertina wire stood between two concrete bunkers.

He stood on the Hong Kong side. Behind him were the New Territories, ahead of him was the People's Republic of China. All around him were the barren brown hills. The only sound was the rushing wind, and he felt the quiet in eerie contrast to the incessant cacophony of Kowloon.

He watched as the guards checked the papers of a young man dressed in a sedate gray suit. They didn't search the bundle the kid carried under his arm. Diplomatic immunity, Graham thought, as the emissary cleared the checkpoint and walked pigeon-toed down the road toward him. Graham stepped forward to meet him.

"Mr. Joseph Graham?"

The boy stole a glance at Graham's arm.

Jesus, he's young, Graham thought. Or maybe I'm just old. They say that grief ages you. They're right.

"Mister Wu?" Graham asked.

The boy bowed. "I wish to express my own sympathy and that of my government."

"Thank you."

"A most tragic and unfortunate accident."

Accident, my ass, he thought. You pricks killed him. Graham wanted to punch him in the mouth, but most of the fight was out of him. Since they'd received the word of Neal's death, he'd felt empty.

"Have you made any progress in recovering the body?"

The boy flushed. "Unfortunately, no. Please understand that the chasm into which Mr. Carey fell is not accessible."

I'll bet.

Graham didn't answer. The boy proffered the bundle, wrapped in brown paper.

"Mr. Carey's belongings."

"He must have been traveling light."

The boy flushed again.

"Can you tell me anything more about why Neal was in—"

"As you are aware, Mr. Graham, our arrangement specifically precludes any discussion of these circumstances. Suffice it to say Mr. Carey died in a climbing accident."

"He was afraid of heights."

"Even so."

Graham gave it up. Neal was dead, and it didn't really matter why or how.

"Thank you for your help," he said.

"You are welcome, and I am sorry for your loss."

They stood looking at each other. The boy seemed to want to say more. Graham waited another moment, and then turned around to start back to the car.

Then he heard Wu say, "Mr. Graham."

Graham turned around.

"Mr. Carey loved literature."

"Yeah?"

"We had delightful conversations about *Huckleberry Finn*."

So what?

"I'm glad," Graham answered.

Wu pointed to the bundle. "Especially the scene on page ninety-four! When Jim meets Huck on the island."

"Okay."

Wu turned and walked back through the checkpoint.

Graham got back in the car and ripped open the brown paper. There was an old shirt, a pair of slacks, and a used paperback copy of *Huckleberry Finn.* He flipped to page ninety-four, and read the underlined passage.

He set the open book in his lap and started to cry. Then he read the passage again:

> Well, I warn't long making him understand I warn't dead. I was ever
> so glad to see Jim. I warn't lonesome, now. I told him I warn't afraid
> of *him* telling the people where I was.

Graham jumped out of the car and ran back toward the checkpoint. He had never read *Huckleberry Finn,* but he had seen the movie. He remembered that Huck had faked his death and disappeared down a river on a raft. But he didn't remember how it ended. He ran up to the chain-link fence and shouted.

"Hey, Wu!"

"Yes?"

"Did Huck Finn ever make it home?"

Wu's smile was as clean and wide as the blue sky.

"Fuck yes!" he said, then he paused. "Oh, yes, Aunt Sally! He makes it home!"

Aunt Sally?! Graham thought. What the hell does that mean? I guess I'd better read the book. He got back in the car, told the driver to take him back to the airport, then started to laugh. He laughed for a while, then cried some more, then laughed again, especially when he read the last line of the book, the one about Aunt Sally.

EPILOGUE

Neal carried a bucket of water in each hand. The buckets were wooden and heavy, and the climb from the creek to the kitchen was steep. But he had made the trip twenty times a day for six months, and his leg and arm muscles were ropy and firm.

He didn't even feel the cold of the snow as he crunched his way up the hill. His brown quilted jacket was warm, and the smell of the fir trees was wonderful. He passed through a side gate, across the small courtyard where some of the monks were sparring, and went into the kitchen. He poured the water into a large kettle suspended over a fire. Then he returned the buckets to the pantry, bowed to the head cook, and walked back through the courtyard.

He stepped outside and climbed the few steps up to a pagoda set on a small knoll. There were many such vistas in the Tiger Taming Monastery, but this was his favorite. The Himalayan peaks rose in the distance above a broad plain. To his left a rocky crag climbed toward the sunset. To his right a waterfall cascaded between groves of giant cedars.

He sat on a bench in the pagoda and watched the sun set. At first it was a fiery red ball above the Himalayas. Soon it fell behind the snowy peaks, leaving the sky a diaphanous sheet of scarlet, then rose, then orange.

He left before darkness fell, padding back through the snow into a long wooden building. He inhaled the incense smoldering by a statue of Buddha, then climbed the staircase and went into his cell, a ten-by-ten cubicle that smelled of pine, and sat down on his *kang*. He lit his kerosene lamp, took *Roderick Random* from under his sleeping mat, and started to read.